Ex Libris

Libri Docent

THERE WAS NO GOING HOME FOR HIM, EVEN TO A PRISON

The Man Without a Country
From the painting by Nella F. Binckley

THE JUNIOR CLASSICS

SELECTED AND ARRANGED BY
WILLIAM PATTEN
MANAGING EDITOR OF THE HARVARD CLASSICS

INTRODUCTION BY
CHARLES W. ELIOT, LL.D.
PRESIDENT EMERITUS OF HARVARD UNIVERSITY, 1869-1909

WITH A READING GUIDE BY
WILLIAM ALLAN NEILSON, PH.D
PROFESSOR OF ENGLISH, HARVARD UNIVERSITY
PRESIDENT SMITH COLLEGE, NORTHAMPTON, MASS, 1917-1939

VOLUME NINE

Stories of To-Day

ORIGINALLY PUBLISHED BY
P.F. COLLIER & SON CORPORATION, NEW YORK, 1918

UPDATED AND EDITED BY
AMANDA KENNEDY, FOR THE HARVARD CLASSICS PROJECT, 2024

Contents

Illustrations	6
Brother Rabbit's Cradle	7
The Little Baxters Go Marketing	14
A Story of Decoration Day for The Little Children of To-Day	18
The Taxes of Middlebrook	23
The Cure of Fear	32
A Christmas Adventure	41
Chased by the Trail	50
Big Timber Beacon	59
How Hilda Got a School	67
The Imp and the Drum	73
The Second String	85
Holding the Pipe	93
The Travelling Doll	100
The Doll Doctor	112
The Idea That Went Astray	123
Gravity Gregg	125
Jonnasen	131
In The Oven	136
On a Slide-Board	141
The Call of the Sea	147
On a Tight Rope	155
Down the Incline	161
The Cost of Loving	164
Ladybird	176
The Drasnoe Pipe-Line	185
Manuk Del Monte	195
The Man Without a Country	203

The Foreman	229
The Gray Collie	238
The Fore-Room Rug	246
Cressey's New-Year's Rent	259
Mr. O'Leary's Second Love	268
Note	280
The Rose and the Ring	281
Reading Guide	**375**
Suggested Books	377
About this Book	**379**
Titles in The Junior Classics Series of Books	380

Illustrations

There was no going Home for him, even to a prison
The Man Without a Country
Frontispiece illustration in colour from the painting by Nella F. Binckley

A Gush of water followed, burying the sled and washing the dogs from their feet
Chased by the Trail
From the drawing by George Giguère

"I'm not your doctor. I'm a doll's doctor."
The Doll Doctor
From the drawing by Carton Moorepark

"Three of us were riding down the Slope of the great, grassy Hills"
Manuk Del Monte
From the drawing by W. H. D. Koerner

"Does Mr. Cressy live here?"
Cressy's New-Year's Rent
From the drawing by Edwin J. Meeker

Bulbo was brought in Chains, looking very uncomfortable
The Rose and the Ring
From the drawing by Wm. Makepeace Thackeray

And the gloomy procession marched on
The Rose and the Ring
From the drawing by J. H. Tinker

Brother Rabbit's Cradle

By Joel Chandler Harris

"I wish you'd tell me what you tote a hankcher fer," remarked Uncle Remus, after he had reflected over the matter a little while.

"Why, to keep my mouth clean," answered the little boy. Uncle Remus looked at the lad, and shook his head doubtfully. "Uh-uh!" he exclaimed. "You can't fool folks when dey git ez ol' ez what I is. I been watchin' you now mo' days dan I kin count, an' I ain't never see yo' mouf dirty 'nuff fer ter be wiped wid a hankcher. It's allers clean—too clean for ter suit me. Dar's yo' pa, now; when he wuz a little chap like you, his mouf useter git dirty in de mornin' an' stay dirty plum twel night. Dey wa'n't sca'cely a day dat he didn't look like he been playin' wid de pigs in de stable lot. Ef he yever is tote a hankcher, he ain't never show it ter me."

"He carries one now," remarked the little boy with something like a triumphant look on his face.

"Tooby sho'," said Uncle Remus; "tooby sho' he do. He start ter totin' one when he tuck an' tuck a notion fer ter go a-courtin'. It had his name in one cornder, an' he useter sprinkle it wid stuff out'n a pepper-sauce bottle. It sho' wuz rank, dat stuff wuz; it smell so sweet it make you fergit whar you live at. I take notice dat you ain't got none on yone."

"No; mother says that cologne or any kind of perfumery on your handkerchief makes you common."

Uncle Remus leaned his head back, closed his eyes, and permitted a heart-rending groan to issue from his lips. The little boy showed enough anxiety to ask him what the matter was. "Nothin' much, honey; I wuz des tryin' fer ter count how many diffunt kinder people dey is in dis big worl', an' 'fo' I got mo' dan half done wid my countin', a pain struck me in my mizry, an' I had ter break off."

"I know what you mean," said the child. "You think mother is queer; grandmother thinks so too."

"How come you to be so wise, honey?" Uncle Remus inquired, opening his eyes wide with astonishment.

"I know by the way you talk, and by the way grandmother looks sometimes," answered the little boy.

Uncle Remus said nothing for some time. When he did speak, it was to lead the little boy to believe that he had been all the time engaged in thinking about something else. "Talkin' er dirty folks," he said, "you oughter seed yo' pa when he wuz a little bit er chap. Dey wuz long days when you couldn't tell ef he wuz black er white, he wuz dat dirty. He'd come out'n de big house in de mornin' ez clean ez a new pin, an' 'fo' ten er-clock you couldn't tell what kinder clof his cloze wuz made out'n. Many's de day when I've seed ol' Miss—dat's yo' great-gran'mammy—comb 'nuff trash out'n his head fer ter fill a basket."

The little boy laughed at the picture that Uncle Remus drew of his father. "He's very clean, now," said the lad loyally.

"Maybe he is an' maybe he ain't," remarked Uncle Remus, suggesting a doubt. "Dat's needer here ner dar. Is he any better off clean dan what he wuz when you couldn't put yo' han's on 'im widout havin' ter go an' wash um? Yo' gran'mammy useter call 'im a pig, an' clean ez he may be now, I take notice dat he makes mo' complaint er headache an' de heartburn dan what he done when he wuz runnin' roun' here half-naked an' full er mud. I hear tell dat some nights he can't git no sleep, but when he wuz little like you—no, suh, I'll not say dat, bekaze he wuz bigger dan what you is fum de time he kin toddle roun' widout nobody he'pin' him; but when he wuz ol' ez you an' twice ez big, dey ain't narry night dat he can't sleep—an' not only all night, but half de day ef dey'd 'a' let 'im. Ef dey'd let you run roun' here like he done, an' git dirty, you'd git big an' strong 'fo' you know it. Dey ain't nothin' mo' wholesomer dan a peck er two er clean dirt on a little chap like you."

There is no telling what comment the child would have made on this sincere tribute to clean dirt, for his attention was suddenly attracted to something that was gradually taking shape in the hands of Uncle Remus. At first it seemed to be hardly worthy of notice, for it had been only a thin piece of board. But now the one piece had become four pieces, two long and two short, and under the deft manipulations of Uncle Remus it soon assumed a boxlike shape.

The old man had reached the point in his work where silence was necessary to enable him to do it full justice. As he fitted the thin boards together, a whistling sound issued from his lips, as though he were letting off steam; but the singular noise was due to the fact that he was completely absorbed in his work. He continued to fit and trim, and trim and fit, until finally the little boy could no longer restrain his curiosity. "Uncle Remus, what are you making?" he asked plaintively.

"Larroes fer ter kech meddlers," was the prompt and blunt reply.

"Well, what are larroes to catch meddlers?" the child insisted.

"Nothin' much an' sump'n mo'. Dicky, Dicky, killt a chicky, an' fried it quicky, in de oven, like a sloven. Den ter his daddy's Sunday hat, he tuck 'n' hitched de ol' black cat. Now what you reckon make him do dat? Ef you can't tell me word fer word an' spellin' fer spellin' we'll go out an' come in an' take a walk."

He rose, grunting as he did so, thus paying an unintentional tribute to the efficacy of age as the partner of rheumatic aches and stiff joints. "You hear me gruntin'," he remarked—"well, dat's bekaze I ain't de chicky fried by Dicky, which he e't 'nuff fer ter make 'im sicky." As he went out the child took his hand, and went trotting along by his side, thus affording an interesting study for those who concern themselves with the extremes of life. Hand in hand the two went out into the fields, and thence into the great woods, where Uncle Remus, after searching about for some time, carefully deposited his oblong box, remarking: "Ef I don't make no mistakes, dis ain't so mighty fur fum de place whar de creeturs has der playgroun', an' dey ain't no tellin' but what one un um'll creep in dar when deyer playin' hidin', an' ef he do, he'll sho be our meat."

"Oh, it's a trap!" exclaimed the little boy, his face lighting up with enthusiasm.

"An' dey wa'n't nobody here fer ter tell you," Uncle Remus declared, astonishment in his tone. "Well, ef dat don't bang my time, I ain't no free nigger. Now, ef dat had 'a' been yo' pa at de same age, I'd 'a' had ter tell 'im forty-lev'm times, an' den he wouldn't 'a' b'lieved me twel he see sump'n in dar tryin' fer ter git out. Den he'd say it wuz a trap, but not befo'. I ain't blamin' 'im," Uncle Remus went on, "kaze 'tain't eve'y chap dat kin tell a trap time he see it, an' mo' dan dat, traps don' allers sketch what dey er sot fer."

He paused, looked all round, and up in the sky, where fleecy clouds were floating lazily along, and in the tops of the trees, where the foliage was swaying gently in the breeze. Then he looked at the little boy. "Ef I ain't gone an' got los'," he said, "we ain't so mighty fur fum de place whar Mr. Man, once 'pon a time—not yo' time ner yit my time, but some time—tuck'n' sot a trap fer Brer Rabbit. In dem days, dey hadn't l'arnt how ter be kyarpenters, an' dish yer trap what I'm tellin' you 'bout wuz a great contraption. Big ez Brer Rabbit wuz, it wuz lots too big fer him.

"Now, whiles Mr. Man wuz fixin' up dis trap, Mr. Rabbit wa'n't so mighty fur off. He hear de saw—er-rash! er-rash!—an' he hear de hammer—bang, bang, bang!—an' he ax hisse'f what all dis racket wuz 'bout. He see Mr. Man come out'n his yard totin' sump'n, an' he got furder off; he see Mr. Man comin' todes de bushes, an' he tuck ter de woods; he see 'im comin' todes de woods, an' he tuck ter de bushes. Mr. Man tote de trap so fur an' no furder. He put it down, he did, an' Brer Rabbit watch 'im; he put in de bait, an' Brer Rabbit watch 'im; he fix de trigger, an' still Brer Rabbit watch 'im. Mr. Man look at de trap an' it satchify him. He look at it an' laugh, an' when he do dat Brer Rabbit wunk one eye, an' wiggle his mustache, an' chaw his cud.

"An' dat ain't all he do, needer. He sot out in de bushes, he did, an' study how ter git some game in de trap. He study so hard, an' he got so errytated, dat he thumped his behime foot on de groun' twel it soun' like a cow dancin' out dar in de bushes, but 'twan't no cow, ner yit no calf—'twus des Brer Rabbit studyin'. Atter so long a time, he put out down de road todes dat part er de country whar mos' er de creeturs live at. Eve'y time he hear a fuss, he'd dodge in de bushes, kaze he wanter see who comin'. He keep on an' he keep on, an' bimeby he hear ol' Brer Wolf trottin' down de road.

"It so happen dat Brer Wolf wuz de ve'y one what Brer Rabbit wanter see. Dey wuz perlite ter one an'er, but dey wan't no frien'ly feelin' 'twix um. Well, here come ol' Brer Wolf, hongrier dan a chicken-hawk on a frosty mornin', an' ez he come up he see Brer Rabbit set by de side er de road lookin' like he done lose all his fambly an' his friends terboot.

"Dey pass de time er day, an' den Brer Wolf kinder grin an' say, 'Laws-a-massy, Brer Rabbit! what ail you? You look like you done had a spell er fever an' ague; what de trouble?' 'Trouble, Brer Wolf? You ain't never see no trouble twel you get whar I'm at. Maybe you wouldn't min' it like I does, kaze I ain't usen ter it. But I boun' you done seed me light-minded fer de las' time. I'm done—I'm plum wo' out,' sez Brer Rabbit, sezee. Dis make Brer Wolf open his eyes wide. He say, 'Dis de fus' time I ever is hear you talk dat-a-way, Brer Rabbit; take yo' time an' tell me 'bout it. I ain't had my brekkus yit, but dat don't make no diffunce, long ez youer in trouble. I'll he'p you out ef I kin, an' mo' dan dat, I'll put some heart in de work.' When he say dis, he grin an' show his tushes, an' Brer Rabbit kinder edge 'way fum 'im. He say, 'Tell me de trouble, Brer Rabbit, an' I'll do my level bes' fer ter he'p you out.'

"Wid dat, Brer Rabbit 'low dat Mr. Man done been had 'im hired fer ter take keer er his truck patch, an' keep out de minks, de mush-rats an' de weasels. He say dat he done so well settin' up night after night, when he des might ez well been in bed, dat Mr. Man prommus 'im sump'n extry 'sides de mess er greens what he gun 'im eve'y day. Atter so long a time, he say, Mr. Man 'low dat he gwineter make 'im a present uv a cradle so he kin rock de little Rabs ter sleep when dey cry. So said, so done, he say. Mr. Man make de cradle an' tell Brer Rabbit he kin take it home wid 'im.

"He start out wid it, he say, but it got so heavy he hatter set it down in de woods, an' dat's de reason why Brer Wolf seed 'im settin' down by de side er de road, lookin' like he in deep trouble. Brer Wolf sot down, he did, an' study, an' bimeby he say he'd like mighty well fer ter have a cradle fer his chillun, long ez cradles wuz de style. Brer Rabbit say dey been de style fer de longest, an' ez fer Brer Wolf wantin' one, he say he kin have de one what Mr. Man make fer him, kaze it's lots too big fer his chillun. 'You know how folks is,' sez Brer Rabbit, sezee. 'Dey try ter do what dey dunner how ter do, an' dar's der house bigger dan a barn, an' dar's de fence wid mo' holes in it dan what dey is in a saine, an' kaze dey have great big chillun dey got de idee dat eve'y cradle what dey make mus' fit der own chillun. An' dat's how come I can't tote de cradle what Mr. Man make fer me mo' dan ten steps at a time.'

"Brer Wolf ax Brer Rabbit what he gwineter do fer a cradle, an' Brer Rabbit 'low he kin manage fer ter git 'long wid de ol' one twel he kin 'suade Mr. Man ter make 'im en'er one, an' he don't speck dat'll be so mighty hard ter do. Brer Wolf can't he'p but b'lieve dey's some trick in it, an' he say he ain't see de ol' cradle when las' he wuz at Brer Rabbit house. Wid dat, Brer Rabbit bust out laughin'. He say, 'Dat's been so long back, Brer Wolf, dat I done fergit all 'bout it; 'sides dat, ef dey wuz a cradle dar, I boun' you my ol' 'oman got better sense dan ter set de cradle in der parler, whar comp'ny comes'; an' he laugh so loud an' long dat he make Brer Wolf right shame er himse'f.

"He 'low, ol' Brer Wolf did, 'Come on, Brer Rabbit, an' show me whar de cradle is. Ef it's too big fer yo' chillun, it'll des 'bout fit mine.' An' so off dey put ter whar Mr. Man done sot his trap. 'Twa'n't so mighty long fo' dey got whar dey wuz gwine, an' Brer Rabbit say, 'Brer Wolf, dar yo' cradle, an' may it do you mo' good dan it's yever done me!' Brer Wolf walk all roun' de trap an' look at it like 'twas 'live. Brer Rabbit thump one er his behime foots on de groun' an' Brer Wolf jump like some un done shot a gun right at 'im. Dis make Brer Rabbit laugh twel he can't laugh no mo'. Brer Wolf, he say he kinder nervous 'bout dat time er de year, an' de leas' little bit er noise 'll make 'im jump. He ax how he gwineter git any purchis on de cradle, an' Brer Rabbit say he'll hatter git inside an' walk wid it on his back, kaze dat de way he done done.

"Brer Wolf ax what all dem contraptions on de inside is, an' Brer Rabbit 'spon' dat dey er de rockers, an' dey ain't no needs fer ter be skeer'd un um, kaze dey ain't nothin' but plain wood. Brer Wolf say he ain't 'zactly skeer'd, but he done got ter de p'int whar he know dat you better look 'fo' you jump. Brer Rabbit 'low dat ef dey's any jumpin' fer ter be done, he de one ter do it, an' he talk like he done fergit what dey come fer. Brer Wolf, he fool an' fumble roun', but bimeby he walk in de cradle, sprung de trigger, an' dar he wuz! Brer Rabbit, he holler out, 'Come on, Brer Wolf; des hump yo'se'f, an' I'll be wid you.' But try ez he will an' grunt ez he may, Brer Wolf can't budge dat trap. Bimeby Brer Rabbit git tired er waitin', an' he say dat ef Brer Wolf ain't gwineter come on he's gwine home. He 'low dat a frien' what say he gwineter he'p you, an' den go in a cradle an' drap off ter sleep, dat's all he wanter know 'bout um; an' wid dat he made fer de bushes, an' he wa'n't a minnit too soon, kaze here come Mr. Man fer ter see ef his trap had been sprung. He look, he did, an', sho' nuff, it 'uz sprung, an' dey wuz sump'n in dar, too, kaze he kin hear it rustlin' roun' an' kickin' fer ter git out.

"Mr. Man look thoo de crack, an' he see Brer Wolf, which he wuz so skeer'd twel his eye look right green. Mr. Man say, 'Aha! I got you, is I?' Brer Wolf say, 'Who?' Mr. Man laugh twel he can't sca'cely talk, an' still Brer Wolf say, 'Who? Who you think you got?' Mr. Man 'low, 'I don't think, I knows. Youer ol' Brer Rabbit, dat's who you is.' Brer Wolf say, 'Turn me outer here, an' I'll show you who I is.' Mr. Man laugh fit ter kill. He 'low, 'You neenter change yo' voice; I'd know you ef I met you in de dark. Youer Brer Rabbit, dat's who you is.' Brer Wolf say, 'I ain't not; dat's what I'm not!'

"Mr. Man look thoo de crack ag'in, an' he see de short years. He 'low, 'You done cut off yo' long years, but still I knows you. Oh, yes! an' you done sharpen you mouf an' put smut on it—but you can't fool me.' Brer Wolf say, 'Nobody ain't tryin' fer ter fool you. Look at my fine long bushy tail.' Mr. Man 'low, 'You done tied an'er tail on behime you, but you can't fool me. Oh, no, Brer Rabbit! You can't fool me.' Brer Wolf say, 'Look at de ha'r on my back; do dat look like Brer Rabbit? Mr. Man 'low, 'You done wallered in de red san', but you can't fool me.'

"Brer Wolf say, 'Look at my long black legs; do dey look like Brer Rabbit?' Mr. Man 'low, 'You kin put an'er j'int in yo' legs, an' you kin smut um, but you can't fool me.' Brer Wolf say, 'Look at my tushes; does dey look like Brer Rabbit?' Mr. Man 'low, 'You done got new toofies, but you can't fool me.' Brer Wolf say, 'Look at my little eyes; does dey look like Brer Rabbit?' Mr. Man 'low, 'You kin squinch yo' eye-balls, but you can't fool me, Brer Rabbit.' Brer Wolf squall out, 'I ain't not Brer Rabbit, an' yo' better turn me out er dis place so I kin take hide an' ha'r off'n Brer Rabbit.' Mr. Man say, 'Ef bofe hide an' ha'r wuz off, I'd know you, kaze 'tain't in you fer ter fool me.' An' it hurt Brer Wolf feelin's so bad fer Mr. Man ter sput his word, dat he bust out inter a big boo-boo, an' dat's 'bout all I know."

"Did the man really and truly think that Brother Wolf was Brother Rabbit?" asked the little boy.

"When you pin me down dat-a-way," responded Uncle Remus, "I'm bleeze ter tell you dat I ain't too certain an' sho' 'bout dat. De tale come down fum my great gran'daddy's great gran'daddy; it come on down ter my daddy, an' des ez he gun it ter me, des dat-a-way I done gun it ter you."

The Little Baxters Go Marketing

By Tudor Jenks

Paul Baxter was too small to be head of the family. He was only seven, while his sister was five, and Paul thought she had a great deal to learn. Mrs. Baxter was the rest of the family, for the father had sailed away with the fishing fleet one foggy morning, and the fleet came back without one boat, and that boat was John Baxter's. They all thought he was drowned, but they were wrong, as you will see. Meanwhile you must pretend you don't know he is alive, or else you can't understand what an unhappy time Mrs. Baxter was living through, and how much rested on Paul's little shoulders while he considered himself the head of the family.

The worst time had not come yet, for the father had saved some money, and he had not been missing more than about two weeks. Mrs. Baxter knew that the money would soon be gone, so she was saving every cent she could.

On the day before Thanksgiving, she told Paul and his sister Kate that "until their father came home again" (for she would not speak as if he were lost), they must be very careful, and so their Thanksgiving dinner would have to be a very plain one.

"No turkey?" Kate asked.

"No, dear," said their mother, "unless you and Paul can catch one somewhere in the street."

They knew this was a joke, for they lived in South Street, New York City, where trucks rumbled about all day.

Paul felt he must get a turkey for a reason Mrs. Baxter didn't know. As John Baxter was bidding Paul good-bye the night before he sailed, Paul had asked whether he would be back for Thanksgiving.

"I think so, my boy, but one can't be sure. If I shouldn't, you must see to the Thanksgiving dinner, and carve the turkey. Will you?"

"Yes," said Paul, very proud, and now how could he, if there was none to carve? Paul made up his mind that it was his business to see that the family had a turkey. Paul had some money in his own small cast-iron bank. And he knew it was right for him to do what he liked with his savings. He had already offered them to his mother, and she had told him they were of no use to her. Kate, too, had some money in her bank; it was just like Paul's except that there was a "K" on the door, made with a red pencil.

While their mother was clearing away the breakfast, Paul beckoned to Kate and proposed that they should put their money together and surprise mother with the biggest, fattest, finest bird in the market.

Kate feared the bird would cost too much.

"Nonsense, child," said Paul, grandly; "why, I have more than seventy-five cents. How much have you?"

"Twenty-eight, I think," said Kate.

"Well, then!" Paul answered; "that's more'n a dollar. You can buy 'most anything for a dollar, child."

They opened the banks, and counted the money three times, to make sure. It came out different every time, but they had about one dollar and fifteen or eighteen cents. It was all in small pieces and looked enough to buy an elephant. Paul tied it all up carefully in the corner of his handkerchief.

Then, after they had helped their mother to tidy the rooms, they got permission to go to market for her. She told them what to buy, and Paul was glad when his mother told them to get some cranberries for sauce, and a plum-pudding that came in a tin can. With their turkey, what a feast these would make!

The market was not far away, but it was so crowded that Paul and Kate had to hold hands tight. For a long time they could get no attention, but at last, by pulling one of the marketmen's aprons, Paul made him listen. Paul bought all the things on their list, and then said, proudly:

"Please show me some of the biggest turkeys."

The marketman, pointing to a long row, remarked:

"There they are—all weighed and marked. Pick out the one you want."

Paul examined the tickets stuck on the turkeys—$2.20, $3.50, $2.40, $4.00 (he was a perfect giant of a gobbler!) and so on. Paul felt a lump in his throat, he was so disappointed! Then little Kate made it worse by pointing to the very biggest and saying, "Oh, Paul, buy that!—it's the best of all!"

Paul whispered to her, "It costs four dollars. Isn't that *awful*? The cheapest one is two dollars! What can we do?"

Kate shook her head. Then she had a bright idea.

"I know!" she said. "If we can't have the biggest, let's get the very littlest that ever was! It will be cunning, and that will make mamma laugh."

"But I don't see any very little ones," Paul replied.

"Ask the man," Kate urged.

It was some time before Paul could get the man's attention, and then the question was put.

"The littlest turkey?" repeated the marketman, with a grin. "That's a queer order, now. Why do you want the littlest one, my boy?"

"'Cause we're buying it for mamma," said Kate eagerly. "She can't get one at all, because papa's gone away, and he *may* not come back, and we got the money out of our banks, and we've only one dollar and fifteen cents, and we can't have the biggest, you see."

"Hello!" said the marketman, "here's a talker for a little one! Haven't I seen you before?"

"Yes, sir," Kate answered. "I'm Katie Baxter, and I used to come with papa."

"You Jack Baxter's girl?" asked the marketman, stooping down and picking the child up.

"Yes, sir," said Kate, "but please put me down." But instead the man called to a marketman in the next stall,

"See here O'Neil, this is the Baxter girl. She's come with another little kid to buy the littlest turkey for her mother. They've got the money out of their banks, and it's a dollar fifteen. Can't we fill the order?"

"Well, I guess we *can*," said the other marketman heartily. "We'll send them a bird—with the stuffing, too!"

"It'll be all right," said the first marketman, putting little Kate on her feet again. "Give me the number, and we'll send the bird around to-morrow."

Paul gave the number, untied the money from his handkerchief, and away they went through the noisy street home.

Paul and Kate had hard work to keep the secret of their marketing, but they did, all that day, and the next.

About four o'clock there was a knock at the door, and when the door was opened, there was nobody there. But there was something. A big, big market-basket, and in it was the giant turkey, and on the turkey's breast a piece of paper, saying:

"From the friends of John Baxter to Mrs. Baxter and the little Baxters, hoping they'll enjoy their Thanksgiving."

And that wasn't all, for the turkey, when Mrs. Baxter came to prepare it, was stuffed with silver dollars.

Then Mrs. Baxter cried; and Paul and Kate were puzzled by that. But she was thankful, for she told them so.

When the great bird was properly browned and smoking, Paul took his place ready to carve. He had just raised the knife and fork when the door opened and a big, hearty sailor came in, saying:

"Here, here, young man, this won't do! That is *my* place!"

And, of course, it was John Baxter; and the turkey was not nearly so hot by the time he had been hugged and kissed (meaning John Baxter, of course), and had told how his boat had been sunk, but he and his mates picked up by a steamer.

That *was* a Thanksgiving dinner.

Next day John Baxter took his boy and girl down to the market, and they made another giving of thanks to the marketmen, and that is a good ending to the story, isn't it?

There is one more thing. The marketmen would not take back their silver, and so it went into the bank—a real bank this time—for Paul and Kate.

A Story of Decoration Day for The Little Children of To-Day

By Elisabeth Harrison

I want you to listen to a sad, sweet story to-day, and yet one that ought to make you glad—glad that such men have lived as those of whom I am going to tell you. It all happened a good many years ago, in fact so long ago that your fathers and mothers were little boys and girls in kilts and pinafores, some of them mere babies in long clothes.

One bright Sunday morning in April the telegraph wires could be heard repeating the same things all over the land, "Tic, tic; tictic; t-i-c; tic, tictic;—tic, t-i-c, tic; t-i-c; tic, t-i-c; t-i-c, t-i-c, tic," they called out, and the drowsy telegraph operators sat up in their chairs as if startled by the words the wires were saying.

"Tic, t-i-c, tic; tictic; tic, tictic; tic; t-i-c, tictic;—tic, tic; t-i-c, tic," continued the wires, and the faces of the telegraph operators grew pale. Any looker-on could have seen that something dreadful was being told by the wires.

"Tic, t-i-c, tic; tictic; tic, tictic; tic; t-i-c, tictic;—tic, tic; t-i-c, tic," again repeated the wires. There was no mistaking the message this time. Alas, alas, it was true! The terrible news was true! Even the bravest among the operators trembled.

Then came the rapid writing out of the fearful words that the slender wires had uttered, the hurrying to and fro; and messenger boys were seen flying to the great newspaper offices, and the homes of the mayors of the cities, and to the churches where already the people were beginning to assemble. For the deep-toned Sabbath church bells high up in the steeples had been ringing out their welcome to all, even the strangers in their midst—"Bim! Baum! Bim!" they sang, which everybody knew meant, "Come to church, dear people! Come! Come! Come!" And the people strolled leisurely along toward the churches—fathers and mothers and little ones, and even grandfathers and grandmothers. It was such a bright, pleasant day that it seemed a joy to go to the house of God and thank Him for all His love and care. So one family after another filed into their pews while the organist played such soft, sweet music that everybody felt soothed and quieted by it.

Little did they dream of the awful words which the telegraph wires were at that very moment calling out with their "Tic, t-i-c, tic; t-i-c; tic, t-i-c; t-i-c, t-i-c, tic;—Tic, t-i-c, tic, tictic, tic, tictic; tic; t-i-c; tictic."

The clergymen came in and took their places in the pulpits. In each church the organ ceased its wordless song of praise. The congregation bowed and silently joined with all their hearts in the petitions which the clergyman was offering to the dear Lord, Father of all mankind, Ruler of heaven and earth. Some of them softly whispered "Amen" as he asked protection for their homes and their beloved country. Did they know anything about the danger which even then hung over them? Perhaps they did.

In many of the churches the prayer was over, the morning hymn had been sung, when a stir and bustle at the door might have been noticed, as the messenger boys, excited and out of breath, handed their yellow envelopes to the ushers who stood near the door ready to show the late comers to unoccupied seats. First one and then the other ushers read the message, and from some one of them escaped, in a hushed whisper, the words, "Oh, God! Has it come to this!"

And all looked white and awe-struck. The head usher hurried tremblingly down the aisle, and without waiting for the clergyman to finish reading the announcements of the week, laid the telegram upon the pulpit desk.

The clergyman, somewhat surprised at such an interruption, glanced at the paper, stopped, gasped, picked it up, and re-read the words written upon it, as though he could not believe his own eyes. Then he advanced a step forward, holding on to the desk, as if he had been struck a blow by some unseen hand. The congregation knew that something terrible had happened, and their hearts seemed to stop beating as they leaned forward to catch his words.

"My people," said he in a slow, deliberate tone, as if it were an effort to steady his voice, "I hold in my hand a message from the President of the United States." Then his eyes dropped to the paper which he still held, and now his voice rang out clear and loud as he read, "*Our Flag has been fired upon! Seventy-five thousand troops wanted at once. Abraham Lincoln.*"

I could not make you understand all that took place the next week or two any more than the little children who heard what the telegram said, understood it. Men came home, hurried and excited, to hunt up law papers, or to straighten out deeds, saying in constrained tones to the pale-faced women, "I will try to leave all business matters straight before I go." There was solemn consultations between husbands and wives, which usually ended in the father's going out, stern-faced and silent, and the mother, dry-eyed but with quivering lips, seeking her own room, locking herself in for an hour, then coming out to the wondering children with a quiet face, but with eyes that showed she had been weeping. There were gatherings in the town halls and in the churches and school houses all over the land. The newspapers were read hurriedly and anxiously.

And when little Robert looked up earnestly into his grandmamma's face and asked, "Why does mamma not eat her breakfast?" grandmamma replied, "Your papa is going away, my dear." And when little Robert persisted, by saying, "But papa goes to New York every year, and mamma does not sit and stare out of the window, and forget to eat her breakfast," then mamma would turn solemnly around and say, "Robert, my boy, papa is going to the war, and may never come back to us. But you and I must be brave about it, and help him get ready." And if Robert answered, "Why is he going to the war? Why does he not stay at home with us? Doesn't he love us any more?" then mamma would draw her boy to her and putting her arms around him, and looking into his eyes, she would say, "Yes, my darling, he loves us, but he *must* go. Our country needs him, and you and I must be proud that he is ready to do his duty."

Then Robert would go away to his play, wondering what it all meant, just as you would have wondered if you had been there.

Soon the papas and uncles, and even some of the grandfathers, put on soldiers' uniforms, and drilled in the streets with guns over their shoulders, and bands of music played military music, and the drums beat, and crowds of people collected on the street corners, and there were more speeches, and more flags, and banners, and stir, and excitement. And nothing else was talked of but the war, the war, the terrible war.

Then came the marching away of the soldiers to the railway stations, and then the farewells and cheers and waving of handkerchiefs and the playing of patriotic airs by the bands of music, and much more confusion and excitement and good-bye kisses and tears than I could tell you of.

Then came the long, long days of waiting and praying in the homes to which fathers and brothers no longer came, and silent watching for letters, and anxious opening of the newspapers, and oftentimes the little children felt their mamma's tears drop on their faces as she kissed them good-night—their dear mamma who so often had sung them to sleep with her gay, happy songs—what did it all mean? They could not tell.

And all this time the fathers, brave men as they were, had been marching down to the war. Oftentimes they slept on the hard ground with only their army blankets wrapped around them, and the stars to keep watch over them, and many a day they had nothing to eat but dry bread and black coffee, because they had not time to cook more, and sometimes they had no breakfast at all because they must be up by daybreak and march on, even if the rain poured down, as it sometimes did, wetting them through and through.

What were such hardships when *their country was in danger?*

Then came the terrible, terrible battles, more awful than anything you ever dreamed of. Men were shot down by the thousands, and many who did not lose their lives had a leg shot off, or an arm so crushed that it had to be cut off. Still they bravely struggled on. It was for their beloved country they were fighting, and for it they must be willing to suffer, or to die.

Then a hundred thousand more soldiers were called for, and then another hundred thousand, and still the bloody war continued. For four long years it lasted, and the whole world looked on, amazed at such courage and endurance.

Then the men who had not been killed, or who had not died of their sufferings came marching home again, many, alas, on crutches, and many who knew that they were disabled for life. But *they had saved their country*! And that was reward enough for their heroic hearts. Though many a widow turned her sad face away when the crowd welcomed the returning soldiers, for she knew that her loved one was not with them, and many little children learned in time that their dear fathers would never return to them.

War is such a terrible thing that it makes one's heart ache to think of it.

Then by and by the people said, "Our children must grow up loving and honouring the heroic men who gave their lives for their country." So in villages and towns and cities monuments were built in honour of the men who died fighting for their country. And one day each year was set apart to keep fresh and green the memory of the brave soldiers; and it has been named "Decoration Day," because on this day all the children, all over the land, are permitted to go to the graves of the dead soldiers and place flowers upon them.

The Taxes of Middlebrook

By Ray Stannard Baker

Up above the pines on the edge to the east the sun was rising and the air smelled of the woods, of the warm sand of the roadsides, of the perfect May morning. Three men in the quaint garb of pioneer foreigners came down the lane from the shoemaker's house and turned into the road. Before they had gone many paces old Peter Walling stopped abruptly.

"There is a warning," he said in Norwegian.

The eyes of the two others followed swiftly to his pointing. In the midst of the sand a twig of willow had been stuck. The top was split, and it held upward a bit of soiled paper. Old Peter seemed undecided whether to touch the message or not, but Halstrom, the shoemaker, plucked it from the stick, and scowled as he tried to make out its meaning. Presently he handed it to his son.

"What does it say, Eric?" he asked.

The message was in English, printed with a lumberman's coarse pencil, and a rude attempt had been made to draw a skull and crossbones at the top of the paper. Eric read it slowly, translating into Norwegian as he went along:

> "Be Ware! All Norwegans and Sweeds are hereby warned not to go to the Town Hall under penalty of death."

It was signed in big letters, "By Order of the Committee."

Eric Halstrom looked up and laughed shortly. "Well," he said, "it means us," and he tucked the message away with some care in his pocket.

"We may need it," he added.

The two older men were silent for a moment. Then Peter Walling spoke faintly: "If there is going to be trouble—if there is danger—"

The old shoemaker straightened his bent shoulders and his eyes flashed angrily. "Peter Walling, will you go or will you stay? I thought we had settled this question once for all."

"I'll go, Jens—yes, yes, I'll go," answered Walling, hurriedly, but his lips protested under his beard.

Halstrom turned without a word and hobbled down the road, determination speaking from every nervous hitch of his twisted frame. He was small and crippled, and in all his life he had never been able to do the work of a strong man. But there was that in his blue eyes which made him a leader in Thingvalla. He had cobbled in the old country, and he had cobbled in this new Northwest among the pines, and every peg he drove had clinched a thought. He was not educated in English; he had emigrated too late for that, but he had seen to it that his son made the best of the scant schooling of a new land, and better still, he had taught him some of the wisdom that comes to a cobbler who thinks.

Eric stood almost six feet tall. His hair was as yellow and curly as a rope end, and his eyes were blue and steady. Although barely twenty years old, he had learned by the hard knocks of a pioneer country how to take care of himself, both with his big right arm and with his tongue.

Over ten miles of sand-hills and corduroy, through vast forests of pine as yet barely notched with the clearings of settlers, the three men came at last in sight of the town hall, the shoemaker and his son in front, and old Peter Walling behind, muttering his fears. The town hall was a log shack, one story high, with a single large room.

As the three approached, they could see that the road was full of men and teams. The men were moving about, and talking with the boisterous pleasantry of backwoodsmen who do not often meet. They had gathered this spring morning for the annual session of the board of review—the board that was to make the final equalisation of the taxes on the property of the township. Eric looked anxiously to see if there were any others present from the Thingvalla settlement, or, indeed, any Scandinavians, but he could not see even one.

"They are all afraid," the shoemaker said, bitterly. "They have come to a free country, and they don't know how to be free."

But the New Antrim settlement was out in force. Eric heard the jolly voices of the young Irishmen, and he knew well that they were spoiling for a fight. Thingvalla was in one corner of the township, New Antrim was in the other, and between the settlements stretched unbroken forests of pine and implacable bitterness. It was one of those settlement differences so common in the backwoods, and the more unfortunate for being unfounded. New Antrim was sure that Thingvalla was trying to control the township, and Thingvalla was equally sure that New Antrim was escaping its share of taxation. And that was the condition on this bright May day, when the three from Thingvalla came down with the warning in Eric's pocket.

"They are too many!" muttered old Peter Walling, tremulously.

They saw Calvin Donohue and his men sporting in the sunshine. Donohue was the man in the otter cap, immensely broad and brawny of shoulders, long of arms and square of chin. He talked in a big, jolly voice; from where they stood they could hear him laugh.

O'Rourke, Callahan and some of the younger men were trying their strength on a huge iron soap-kettle that stood in front of the blacksmith shop. They were testing their muscles to see which could lift it from the ground with one hand. There were few who could do it, but Calvin Donohue put it as high as his shoulder as if it were only a feather. Others were pitching quoits with horseshoes, and one group was watching a pulling contest between O'Rourke and Davy, who were sitting, feet to feet on the ground, tugging on a crowbar.

The shoemaker, who had been resting by the roadside, now rose, and without a word set off down the hill toward the crowd, with his chin thrown up and his eyes looking neither to the right nor to the left.

The moment the men of New Antrim saw them, a gleeful shout went up. Here was new sport for them. A powerful man in a lumberman's red jacket seized a heavy oak swingletree from the blacksmith's door, sprang out into the road, and shouted:

"Come on, boys, we've got 'em!"

Eric and his father did not stop, but old Peter Walling wavered, then turned and ran back up the road as fast as his legs could carry him. It was two against thirty, but the two stood their ground. While they were exchanging challenges, a man opportunely stepped from the doorway of the town hall and began to rap on the logs with a stake, announcing that the board had been called to order.

At once there was a rush for the benches, and Eric and his father reached the door without opposition.

The shoemaker made as if to enter, but Jim O'Rourke barred the door with his arm.

"No Swedes admitted," he said, gruffly.

The shoemaker, paying no attention to the order, again endeavoured to enter. He was thrown back violently, and if it had not been for Eric, he would have fallen. The shoemaker tried to speak, but his English was hopelessly confused and broken. Eric was white to the lips, but he controlled himself.

"We are citizens of this township," he said, "and we have a right in this meeting."

"Go wan!" was the answer. "We won't have any foreigners here."

"We are as much Americans as you are!" responded Eric, hotly. "Be cool," cautioned the shoemaker, in his native tongue.

"I tell you, Jim O'Rourke," continued Eric, more steadily, "there's no need of our quarrelling this way, and if you'd let us explain we'd show you why we should all be friends—"

"Friends! Let me give you a friendly hint. You get out of here double-quick."

By nature the Scandinavian is peaceable. He hates fighting as much as he loves his home; and yet, for being slow to wrath, he is the more terrible when roused. Eric took one step forward and drove up O'Rourke's arm with a stinging blow that sent him spinning into the room. Then he and his father entered. O'Rourke, recovering himself, rushed upon Eric and dealt him a terrific blow in the breast. The two men were just closing in a desperate encounter when Caxton, the chairman, rose, ordering silence and preparing to enforce his decree with a stout oak stake.

"What's the trouble here?" he demanded, when quiet had been restored.

"We are citizens of this township," said Eric, panting, "and we have a right to attend this meeting. This man tried to shut us out."

Caxton paused a moment.

"Put out the Norsks!" roared a voice.

"No," said Caxton. "They have a right to be here and to be heard on the subject of their taxes."

"Thank you!" said Eric, eagerly. "I want to explain—"

"You will be given a chance in due time," was the answer, given so coldly that it indicated the chairman's position against them beyond a doubt. There were many whispered threats, but Eric and his father firmly stood their ground. The business of the board of review is to hear the complaints of those who think they have been unfairly taxed. Apparently there were to be few complaints at this meeting. An old man who spoke with the unmistakable inflection of the Irishman commended the assessment and praised the assessor. He thought every one in the township had been satisfied. He was pleased to know that this was so. As he sat down, a small, loosely jointed man, with fiery red hair, rose from his chair.

He wore a diamond shirt-stud which, if genuine, would have purchased every stitch of personal apparel in the room. He drawled pleasantly in his talk. Every one knew him. His name was William P. Ketchum, or more familiarly, Billy Ketchum. Eric's eyes fastened hard upon him and watched him as a catamount might watch a squirrel, and with much the same motive.

Billy Ketchum was the representative of the great logging concern of Miller, Knees & Dye, which owned all the pine lands in the township, and, indeed, in nearly all the county. He complimented the assessor in his softest manner, he complimented the board down from Caxton to Severn, through Holt, and then he complimented them up again from Severn to Caxton. He mentioned New Antrim and brought in a deft reference to the shamrock and the old sod, and then—he suddenly caught the eye of Eric Halstrom burning at him above the heads of the crowd. For a single instant he seemed trying to pull himself together, and then he went on with his pleasant drawl:

"As representing the largest taxpayers in Middlebrook," he said, "I am deeply interested in its welfare. We pay our taxes gladly, knowing that they have been honestly levied and that they will be honestly collected—"

At this Eric Halstrom came shouldering nearer, with the shoemaker close behind him.

"It's not so!" Eric gasped, excitedly. "I tell you it's not so. He's the man who's caused all the trouble."

"I was not aware," put in Billy Ketchum, in his smoothest voice, "that you allowed your meetings to be broken up by a brawling—"

His last words were drowned in shouts, and it was some moments before Mr. Caxton, pounding on the table, could restore peace.

Calvin Donohue whispered in the chairman's ear, and Mr. Caxton said aloud to Eric, "We'll hear what you have to say right away."

The shoemaker pushed Eric forward eagerly. The boy stood up before the crowd, blushing and stammering. His big hands fumbled in his pockets and his tongue refused to stir. He had not been particularly afraid to face the assembled forces of New Antrim in the road, but he was afraid to make a speech.

"I—I wanted to—explain about the taxes," he stammered.

"So I suppose," was Mr. Caxton's cool reply.

Eric pulled a piece of chalk out of his pocket and looked round.

"I—I've got to have something to write on," he said, at which the New Antrimites shouted with laughter.

If it had not been for the wise old shoemaker at that moment, Eric would have been lost, laughed to defeat. Nothing will floor a speaker more quickly than the wit of an Irish audience. But the shoemaker spoke in Norwegian. Eric turned quickly; he was only a step from the door. There, outside in the sand, stood the old iron kettle. He stooped, picked it up, and set it on a bench, which the shoemaker had swung into place. It was all done so swiftly that New Antrim forgot it's fun in its astonishment.

And when Eric drew a big white square on the kettle with his chalk, a voice rose hoarsely from the back of the room:

"Well, I'll be jiggered!"

At that all the Irishmen laughed, and then sat still again, out of respect, being "jiggered."

Eric divided the white square into many smaller squares. In one corner he drew a number of crosses; in the opposite corner he did the same. One of these groups of crosses he labelled T.

"That is the Thingvalla settlement," he said, "and this—is New Antrim."

Then he swept his hand between the two and glanced at Billy Ketchum. "And all this in here is the pine owned by Miller, Knees & Dye."

The shoemaker whispered in his ear, and he turned to the chairman, and said in a sterner voice: "I want to show who is to blame for all this trouble between the settlements."

"We are not dealing with quarrels," was the response. "We are here to equalise taxes."

"That's it, that's what I want to do. I want to show that the taxes aren't equal."

Then he fumbled in his pocket and drew out a much-folded paper. With this to support him, he forgot all about himself, and talked rapidly and earnestly.

He told how he had figured up all the land owned by the Scandinavians of Thingvalla, and all that owned by New Antrim, and all that owned by the lumber company.

"Thingvalla has two thousand two hundred and forty acres in farms; New Antrim has two thousand nine hundred and twenty acres," he explained, "while the lumber company has more than twelve thousand acres of pine. Thingvalla is assessed at an average of four dollars and sixty cents an acre; New Antrim is assessed at four dollars and fifteen cents an acre—a little less, but not enough to count. But here is this lumber company assessed for only one dollar and ninety cents an acre—"

Here Billy Ketchum sprang excitedly to his feet. "But this is wild land—not a foot of it is cultivated. I tell you such a comparison is unfair—"

"Yes, but your pine is worth more to the acre than our farms with all our crops and buildings on them."

"I tell you—"

"I know!" broke in Eric, excitedly. "I tell you, I know! Look here—"

He drew from his pocket a pack of little strips of paper, each with a section map at the top, upon which different "forties" of land were checked up in red and blue pencil.

He turned again to the table and marked out a square about midway between the settlements.

"Here's section ten, township forty, range twelve. Last fall I was hired to go over this land with the company's explorer, and estimate the pine. We travelled together for two months, counted all the trees, and estimated the number of feet of lumber they would make. That pine as it stands is worth from four dollars to six dollars a thousand feet, and some of the single forties have more than two hundred thousand feet of timber on them. That makes a cash value of from eight hundred dollars to twelve hundred dollars—or twenty dollars to thirty dollars an acre—and that's more than the best improved farm in this county is worth—"

"I tell you—" roared little Billy Ketchum, wild with excitement.

"And you know it," added Eric. "Here are these slips, which will prove just what I say. They are the company's own valuation of its property. You can see for yourselves that our farms are assessed for more than twice as much as this pine land, although it is worth five or six times as much. And that will show you who is dodging taxes. Billy Ketchum says that he represents the biggest taxpayers in the township, and that he is well contented with the assessment. Of course he is contented, but he is wrong about representing the largest taxpayers. As the assessments now are, we represent the biggest taxpayers—and we are not contented, for we pay ten times the taxes that we should. All I ask is that the assessments be fair, and Thingvalla and New Antrim will not quarrel."

Billy Ketchum, purple of face, tried in vain to make himself heard, but the Irishmen of New Antrim drowned him out of the discussion. The explorer's slips were passed back and forth and referred to the diagram on the iron kettle, and for a few moments pandemonium reigned.

"What's more," shouted Eric, in the flush of victory, "I can prove that Billy Ketchum is at the bottom of this quarrel!"

There was silence again.

"If it hadn't been for him, we'd have been good friends to-day. He's kept us enemies so that we couldn't get together and assess the pine lands as they ought to be assessed."

Ketchum sprang to his feet.

"It's not so!" he shouted. "We've been perfectly fair to every one. Why should I mix up in neighbourhood quarrels?"

He poured out an impassioned speech, the drawl all gone, and the words crowding so fast that he could hardly utter them plainly. He called the Irishmen "Billy" and "Calvin" and "Pete" familiarly, and spoke of their warm friendship, but somehow they did not rouse to enthusiasm as he had expected. They were thinking.

Presently Eric made himself heard again.

"Who left that warning in the Thingvalla road last night?" he asked, facing Ketchum.

"Who? How should I know?"

At this, New Antrim leaned forward to a man with curiosity. Eric drew out the warning and told where he had found it. Then he passed it gravely to Mr. Caxton.

"Billy Ketchum left that in the road," said Eric. "He did it to keep us away from the meeting. He tried to make us think that the New Antrim settlement was against us. He had found out that I knew the real value of those pine lands."

Again Billy hopped up. "I dare him to prove it, Mr. Chairman! I didn't come here to be insulted. I tell you—I dare him to prove it!"

"Well, I will," said Eric, coolly.

At that the shoemaker stepped round behind the table and picked up a long, slender, paper-covered roll and handed it to Eric. Eric held it up, and pointed to Ketchum's name written upon it, for it was a roll of maps.

Ketchum rushed at Eric and tried to grasp his property, but Eric brushed him aside.

Then he unrolled the manila covering of the maps a few inches and held it up. One corner was torn off. He took the warning notice from Mr. Caxton's desk and held it in the place of this torn corner. It fitted perfectly.

"My father happened to see this when he came in," explained Eric. "What more proof do you want?"

For a moment the room was still. Then the same deep voice which had spoken once before burst out:

"I'll be jiggered!"

Calvin Donohue turned to Billy Ketchum and said, none too pleasantly:"You get out! We can manage our own affairs!"

Callahan suggested taking him out triumphantly in the iron kettle, but Billy disappeared with such haste they could not catch him.

Then the whole assembly took up seriously the problem of assessments, and before the day was out, the township of Middlebrook was equalised, and the taxes of the settlers, New Antrim and Thingvalla alike, were cut down to their just proportions, no more, no less, and the pine lands were assessed strictly in accordance with Eric's estimate slips.

The Cure of Fear

By Norman Duncan

Like many another snug little harbor on the northeast coast of Newfoundland, Ruddy Cove is confronted by the sea and flanked by a vast wilderness; so all the folk take their living from the sea, as their forebears have done for generations.

It takes courage and a will for work to sweeten the hard life of those parts, which otherwise would be filled with dread and an intolerable weariness; and Donald North, of Ruddy Cove, was brave enough till he was eight years old. But after that season he was so timid that he shrank from the edge of the cliffs when the breakers were beating the rocks below, and he trembled when the punt heeled to a gust.

Now he was a fisherman's son, and in the course of things must himself be a paddle-punt fisherman; thus the mishap which gave him that great fear of the sea cast a dark shadow over him.

"Billy," he said to young Topsail, on the unfortunate day, "leave us go sail my new fore-an'-after. I've rigged her out with a grand new mizzens'l."

"Sure, b'y!" said Billy. "Where to?"

"Uncle George's wharf-head. 'Tis a place as good as any."

Off Uncle George's wharf-head the water was deep—deeper than Donald could fathom at low tide—and it was cold, and covered a rocky bottom, upon which a multitude of starfish and prickly sea-eggs lay in clusters. It was green, smooth and clear, too; sight carried straight down to where the purple-shelled mussels gripped the rocks.

The tide had fallen somewhat and was still on the ebb. Donald found it a long reach from the wharf to the water. By and by, as the water ran out of the harbour, the most he could do was to touch the mast tip of the miniature ship with his fingers. Then a little gust of wind crept round the corner of the wharf, rippling the water as it came near. It caught the sails of the new fore-and-after, and the little craft fell over on another tack and shot away.

"Here, you!" Donald cried. "Come back, will you?"

He reached for the mast. His fingers touched it, but the boat escaped before they closed. He laughed, hitched nearer to the edge of the wharf, and reached again. The wind had failed; the little boat was tossing in the ripples, below and just beyond his grasp.

"I can't catch her!" he called to Billy Topsail, who was back near the net-horse, looking for squids.

Billy looked up, and laughed to see Donald's awkward position—to see him hanging over the water, red-faced and straining. Donald laughed, too. At once he lost his balance and fell forward.

This was in the days before he could swim, so he floundered about in the water, beating it wildly, to bring himself to the surface. When he came up, Billy Topsail was leaning over to catch him. Donald lifted his arm. His fingers touched Billy's, that was all—just touched them. Then he sank; and when he came up again, and again lifted his arm, there was half a foot of space between his hand and Billy's. Some measure of self-possession returned. He took a long breath, and let himself sink. Down he went, weighted by his heavy boots.

Those moments were full of the terror of which, later, he could not rid himself. There seemed to be no end to the depth of the water in that place. But when his feet touched bottom, he was still deliberate in all that he did.

For a moment he let them rest on the rock. Then he gave himself a strong upward push. It needed but little to bring him within reach of Billy Topsail's hand. He shot out of the water and caught that hand. Soon afterward he was safe on the wharf.

"Sure, mum, I thought I was drownded that time!" he said to his mother, that night. "When I were goin' down the last time I thought I'd never see you again."

"But you wasn't drownded, b'y," said his mother, softly.

"But I might ha' been," said he.

There was the rub. He was haunted by what might have happened. Soon he became a timid, shrinking lad, utterly lacking confidence in the strength of his arms and his skill with an oar and a sail; and after that came to pass, his life was hard. He was afraid to go out to the fishing-grounds, where he must go every day with his father to keep the head of the punt up to the wind, and he had a great fear of the wind and the fog and the breakers.

But he was not a coward. On the contrary, although he was circumspect in all his dealings with the sea, he never failed in his duty.

In Ruddy Cove all the men put out their salmon-nets when the ice breaks up and drifts away southward, for the spring run of salmon then begins. These nets are laid in the sea, at right angles to the rocks and extending out from them; they are set alongshore, it may be a mile or two, from the narrow passage to the harbour. The outer end is buoyed and anchored, and the other is lashed to an iron stake which is driven deep into some crevice of the rock.

When belated icebergs hang offshore a watch must be kept on the nets, lest they be torn away or ground to pulp by the ice.

"The wind's haulin' round a bit, b'y," said Donald's father, one day in spring, when the lad was twelve years old. "I think 'twill freshen and blow inshore afore night."

"They's a scattered pan of ice out there, father," said Donald, "and three small bergs."

"Iss, b'y, I knows," said North. "'Tis that I'm afeared of. If the wind changes a bit more, 'twill jam the ice agin the rocks. Does you think the net is safe?"

It was quite evident that the net was in danger, but since Donald had first shown signs of fearing the sea, Job North had not compelled him to go out upon perilous undertakings. He had fallen into the habit of leaving the boy to choose his own course, believing that in time he would master himself.

"I think, zur," said Donald, steadily, "the net should come in."

"'Twould be wise," said North. "Come, b'y, we'll go fetch it."

So they put forth in the punt. There was a fair, fresh wind, and with this filling the little brown sail, they were soon driven out from the quiet water of the harbor to the heaving sea itself. Great swells rolled in from the open and broke furiously against the coast rocks.

The punt ran alongshore for two miles keeping well away from the breakers. When at last she came to that point where Job North's net was set, Donald furled the sail and his father took up the oars.

"'Twill be a bit hard to land," he said.

Therein lay the danger. There is no beach along that coast. The rocks rise abruptly from the sea—here, sheer and towering; there, low and broken.

When there is a sea running, the swells roll in and break against these rocks; and when the breakers catch a punt, they are certain to smash it to splinters.

The iron stake to which Job North's net was lashed was fixed in a low ledge, upon which some hardy shrubs had taken root. The waves were casting themselves against the rocks below, breaking with a great roar and flinging spray over the ledge.

"'Twill be a bit hard," North said again.

But the salmon-fishers have a way of landing under such conditions. When their nets are in danger they do not hesitate. The man at the oars lets the boat drift with the breakers stern foremost toward the rocks. His mate leaps from the stern seat to the ledge. Then the other pulls the boat out of danger before the wave curls and breaks. It is the only way.

But sometimes the man in the stem miscalculates—leaps too soon, stumbles, leaps short. He falls back, and is almost inevitably drowned. Sometimes, too, the current of the wave is too strong for the man at the oars; his punt is swept in, pull as hard as he may, and he is overwhelmed with her. Donald knew all this. He had lived in dread of the time when he must first make that leap.

"The ice is comin' in, b'y," said North. "'Twill scrape these here rocks, certain sure. Does you think you're strong enough to take the oars an' let me go ashore?"

"No, zur," said Donald.

"You never leaped afore, did you?"

"No, zur."

"Will you try it now, b'y?" said North quietly.

"Iss, zur," Donald said, faintly.

"Get ready, then," said North.

With a stroke or two of the oars Job swung the stem of the boat to the rocks. He kept her hanging in this position until the water fell back and gathered in a new wave; then he lifted his oars. Donald was crouched on the stern seat, waiting for the moment to rise and spring.

The boat moved in, running on the crest of the wave which would a moment later break against the rock. Donald stood up, and fixed his eye on the ledge. He was afraid; all the strength and courage he had seemed to desert him. The punt was now almost on a level with the ledge. The wave was about to curl and fall. It was the precise moment when he must leap—that instant, too, when the punt must be pulled out of the grip of the breaker, if at all.

He felt of a sudden that he must do this thing. Therefore why not do it courageously? He leaped; but this new courage had not come in time. He made the ledge, but he fell an inch short of a firm footing. So for a moment he tottered, between falling forward and falling back. Then he caught the branch of an overhanging shrub, and with this saved himself. When he turned, Job had the punt in safety; but he was breathing hard, as if the strain had been great.

"'Twas not so hard, was it, b'y?" said Job.

"No, zur," said Donald.

Donald cast the net line loose from its mooring, and saw that it was all clear. His father let the punt sweep in again. It is much easier to leap from a solid rock than from a boat, so Donald jumped in without difficulty. Then they rowed out to the buoy and hauled the great, dripping net over the side.

It was well they went out, for before morning the ice had drifted over the place where the net had been. More than that, Donald North profited by his experience. He perceived that if perils must be encountered, they are best met with a clear head and an unflinching heart.

That night, when he thought it over, he was comforted.

In the gales and high seas of the summer following, and in the blinding snowstorms and bitter cold of the winter, Donald North grew in fine readiness to face peril at the call of duty. All that he had gained was put to the test in the next spring, when the floating ice, which drifts out of the north in the spring break-up, was driven by the wind against the coast.

Job North, with Alexander Bludd and Bill Stevens, went out on the ice to hunt seal, and the hunt led them ten miles offshore. In the afternoon of that day the wind gave some sign of changing to the west, and at dusk it was blowing half a gale offshore. When the wind blows offshore it sweeps all this wandering ice out to sea, and disperses the whole pack.

"Go see if your father's comin', b'y," said Donald's mother. "I'm gettin' terrible nervous about the ice."

Donald took his gaff—a long pole of the light, tough dogwood, two inches thick and shod with iron—and set out. It was growing dark, and the wind, rising still, was blowing in strong, cold gusts. It began to snow while he was yet on the ice of the harbour, half a mile away from the pans and clumpers which the wind of the day before had crowded against the coast.

When he came to the "standing ice,"—the stationary rim of ice which is frozen to the coast,—the wind was thickly charged with snow. What with dusk and snow, he found it hard to keep to the right way. But he was not afraid for himself; his only fear was that the wind would sweep the ice-pack out to sea before his father reached the "standing edge." In that event, as he knew, Job North would be doomed.

Donald went out on the standing edge. Beyond lay a widening gap of water. The pack had already begun to move out.

There was no sign of Job North's party. The lad ran up and down, hallooing as he ran; but for a time there was no answer to his call. Then it seemed to him he heard a despairing hail, sounding far to the right, whence he had come. Night had almost fallen, and the snow added to its depth; but as he ran back, Donald could still see across the gap of water to that great pan of ice, which, of all the pack, was nearest to the standing edge. He perceived that the gap had considerably widened since he had first observed it. "Is that you, father?" he called.

"Iss, Donald!" came an answering hail from directly opposite. "Is there a small pan of ice on your side?"

Donald searched up and down the edge for a detached cake large enough for his purpose. Near at hand he came upon a thin, small pan, not more than six feet square.

"Haste, b'y!" cried his father.

"They's one here," he called back, "but 'tis too small! Is there none there?"

"No, b'y! Fetch that over!"

Here was a desperate need. If the lad was to meet it, he must act instantly and fearlessly. He stepped out on the pan, and pushed off with his gaff.

Using his gaff as a paddle—as these gaffs are constantly used in ferrying by the Newfoundland fishermen—and helped by the wind, he soon ferried himself to where Job North stood waiting with his companions.

"'Tis too small," said Stevens. "'Twill not hold two."

North looked dubiously at the pan. Alexander Bludd shook his head in despair.

"Get back while you can, b'y," said North. "Quick! We're driftin' fast. The pan's too small."

"I think 'tis big enough for one man and me," said Donald.

"Get aboard and try it, Alexander," said Job.

Alexander Bludd stepped on. The pan tipped fearfully, and the water ran over it; but when the weight of the man and the boy was properly adjusted, it seemed capable of bearing them both across. They pushed off.

When Alexander moved to put his gaff in the water the pan tipped again. Donald came near losing his footing. He moved nearer the edge, and the pan came to a level. They paddled with all their strength, for the wind was blowing against them, and there was need of haste if three passages were to be made. Meanwhile the gap had grown so wide that the wind had turned the ripples into waves, which washed over the pan as high as Donald's ankles.

But they came safe across. Bludd stepped quickly ashore, and Donald pushed off. With the wind in his favour, he was soon once more at the other side.

"Now, Bill," said North, "your turn next."

"I can't do it, Job," said Stevens. "Get aboard yourself. The lad can't come back again. We're driftin' out too fast. He's your lad, an' you've the right to—"

"Iss, I can come back," said Donald. "Come on, Bill! Quick!"

Stevens was a lighter man than Alexander Bludd, but the passage was wider, and still widening, for the pack had gathered speed.

When Stevens was safely landed, he looked back.

A vast white shadow was all that he could see. Job North's figure had been merged with the night.

"Donald, b'y," he said, "you got to go back for your father, but I'm fair feared you'll never—"

"Give me a push, Bill," said Donald. Stevens caught the end of the gaff and pushed the lad out.

"Good-by, Donald!" he said.

When the pan touched the other side, Job North stepped aboard without a word. He was a heavy man. With his great body on the ice-cake, the problem of return was enormously increased, as Donald had foreseen.

The pan was overweighted. Time and again it nearly shook itself free of its bad load and rose to the surface.

North stood near the centre, plying his gaff with difficulty, but Donald was on the extreme edge. Moreover, the distance was twice as great as it had been at the first, and the waves were running high, and it was dark.

They made way slowly, and the pan often wavered beneath them; but Donald was intent upon the thing he was doing, and he was not afraid.

Then came the time—they were but ten yards off the standing edge—when North struck his gaff too deep into the water. He lost his balance, struggled desperately to regain it, failed—and fell off. Before Donald was awake to the danger, the edge of the pan sank under him, and he, too, toppled off.

Donald had learned to swim now. When he came to the surface, his father was breast-high in the water, looking for him.

"Are you all right, Donald?" said his father.

"Iss, zur."

"Can you reach the ice alone?"

"Iss, zur," said Donald quietly.

Alexander Bludd and Bill Stevens helped them up on the standing edge, and they were home by the kitchen fire in half an hour.

"'Twas bravely done, b'y," said Job.

So Donald North learned that perils feared are much more terrible than perils faced. He has a courage of the finest kind, in these days, has young Donald.

A Christmas Adventure

By J. E. Chamberlin

Having lived all his fourteen years in New York City, making occasional visits to his grandfather's house in Connecticut, Horace Mason had often sighed for an adventure, and lamented because life in the eastern part of the country is so tame and uninteresting. It had certainly never occurred to him that the chance for a pretty thrilling adventure existed in the quiet country neighbourhood in which his grandfather lived.

About a week before Christmas Horace's mother took him to his grandfather's farm for the holidays—he had seldom been there in winter.

The weather became remarkably cold and rough, but Horace found pleasure in walking about woods and pastures in rubber boots and ulster, and noting how odd the familiar scenes looked when covered with snow and ice, instead of dressed in green.

A tree was to be set up on Christmas Eve in the old homestead; but Uncle John, on the afternoon of the twenty-third, brought in for the celebration a rather scraggly little red cedar, brown rather than green, which Horace deemed totally unfit for the dignity of a Christmas celebration.

"Why didn't you get a fir balsam, with a nice even top to it?" Horace asked his uncle.

"Don't grow around here."

"But there are some over in the Big Swamp," said Horace.

"Never noticed 'em," said Uncle John.

Horace said nothing to this, because he was aware that he had often noticed things about the region, in the way of trees, plants and birds, which were apparently quite unobserved by the residents.

"You won't be offended if I go after one to-morrow, will you, Uncle John?"

"Bless your heart, no!"

The next morning a blizzard raged. Horace, looking out, saw nothing but the whirling fine snow; the wind rattled all the shutters on the old house; it shook the building to its very foundations.

Horace thought it would be great fun to go out into this storm, with ulster, high rubber boots, and cap over his ears, looking for a Christmas tree in the Big Swamp. It did not occur to him that he needed to get his mother's permission for the expedition, and it certainly did not occur to her that the boy would start out in such a storm.

Shortly after breakfast he took an ax from the wood-shed, and was gone. On the way he thought for a time that he must turn back—the storm buffeted him so terribly, and the cold, in spite of his warm coverings, was so intense. But he fought his way along, and at last came to the borders of the swamp, a flat tract of perhaps a hundred acres, lying in a hollow between hills.

In the spring this level expanse was mostly covered with water, up through which grew many low red maples, some scattered firs and cedars, and a jungle of alders. Horace had often wished that he might explore the gloomy depths of this swamp, but in midsummer mosquitoes and pools forbade. Now, with the ground and the pools frozen, he had no doubt he could pass through the swamp from end to end.

He left the wood road, and plowed through the deep snow along the margin of the swamp, looking out for firs. But he could see nothing more than a rod or two away. The storm did not diminish, and all about him the snow seemed extraordinarily deep. He sank into it up to his knees, and sometimes it was deeper still. He walked thus a long way on the edge of the swamp woodland, not caring to plunge into the swamp until he should have spied out a balsam.

At last he saw, through the cloud of snow, the tapering head of an unmistakable fir balsam. He struck into the swamp after it, parting the alder branches with the ax held with both hands before him, and sinking two or three inches deeper into the snow.

The fir proved to be too irregular for a Christmas tree. Then, through the snow, he saw another farther in the swamp. He penetrated to that, and found one side of it lacking. Beyond were other firs, and he fought his way deeper and deeper into the swamp.

He discovered now a circumstance that aided him somewhat in working his way through the jungle. The matted alders seemed to lean away in masses from the hummocks of earth upon which they grew, in such a way as to make crooked arched-over passageways, which, Horace thought, were curiously like the paths moles make under matted grass. He had often amused himself in summer digging out these mole-paths, and wondering why the crooked ways were constructed.

These avenues through the alder thickets, away down in the bottom of a swamp quite impenetrable without them, often came to an abrupt end. Then Horace, floundering on hands and knees in the deep snow, sometimes thrusting his foot down into a watery depth, had to break his way with his ax through to another opening.

He found the seclusion somewhat interesting. Down here there was no wind, and his clothing and his laborious exercise made him warm—even uncomfortably so. He lay a few minutes on his back, in a place where he could look up through an opening in the branches, and marvelled at the sight of the stormy maelstrom overhead.

The whirling snow looked black. For a moment the current of it seemed flowing like a river all one way; then it appeared to turn, to cross itself, and to twist about in a circle, from which it soon disentangled itself, to resume its swift and steady march in one direction.

All at once it occurred to Horace to ask himself, Which direction was that? He thought first that he could not get lost in the swamp so long as he could see which way the snow was driving; but a chill ran over him when he reflected that he had not noticed, in his eagerness all the morning to be out in the storm, which way the wind was blowing. He tried now to think which way it had come as he walked to the swamp, but all he could recall was that the storm seemed to be coming from all directions at once.

He started up with a sudden alarm; and then, noticing the deep track he had made as he floundered to the place where he lay now, he began to laugh. To get out of the swamp, he had only to follow his tracks back.

He had come in here to find a nice young fir for a Christmas tree, and he was bound to get one. As he sat up, preparatory to rising, he saw that the snow, sifting down straight and steady from the eddying masses above the tops of the alders, had covered his coat and trousers with a deposit half an inch thick. And the minute of inaction had made him feel cold and stiff. He must be stirring.

He plowed along farther into the swamp. Coming out on the surface of one of the pools, he was rejoiced to see some balsam tops that seemed not more than a rod or two from the other edge of the pool. He struck through to them, but found here not even a mole-path; he had to cut and slash with his ax to get to the trunks of the firs.

Although the butts were five or six inches thick, the tops seemed tapering and even, and he set about cutting down one of the trees. Very soon he had the trunk cut in two, and it settled down into the snow; but fall it certainly could not, so dense was the growth all about it. He had to drag the butt through the bushes, still fighting his way with the ax, until the tree lay nearly flat on the ground; and then he found that the shape did not suit him at all.

He left this fir on the ground and went plowing after another.

Before long, traversing one of the tunnels under the alders, he came upon the very fir he wanted—a beautiful, even little tree, thick and green. He cut it down eagerly; but in another moment he found that it was as impracticable to drag that bushy-headed young tree through the alder jungle as it would have been to move a house through the same wilderness. Horace had literally to carve a way for it. He slashed and chopped and worked the tree along a rod or two, and this took him at least half an hour.

Horace sat down, quite out of breath, on the butt of the little tree to think it over. How could he get the tree out? He pondered a good while, and began to feel very cold, and then looked up to see if the storm was still raging violently. It certainly was. The space above the treetops was black with clouds of snow.

Then, chancing to look away in the direction from which he had come, he noticed that his tracks were already filled with snow! Horace jumped up, quite willing to leave his Christmas tree behind, and dragging his ax, rushed through the tunnel toward the pool that he had crossed less than an hour before. The track disappeared completely before he had reached this small open space. Although the alder branches were so thick, they held up very little of the snow. Leafless and wiry, they afforded little surface for the hard snow to cling to.

Nevertheless, Horace found his way to the pool, and there the storm struck him full in the face. It was blinding. He could no longer see the fir tops that had beckoned him on an hour ago! Every track that he had made in coming in was completely obliterated!

Perhaps if he beat round the outskirts of the pool he could find the tracks where he came in, among the bushes on the other side. So he began to walk round and round the little open space, searching in vain for the tracks, and finding nothing but those by which he had just come out of the alders where he had cut the tree; and even these tracks were rapidly being covered.

He began to feel decidedly queer, for he had not the slightest idea now which was the way out of the swamp. But he must be able to reach some place where he could see the woods; and once out of the swamp and into these, he could easily enough find his way back to the house.

So for more than an hour—it seemed longer to him, but he had left his watch at home, and had no way of telling the time—he dragged himself through the tunnels under the alders, or slashed to right and left with his ax. He struggled and grew desperate, and never once did he catch sight of anything that looked like the woods or the margin of the swamp.

The snow grew deeper and deeper, and made the arching tops of his mole-paths lower and lower, while the labour of floundering and dragging himself through them became more terrible. Once he felt a thrill of relief upon coming on a track which he knew must be his own. He supposed that it was the track by which he had come into the jungle in the morning, strangely left uncovered by some better protection than the thicket had provided elsewhere. So he started back on it quite joyfully. And he followed it until he came to the trunk of a little maple-tree which he knew he had cut down not fifteen minutes before to clear a path.

Then he knew he was winding about and had crossed his own tracks. If he followed them farther, they would simply bring him back to where he stood now.

Meanwhile he had grown very faint—he was almost too badly scared to be aware that he was hungry.

But he felt that it must be afternoon; and on such a day, and at this time of year, the darkness would fall by half past three. He felt himself hopelessly lost—and abandoned, too, for why did not the people at the house miss him, and know that, having gone after a Christmas tree, he must be lost in the Big Swamp? Why did they not send after him?

They must come! But if he sat down and waited for them he would get chilled. Already, in spite of his efforts, he felt a numbness creeping over him. The sense of it filled him with horror. He hurled himself against the bushes; he threw himself on his hands and knees, and worked his way through the narrow passages. His mind went over and over various futile schemes for tracing his way.

All at once he stopped and pondered. If he was really going round in a ring when he thought he was going straight, could it be possible that he would go straight if he tried to go round in a ring? And if he found his way back to his track and made a ring, why not start out anew and deliberately add another ring to that? Enough circles made thus, placed side by side, would reach at last the edge of the swamp.

He went back on his tracks, and was pleased to find that the snow had not yet covered them so deeply but that he could find the place where he had branched off from the ring he had made.

Walking back on this a few steps, Horace went off to the left, purposely intending to make another circle and come back to this one. But after threading and pushing his way a long time, he convinced himself that he was not returning to it; no more tracks did he find. Did this mean that he was now following a straighter line, or merely that he was making a larger circle, and going entirely round the inner one?

A terrible fear of the snow and the earth came over him, and he could not bear to get down on his hands and knees to follow the tunnels under the bushes. But he was too weak to fight his way upright through the thicket. His brain reeled as he strained his eyes for the five-hundredth time for some sign of the trees of the woods.

It reeled still more when it seemed to him that he saw something large and black and shapeless through the gloom—some strange and threatening object descending upon him.

The boy was so weak and tired and dazed by the long beating about and the everlasting swirl of the storm above his head, that he could not bring his reason to bear upon the consideration of the question what this thing might be. It seemed to dash forward at him, and the formless black mass then divided as if it were the mouth of a crocodile, and then it drew back; it shook angrily from side to side; now it dashed at him again, and opened its terrible mouth.

Horace felt himself swooning in horror, and he knew that if he fainted here it would be the last of him. Oh, why had not his mother sent for him?

Then a thought of shame came over him, that he should be fainting with terror over something that could not be real.

Out of this shame grew a resolution, and suddenly the resolution mended his reason, and enabled him to see that this terrible shapeless object was a great pine-tree, whose dark branches were waving and bending and opening in the storm, seen dimly through the thick snow.

Then he was at the edge of the woods! He tore through the bushes, and came out on the clear space about the tree, and rushed up to it. He dropped the ax and put his arms round the tree. Now he had to pull himself together to save himself from swooning with joy. But in another minute he felt much better. He had no idea on which side of the swamp he was, but that did not matter. He could find his way well enough now.

After a little search, he found that he was exactly on the opposite side of the swamp from that on which he had gone in. And as he was skirting the edge of it, feeling fearfully hungry as well as weak, he saw, growing quite within his reach, a fine young fir-tree.

Then he remembered that he had dropped the ax at the foot of the pine-tree, and he had to go back and get it before he could cut down the little tree. But he did cut it down, and staggered home with it, weak but triumphant.

He found that it was three o'clock, and his mother was very much agitated, and Uncle John had gone away, by the road, to the Big Swamp about half an hour before. The boy had been so much accustomed to going off by himself that his mother had not worried until he had failed to return for the midday meal. Nor had she any idea what sort of a place the Big Swamp was.

When Uncle John got it through his somewhat slow head that Horace had in all probability actually gone there, he, too, had become alarmed, and after slow preparations, had started. Horace had missed him by coming home across the pastures.

But Uncle John was brought home in an hour by the hired man, and as Horace felt much better after a good meal and a rest, the tree that he had brought was dressed, and the Christmas festival merrily celebrated by its aid.

A GUSH OF WATER FOLLOWED, BURYING THE SLED
AND WASHING THE DOGS FROM THEIR FEET

Chased by the Trail

From the drawing by George Giguère

Chased by the Trail

By Jack London

Walt first blinked his eyes in the light of day in a trading post on the Yukon River. Masters, his father, was one of those world missionaries who are known as "pioneers," and who spend the years of their life in pushing outward the walls of civilization and in planting the wilderness. He had selected Alaska as his field of labour, and his wife had gone with him to that land of frost and cold.

Now, to be born to the moccasin and pack-strap is indeed a hard way of entering the world, but far harder it is to lose one's mother while yet a child. This was Walt's misfortune when he was fourteen years old.

He had, at different times, done deeds which few boys get the chance to do, and he had learned to take some pride in himself and to be unafraid. With most people pride goeth before a fall; but not so with Walt. His was a healthy belief in his own strength and fitness, and knowing his limitations, he was neither overweening nor presumptuous. He had learned to meet reverses with the stoicism of the Indian. Shame, to him, lay not in the failure to accomplish, but in the failure to strive. So, when he attempted to cross the Yukon between two ice-runs, and was chased by the trail, he was not cast down by his defeat.

The way of it was this. After passing the winter at his father's claim on Mazy May, he came down to an island on the Yukon and went into camp. This was late in the spring, just before the breaking of the ice on the river. It was quite warm, and the days were growing marvellously long. Only the night before, when he was talking with Chilkoot Jim, the daylight had not faded and sent him off to bed till after ten o'clock. Even Chilkoot Jim, an Indian boy who was about Walt's own age, was surprised at the rapidity with which summer was coming on. The snow had melted from all the southern hillsides and the level surfaces of the flats and islands; everywhere could be heard the trickling of water and the song of hidden rivulets; but somehow, under its three-foot ice-sheet, the Yukon delayed to heave its great length of three thousand miles and shake off the frosty fetters which bound it.

But it was evident that the time was fast approaching when it would again run free. Great fissures were splitting the ice in all directions, while the water was beginning to flood through them and over the top. On this morning a frightful rumbling brought the two boys hurriedly from their blankets. Standing on the bank, they soon discovered the cause. The Stewart River had broken loose and reared a great ice barrier, where it entered the Yukon, barely a mile above their island. While a great deal of the Stewart ice had been thus piled up, the remainder was now flowing under the Yukon ice, pounding and thumping at the solid surface above it as it passed onward toward the sea.

"To-day um break um," Chilkoot Jim said, nodding his head. "Sure!"

"And then maybe two days for the ice to pass by," Walt added, "and you and I'll be starting for Dawson. It's only seventy miles, and if the current runs five miles an hour and we paddle three, we ought to make it inside of ten hours. What do you think?"

"Sure!" Chilkoot Jim did not know much English, and this favourite word of his was made to do duty on all occasions.

After breakfast the boys got out the Peterborough canoe from its winter cache. It was an admirable sample of the boat-builder's skill, an imported article brought from the natural home of the canoe—Canada. It had been packed over the Chilkoot Pass, two years before, on a man's back, and had then carried the first mail in six months into the Klondike. Walt, who happened to be in Dawson at the time, had bought it for three hundred dollars' worth of dust which he had mined on the Mazy May.

It had been a revelation, both to him and to Chilkoot Jim, for up to its advent they had been used to no other craft than the flimsy birch-bark canoes of the Indians and the rude poling-boats of the whites. Jim, in fact, spent many a happy half-hour in silent admiration of its perfect lines.

"Um good. Sure!" Jim lifted his gaze from the dainty craft, expressing his delight in the same terms for the thousandth time. But glancing over Walt's shoulder, he saw something on the river which startled him. "Look! See!" he cried.

A man had been racing a dog-team across the slushy surface for the shore, and had been cut off by the rising flood. As Walt whirled round to see, the ice behind the man burst into violent commotion, splitting and smashing into fragments which bobbed up and down and turned turtle like so many corks.

A gush of water followed, burying the sled and washing the dogs from their feet. Tangled in their harness and securely fastened to the heavy sled, they must drown in a few minutes unless rescued by the man. Bravely his manhood answered.

Floundering about with the drowning animals, nearly hip-deep in the icy flood, he cut and slashed with his sheath-knife at the traces. One by one the dogs struck out for shore, the first reaching safety ere the last was released. Then the master, abandoning the sled, followed them. It was a struggle in which little help could be given, and Walt and Chilkoot Jim could only, at the last, grasp his hands and drag him, half-fainting, up the bank.

First he sat down till he had recovered his breath; next he knocked the water from his ears like a boy who has just been swimming; and after that he whistled his dogs together to see whether they had all escaped. These things done, he turned his attention to the lads.

"I'm Muso," he said, "Pete Muso, and I'm looking for Charley Drake. His partner is dying down at Dawson, and they want him to come at once, as soon as the river breaks. He's got a cabin on this island, hasn't he?"

"Yes," Walt answered, "but he's over on the other side of the river, with a couple of other men, getting out a raft of logs for a grub-stake."

The stranger's disappointment was great. Exhausted by his weary journey, just escaped from sudden death, overcome by all he had undergone in carrying the message which was now useless, he looked dazed. The tears welled into his eyes, and his voice was choked with sobs as he repeated, aimlessly, "But his partner's dying. It's his partner, you know, and he wants to see him before he dies."

Walt and Jim knew that nothing could be done, and as aimlessly looked out on the hopeless river. No man could venture on it and live. On the other bank, and several miles up-stream, a thin column of smoke wavered to the sky. Charley Drake was cooking his dinner there; seventy miles below, his partner lay dying; yet no word of it could be sent.

But even as they looked, a change came over the river. There was a muffled rending and tearing, and, as if by magic, the surface water disappeared, while the great ice-sheet, reaching from shore to shore, and broken into all manner and sizes of cakes, floated silently up toward them. The ice which had been pounding along underneath had evidently grounded at some point lower down, and was now backing up the water like a mill-dam. This had broken the ice-sheet from the land and lifted it on top of the rising water.

"Um break um very quick," Chilkoot Jim said.

"Then here goes!" Muso cried, at the same time beginning to strip his wet clothes.

The Indian boy laughed. "Mebbe you get um in middle, mebbe not. All the same, the trail um go down-stream, and you go, too. Sure!" He glanced at Walt, that he might back him up in preventing this insane attempt."You're not going to try and make it across?" Walt queried.

Muso nodded his head, sat down, and proceeded to unlace his moccasins.

"But you mustn't!" Walt protested. "It's certain death. The river'll break before you get half-way, and then what good'll your message be?"

But the stranger doggedly went on undressing, muttering in an undertone, "I want Charley Drake! Don't you understand? It's his partner, dying."

"Um sick man. Bimeby—" The Indian boy put a finger to his forehead and whirled his hand in quick circles, thus indicating the approach of brain fever. "Um work too hard, and um think too much, all the time think about sick man at Dawson. Very quick um head go round—so." And he feigned the bodily dizziness which is caused by a disordered brain.

By this time, undressed as if for a swim, Muso rose to his feet and started for the bank. Walt stepped in front, barring the way. He shot a glance at his comrade. Jim nodded that he understood and would stand by.

"Get out of my way, boy!" Muso commanded, roughly, trying to thrust him aside.

But Walt closed in, and with the aid of Jim succeeded in tripping him upon his back. He struggled weakly for a few moments, but was too wearied by his long journey to cope successfully with the two boys whose muscles were healthy and trail-hardened.

"Pack um into camp, roll um in plenty blanket, and I fix um good," Jim advised.

This was quickly accomplished, and the sufferer made as comfortable as possible. After he had been attended to, and Jim had utilised the medical lore picked up in the camps of his own people, they fed the stranger's dogs and cooked dinner. They said very little to each other, but each boy was thinking hard, and when they went out into the sunshine a few minutes later, their minds were intent on the same project.

The river had now risen twenty feet, the ice rubbing softly against the top of the bank. All noise had ceased. Countless millions of tons of ice and water were silently waiting the supreme moment, when all bonds would be broken and the mad rush to the sea would begin. Suddenly, without the slightest apparent effort, everything began to move down-stream. The jam had broken.

Slowly at first but faster and faster the frozen sea dashed past. The noise returned again, and the air trembled to a mighty churning and grinding. Huge blocks of ice were shot into the air by the pressure; others butted wildly into the bank; still others, swinging and pivoting, reached inshore and swept rows of pines away as easily as if they were so many matches.

In awe-stricken silence the boys watched the magnificent spectacle, and it was not until the ice had slackened its speed and fallen to its old level that Walt cried, "Look, Jim! Look at the trail going by!"

And in truth it was the trail going by—the trail upon which they had camped and travelled during all the preceding winter. Next winter they would journey with dogs and sleds over the same ground, but not on the same trail. That trail, the old trail, was passing away before their eyes.

Looking up-stream, they saw open water. No more ice was coming down, although vast quantities of it still remained on the upper reaches, jammed somewhere amid the maze of islands which covered the Yukon's breast. As a matter of fact, there were several jams yet to break, one after another, and to send down as many ice-runs. The next might come along in a few minutes; it might delay for hours. Perhaps there would be time to paddle across. Walt looked questioningly at his comrade.

"Sure!" Jim remarked, and without another word they carried the canoe down the bank. Each knew the danger of what they were about to attempt, but they wasted no speech over it. Wild life had taught them both that the need of things demanded effort and action, and that the tongue found its fit vocation at the camp-fire when the day's work was done.

With dexterity born of long practice they launched the canoe, and were soon making it spring to each stroke of the paddles as they stemmed the muddy current. A steady procession of lagging ice-cakes, each thoroughly capable of crushing the Peterborough like an egg-shell, was drifting on the surface, and it required of the boys the utmost vigilance and skill to thread them safely.

Anxiously they watched the great bend above, down which at any moment might rush another ice-run. And as anxiously they watched the ice stranded against the bank and towering a score of feet above them. Cake was poised upon cake and piled in precarious confusion, while the boys had to hug the shore closely to avoid the swifter current of mid-stream. Now and again great heaps of this ice tottered and fell into the river, rolling and rumbling like distant thunder, and lashing the water into fair-sized tidal waves.

Several times they were nearly swamped, but saved themselves by quick work with the paddles. And all the time Charley Drake's pillard camp smoke grew nearer and clearer. But it was still on the opposite shore, and they knew they must get higher up before they attempted to shoot across.

Entering the Stewart River, they paddled up a few hundred yards, shot across, and then continued up the right hank of the Yukon. Before long they came to the Bald-Face Bluffs—huge walls of rock which rose perpendicularly from the river. Here the current was swiftest inshore, forming the first serious obstacle encountered by the boys. Below the bluffs they rested from their exertions in a favorable eddy, and then, paddling their strongest, strove to dash past.

At first they gained, but in the swiftest place the current overpowered them. For a full sixty seconds they remained stationary, neither advancing nor receding, the grim cliff base within reach of their arms, their paddles dipping and lifting like clockwork, and the rough water dashing by in muddy haste. For a full sixty seconds, and then the canoe sheered in to the shore. To prevent instant destruction, they pressed their paddles against the rocks, sheered back into the stream, and were swept away. Regaining the eddy, they stopped for breath. A second time they attempted the passage; but just as they were almost past, a threatening ice-cake whirled down upon them on the angry tide, and they were forced to flee before it.

"Um stiff, I think yes," Chilkoot Jim said, mopping the sweat from his face as they again rested in the eddy. "Next time um make um, sure."

"We've got to. That's all there is about it," Walt answered, his teeth set and lips tight-drawn, for Pete Muso had set a bad example, and he was almost ready to cry from exhaustion and failure. A third time they darted out of the head of the eddy, plunged into the swirling waters, and worked a snail-like course ahead. Often they stood still for the space of many strokes, but whatever they gained they held, and they at last drew out into easier water far above. But every moment was precious. There was no telling when the Yukon would again become a scene of wild anarchy in which neither man nor any of his works could hope to endure. So they held steadily to their course till they had passed above Charley Drake's camp by a quarter of a mile. The river was fully a mile wide at this point, and they had to reckon on being carried down by the swift current in crossing it.

Walt turned his head from his place in the bow. Jim nodded. Without further parley they headed the canoe out from the shore, at an angle of forty-five degrees against the current. They were on the last stretch now; the goal was in fair sight. Indeed, as they looked up from the toil to mark their progress, they could see Charley Drake and his two comrades come down to the edge of the river to watch them.

Five hundred yards; four hundred yards; the Peterborough cut the water like a blade of steel; the paddles were dipping, dipping, dipping in rapid rhythm—and then a warning shout from the bank sent a chill to their hearts. Round the great bend just above rolled a mighty wall of glistening white. Behind it, urging it on to lightning speed, were a million tons of long-pent water.

The right flank of the ice-run, unable to get cleanly round the bend, collided with the opposite shore, and even as they looked they saw the ice mountains rear toward the sky, rise, collapse, and rise again in glittering convulsions. The advancing roar filled the air so that Walt could not make himself heard; but he paused long enough to wave his paddle significantly in the direction of Dawson. Perhaps Charley Drake, seeing, might understand.

With two swift strokes they whirled the Peterborough down-stream. They must keep ahead of the rushing flood. It was impossible to make either bank at that moment. Every ounce of their strength went into the paddles, and the frail canoe fairly rose and leaped ahead at every stroke. They said nothing. Each knew and had faith in the other, and they were too wise to waste their breath. The shore-line—trees, islands and the Stewart River—flew by at a bewildering rate, but they barely looked at it.

Occasionally Chilkoot Jim stole a glance behind him at the pursuing trail, and marked the fact that they held their own. Once he shaped a sharper course toward the bank, but found the trail was overtaking them, and gave it up.

Gradually they worked in to land, their failing strength warning them that it was soon or never. And at last, when they did draw up to the bank, they were confronted by the inhospitable barrier of the stranded shore-ice. Not a place could be found to land, and with safety virtually within arm's reach, they were forced to flee on down the stream. They passed a score of places, at each of which, had they had plenty of time, they could have clambered out; but behind pressed on the inexorable trail, and would not let them pause.

Half a mile of this work drew heavily upon their strength; and the trail came upon them nearer and nearer. Its sullen grind was in their ears, and its collisions against the bank made one continuous succession of terrifying crashes. Walt felt his heart thumping against his ribs and caught each breath in painful gasps. But worst of all was the constant demand upon his arms.

If he could only rest for the space of one stroke, he felt that the torture would be relieved; but no, it was dip and lift, dip and lift, till it seemed as if at each stroke he would surely die. But he knew that Chilkoot Jim was suffering likewise; that their lives depended each upon the other; and that it would be a blot upon his manhood should he fail or even miss a stroke.

They were very weary, but their faith was large, and if either felt afraid, it was not of the other, but of himself.

Flashing round a sharp point, they came upon their last chance for escape. An island lay close inshore, upon the nose of which the ice lay piled in a long slope. They drove the Peterborough half out of water upon a shelving cake and leaped out. Then, dragging the canoe along, slipping and tripping and falling, but always getting nearer the top, they made their last mad scramble.

As they cleared the crest and fell within the shelter of the pines, a tremendous crash announced the arrival of the trail. One huge cake, shoved to the top of the rim-ice, balanced threateningly above them and then toppled forward.

With one jerk they flung themselves and the canoe from beneath, and again fell, breathless and panting for air. The thunder of the ice-run came dimly to their ears; but they did not care. It held no interest for them whatsoever. All they wished was simply to lie there, just as they had fallen, and enjoy the inaction of repose.

Two hours later, when the river once more ran open, they carried the Peterborough down to the water. But just before they launched it, Charley Drake and a comrade paddled up in another canoe.

"Well, you boys hardly deserve to have good folks out looking for you, the way you've behaved," was his greeting. "What under the sun made you leave your tent and get chased by the trail? Eh? That's what I'd like to know."

It took but a minute to explain the real state of affairs, and but another to see Charley Drake hurrying along on his way to his sick partner at Dawson.

"Pretty close shave, that," Walt Masters said, as they prepared to get aboard and paddle back to camp.

"Sure!" Chilkoot Jim replied, rubbing his stiffened biceps in a meditative fashion.

Big Timber Beacon

By John L. Mathews

There were three government beacon-lights in Big Timber Bend, and the uppermost of them was Barney Layton's. It was nothing more than a lantern set in a frame against a white target on the top of a post, fifty feet from the edge of the deep bank of the Mississippi River. It was at the very head of the bend, at the foot of the "crossing" by which the channel came from the lower end of Silverplate Bend over into Big Timber. It stood there so that the pilots on river steamers, coming down, could set the bows of their boats toward it, and run straight and true in the channel between the lower end of McAlpin's Bar and the head of Nodaway Towhead.

When the river was low, this channel was both shoal and narrow, and the white target by day and the bright lantern by night had been gladly welcomed by pilots who had figured their way over the crossing in old days by sounding-pole and luck.

Every night at sunset Barney climbed the levee in front of his mother's cabin, walked the half-mile down to the head of Big Timber, and out by a path he had made through the big timber itself to his light-post, carrying the lantern, which he set in place and lighted. Every morning he came early to put it out and carry it home for cleaning and filling. For this the government paid his mother seventy-five dollars a year, besides furnishing the oil and other supplies; and seventy-five dollars a year is a considerable amount behind a levee in lower Arkansas.

The work was not always as easy as it sounds. Some years the Mississippi never rises out of its banks—and some years it does. When it did, it filled all the big timber in front of the levee with a rushing current, and Barney Layton had to use main strength as well as his wits getting out in his skiff to tend his light. Sometimes he would be carried by, and washed a mile down-stream before he could get out of the current and start home again; and with the river out of its banks, he was always rather glad when the post, too, was submerged, and the support for his light was either nailed on a tree in the front of the big timber or abandoned altogether for a week or two.

Big Timber Bend had been stable for several years. The swift current of the river sweeping by its front had apparently taken not a foot of soil from it. The light-post had been shifted hardly a rod in two seasons. The crossing seemed to hold its place.

But at last came a big water out of the Ohio, which found the river already full and the lower tributaries high. For weeks it stood over the banks and against the levees, and when at last it went down, it left the earthen banks saturated with water, so that they could with difficulty sustain their own weight without collapsing.

Then Silverplate Bend began to cave. As the pressure of the water on its front was withdrawn, the bank began to topple over and settle into the river in great slices, eating back farther and farther, changing the shape of the bend, and altering the set of the current over the crossing. The deflected swift water ate up into McAlpin's Bar, and struck Big Timber Bend a hundred yards above the light; and one night the *Rupert Lee*, coming up, and steering by Barney's beacon, as it turned where the crossing used to be, ran hard on a new bar at the head of Nodaway Towhead. She got off before morning, and lay up at the light till the crossing could be sounded, and Barney had a chat about it with pilot Ned Hinckley.

"Better get your light shifted," said the pilot, banteringly. "If we'd been coming down and struck that bar with the current, the *Rupert* would have left her bones in it. What good's a false beacon, youngster?"

"A false beacon?" Barney took that very much to heart. He told his mother about it, and she forthwith wrote to the lighthouse inspector; but the letter was forestalled the next day, when the tender *Lily* herself arrived with the inspector on board, sounded out a new channel, and moved Barney's light up the bank to mark it.

"Now, Barney," said the inspector, "you've got to be on watch. That bank in Silverplate is going to make trouble below. Big Timber Bend will begin caving before many days. It can't stand this.

The water is seventy feet deep right in front of this bank, and it must be cutting pretty steep now. The snag boat will be along pretty soon and cut the timber off quite away back, and then we'll set the light farther inland. But till then you must watch, and if the bank where the light is starts to go, get the target and nail it to the front of that big gum-tree right behind it. If that goes, keep on working straight back till we get here. The crossing is moving up so you'll be about right."

Barney promised faithfully—and he kept his word. He was only a boy of fifteen, and it was a good deal of responsibility to have on his shoulders; but Barney was used to all kinds of responsibility, from taking care of his mother to hauling his cotton to the gin. He would keep this beacon true.

The inspector's prophecy was promptly verified. Within a week Big Timber Bend was caving, and caving badly. When Barney came to put the light out one morning, he heard the roar of it—a roar that made him run, for it was more than the noise of earthen banks going in; it was the sound of trees crashing into the river.

He hurried through the woods and found his light still standing, but so close to the edge that it seemed saved by a miracle. The bank before it had given and slipped into the water, leaving not over a foot of earth before the post, and the ladder by which he usually mounted stuck out over empty air.

Barney approached cautiously, knowing that the whole section on which he stood might at any moment sink into the deep water. As he neared the edge, there was a roar, and a big section ten rods down-stream went under. Barney felt chills run up and down his spine, but he stayed to get his light. Foot by foot he advanced, waiting to see if anything would happen after each step, and reached at last the six-foot post, "shinned" cautiously up it, grasped the lantern, and retired to safer ground.

Then he thought of the target. To get it was a task, for he might shake the post free and precipitate himself into the eddying water thirty feet below. But he must have the target. So cautiously he went back, and cautiously he tugged and wrenched until he had the white board loose. Then he went back to the house for nails and a hammer; and later in the day he came back to fix a new mounting, and brought the lantern with him.

Meanwhile the river had not been idle. Barney had left the white target at the foot of the big gum-tree on which it was to be nailed; but the river had evidently desired the piece of bank on which that gum-tree stood, and had undermined it. It had cracked off fifty feet back of the tree, and an acre at more had slumped down about four feet. There it had stopped, but Barney knew that the slightest jar might be enough to start the whole piece settling again beneath the river. Did he dare jump down on it, run out, get his target, and scramble back? Did he dare?

Barney thought about false beacons, and scarcely hesitated. The bank on which he stood had cut away as sharply as if chiselled, and the soil that formed the edge was still wet and smooth. Over it slipped Barney to the lower part, and hastened toward the gum.

He had just reached it when he felt a peculiar trembling of the earth, and heard a series of loud splashes at the waterside. A quick glance told him what was happening. The whole loose segment on which he stood had started slipping again. It went slowly down, while Barney raced for the firm bank; but when he reached the edge of the slipping piece he was already confronted by a precipice at least fifteen feet in height, to scale which was impossible.

Badly frightened, but not panic-stricken, he made two or three futile attempts, only to bring the earth crashing down with him; and realising that this was to invite immediate sinking of the part he stood on, he looked for another plan. Up- and down-stream ran the precipice which baulked him. All round the other sides the land gave sharply down into the river, and at its feet washed that swift current, which, within a short distance of the edge, was seventy feet deep.

Barney went carefully back to the big gum-tree, wondering how he would get off. As he stood by it the earth slipped five or six feet lower, and Barney realised that another six feet would put him under water. Then he had an idea. There was one route to possible safety—up the big gum-tree!

Sometimes when the bank goes in, such trees roll over and drift away, their roots free of earth. Sometimes they turn their roots up, embed their branches in the bottom, and form dangerous snags. But sometimes they stand upright for days, even weeks, their tops out of water, their main trunk and roots hidden deep beneath the flood. This was going down so straight that Barney hoped it might take that course.

It was a big tree and the nearest fork was at least twenty feet up. But Barney had brought his hammer and a pocketful of four-inch nails for the target. He picked the target up, and with two of them nailed it firmly to the tree five feet above the ground. He took a cord from his pocket and hung his lantern over his shoulder, drove a spike two feet from the ground for a step, mounted on it and threw a knee over the target, and drove another two feet above that.

Sitting on the target, he drove another still higher, and then standing, drove another above that. They were not directly in line, but formed a sort of ladder for him, although a ladder difficult to cling to.

He was still standing on the target when the earth slipped again, and this time tilted, so that the shore edge was below water-line; but the outer edge was a foot or two above the eddies, and the tree tilted shoreward slightly. That made climbing easier. He was on the upper side, and could lean somewhat against the tree. Nail after nail he drove, and climbed steadily upward until, as he reached the crotch and found branches on which he could mount more easily, the land in which the tree was rooted caved easily down into the turbulent water!

Had a mad dog suddenly learned how to climb a tree, and scrambled up after him, Barney could not have climbed faster than he now went up the rest of the big gum. He fairly jumped from branch to branch, warned of the need of haste by the gurgle of water below.

The bank went down steadily as he went up, but at last it came to rest again, leaving Barney ten feet above the water, and on the highest branch on which he dared to risk his weight.

Looking about him, he discovered himself in a dreadful plight. All round rushed the swift water of the channel current, bending and swaying his treetop till he feared it would be torn away. Fifty feet of angry water lay between him and the shore, and the shore itself was a frowning cliff almost perpendicular and thirty feet high. It was three miles down to the foot of Big Timber Bend, and Barney could see no prospect of being able to swim out.

He cogitated until dusk came, and could not imagine how any one would come to rescue him.

He had kept his hammer, thrust into his outside pocket, when he sprang into the branches, and with his last nail he made a hook for his lantern on the swaying tree. Then he lighted and hung the beacon.

"Must keep that true," he said aloud, as he did so.

Then settling himself in the most nearly comfortable position he could find, he prepared to wait until some solution of his difficulty was thrust upon him, either by the final collapse of the tree or by the arrival of rescue. As it was a warm summer night, even the cool of the river could not make his position impossible, and there was nothing for him to do but wait.

When the big steamboat *Rupert Lee*, bound down, swung into the head of Silverplate Bend long after midnight, pilot Ned Hinckley prepared for trouble.

"Landing's gone," he said to his helper on the other side of the big wheel. "I saw Jim Higgins, who came up in the *Walsh Honsell*, and he says it has cut back a quarter of a mile. The whole bend has gone. The two houses at the landing—the people hardly got out. That's what they get for living outside the levee. I wish I knew what we'll find in the crossing below. Like as not, Big Timber Beacon has gone into the river before now."

The big side-wheeler coughed her way down through the Silverplate Bend cautiously enough, feeling it by the loom of the shore, since the lights at the head and middle of it were gone.

Only a solitary beacon at the foot remained, and as they swept the curve the pilot reached for a lever and threw on the search-light, and with it lighted up the bend.

All along its front, tree trunks cluttered a ragged bank, and the water rustled through their tops as they lay fallen half-over. He cut the light off, and brought the steamboat a little farther out.

"Hate to take chances on McAlpin's Bar," he said. "But there are some nasty snags there, and the bar is the lesser evil."

So they came down to the foot of the bend and to the solitary beacon. Then the pilot cast a glance across the river.

"Well, by hokey!" he exclaimed. "Big Timber Light is still standing. I'm glad of that. The *Lily* reset it, and if ever I was glad to see a light I am glad to see that one now."

He brought the big wheel spinning over toward him, and the *Rupert Lee* swung its nose out from the bank, and slowly turned its huge bulk till it was headed toward the Big Timber Beacon. The current swept it downward as it turned, so that as it finally "straightened out," the two lights bore almost directly ahead and astern, the proper line for a run through the thread of channel below McAlpin's Bar. Hinckley thoughtfully eyed the Big Timber Beacon.

"Tommy," he said, "does that light seem to be as high up as usual?"

"Pretty low," commented Tommy, peering out into the darkness. "Looks to me like it ain't steady, either."

The light was, indeed, swaying with the motion of the tree, but a moment later it swayed much more violently. Barney had taken it from its nail, and was swinging it to and fro in a long arc, in the usual manner of hailing a passing steamboat.

"It ain't the beacon at all—or else some one is using it for a signal-light!" exclaimed the pilot.

He threw the lever, and the search-light blazed out. A turn of a little wheel overhead directed the beams, and out of the darkness leaped the picture of a caved bank, a treetop waving in the water, and the figure of some one in the treetop swaying the light.

"It's the beacon all right," said the pilot, "or it's where the beacon was."

He reached for a rope, and sounded loudly three long blasts of the whistle, two short and another long. On the lower deck all was activity at once.

"What's the landing, Mr. Hinckley?" came a deep voice from the darkness below. The pilot leaned out of the window and answered:

"Head of Big Timber Bend, captain. Something wrong with the beacon—some one in the water."

He signalled the engine-room and the wheels stopped, and again the *Rupert Lee* swung round.

Hinckley took a quick survey of the bank up and down the bend, then turned his light on the beacon tree. The figure of Barney stood out in bold detail.

"Hello!" said the pilot. "It's the kid that tends the light. Lower the stage on deck there, and brace the inner end of it. Send some one out to pick the boy out of that tree. We will have to do it quick. Don't miss him, now."

The *Rupert Lee* was broadside to the current, and drifting swiftly down-stream. The wheels were barely turning.

The port landing-stage was run out forward and lowered, a dozen negro hands were stationed on the inboard end of it, and a stout "rouster" and the mate ran to the outer end, where they hung out over the water. Barney saw them coming and made ready to be caught.

He hung the lantern on its nail, freed himself from the branches, and as Hinckley, with the skill of a lifelong experience, set the wheels of the steamer back to clear the nest of fallen trees, Barney reached out, and the two on the landing-stage caught him and dragged him on board. The steamer backed away and turned down-stream, and Barney, after hearty congratulations from the lower deck, was escorted to the pilot-house.

"Hello, bub!" said the pilot, as he came in. "No false light about you, is there? You guided us over that crossing straight as a die, and I'll report the way you did it to the department."

He did report him, too, and things came of that; but the ending of this story came when Barney had been put aboard the *Kate Clancy* in the bend below, to be carried back home. And as the *Kate Clancy* came up through Big Timber Bend, to drop him at the foot of McAlpin's Bar, he and her captain surveyed the scene of his adventure, and found no sign of the beacon, for the big gum-tree and the lantern had gone into the river.

How Hilda Got a School

By Lelia Munsell

"Well, Hilda, do you want to try again?"

Mr. Kenyon had hung up his overcoat and cap and was standing with his back to the fire, which Hilda had quickened when she heard him coming. She knew he would be chilled, for it was a cold February night.

"Johnston told me that there would be a change for the spring term down here in Hazel Row," he went on. "The board is going to meet next Monday, he said. So if you want to try again we'd better get in your application within a day or two."

Mrs. Kenyon heard her husband's question, and came in from the kitchen to hear what further he might have to say, while the two younger children dropped their play to listen. They were all interested in Hilda's attempt to get a school.

"You could board at home if you got that," said Mrs. Kenyon. "It's only two miles."

Mr. Kenyon laughed. "Better catch your hare before you cook it. Perhaps Hilda doesn't even want to try again."

"Papa," cried Hilda, indignantly, "you know I want to try again! But now listen, you and mamma both. And please don't think I don't appreciate what you have done to help me; but I want to go all alone this time. If I am ever going to make a teacher, I must learn to depend upon myself. I can't always have you to do things for me. And besides, I don't blame a school board for not hiring a teacher who hasn't grit enough to apply alone. You know I can't say anything for myself when you are along, papa. I can talk before a stranger lots better than I can before you."

"I don't see why you should feel that way," interposed Mrs. Kenyon. "You surely are not afraid of your father."

"I'm not afraid of him in one sense, but in another sense I am. I can't talk to the directors before him as I could if I were alone. I let papa apply for me last fall, and I let him go along twice this spring, and I haven't a school yet."

Mrs. Kenyon started to speak, but her husband shook his head at her. "I guess we'll have to let you have your way this time," he said. "We'll see if you succeed any better than I did."

Hilda gave him a grateful look.

"But how are you going?" he asked.

"Couldn't I walk? It isn't far."

"No, indeed. Johnston, of course, is less than two miles away, but Mr. Andrews lives four or five miles northeast, and Smith is as far in the other direction. You'll have twelve or fourteen miles to travel by the time you get back home. There is too much snow for you to walk, anyway, even if it wasn't too far. And I can't trust you to drive the team alone as cold as it is."

"I can ride old Selim. He's safe enough."

"Yes, he's safe enough. But you will find it pretty cold, riding so far on horseback."

"You'd better let your father take you in the buggy," said Mrs. Kenyon. "You'll freeze to death on Selim."

"Now, mamma, please!" begged Hilda, and her mother said no more.

Hilda had many ambitions, but the nearest and most absorbing one was to get a school. Beyond that lay a college course, and beyond that—she hardly dare to think of all the good things the future might hold for her and hers if only she might go to college.

But she knew that the money for a college course must come from her own efforts.

She had been a very proud girl when her first certificate came. It was only for a year, of course. According to the laws of the state, one must have taught three months to receive a certificate for a longer time than that. But her grades were high enough to entitle her to a second class.

The county superintendent had enclosed a kind little note with the certificate, and had spoken personally to her father, commending her work very highly. Hilda felt that she had a right to be proud.

But the certificate in itself was not worth much. Its chief value lay in the fact that it entitled her to teach if she could get a school. And how she did want a school! She dreamed of it by night and talked of it by day.

Her father's announcement that there was a vacancy so near home raised her hopes again. If she could get the place she could save all her salary, for the schoolhouse was so near that she could board at home, as her mother had said. She must get it, that was all. And she felt that she must go alone. Mr. Kenyon made no objection this time, and Mrs. Kenyon consented on the condition that Hilda would allow herself to be well bundled up for the long, cold ride.

Hilda readily consented to this, but she almost rued her bargain in the morning when her mother insisted on putting a large coat of her own over Hilda's and in tying a scarf over the warm hood, and when the girl had climbed on the horse she had wrapped a warm shawl about her.

"How in the world am I to get on and off again with all this stuff, mamma?" she asked. "I feel as wrapped up as a mummy. I know I'll frighten all the horses I meet."

It was well, perhaps, that she could not see herself, for she certainly cut rather a ridiculous figure. Added to all the rest, she was riding her father's saddle. The right stirrup had been thrown over, and in this her foot rested, while the left stirrup dangled below. She had never been fortunate enough to possess a side-saddle, and had often ridden in this way about the farm.

But she could not help feeling a little sensitive about her appearance on this occasion, which meant so much to her, and she wished her mother would not be so fussy.

As she drew near Mr. Johnston's house, she considered.

It would take her some time to disentangle herself from her many wrappings, and to any one watching from the house she would present rather a ridiculous appearance in her necessarily clumsy efforts to dismount.

So she halted old Selim some distance from the front gate, and here, hidden by the trees, she divested herself of her extra garments.

Her heart was pounding away vigorously as she knocked and inquired if Mr. Johnston was in. She had known him ever since she could remember, but he seemed suddenly to have become almost a stranger. Outwardly, however, it was a very dignified young lady who presented her case before him.

It seemed to her that he looked at her for fully five minutes without speaking.

"So you want to teach?" he asked at last. "Pretty young, aren't you? How old are you? Seventeen?"

"Yes, sir," answered Hilda. "I suppose that isn't very old, but I have a good certificate, and I am pretty sure that I can teach a good school. At least, I'd try my best if you would give me a chance."

"That's what they all say," remarked Mr. Johnston.

"I know. But that is all I *can* say till somebody gives me a chance to show what I can do."

"You have had no experience, of course."

"No. But if I am ever to make a teacher, I'll have to teach my first school sometime and somewhere."

"I guess that's so. Got some pretty good grades here." He had been examining the certificate she had handed him.

"Yes, sir," answered Hilda, modestly.

Again he was silent. Then he handed her back her certificate. "Well, I'll tell you, Hilda. So far as I am concerned, I am willing to give you a chance. I've known you ever since you were a baby, and I know you are a wide-awake, energetic little girl. But I'm only one of three, and I am afraid you won't stand the best of chances with the other two. You don't know either of them personally, do you? I thought not. Andrews wants the place for a cousin of his, and Smith will think you are too young. But go and see both of them. Don't tell them what I've said. Simply say that you spoke to me about it. Smith is president of the board."

Hilda thanked him and went her way, much encouraged in spite of what he had said about her possible reception by the other two members. She experienced some difficulty in mounting and dismounting each time, encumbered as she was, but that did not trouble her much now, although she was careful at both places to stop far enough away from the house, as she had done at Mr. Johnston's, to enable her to accomplish this feat without being seen.

And she was truly thankful that no one asked her how she came. She much preferred that the men whose interest she was trying to enlist should not see her perched up on old Selim, like a big round bump on a log, as her father had expressed it.

Fortunately, she found both Mr. Andrews and Mr. Smith at home, but she did not receive the encouragement from them that she had done from Mr. Johnston.

Indeed, Mr. Andrews told her that the school was as good as engaged, and that it was useless for her to see Mr. Smith. Hilda, remembering what Mr. Johnston had told her about the cousin, made no reply, but resolved to call upon Mr. Smith.

Mr. Smith listened to her courteously and quietly. "Pretty young, aren't you?" he asked.

Hilda laughed. "I expected you to say that. But it isn't always age and experience that make success. I have always wanted to teach, and I've always thought I could teach, and I believe I can, if I *am* young."

"I don't know but that's the right way to talk. We've got to believe in ourselves before we ever amount to much. How much would you want a month?"

She was not prepared for this question. In her heart she knew that she would take the school at whatever they might offer. But she reflected that it would not be policy to say so, so she answered:

"Whatever you have been paying for your spring term."

"Well, we'll talk over your application Monday. If we want you, we will let you know. You needn't come to see us about it again."

Hilda was obliged to be content with this. She thanked him, and then, behind the grove where she had tied her horse, she bundled herself up for the ride home, where an eager audience listened to her story while she thawed out her fingers and toes.

The next six days seemed interminably long to her, but Monday came at last. All day she listened expectantly for a step on the front porch, but no one came that day or the next. Wednesday morning she was helping her father about the barn, when she heard some one behind her, and turned to face Mr. Johnston.

"Hello!" he cried. "So you concluded to try farming if you couldn't get a school?"

Hilda smiled in reply. She could not trust herself to speak. So she had failed again.

Mr. Johnston chatted with her father for a time, while she went bravely on with her work. It would never do to let him know how disappointed she was.

"Well, Hilda," he said, finally, "I'll expect you to do me credit this spring."

Hilda looked up, surprised.

"We concluded we would try you," he continued. "Andrews stuck out for his cousin, but Smith went with me. Smith was quite taken with you. Andrews' cousin had let him attend to her application, and had never come to see one of us about it. Smith didn't like that way of doing things, and I confess I don't, myself. You'll get thirty-five dollars for three months. If that is satisfactory, I guess we might as well go to the house and sign the contract now."

Hilda felt that she was treading on air as she followed him to the house, and when she saw her name signed to the little slip of paper, the contract between herself and District No. 33, she secretly pinched herself to see if she were awake. She wanted to shout, but of course that would not do. But the moment Mr. Johnston was gone she seized her mother about the waist and whirled her round the room.

"Just think, mamma! Just think!" she cried. "I've actually got a school. One hundred and five dollars, and no board to pay. Maybe, now, I won't have to wait any longer to go to college than I had expected to do in the first place. And, mamma," she drew her mother close and whispered in her ear, "when I get to be a professor in some big university you won't have to work any more, and I can give you the things that I've wanted and wanted so long to give you."

The Imp and the Drum

By Josephine Dodge Daskam Bacon

It never would have happened but for Miss Eleanor's mission class. Once a week through the winter she went in the cars to a town not far from the city, where there were a great many mills, but few schools, and talked to a crowd of the mill-hands' little children. She did not give them lessons, exactly, but she told them stories and sang songs with them and interested them in keeping themselves and their homes clean and pretty. They were very fond of her and were continually bringing in other children, so that after the first year she gave up the small room she had rented and took them up two flights into an old dancing-hall, a little out of the centre of the town.

The Imp had been from the beginning deeply interested in this scheme, and when he learned that many of the boys were just exactly eight and a half—his own age—and that they played all sorts of games and told stories and sang songs, and had good times generally, his interest and excitement grew, and every Thursday found him begging his mother or big aunty, with whom they spent the winter, to telephone to his dear Miss Eleanor that this time he was to accompany her and see all those fascinating children: big Hans, who, though fourteen, was young for his years and stupid; little Olga, who was only eleven, but who mothered all the others, and had brought more children into the class than anyone else; Pierre, who sang like a bird, and wore a dark-blue jersey and a knitted cap pulled over his ears; red-headed Mike, who was all freckles and fun; and pretty, shy Elizabeth, with deep violet eyes and a big dimple, who was too frightened to speak at first, and who ran behind the door even now if a stranger came.

But it was not till the Imp gave up being eight and a half and arrived at what his Uncle Stanley called quarter of nine that Miss Eleanor decided that he might go if his mother would let him.

"I used to think," she said, "that it wouldn't be wise to take him. I thought they'd feel awkward; for of course he's better dressed, and I don't want them to feel that they're being shown off or made an exhibition of, even to a child. But I know them so well now, and I've told them about him and how he loves to play games, and wants to come, and I think it may really be a good thing—for both sides."

So on one delicious Thursday in early February, the Imp boarded the train proudly, and they steamed out of the big station. He had gone over the entire afternoon, in anticipation, with Harvey, his little lame friend, who could not go to school, but did his lessons with a tutor, and with whom the Imp studied every morning during the three or four months they spent in the city; and Harvey was as interested as he, and sent his best love to them all.

From the moment of the Imp's entrance, when his cheerful "Hullo!" made him any number of friends, and his delight at being there made them all delighted to have him, he was a great success; and when big Hans, with a furtive glance at the Imp's clean hands, went quietly off to the ever-ready basin and washed his own, Miss Eleanor regretted that she had not brought him sooner.

When they had finished the story about Washington at Valley Forge—for Miss Eleanor was quietly teaching them history—she got them into a long line that reached quite around the room, and went out for a moment, returning with a drum in her hand: not a play drum, but a real one, with polished black sticks and a fascinating strap to cross over the shoulder.

"Now," said she, "we're going to learn the fire-drill, and we'll take turns at the drum."

The children were delighted, and stood still as mice while she explained the order of affairs. In the big city public schools, she had been told, they practised going out in line at a mock alarm of fire, and the boy or girl who broke out of line or dashed for the door before the drum-tap was disgraced for days in the eyes of the school. Everything must be quiet and in order; every child must have his place and take it; no one must cry out, or run ahead, or push, or try to hurry matters; and what was most important, all must keep step—which was why the drum came to be there.

She arranged them carefully: little one first, then girls, last of all the boys, with big Hans at the rear, and Olga managing a crowd of the little ones.

"Now," she said, "we won't leave the room this first time; we'll just march round and round till we can all keep step, and later we'll practise going through the halls and downstairs. I'll drum the first time, and then the best boy shall be drummer."

The friend who had suggested the fire-drill when Miss Eleanor had begged her for some new game to play, had never seen one, and did not know the exact details, but she knew the general idea of it, and she knew, too, that it was not at all easy for people to keep in step, even to a drum. This had surprised Miss Eleanor greatly. She supposed that anybody could keep step, and she was much inclined to doubt her friend's statement that a large number of grown people, even, found it difficult.

But there was a still greater surprise in store for her. When she slung the strap over her pretty red waist and hit the drum a resounding blow, a very different sound from what she had expected was the result—a muffled, flat noise, with nothing inspiring about it whatever. She bit her lip and tried again, the children watching her attentively from the sides of the big room.

Bang!

Bang!

Bang, bang, bang!

A few feet began to keep time, but the sound was not very different from that produced by a stick hit against the wall, and big Hans, whose father played in a band, and who had attended many rehearsals—it was from him the drum had been procured—shook his head solemnly.

"Not so! Not so!" he said in his thick, gruff voice. "You no hit good! You no hit hard!"

"Oh, Hans, can *you* play it?" cried Miss Eleanor eagerly. "Here, take it!" And she flung the strap over his shoulder.

Hans shambled out to the centre of the room, and struck a mighty blow. The familiar deep sound of a drum filled the place, and Miss Eleanor sighed with relief, but alas! her joy was short-lived, for poor Hans had no idea of time, and could only pound away like a hammer. In vain she held his hand and tried to guide his strokes. The noise was deafening, but no more to be marched to than thunder.

Little Pierre tried next, but though he kept perfect time, and looked very cunning in his little blue blouse, his taps were too light to cover the sound of the tramping feet.

Miss Eleanor's cheeks were red with vexation. Her arm ached, and the children were getting restless. She did not know what to do.

"Oh, dear! *Who* would have thought it was so hard?" she exclaimed pathetically. And then she noticed the Imp, who was fairly holding his lips in his effort to keep silence. For he had solemnly promised his mother not to put himself forward, nor suggest anything, nor offer to do a single thing till he was asked, on pain of never coming again.

"What is it, Perry?" she asked.

"*I* can—*I* can play a drum, Miss Eleanor!" he burst out.

She looked doubtful: the Imp was given to thinking that he could do most things.

"This isn't a play drum, you know, dear; it's a real one," she said. "But I can play a real one. Truly I can! Mr. Archer taught me—he was a truly drummer-boy in the war; he showed me how. He said I could hit it up like a good 'un!" the Imp exploded again.

Miss Eleanor dimly remembered that among the Imp's amazing list of acquaintants, a one-legged Grand Army man, who kept a newspaper-stall, had been mentioned, and decided that it could do no harm to let him try.

"Well, put it on," she said, and the Imp proudly assumed the drum, grasped the sticks loosely between his fingers, wagged his head knowingly from side to side, and began.

Brrrm!

Brrrm!

Brrrm! brrrm! brrrm!

The straggling line straightened, the children began to grin, and little Pierre, at the head of the line, stamped his foot and started off. Miss Eleanor's forehead smoothed, and she smiled encouragingly at the Imp.

"That's it, that's it!" she cried delightedly. "How easy it looks!"

But the Imp stopped suddenly, and the moving line stopped with him.

"Wait! I forgot!" he said peremptorily. "You mustn't start till I do this."

And with a few preliminary taps he gave the long roll that sends a pleasant little thrill to the listener's heart.

Brrrm!

Brrrm!

Brrrrr—*um* dum!

The children jumped with delight, and the line started off, the Imp drumming for dear life around the inside of the big square, and Miss Eleanor keeping the hasty ones back and hurrying the stragglers, trying to make big Hans feel the rhythm, and suppressing Pierre's happy little skips.

After a half-hour of this they begged to try the halls and stairs, and the Imp stood proudly on the landings, keeping always at about the middle of the line, stamping his right foot in time with his sticks, his eyes shining with joy, his little body straight as a dart.

Miss Eleanor was delighted. The boys responded so well to her little talk on protecting the girls and waiting till they were placed before taking their own stand in the line, the girls stood so straight, the little ones entered so well into the spirit of the thing, that she felt that afternoon to have been one of the best they had had, and confided as much to the Imp on their journey home.

As for the Imp, he had a new interest in life, and talked of little else than the fire-drill for days. There was no question as to his going the next Thursday, and he and his drum formed the chief attraction of the day, for the drill proved the most popular game of all, and after the proclamation had gone forth that none but clean-handed, neatly dressed, respectful boys need aspire to head the line, such boys were in a great and satisfying majority.

For a month they had been practising regularly, and by the end of that time every child knew his place and took it instantly at the opening tap. It was pretty to see little Olga shake back her yellow pigtails and marshal her tiny brood into line; even the smallest of them kept step nicely now.

Only big Hans could not learn, and Pierre walked by his side in vain, trying to make him feel the rhythm of the Imp's faithful drumsticks.

There was one feature of the drill that amused Miss Eleanor's friends greatly. Of course there was no fire-alarm in the old hall, and she would not let anyone cry out or even pretend for a moment that there was any real danger. She merely called sharply, "*Now!*" when they were to form, and it was one of the suppressed excitements of the afternoon to wait for that word. They never knew when it would come.

For Miss Eleanor's one terror was fire. Twice, as a little girl, she had been carried out of a burning house; and the flames bright against the night, the hoarse shouts of the firemen, the shock of the frightened awakening, and the chill of the cold winter air had so shaken her nerves that she could hardly bear to remember it. Burglars had little terror for her; in accidents she was cool and collected; more than once, in a quiet way, she had saved people from drowning; but a bit of flaming paper turned her cheeks white and made her hands tremble. So though big Hans begged to be allowed to call out "Fire!" she would never let him, and though she explained the meaning of the drill to them, it is to be doubted if they attached much importance to the explanation, as she herself did not care to talk about it long.

One fine, windy Thursday—it was the second Thursday in March, and the last Thursday the Imp would be able to spend with his new friends, for he was going back to the country—they started out a little depressed in spirits: the Imp because it was his last visit, Miss Eleanor because she was afraid her children were in danger of a hard week. The hands of three of the largest factories were "on strike," and though they were quite in the wrong, and were demanding more than any but the ring-leaders themselves felt to be just, they were excited to the pitch of rage that no reasoning can calm, and as the superintendents had absolutely refused to yield any further, affairs were at a deadlock.

One or two of Miss Eleanor's friends had grown alarmed, and urged her not to go there till the matter was settled, but she would not hear of this.

"Why, this is the very time I want to keep the children out of the streets!" she said. "They all know me—nobody would hurt me. They know I love the children, and I have nothing to do with their quarrel. I should be willing to trust myself to any of them. They have always been very polite and respectful to me, and they've been getting ready for this for two weeks, for that matter."

Her father agreed to this, and assured the Imp's mother that any demonstration that might take place would be at the other end of the town, near the mills, and that it was very unlikely that anything further than a shut-down for a few days would result, at most.

"They're in the wrong, and most of them know it, I hear," he said. "They can't hold out long: nobody else will hire them."

This may have been true, but it did not add to their good-humour. As the Imp and Miss Eleanor walked up through the village, the streets were filling rapidly with surly, idle men. Dark-eyed Italians, yellow-haired Swedes, shambling, gesticulating Irish, and dogged, angry English jostled each other on the narrow walks, and talked loudly. Miss Eleanor hurried the Imp along, picking up a child here and there on the way, and sighing with relief as she neared the old hall.

Some of the excitement had reached the children, and though they had come in large numbers, for they knew it was the Imp's last visit for some time, and there had been hints of a delightful surprise for them on this occasion, they were restless and looked out of the windows often. There was a shout of applause when, the Imp suddenly becoming overwhelmed with shyness, Miss Eleanor invited them all out to his home for one day in the summer; but the excitement died down, and more than one of the older children glanced slyly at the door. The men from that end of the town were filing by, and most of the women were following after.

Miss Eleanor racked her brains for some amusement.

It was cold in the room, for the boy who had charge of the clumsy old-fashioned stove was sick that day, and there was no fire. So partly to keep them contented, and partly to get them warm, she proposed a game of blindman's-buff. There was a shout of assent, and presently they were in the midst of a tremendous game. The stamping feet of the boys and the shrill cries of the girls made a deafening noise; the dust rose in clouds; the empty old building echoed confusingly. The fun grew fast and furious; the rules were forgotten; the boys began to scuffle and fight, and the little girls danced about excitedly.

Miss Eleanor called once or twice to quiet them, but they were beyond control; they paid no attention to her.

With a little grimace she stepped out of the crowd to breathe, and took out her watch.

"Twenty minutes!" she said to little Olga, who followed her about like a puppy. "I'll give them ten more, and then they *must* stop!"

Little Olga began to cough, and looked doubtfully at the old stove, which was given to smoking.

"It smells bad just the same, don't it?" she called. They had to raise their voices to be heard above the noise.

"No, child, it's the dust. Isn't it dreadful?" Miss Eleanor called back, coughing herself. "But it smells just like smoke. How horrid it is! And how hot!" she added after a moment. "With the windows open, too! We'll all take cold when we go out. They *must* stop! Boys, boys! Hans, come here to me!"

She rang a little bell that was the signal for quiet, and raised her hand. "Now I'm going to open the door, to get a thorough draft, and then we'll quiet down," she said, and pushed through the crowd to the door.

As she opened it wide, a great cloud of brown, hot smoke poured into the room, a loud roaring, with little snapping crackles behind it, came from below, and Miss Eleanor suddenly put her hand to her heart, turned perfectly white, and half fell, half leaned against the door.

For a moment the children were quite still, so still that through the open door they could hear the roar and the crackle. Then suddenly, before she could prevent him, little Pierre slipped through and started down the hall. With a cry she went after him, half the children following her, but in a moment they crowded back, screaming and choking. The stairs at the end of the long hall were half on fire!

Miss Eleanor tried to call out, but though her lips moved, she could not speak above a whisper. She shut the door and leaned against it, and the look in her eyes frightened the children out of what little control they had.

"Call," she said hoarsely, "call 'Fire!' out of the window. Quick! Call, all of you!"

But they stumbled about, crying and gasping, some of them struggling to get by her out of the door. She was trembling violently, but she pushed them away and held the door-knob as tightly as she could.

Only Olga ran to the open window, and sent a piercing little shriek out into the quiet street:

"*Fire! Fire! Come along! Fire!*"

For a moment there was no answer, and then a frightened woman ran out of her house and waved her hand.

"Come out! Come out, you!" she called.

"Our stairs is burnt all up! We can't!" screamed Olga.

The woman ran quickly down the empty street, calling for help as she ran, and the children surged about the door, a crowd of frightened little animals, trying to drag Miss Eleanor away from it.

"Wait," she begged them, "wait! You can't go that way—they'll bring ladders! Oh, *please* wait!"

Her knees shook beneath her, the room swam before her eyes. The smell of the smoke, stronger and stronger, sickened her. With a thrill of terror, she saw big Hans drag a child away from the window, and deliberately pushing her down, prepare to climb out over her, almost stepping on her little body.

Suddenly she caught sight of the Imp. He was pushing his way through the crowd valiantly, but not toward her.

"Come here, Perry!" she said weakly. But he paid no attention. He had been dazed for a moment, and like all the other children, her terror had terrified him quite as much as the fire. Now as he caught her eye, and saw the helpless fear in her face as she watched Hans, something sent him away from her to a farther corner, and as the smoke began to come up between the boards of the floor, and the same deadly stillness reigned outside, while the confusion grew greater in the hot, crowded room, a new sound cut through the roar and the crackle.

Brrrm!

Brrrm!

Brrrm, brrrm, brrrm!

The children turned. Big Hans, with one leg out of the window, looked back. There was a little rush, half checked, for the sides of the room, and Olga instinctively looked about for her small charges.

But they wavered undecidedly, and as the sound of steps outside and the clattering of horses' feet reached them, a new rush for the door began, and Miss Eleanor's hand slipped from the knob, and she half fell beside it.

Brrrm!

Brrrm!

Brrrm—*um* dum!

That familiar long roll had never been disobeyed; the habit of sudden, delighted response was strong; and with a quick recollection that he was to be head boy, big Hans slipped from the window-sill and jumped to the head of a straggling line. Olga was behind him in a moment, and Pierre, proud of his position as rear-guard and time-keeper for the little boys, pushed them, crying and coughing, into place.

Miss Eleanor must have been half unconscious for a moment. When she struggled to her feet, no scrambling crowd, but an orderly, tramping line pushed by her, and above the growing tumult outside, above the sickening roar of the fire below, came the quick, regular beat of the faithful drum.

Brrrm!

Brrrm!

Brrrm, brrrm, brrrm!

The children marched as if hypnotized. The long line just filled the sides of the room, and they were squeezed in so tightly that they forced each other on unconsciously. The Imp in his excitement beat faster than usual, and his bright red cheeks, his straight little figure, as he walked his inside square, his quick, nervous strokes, were an inspiration to the most scared laggard. Big Hans, elated at his position—his for the first time—never took his eyes off the black sticks, and worked his mouth excitedly, keeping time to the beats, the Imp frowning at his slightest misstep.

Miss Eleanor, the door hot against her back, forced her trembling lips into a smile, and cheered them on as they tramped round and round. Was nothing being done? Would no one come?

Suddenly there was a thundering, a clanging, and a quick, sharp ringing gong came closer with every stroke; the sound of many running feet, too, and loud, hoarse orders. The line wavered, seemed to stop. She summoned all her strength, and called out aloud for the first time:

"Don't stop, children! Keep right on! Stand straight, Hans, and show them how well you can lead!"

Hans tossed his head, glared at a boy across the room who had broken through, and forged ahead. There was a succession of quick blows on the sides of the room, a rush, and in another moment three helmeted heads looked through three windows. At the same moment a sharp hissing sound interrupted the roaring below, and though the door was brown behind her now, and a tiny red point was glowing brighter in the wall near by, Miss Eleanor's strength returned at the sight of the firemen, and she stood by the side of the Imp and encouraged the children.

"Don't stop, Hans! Remember, little ones first! Olga's children first!"

And with a grunt of assent Hans marched on, the line following, closing up mechanically over the gaps the men made, who snatched out the children as they passed by the windows, and handed them rapidly down the long ladders. In vain the firemen tried to get the boys. They wriggled obstinately out of their grasp, as they went round, till every girl was lifted out, Olga standing by the window till the last of her charges was safe.

The door fell in with a bang, and in spite of the hose below, the smoke rolled up from between the cracks in the floor, thicker and thicker. As the plaster dropped from the walls in great blocks, Miss Eleanor dragged the line into the centre of the room, and motioned one of the men to take the Imp as he passed by. For so perfect was the order that the men never once needed to step into the room, only leaning over the sills to lift out the children. The Imp felt a strong grasp on his arm, and pulled away; the man insisted.

"Hurry now, hurry, let go!" he commanded gruffly. The despair in the Imp's eyes as he drummed hard with his other hand grew to rage, and he brought down his free stick with a whack on the man's knuckles. With a sharp exclamation the man let go, and the Imp pressed on, his cheeks flaming, his eyes glowing. His head was high in the air, he was panting with excitement. The line was small now; another round and there would be but a handful. The floor near the door began to sag, and the men took two at a time of the bigger boys, and left them to scramble down by themselves. With every new child a shout went up from below. As Hans slipped out by himself, and two men lifted Miss Eleanor out of one window, a third meanwhile carrying the Imp, kicking in his excitement, and actually beating the drum as it dangled before him, while a fourth man took a last look, and crying "O. K.! All out!" ran down his ladder alone, the big crowd literally shouted with thankfulness and excitement.

As for the Imp, he felt tired and shaky, now that somebody had taken away his drum, and all the women were trying to kiss him; and he watched the blackened walls crash in without a word. His knees felt hollow and queer, and there was nobody to take him in her lap like the other children, for Miss Eleanor had quietly fainted in the firemen's arms, and they were sprinkling her with water from the little pools where the big hose had leaked.

They took them to the station in a carriage, and the Imp sat in Miss Eleanor's lap in a drawing-room car, and she cuddled him silently all the way home. Her father, dreading lest she should be hurt somehow after all in the crowded streets, passed them in an express going in the other direction, to find out that they were safe, and that the strike was off. The recent danger had sobered the men, and their thankfulness at their children's safety had softened them, so that their ring-leaders' taunts had no effect on their determination to go back to work quietly the next day.

It was at her father's request that they refrained from any more costly gift to Miss Eleanor than a big photographic group of the children, framed in plush, "as an expression of their deep gratitude for her presence of mind in keeping the children in the room away from the deadly flames beneath." But to the Imp the Mill Town drum corps and military band formally presented "to master Perry S. Stafford the drum and sticks that he used on the occasion when his bravery and coolness made them proud to subscribe themselves his true friends and hearty well-wishers."

The Second String

By James B. Connolly

The Interscholastic Athletic Association was holding its annual track meeting. In the athletic building a hundred lads or more were dressing or rubbing in preparation for the different events. The clerk of the course, sticking his head within the door, shouted, "Last call for the hundred yards final! Last call! Hurry now, fellows!"

The graduate coach of Webster High School cut short his instructions to a medium-sized, heedful, earnest-looking lad. "There now, I'll have to go and see how Prouty runs in the hundred. But bear in mind, Haskins, what you're to do when your race comes. Keswick is out to run the field off its feet. And if they follow him he'll do it. You are to get the inside track—on the first run get the pole, mind, if you have to do forty yards in record time to do it. That will start a break in Keswick's plans. Then you make the pace—with an eye all the way to Stevenson. Perhaps you'll carry Sullivan off his feet, too, at the same time. That's not likely, though. Anyway, carry Stevenson along—clear round to the home-stretch, and make it so hot for Keswick on the way that he'll be done up at that point. Land Stevenson in the straight in good shape and your work will be done. Drop out then if you want to, and I guess you'll want to drop. You've an hour yet. When Stevenson comes from the rubbing board, jolly him along a bit. He's apt to get—nervous—you know. Got it all?"

"I think so." Haskins lay back on his mat for rest and meditation.

Pretty soon Stevenson, a tall, rangy lad, came over from the other side of the room. He halted above Haskins, and looked about, as if seeking a place to lie.

Haskins caught his glance. "They're all in use, I guess, Stevie. Take this place. You'll want all the rest you can get for your race."

"You're not done? You've got to run, too."

"O shucks—me—second string—I'm only to make pace for you. Mr. Ludwig just told me."

"Well, all right—thanks. Think you can do it right?"

"I don't know. It'll be hard getting the pole from Keswick. He's in for the same game—making way for Sullivan. We'll have a great time of it, Keswick and I. I wonder which will flop first? But I'll make for that pole—though Keswick's a hound for a quick start—and try to hold on for the straight again. That'll do, won't it? If I kill off Keswick so he won't be of any use, you can give all your attention to Sullivan? He's a good man, Sullivan, but you can give him yards and a licking any day in the week, Stevie."

"Think so, Dickie?"

"Think? I know it. He hasn't your stride, your speed, or your head, and you're in great shape to-day, Mr. Ludwig says. Beat him? You'll flag him. Oh, I wish I had your speed! I'd make Sullivan and Keswick look like busted automobiles. I know just how I'd do it, too. But what's the use? I haven't the speed. I'm only second string and lucky to be that, but

I'll go through three hundred yards of that quarter to-day for every little ounce in me, and I don't care if they carry me off afterward."

The little lad was cuddled up on the floor, back to a locker, knees up to his chin, bath-robe tucked in round him. His regard was all for his school champion. In common with most of the boys of the school, he had the deepest admiration for Stevenson's running power. Never before had such a quarter-miler come out of Webster—no, nor out of the state! All he needed was a little more growth and experience and a little more—well, confidence in himself, and he would beat the world! So his schoolmates phrased it.

Stevenson placidly accepted Haskin's devotion. He had been used to that sort of thing for some time now, and it did not fluster him. He did not even acknowledge the care with which his friend tucked in the wandering folds of his blanket, saying, "It's drafty here, Stevie, and you want to keep your legs covered or you'll stiffen up. Mustn't stiffen up, you know."

They waited for their time to come—Stevenson on the mat, Haskins snuggled up against the locker. The young athletes in the room kept going and coming. They would go out fresh and strong, some nervous, some confident, a few absolutely in fear—ready to draw back only that shame forced them on. They came back tired, winded, used up, some of them jubilant, some depressed, a few crying. With each returning batch some new details of the progress of things were shouted round the room.

At last the coach, Ludwig, came back. "Your quarter's coming soon, fellows. Looks like Scotia and Webster again. Sullivan's just run the two-twenty; that'll take the edge off him for the quarter-mile, Stevenson. How do you feel? And you, Dickie? It'll be up to you soon. Feel fit for the fastest three hundred you ever ran in your life? Of course you do."

"I wish Dickie had the other's speed," Ludwig whispered to MacArthur, high jumper and team captain.

"H-m-m, Mr. Ludwig—Dickie's heart and Stevenson's legs! Rather a lot for one package, wouldn't it be?"

The clerk of the course here made an entrance. "Quarter-mile comes last of the track events. Sullivan of Scotia wants to get rested from the two-twenty, and judges agreed. All out for the long jump and hammer."

Stevenson made a pettish face. "I suppose Sullivan and the Scotians can have things cooked to their order and the rest of us take what we can get. I think you ought to protest, Mr. Ludwig."

Ludwig shook his head. "I can't change the order of events, Stevenson. Besides, it's only fair to give a man a rest after he's been through a hard two-twenty. Take it easy, like Dickie, there. Go to sleep if you can. Dickie, can't you find a mat to lie on? You have an hour to wait yet, and I don't like to have you hugging the floor like that."

"Oh, this is nice. Here's my suit case for a pillow. I could go to sleep here."

All things come to an end. The busy clerk of the course rushed in for the last time. "Quarter-mile now! Only one call—all out!"

Stevenson and Dickie promptly rose—Stevenson anxious in manner, fussy; Dickie serious, calm. Together they walked across the field, MacArthur and Ludwig in attendance. Every event had been finished except the pole-vault, always a lengthy affair. The audience was in a fine state of expectancy.

Just before reaching the track, Ludwig drew the boys' heads together. "Now, Stevenson, this meet depends on you. We win it if you capture the five points for first place in the quarter. We lose it if you don't. Dickie here is to be sacrificed for you. Keep your eye on Dickie; he'll swing out and tell you when.

"And you, Dickie," Ludwig went on, "make a way for Stevenson and balk Keswick. See that you have the pole on the last turn. Now go along. O Dickie, a moment!"

Ludwig dropped his arm round the boy's neck. "This is in confidence, Dickie. MacArthur and I are afraid that Stevenson isn't any too fond of his job to-day—that he doesn't quite fancy a tilt with Sullivan. What do you think?"

"Stevenson afraid? Oh, no, Mr. Ludwig! Stevie's nervous—that's natural. Why, I'm nervous, for all you crack up my coolness. I'm nervous as I can be, but I try not to show it, and Stevie lets his out. Stevie will win. Look at him up on his toes now! Style! He's won three-quarters of the crowd already, just the gait of him. Don't worry, Mr. Ludwig, Webster'll win this quarter-mile."

"Well, all right, Dickie. I hope you're right. Hope he's only nervous. Look out for him, anyway. But don't try to do it too fast—don't kill yourself. If you can, you might just as well finish; you don't know, somebody might drop and you pick up a point. Not much of a chance for you, but—"

"But Sullivan and Stevie and the rest of them *might* drop—used up! Ha, that's good! Imagine me a quarter-mile champion! It's too strange to think of."

"Strange things, Dickie. There, that's for you."

In the line of starters Dickie was second from the pole. Big Keswick was inside him, Stevenson outside, and Sullivan second outside Stevenson. Dickie at once made himself acquainted with Keswick's tactics. One or two false starts convinced him that Keswick's right elbow was intended for a prominent part in the contest. Dickie knew that Keswick expected to have it all his own way when it came to close quarters. But there was a way. Dickie had no notion of letting Keswick's cruel elbow rob him of the pole. There was always a way to deal with such tactics.

"Starters ready?"

"Ready!"

"Timers ready?"

"Ready—ready, all ready!"

"Get on your marks. Set—stea-a-d-d-y. Come up. Man at the pole, be careful. Now—on your marks. Get set—"

Bang! Dickie promptly caught the hook of Keswick's plunging right elbow in the angle of his own left. Keswick was spun half-round and Dickie shot in. "That for Kessie!" muttered Dickie. The judges saw it, but it raised only a smile all round and an appreciative comment from one. "That big fellow tried it that time, didn't he? An old trick of his, Ludwig says, but the little fellow was too clever."

Dickie ran like mad for the turn. He got it, with Stevenson outside him, a little back, and Keswick directly behind. All the runners turned the curve in fine style. It promised to be a hot race. The audience was already applauding vigorously.

Dickie motioned to Stevenson. "I'll cut loose the whole length of the back-stretch. Don't try to keep up—let Keswick chase me if he cares to; watch Sullivan, and wait for the turn." That was not put in so many words, but had it been written out, Stevenson could not have read the motions more plainly.

It was a rare pace that Dickie set. The bunch tore round the lower curve as if they were to run only two hundred and twenty yards.

"This is going to be warm," said a group of old-timers under the willows.

"Look at that!" yelled the crowd. Dickie had shot away from the others. Big Keswick was at his heels. Keswick's plans had been interfered with. He was there to take care of Haskins, but things had been changed. This pace was a "scorcher." What did it mean?

It was a beautiful sprint the whole length of the back-stretch. Dickie was ten yards, Keswick eight yards in front. Stevenson and Sullivan were running stride for stride, the Webster man inside, a yard or two ahead of Sullivan.

Swinging into the upper curve, Dickie signalled to Stevenson, and then imperceptibly slowed up the pace. Keswick naturally trailed behind. Without understanding how it was brought about, he felt the relief, and was well content to take it. Dickie knew Keswick was in no trim to interfere with what was soon going to happen.

Dickie felt Stevenson coming easily. Again he signalled, this time looking back to see that all was well. Stevenson moved up to Keswick's flank and nodded. The last turn was before them. Dickie, suddenly darting forward, opened up several yards. Keswick was too surprised and too tired to understand at once. Stevenson strode past him and dropped into Dickie's tracks. Dickie, on the corner, swung wide and Stevenson slid inside. The pole and the lead were his.

Sullivan had his choice of following Stevenson or running outside Dickie. He chose to follow Stevenson. To let him by, Keswick was compelled to pull up and lose his chance for a place. Dickie, seeing how

Sullivan had chosen, promptly dropped back a yard to Sullivan's flank. That put Sullivan in a close pocket.

It was all most prettily done. The grand stand got up on its toes to cheer it. The experts under the willows hurled big words of praise out to Dickie.

After that manoeuvre, Dickie felt that he had no more strength left. It was an immense relief to him to think that the strain of his work was past, and that Stevie was in a good way now to win the race. But he must give a final word of cheer to Stevie before he was left behind.

"Go in, Steve, go in now! That's the boy! All right, you've got it cinched. Go on! What's the matter?"

Dickie, looking up at his chum's face, saw an expression that made his heart sink. There was despair in Stevenson's eyes.

Others saw, and understood. From under the willows came encouraging cries to Sullivan: "Go in, Scotia! You've got him! He's all in! He's a quitter, anyway, and the little fellow's used up. Come out of that box, Sully, and win!"

Dickie heard this. Stevenson heard it, too, and it did him no good. Sullivan heard, also, and acted on it. He worked out of the pocket to Dickie's side. Dickie looked at Sullivan, saw only a grim resolve there, and in despair appealed to Stevenson.

"O Stevie, go in! Only half the stretch! You can do it! Go in!"

Stevenson made no answer, but to Dickie's dismay, fell down, as if exhausted, on the grass.

Dickie, without looking again, felt the courage of the Scotian beside him. There was no giving in there. The race was lost!

But was it lost? He did what had never entered his head until that instant. The import of Ludwig's last words flashed on him. Had Stevenson really quit? He did not seem used up. And after everything had worked so nicely! What a shame for Webster!

It was in the blindest kind of way that Dickie pegged on beside Sullivan. Only for that work on the turn and Sullivan would have been yards ahead! What a runner this Sullivan was! Dickie was marvelling that he held up with him.

The audience was marvelling, too. They were frantic, some for Sullivan, but most for Dickie, because he was so small and had borne his previous share so nobly. Their yells were deafening. But Dickie never heard them. He was taken up with a different thing—with the unbearable strain of the race. Every nerve in his body quivered under the rack of his effort. Every little molecule and atom was crying out with the torture of it—but would not Webster be disgraced if he did not win? He knew what they would all say. Could he make it? Still behind—what a hard fighter—this Sullivan! He would never underrate a Scotian again.

One foot and twenty yards to go. Now then! No use. O Dickie! Who called? All Webster was calling. O Dickie! What a horrible thing! Hot, heavy iron in his loins—great lead weights on his feet—and his chest! What an awful collapse in his chest! Would it hold out? And his knees—if they would but keep off the ground he would win yet.

A foot, still a foot—what an awful lot to make up! Half a foot! Was Sullivan going, too? Ten yards—even! Was it even? Was it worth this awful agony? Even—one more, two more, another—and—sh-h-h!

It was the frenzied Ludwig who caught him as he fell. And it was Ludwig and MacArthur who bore him in a blanket across the field and laid him on two thicknesses of mats in the athletic building. It was these two, and a doctor from among the officials, who worked on him until he knew where he was.

It was Ludwig on one side, sponging his face, and MacArthur on the other, drying him off, when he looked up with the first sign of intelligence.

"There you are, you little bronco! Changed your mind and came back to life, did you? Know what we've a good mind to do to you? A little of this, now—there, how's that? That's witch-hazel we're rubbing on. Sniff it up, that's right. Fine, eh? Feel better than when you crossed the tape-rather! Get up? Not for a while yet—not till the carriage comes.

"Who won? Why, you, of course!"

"I didn't know. I was almost afraid to ask—afraid it was Sullivan. Last I remember he was ahead. Couldn't see—"

"Ahead? I should say he was ahead until a yard from the string, and then a miracle happened. Of course you couldn't see. Wonder you could breathe after that finish—and setting the pace all the way round! Why, your knees weren't six inches off the ground! You crossed on your hands and knees—crossed, no, you never crossed—you fell over, and Sullivan fell alongside. Wait till Webster gets hold of you."

"Poor Sullivan, wasn't he game? And we beat Scotia?"

"Beat them, yes, and won the banner—champions again."

"Won the banner—that's good. And Richard L. Haskins won the quarter. That'll look fine in the morning paper. Won't the people at home read that, though? But, Mr. Ludwig—Stevie—how's Stevie?"

"Stevenson's all right. No, lie down—he's not here. He's gone to the station to catch an early train home."

"Poor Stevie—I know—you don't want to tell me," whispered Dickie.

"Now, now, Dickie, I'll handle the sponge."

Ludwig bent lower. "Sh-h-h! There, there, let Mac pull the hood over, and nobody will know. Go ahead, don't mind me and Mac; we understand."

Ludwig plied the sponge and MacArthur the towel. And so deftly did they work that in all that room no other knew that under the hood of the bath-robe they were wiping away Dickie's tears of pity for Stevenson.

Holding the Pipe

By Albert W. Tolman

As the father of Billy and Jack Remfry emerged from the sitting-room closet with the checker-board, the two boys sidled up to him. Billy hugged an armful of rockets, while Jack was generously laden with firecrackers and Roman candles. "Aren't you going with us to Steel Bridge? You promised."

Tom Remfry hesitated. Fourth of July night though it was, he could not forego his weekly battle with Lon Penfield, his fellow fireman and ancient checker foe. So he compromised. "Run along, boys. I'll come after just one game. Don't point those rockets toward the city."

Whooping, the boys made off. Tom and Lon sat down to the board, undisturbed by the noise outside. This game was unusually important, for Lon's victory the Saturday before had tied them with seventeen apiece.

While they whittled down each other's forces, Henry Marcot, watchman in Bustin's lumber-yard, was uneasily watching three boys with firecrackers just outside the fence. So engrossed was Henry with the foe in front that he did not observe a flaming rocket-stick which, after soaring far and high, dropped quietly upon a hard-pine board-pile behind him. Startled by a sudden crackling, he looked back to see the whole pile ablaze.

When the rocket fell, Remfry's four kings were beleaguering Penfield's remaining three in the latter's dodge-corner. Marcot pulled the yard alarm just as an incautious onslaught cost the besieger two pieces to his enemy's one, and left the game a draw.

Clang! Clang!

Over went the board and up leaped both call-men. Out they darted, Remfry snapping his spring-lock, and ran at top speed for the house of Hose 5. The cart was rattling into the street when they jumped abroad.

"Where's the fire?" halloed Remfry to Louville Craig, his elbow neighbour on the swaying wagon.

"Bustin's lumber-yard!" Craig shouted. "They say a rocket from Steel Bridge started it."

Remfry caught his breath as if doused with cold water. Steel Bridge! One of his boys' rockets! His heart went down like lead. Oh, why had he not gone with them and given up his game! But it was too late now. That very thing had been the nightmare of the fire department ever since he joined it—a blaze in the worst place and under the worst conditions.

The city stood west of the river on three terraces. The first contained lumber-yards, coal-sheds and mills; the second, thirty feet higher, held the railroad-tracks and business section; while the third, thirty feet higher still, was covered with residences. Unless the flames were checked, the east wind would drive them against an oil-tank right above the yard on the edge of the second terrace. That once afire, the whole city might be wiped out.

As Hose 5 clattered across the railroad gridiron between hurrying crowds, Remfry sighted the yard, and felt sick. The pine was blazing fiercely, sending out a dense yellowish-black smoke. The second alarm began to clang, calling out the whole force.

The cart stopped near the engine, which was already in position. The two call-men rapidly donned rubber coats and helmets, while their mates took the butt of the hose off the wagon and rushed it to the hydrant.

"Run a line up Adams Street, you two, back of the yard!" shouted Capt. Joe Porter. It was the post of responsibility in the very track of the flames, and he picked his best men for it. Penfield and Remfry again jumped on the hose-cart.

"Go ahead!" yelled the hydrant man to the driver. Off rattled the wagon, dropping a lengthening trail of hose. The instant they stopped, the firemen screwed on the pipe and began to drag the line toward the yard.

Close by stood the oil-tank, big and black, with the smoke eddying thickly round it. Thirty feet below lay the lumber piles. Dropping their hose over the edge of the stone wall, they slid down to the ground.

"Play away, 5!" shouted Remfry, pulling down more line. They were in a space between high board-piles, and a strong wind was driving the fire and smoke toward them. The spot might easily become a dangerous trap.

"Come on, Tom!" bellowed Penfield, tugging at the pipe. "Let's get well in before the water comes."

The piles were twenty feet apart. Round a corner twice as far ahead red tongues were spurting. Already the air was hot and thick. Crouching, they dragged the line along several yards. Remfry was wild with impatience. He was responsible for that fire. He must put it out.

"Far enough!" he gasped at last. "Isn't that water ever coming?"

It was fully five hundred feet to the engine. A few lengths from it the three-inch hose was "Siamesed" off into two smaller lines, one of which ran to the impatient call-men. Suddenly a tremor shook the closely woven cotton.

"Here it is!" exclaimed Penfield.

Psht! Psht! hissed the nozzle. Spasmodically at first, but in a few seconds foaming strongly under a two-hundred pound pressure, the water came. The two rested the pipe over their knees, grasping the handles firmly, interlocking fingers under the tip. A powerful white jet was soon bombarding the burning pine.

The hose stiffened under their hands, responsive to every impulse from the engine. It was like a live thing, struggling to escape. But they knew its tricks, and held it hard. Three years they had been together on the pipe, and never once had it got away from them.

At the very apex of the fire they literally held the safety of the city in their hands. Behind them loomed the gaunt, black oil-tank. Should the flames reach its ten thousand gallons nothing could save the city.

Remfry groaned at the thought. He envied Penfield. Penfield had only the fire to think of. That was bad enough, to be sure. But it was tenfold worse for him, Tom Remfry, to feel that he might have prevented all this, had he only gone to Steel Bridge with his boys.

Low as they might stoop, they could not avoid the smoke. Their smarting eyes could barely see to direct the jet. Both were choking. Penfield leaned forward and thrust his hand into the stream to spray his face.

His foot slipped; he lost his balance; his grip on the handle loosened.

With a tremendous leap the pipe wrenched out of the men's grasp, and disappeared straight up in the thick smoke.

A deluge burst above the firemen. The hose had changed from their best friend to their worst enemy. It whipped the board-piles; it slapped full length on the ground to their right; vanishing, it dropped a moment later on their left. Fearful in plain sight, it was doubly, trebly terrible in that impenetrable pitchiness. One rap from the crazy nozzle would smash a man's skull.

Remfry grabbed Penfield's shoulder. Their first impulse was to run; but where? Straight ahead was the only way out; and the fire barred that. Behind rose the thirty-foot wall.

Instinct told Remfry the only spot where for a brief period they might be comparatively safe.

"Back to the corner!" he whispered, hoarsely; and the two ran for their lives. Once the nozzle jabbed Penfield in the spine. Then Remfry ducked in time to lose only his helmet from a flying loop of hose. Soon they were crouching in the angle between the wall and a board-pile.

But the flames would soon drive them from this refuge. Besides, the chief counted on them to fight back the fire from the oil-tank. The force had its hands full. Every man and every line were busy. Somehow they must signal the engine to shut the water off, until they could regain control of the pipe.

"Hold on, 5!" shrieked Remfry. And Penfield seconded him with:
"Shut that line down!"

But no answering cry came back. It was not strange. Two men under a high wall, throats full of smoke and cinders, could hardly make themselves heard above the roar of the flames and the hissing of water, capped by the whirring and puffing of seven engines.

Desperate as was their own situation, the firemen's first thought was of the ruin threatened by the fire. The destruction of the lumber-yard was bad enough, but the whole city—every business block, every dwelling, their own homes—it was horrible! Remfry remembered he had just paid for his house, and that he had no insurance.

Meanwhile the fire was growing hotter; shrivelling blasts swept against the wall. Hot, stinging pitch-pine smoke filled their eyes and lungs. The nozzle was vainly cascading every spot except the one that needed it. It maddened Remfry to see so much good water wasting. Every gallon was priceless. He could stand it no longer.

"No use, Lon!" he croaked, putting his mouth close to his comrade's ear. "We can't make 'em hear. We've got to catch that pipe."

Both knew well the peril they risked. Three months before, a flying nozzle snapped Billy Bowen's leg! But they must take chances. Remfry slunk along the right-hand board-pile; Penfield followed the left. Should one get his hands on the hose, the other was to spring to his help.

The dense smoke thinned, and they glimpsed the line, slatting like a maddened python. Three or four clutches at the elusive loops resulted only in their being flung down and dragged in the dirt.

Through those moments of exhausting struggle, of harrowing suspense, dread of the fire creeping ever nearer the oil, destruction menacing the entire city, Remfry's brain was busy with the terrible thought that he and his boys were responsible for it all.

The clouds lifted. Remfry saw the coil whip toward Penfield. There came a thud. Lon was swept off his feet, and dashed against the board-pile. Dropping like a lump of clay, he lay motionless. Remfry thought his mate was killed. He faced the hose with sudden fury.

Just then it caught for an instant under the end of a board. His chance! Hurling himself upon it, he wound both arms about the swelling tube just as it got away again.

Twining arms and legs round the hose, he hitched slowly forward. The whole thing now was on him, *him*! Lon could not help any more. Inch by inch he crept along the squirming tube, hugging it bearishly. It flirted him from one side to the other, rolling him in the dirt. It humped itself like a bucking bronco. Once it tossed him against the boards, almost fracturing his ribs. In spite of all he did not let go; for he knew he could never get hold again.

A weak cry made him look back. Under the smoke he caught sight of Penfield, struggling to rise. He had only been stunned. A great weight fell from Remfry's mind, and he clung with fresh strength.

"Take your time, Lon!" he shouted. "I'll hold it down."

Huge, black, formless, fiery-eyed, spitting forky flame, the conflagration overshadowed him, like a gigantic Chinese dragon, the spirit of ruin personified. Against its searing breath he crawled, now prone, now tossed aloft, battered, smoke-stifled, but creeping steadily on.

The end of the big tube was not far away. Remfry could tell that, for its oscillations were growing shorter and more violent. The part conquered lay quiet behind him. But somewhere in the smoke in front the metal pipe was brandishing like the snapper of a whip-lash.

With lightning suddenness down it smashed on the hose not three inches before his fingers. Had it struck his hand, it would have splintered every bone. The polished brass glinted as it gyrated wildly away. The next few feet would be the most perilous, for at any second the nozzle might crack his skull.

The hot black smoke puffed along the ground. Remfry butted blindly into it, lowering his face, till his lips brushed the dirt. Inch after inch of hard round tube slipped back under him and grew quiet. With eyes closed tight he wriggled on. When he was within a yard of the pipe, he knew it would stop slatting.

The moment came sooner than he had expected. With one final flirt the nozzle gave up, conquered, and the jet began to furrow the chips and dirt. A second later Remfry's fingers touched the brass handles.

Soon Penfield was beside him, his strength and consciousness fully restored; and they took up once more their battle with the flames.

It was well toward morning before the fire was out, and the two started for home. Remfry felt better. The city was safe. Still the thousands of dollars' worth of lumber that had gone up in smoke hung, a black, heavy pall, above his conscience. He dreaded to meet Jack and Billy.

As he stumbled on, a sentence from a passer-by caught his ear:

"Started by a rocket from Triangle Hill, across the river."

He gripped the man's arm.

"Are you sure?" he almost shouted.

"Sure," briefly rejoined the stranger, looking in surprise at his begrimed, excited questioner.

Remfry dropped his arm. So his boys were not responsible, after all. Bruised, muddy, saturated with pitch-pine smoke, every muscle aching, he resumed his way homeward, his mind at peace.

The Travelling Doll

By Evelyn Snead Barnett

Before the serpent came in the guise of a French doll, it was a gay little Eden of a shanty-boat. Its doors were plaid-panelled in red, green and blue; its tiny square window-frames were painted blue on one side of the house, red on the other, and green at the back. Here, to be sure, the paint grew thin and failed to hold out for the walls, although gathering with a mixture of its three tints it sprawled in a final effort to tell that the name of the little home was *The Wing*.

But a short distance from the mainland *The Wing* rested, anchored to a green island. A skiff was tied to its front mast and a single plank connected the shanty-boat with the great world—typical of the slender thread that bound the floating family to their kind, for the Wings did not consort with other shanty-boaters.

Inside, the little abode was as gay as its exterior, and far more tidy. The stove and its tins were polished "to the nines," the strips of rag carpet were bright and clean, the table was scoured white, the bed was neatly made, and under it the family wardrobe was out of sight in a long, black, brass-nailed box. A gaudy clock ticked noisily from a shelf; a tall lamp, in a rainbow-paper shade, the pride and glory of the home, sat by its side. The wall was covered with bright posters; everywhere were gay colours and shining cleanliness.

And they were a satisfied family,—before the serpent came,—Father Wing being a sturdy, silent fisherman, who could always be counted upon to make a living, catching it on water and spending it on land, and finding comfort in his gentle wife and ten-year-old daughter.

To-day he was off fishing, and Mrs. Wing sat inside the sill of the plaid doorway, sewing on a high-necked, long-sleeved gingham apron, her head turned in a listening attitude that was habitual. Outside on the little deck piazza, in a starched mate to the apron her mother was making, little Almira sat, hugging Botsey and feeling rather lonely; for although her father had left the skiff and taken Wally Jim away, Sweeping had surreptitiously followed.

Almira was barelegged and towheaded, but she had a fair skin that defied exposure, and her face had never lost its baby curves. Her eyes were as blue as the river on a clear day, and her mouth had a tender droop, as if she were always feeling sorry for something or some one. She was tilting her little stool, humming a song to Botsey, when her mother said:

"I hear voices. Who's on shore, Almira?"

Almira looked. "They's two of 'em, ma. They're beck'ning me to come for 'em. One's Miss May, and the other's got lace on her petticoat and fuzzy things round her neck."

"I reckon Miss May's coming about school again. I'm going to show her that last copy of yours. I wish I could spare you to get an education like my mother gave me, but I can't. Still, it ain't every child with eyes can read raised point."

Almira was untying the boat. "I wouldn't let you spare me. You'd catch afire or you'd fall into the river. We'd rather stay here, wouldn't we?" She was talking to Botsey now. "No, you can't go with me." Jumping nimbly into the skiff, she began to cross the narrow strip of water.

"That baby row us?" she heard the lace lady ask. So she ran the boat in skilfully.

Miss May stepped lightly in; the lace lady hesitated, then followed with a laugh. Almira could hardly work the oars for looking at her soft brown eyes and the little brown curl that fluttered on her cheek.

A few strokes brought the skiff to the boat. "Good morning, Mrs. Wing!" called Miss May. "Here's somebody you want to meet. Guess!"

"Is it Mrs. Lenox, who sends the raised point books in the travelling library?"

"You're a witch!" cried the girl.

The woman smiled brightly. Her blue eyes, with the white, sightless pupils, turned toward the stranger. "I'm glad to see you at last. We heard you were coming. Almira, have you brought seats for the ladies?"

The child, keeping her eyes on the beautiful stranger, brought forward two soap-boxes upholstered in gay calico. If Botsey only had something like that for her neck! And she caught up the bottle in its crude skirt and blue crocheted shawl with an emphatic hug.

"Is that your doll?" asked Mrs. Lenox.

"No, ma'am. It's Botsey."

"It's the bottle I've fixed up for her. I don't know how she'd pass the time if it wasn't for Botsey. You see, being so helpless, I try to make her enjoy staying with me. You know how helpless I am without her, Miss May."

"I know how helpful you are and what a good housekeeper," said Miss May, looking about at the tidy interior.

Then she told her errand. Almira was invited to the schoolhouse reception party the next Wednesday. Wally Jim had offered to fish near *The Wing*, if Mr. Wing should have to be filling orders in town.

Almira, her eyes still fixed on the beautiful lady's face, said, "I went once. Miss May had an Easter just after we first come here. May I bring Botsey?"

But Miss May said no. A new library was due, and if it reached the village in time Almira would have books to bring her mother.

Mrs. Wing smiled softly. "How good of you! The last one was about little Nell. Why is it our books are so much better than books for people that can see? Jack thinks so, and so does Almira. How I bless you, ma'am!"

Mrs. Lenox could say nothing. May had told her the story of the young mother, attacked by the scarlet fever that left her sightless ten years before.

"I'll let her come on Wednesday," pursued Mrs. Wing, "but I'll never budge from this chair till she gits back. It's not as if I'd never seen how dangerous things are."

With the school party this tale has naught to do. The child reached home betimes, carrying a package of books and a pasteboard box that seemed almost as long as herself. She was trembling with excitement.

"The library's come, ma! And here's two books and some cake and candy and—O ma, just guess what's in the box?"

The mother felt, smiled, and shook her head.

"A little girl—a live little girl-baby doll!" And she lifted it from its shell. "And Miss May—she's sometimes so funny!—she said at first she believed she'd rather I wouldn't have her, but the lady said she wanted me to."

The mother held out her arms for the doll, almost as excited as the child.

Almira expounded, "Its dress is blue, with buttons and buttonholes, and her hair's real; put your hand here. It's brown, and these teenty brown curls slant on her cheeks, and her eyes are brown, and she can shut them and go to sleep just like you and me."

"Well, I never!" said the mother, feeling. "And what is this paper pinned on her dress?"

"It's a letter," answered Almira, sagely. "It begins in print and ends in writing, but I can't make it all out. It says, 'Patent, unbreakable, celluloid. Made in France.' I'll ask daddy the rest when he comes. And feel the petticoat, ma! Lace!"

"And tucks," added the mother. "And see how fine the stuff is. Are these slippers?"

"With heels, real heels!" gurgled Almira. "And stockin's! And in the box here's a hat and feather and a white nightgown!" Almira's emotion got the better of her, and she flung herself into her mother's arms and rocked in ecstasy.

Then came a familiar bark, and Sweepins preceded the husband and fell to sniffing the doll immediately. "It's mine, Sweepins," cried the child. "Look, daddy!"

But the fisherman was too hungry to notice dolls, so the trio prepared the supper of frizzled bacon, corn, hoe-cakes and weak coffee. Afterward was bedtime, and the little feather bed was pulled from the big one to the floor, and made up with clean quilts for the child. But first she undressed the doll, carefully plaiting its hair in two nice plaits, putting the front in curl-papers, and robing it in the night-dress fine enough for day. Mrs. Lenox had cautioned her to teach her child tidy ways like its grandmother's. Poor Botsey, hitherto her constant bedfellow, stood motionless outside the door.

When morning came, and she was helping, her mother asked, "What are you going to name her?"

"It ought to be something pretty. I thought of Queeny."

"Queeny'll be fine," agreed Mrs. Wing. "But where's the paper? Maybe she's already named."

Outside "daddy" was mending a net when Almira brought him the paper. He read:

"'Patent, unbreakable, celluloid. Made in France.' That's in print, and here in writing is, 'This travelling doll goes with Travelling Library Number Ten to any child selected by persons responsible for the distribution of the books. It is the reward for good behaviour or special merit in the place of a medal, and is to belong to the child until the library is ready to go on, when the dolly in neat condition and clean, her hair combed, her clothing washed and ironed, must be put back in her box and packed for the next child on the circuit.'"

Almira snatched at the paper and ran into the boat. She laid Queeny on her mother's lap and crept out to the little deck. Botsey, again on guard, stood by the door. Almira seized her fiercely, tore off the blue shawl, dragged at the soiled skirt. An old greasy bottle! How could it ever be taken back as her very own child when Queeny had to go?

"Almira," called the mother, scenting tragedy, "don't you want me to play grandmother with you and Queeny?"

"What's the use? She's like your books. She ain't mine, and I never had a real child before. The paper says she must travel with the books."

But the placid cheeriness of the blind woman smoothed matters: "But she's yours now, and sometimes the books stay for weeks and weeks."

Here was some comfort. One week was a long time; a month so long that Almira could hardly remember it. And Queeny was beautiful. Why not love her and be happy?

And she was, for weeks and weeks that went by like a dream. She quite forgot what had to happen until one day Wally Jim stopped with a note from Miss May—in printing writing that Almira could read. It said:

"Will you let Queeny go on to-morrow? There's a dear little girl just your age up in the mountains who may have to walk on crutches all her life. She is expecting the doll every day now, so have it looking clean and pretty."

"Almira?" questioned the mother. But the child did not answer. Fortunately no one was near but Wally Jim to see her screwed-up face as she gulped once or twice. She handed him the paper to read, making a sign of silence. Whatever her emotions, she always instinctively spared her sympathetic mother.

"I wouldn't let her go!" blurted Wally Jim, kicking one cowhide boot so hard against the tying-post that he rocked the house.

Almira's head shook in mournful dissent. "When I took her I knew I had to let her travel with the books," she said, with wonderful logic.

Wally Jim would not look at her. "You take my advice—kick about it. 'Twon't do any harm." He got into his skiff, with head turned from Almira's drawn face. "But if you're bound to send her, I'll be round to-morrow for her and the books."

"What's that he said about the books?" called the mother. "Are some more coming?"

"I suppose so. These have to go back."

"And the doll? O baby!"

"Of course," answered Almira, shortly. "We'll wash her clothes to-day, for it says, 'Returned clean and neat.'"

It was all right while the work went on. Queeny was washed, combed, braided and dressed. Almira touched her as little as possible.

When Queeny was laid in her box, wearing a blue hood knitted by the mother, and tied with the tapes that had held her still on her former journey, Almira thought she looked as if she were in her coffin. Then Almira caught sight of Botsey, as usual on guard outside the door. Before Queeny came Botsey was ever so much sweeter. If she had never seen Queeny! Why could not the little girl in the mountains on crutches have a Botsey? They do all right until you've seen the other kind.

Almira's character was one of quick decision. With a furtive look at her mother, she took Queeny from her nest and removed her hood, dress, shoes, stockings. Then she stripped Botsey of her old skirt and blue shawl, putting Queeny's clothes on Botsey after a painful fashion, put the blue woollen hood over Botsey's green glass countenance, and folded Queeny's freshly starched nightgown on Botsey's chest. She viewed her work critically, and with an access of turpitude, stuffed empty sleeves and stockings with paper, putting on the slippers so that they stuck quite naturally from beneath the blue frock: and right over the place where Queeny's face should have looked from the hood, she pinned the paper. Then she tied the tapes, tied them with a vicious screw of her mouth in hard, hard knots, put the lid on the box, and brought all to her mother, saying, in the evenest of tones:

"I want you to help me wrap her up."

"Poor baby!" said the mother. "Maybe some day Mrs. Lenox will send another."

"Never want another!" said the child, sullenly.

Going out to her stool in front, she dressed Queeny in the old skirt, put the shawl over her head, and tried to stand her on guard, Botsey fashion. But Queeny doubled up, and refused. So she held her in her arms with a savage satisfaction, thinking, "Queeny isn't any bottle doll."

Once the mother brushed the wool of the little shawl as the child passed her on some household task.

"You've done gone back to Botsey? That's right. You've the sense of a grown-up."

The afternoon brought a scare. Miss May herself came for the packages. Suppose! Oh, suppose! Almira barely had time to plump Queeny between the feather beds before Miss May landed in Wally Jim's skiff. Almira was glad that she had been prompt, and that the string was tied in hard knots. Miss May praised her for being a good little girl, and made her wince by depicting the gladness of that lame child in the mountains when Queeny should arrive.

But Almira did not repent for a minute. She even said, "Poor little girl!" with a hard-hearted irony. Miss May puckered her forehead, as she always did when she was thinking.

That night Almira tossed and tumbled, unable to sleep. Then the moon rose and sent a straight shaft of light through one of the little square windows on the doll's face. Almira smothered a scream. One of Queeny's eyes was asleep, the other wide open, staring at her. She shook her hard, but that eye would not sleep. She held her up, but although the shut eye opened, the open eye shut, giving the effect of a wicked wink.

How she longed for dear, blind Botsey! Where was Botsey now? Could she feel, and did she know what had been done? No, Botsey was only a bottle.

But *Queeny knew*! And Queeny was watching her with one eye to see what other wicked things were going to happen; and there was Miss May praising her and trusting her, and that little lame girl in the mountains expecting a doll, and getting—

Almira could not have called this a protest of conscience, but she knew she was utterly miserable. Furthermore, she realised that Queeny's ability to bring pride and happiness was gone, and that she herself would always have this something gnawing her inside.

But must she? Perhaps it was not too late. Jim would help her. To-morrow she would get him to stay near her mother while she went ashore with Queeny, the glaring Queeny, to Miss May, telling her how bad she had been. Perhaps Number Ten had not gone on, and Botsey could be stopped on her deceitful way.

This resolve so comforted Almira that as the moon went down and darkness hid the staring eye, she fell asleep.

She was awakened by voices and a motion she knew well. The daylight came broadly through the windows. She heard a clanging and creaking.

A sick realisation overwhelmed her. They had left the island, they were in the broad bed of the river, skimming away who knew where?—away from Miss May and the chance of making things all right.

She dressed herself, asking no questions; but her mother, holding to the arms of her chair, explained:

"Your pa thinks he'll do better off a larger town, so he came in before day and raised sail to get into the current while this good wind's blowing."

Almira sat limply on her little stool. Queeny could not go back to Miss May, but she should not glare at her with her one eye for the rest of her life. Botsey could swim, but Queeny—Queeny could drown! And this time there was no deliberation. She snatched at the doll, and going to the back of the boat, hurled it as far as she could into the river!

Then she fell to helping her mother assiduously, being extra loving and attentive, giving little pats and squeezes as she passed her in her morning tasks, even running to hug her whenever the boat rocked in the waves made by passing craft. Mrs. Wing did the washing, Almira hung the clothes to dry in the bright, breezy sunshine. She scoured the already bright tins, she shook up the beds, hung the quilts to air, washed the floor, the deck. It was work she wanted, hard work. She made the discovery that work brought forgetfulness. She would have liked to scrub the floor of the world.

Day was all right, but for all her bodily fatigue she slept but fitfully that night. She wished people could work at night.

Although they soon reached a place that her father called the Point, and anchored a little way up a creek, where things stopped shaking and were quiet, her eyes would not close.

This Point place was not like the green island. There were smells. They were far enough inland to see a street with people walking; indeed, they were almost under a bridge that let the street-cars go by. "Daddy" left early. After putting the cabbage on to boil, her mother sat down to her seams and hems in the checked blue gingham. Almira, empty-handed, moped on her little three-legged stool at the door. Sweepins, wringing wet, snored on the sunny deck.

A skiff came up the stream; in it Wally Jim. "I've brought you something!" he called. "Miss May got to thinking after she got home, and she says she'll get another doll for that mountain kid, and you can have Queeny back." He reached under the seat, and with dramatic effect drew out the long box.

At the sight of it Almira's self-control gave way. Here was punishment, indeed! To her mother's arms she rushed, blurting out the truth with sobs.

"Wally Jim," asked Mrs. Wing, "how far is Miss May's from here?"

"Not so very far, and she's down in town to-day—said she was coming."

"Take the box back to her, Wally Jim!" sobbed Almira. "Let her see it just as it is, because she hasn't opened it, and she thinks she's sending me Queeny. And I'll write a letter besides."

"I'll take all the letters you want, but I won't take the box, because whatever's in it, it's yours." There was something different and set about Wally Jim this morning. Almira sighed resignedly, and with painstaking labour proceeded to print her letter of repentance.

"You have got back Botsey, dear," said the mother, "so try to forget."

"I'll never play with Botsey again. I'll give her away first."

In an incredibly short time they heard Jim's oars again, and Miss May stepped on deck. She was holding out her arms to Almira, and there were tears in her eyes.

"Dear child, I didn't like the idea from the very first, but Mrs. Lenox does so much for us. You'll be all the better for the sharp experience, and you have really shown your repentance. Now let's open the box and see exactly what you did."

Quite cheerfully, all the miserable feeling gone, Almira brought scissors, cut strings, pointing out the while the iniquities of hard knots and covered features.

What! Queeny! From the bottom of the river, dry, clothed, and with her two eyes shut! Almira looked at Miss May and at Wally Jim, grinning over Miss May's shoulder.

"What has happened now?" asked Mrs. Wing.

"Tell your story, Jim," said Miss May.

"I was drifting some way off behind you all," said Jim, "and maybe sleeping some, when who should swim up to the skiff with something in his mouth but Sweepins. It was Queeny, but as she's cellyloid, only her clothes were wet. I puzzled out that somehow she hadn't gone back to Miss May, and that she ought to. So I took her, and Miss May says, 'If this is Queeny, what's in Almira's box?' And we looked, and there was Botsey."

"And oh, I was so sorry," said Miss May, taking up the tale, "though I'd known all along that a travelling doll would cause heartache—and this proved it would do worse. I sent Queeny back, after having her doctored, knowing that my little Almira was good before temptation came, and wishing to know what it had made of her. I'm satisfied," and Miss May hugged the child once more.

The blind mother was smiling. "Miss May, she's only a child, you know, but she suffered like a grown-up, and with it all, helped me just the same as ever."

Almira dug her bare toes into the rag carpet. "Where'd Botsey go to?" she asked, without looking up.

"If I were you, I'd look under the seat of my boat," said Wally Jim.

"I'M NOT YOUR DOCTOR. I'M A DOLL'S DOCTOR."

• *The Doll Doctor*

From the drawing by Carton Moorepark

The Doll Doctor

By E. V. Lucas

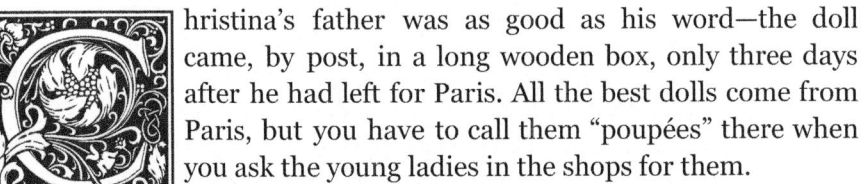

Christina's father was as good as his word—the doll came, by post, in a long wooden box, only three days after he had left for Paris. All the best dolls come from Paris, but you have to call them "poupées" there when you ask the young ladies in the shops for them.

Christina had been in the garden ever since she got up, waiting for the postman—there was a little gap in the trees where you could see him coming up the road—and she and Roy had run to meet him across the hay-field directly they spied him in the distance. Running across the hay-field was forbidden until after hay-making; but when a doll is expected from Paris!...

Christina's father was better than his word, for it was the most beautiful doll ever made, with a whole wardrobe of clothes, too.

Also a tiny tortoiseshell comb and a powder puff. Also an extra pair of bronzed boots. Her eyes opened and shut, and her eyebrows were real hair. This is very unusual in a doll. "She shall be called Joan Shoesmith," said Christina, who had always loved the name; it had been her first nurse's.

Christina took Joan to her mother at once, Roy running behind her with the box and the brown paper and the string and the wardrobe, and Chrissie calling back every minute, "Don't drop the powder puff whatever you do!" "Hold tight to the hand-glass!" and things like that.

"But it's splendid!" Mrs. Tiverton said. "There isn't a better doll in the world; only, Chrissie dear, be very careful with it. I don't know but that father would have done better to have got something stronger—this is so very fragile. I think, perhaps you had better have it only indoors. Yes, that's the best way; after to-day you must play with it only indoors."

Thus Joan Shoesmith came to Mapleton.

How Christina loved her doll that first day! She carried it everywhere and showed it everything—all over the house, right into the attics; all over the garden, right into the little black stove place under the greenhouse; into the village, to introduce her to the postmistress, who lived behind a brass railing in the grocer's shop; into the stables, to kiss General Gordon, the old white horse. Jim, who groomed the General, was the only person who did not admire the doll properly, but how could you expect a nice feeling from a boy who sets dogs on rats?

It was two or three days after this that Roy went down to the river to fish. He had to go alone, because Christina wanted to play with Joan Shoesmith in the nursery; but not more than half an hour had passed when he heard footsteps in the long grass behind him, and, looking up, there was Christina. Now, as Christina had refused so bluntly to have anything to do with his fishing, Roy was surprised to see her, but more surprised still to see that Joan Shoesmith had come too.

"Why, did mother say you might bring Joan?" he asked.

"No," said Christina, rather sulkily, "but I didn't think she'd mind."

Roy looked troubled: his mother did not often make rules to interfere with their play, and when she did she liked to be obeyed. She had certainly forbidden Christina to take Joan Shoesmith out of the house. He did not say anything. Christina sat down and began to play. She was not really at all happy, because she knew it was wrong of her to have disobeyed, and she was really a very good girl. Roy went on fishing.

"Oh, do do something else," Christina cried pettishly, after a few minutes. "It's so cold sitting here waiting for you to catch stupid fish that never come. Let's go to the cave." The cave was an old disused lime-kiln, where robbers might easily have lived.

"All right," Roy said.

"I'll get there first," Christina called out, beginning to run.

"Bah!" said Roy and ran after. They had raced for a hundred yards, when, with a cry, Christina fell. Roy, who was still some distance behind, having had to pack up his rod, hastened to Christina's side. He found that she had scrambled to her knees, and was looking anxiously into Joan Shoesmith's face.

"Oh, Roy," she wailed, "her eyes have gone!"

It was too true. Joan Shoesmith, lately so radiantly observant, now turned to the world the blankest of empty sockets. Roy took her poor head in his hand and shook it. A melancholy rattle told that a pair of once serviceable blue eyes were now at large. Christina sank on the grass in an agony of grief—due partly, also, to the knowledge that if she had not been naughty this would never have happened. Roy stood by, feeling hardly less unhappy. After a while he took her arm. "Come along," he said, "let's see if Jim can mend her."

"Jim!" Christina cried in a fury, shaking off his hand.

"But come along, anyway," Roy said.

Christina continued sobbing. After a while she moved to rise, but suddenly fell back again. Her sobbing as suddenly ceased. "Roy!" she exclaimed fearfully, "I can't walk."

Christina had sprained her ankle.

Roy ran to the house as fast as he could to find help, and very soon old Stedder, the gardener, and Jim were carrying Christina between them, with mother and nurse walking by her side. Christina was put to bed at once and her foot wrapped in bandages, but she cried almost incessantly, no matter how often she was assured that she was forgiven. "Her sobs," the cook said, coming downstairs after her twentieth visit to the nursery, "her sobs are that heart-rending I couldn't stand it; and all the while she asks for that blessed doll, which its eyes is rattling in its head like marbles through falling on the ground, and Master Roy and Jim's trying to catch them with a skewer."

Cook was quite right. Roy and Jim, with Joan Shoesmith between them, were seated in the harness-room, probing tenderly the depths of that luckless creature's skull. A housemaid was looking on without enthusiasm. "You won't do it," she said every now and then; "you can't mend dolls' eyes with skewers. No one can. It's impossible. The king himself couldn't. You ought to take it to the Miss Bannisters' brother at Dormstaple. He'd mend it in a jiffy—there's nothing he can't do in that way."

Roy at last gave up in despair. "I'll take it to the Miss Bannisters' brother," he said, rising with Joan Shoesmith in his arms; "it's only six miles." But a sudden swoop from a figure in the doorway interrupted his bold plan.

"You'll do nothing of the kind," cried nurse, seizing the doll, "with that angel upstairs crying for it every minute, and the doctor saying she's in a high fever with lying on the wet grass"; and with a swirl of white skirts and apron, nurse and Joan Shoesmith were gone.

Roy put his hands in his pockets and wandered moodily into the garden. The world seemed to have no sun in it any more.

The next day Christina was really ill. It was not only the ankle, but she had caught a chill, the doctor said, and they must be very careful with her. Roy went about with a sad and sadder face, for Christina was his only playmate, and he loved her more than anything else; and, also, it seemed so silly not to be able to mend a doll's eyes. He moped in and out of the house all the morning, and was continually being sent away from Christina's door, because she was too ill to bear anyone in the room except nurse. She was wandering in her mind, nurse said, and kept on saying that she had blinded her doll, and crying to have its eyes made right again; but she would not let a hand be laid upon her, so that to have Joan Shoesmith mended seemed impossible. Nurse cried too as she said it, and Roy joined with her. He could not remember ever having been so miserable.

The doctor looked very grave when he was going away. "That doll ought to be put right," he said to Mrs. Tiverton. "She's a sensitive little thing, evidently, and this feeling of disobeying you and treating her father's present lightly is doing her a lot of harm, apart altogether from the chill and the sprain. If we could get those eyes in again she'd be better in no time, I believe."

Roy and his mother heard this with a sinking heart, for they knew that Christina's arms locked Joan Shoesmith to her side almost as if they were bars of iron.

"Anyway," the doctor said, "I've left some medicine that ought to give her some sleep, and I shall come again this afternoon." So saying, the doctor touched up his horse, and Mrs. Tiverton walked into the house again.

Roy stood still pondering.

Suddenly his mind was made up, and he set off for the high road at a good swinging pace. At the gate he passed Jim. "If they want to know where I am," he called, "say I've gone to the Miss Bannisters' brother."

Miss Sarah Bannister and Miss Selina Bannister had lived in Dormstaple as long almost as anyone could remember, although they were by no means old. They had the red house with white windows, the kind of house which one can see only in old English market towns. There was a gravel drive before it, in the shape of a banana, the carriages going in at one end and out at the other, stopping at the front door steps in the middle. The blinds were of that kind through which no one who is outside can see anything, and all who are inside can see everything. The door knocker was of the brightest brass. Behind the house was a very large garden, with a cedar in the midst; and a very soft lawn on which hundreds of birds used to settle every morning in winter for the breakfast that the Miss Bannisters provided. The cedar and the other trees had cigar boxes nailed to them, for tits or wrens to build in, and half cocoa-nuts and lumps of fat were always hung just outside the windows. At one side of the house was the stable and coach-house, on the other side a billiard-room, now used as a workshop. And his workshop brings us to the Miss Bannisters' brother.

The Miss Bannisters' brother was an invalid, and he was also what is called an eccentric. "Eccentric, that's what he is," Mr. Stallabrass, who kept the King's Arms, had said, and there could be no doubt of it after that. This meant that he wore rather shabby clothes, and took no interest in the town, and was rarely seen outside the house or the garden.

Rumor said, however, that he was very clever with his hands, and could make anything. What was the matter with the Miss Bannisters' brother no one seemed to know, but it gradually kept him more and more indoors.

No one ever spoke of him as Mr. Bannister, they always said the Miss Bannisters' brother. If you could see the Miss Bannisters, especially Miss Selina, you would understand this; but although they had deep, gruff voices they were really very kind.

As time went on, and the Miss Bannisters' brother did not seem to grow any better, or to be likely to take up his gardening again, the Miss Bannisters had racked their brains to think of some employment for him other than reading, which is not good for anyone all day long. One evening, some years before this story, while the three were at tea, Miss Selina cried suddenly, "I have it!"—so suddenly, indeed, that Miss Sarah spilt her cup, and her brother took three lumps of sugar instead of two.

"Have what?" they both exclaimed.

"Why," she said, "I was talking to-day with Mrs. Boniface, and she was saying how nice it would be if there were someone in the town who could mend toys—poor Miss Piper at the Bazaar being so useless, and all the carpenters understanding nothing but making book-shelves and cucumber frames, and London being so far away, and I said 'Yes,' never thinking of Theodore here. And, of course, it's the very thing for him."

"Of course," said Miss Sarah. "He could take the old billiard-room."

"And have a stove put in it," said Miss Selina.

"And put up a bench," said Miss Sarah.

"And some cocoa-nut matting on the floor," said Miss Selina.

"Linoleum," said Miss Sarah.

"Cocoa-nut matting," said Miss Selina.

"And we could call it the Dolls' Hospital," said Miss Sarah.

"Infirmary," said Miss Selina.

"I prefer Hospital," said Miss Sarah.

"Infirmary," said Miss Selina. "Dr. Bannister, house surgeon, attends daily from ten till one."

"It would be the prettiest and kindliest occupation," said Miss Sarah, "as well as a useful one."

"That's the whole point of it," said Miss Selina.

And that is how—five or six years ago—the Miss Bannisters' brother came to open the Dolls' Infirmary. But he did not stop short at mending dolls. He mended all kinds of other things too; he advised on the length of tails for kites; he built ships; he had even made fireworks.

Roy walked into Dormstaple at about one o'clock, very tired and hot and dusty and hungry; and a little later, after asking his way more than once, he stood on the doorstep of the Miss Bannisters' house. The door was opened by old Mary, and as the flavour of roast fowl rushed out, Roy knew how hungry he was. "I want to see the Miss Bannisters' brother," he said, "please."

"You're too late," was the answer. "Come to-morrow morning. Mr. Theodore never sees children in the afternoon."

"Oh, but I must," Roy almost sobbed.

"Chut, chut!" said old Mary, "little boys shouldn't say must."

"But when they must, what else is there for them to say?" Roy asked.

"Chut, chut!" said old Mary again. "That's imperent! Now run away, and come to-morrow morning."

This was too much for Roy. He covered his face with his hands, and really and truly cried—a thing he would scorn to do on his own account.

While he stood there in this distress a hand was placed on his arm, and he was drawn gently into the house. He heard the door shut behind him. The hand then guided him along passages into a great room, and there he was liberated. Roy looked round; it was the most fascinating room he had ever seen. There was a long bench at the window with a comfortable chair before it, and on the bench were hammers and chisels and all kinds of tools. A ship nearly finished lay in one place, a clockwork steamer in another, a pair of rails wound about the floor on the cocoa-nut matting—in and out like a snake—on which a toy train probably ran, and here and there were signals. On the shelves were coloured papers, bottles, boxes, and wire. In one corner was a huge kite, as high as a man, with a great face painted on it. Several dolls, more or less broken, lay on the table.

All this he saw in a moment. Then he looked at the owner of the hand, who had been standing beside him all the while with an amused expression on his delicate, kind face. Roy knew in an instant it was the Miss Bannisters' brother.

"Well," said the Miss Bannisters' brother, "so when one must, one must?"

"Yes," Roy said, half timidly.

"Quite right too," said the Miss Bannisters' brother. "'Must' is a very good word, if one has the character to back it up. And now tell me, quickly, what is the trouble. Something very small, I should think, or you wouldn't be able to carry it in your pocket."

"It's not in my pocket," Roy said, "it's not here at all. I want—I want a lesson."

"A lesson?" Mr. Theodore asked in surprise.

"Yes, in eye mending. When eyes fall inside and rattle, you know."

The Miss Bannisters' brother sat down and took Roy between his knees. There was something about this little dusty, nervous boy that his clients (often tearful enough) had never displayed before, and he wished to understand it. "Now tell me all about it," he said.

Roy told him everything, right from the first.

"And what is your father's name?" was the only question that had to be asked. When he heard this, the Miss Bannisters' brother rose. "You must stay here a minute," he said.

"But—but the lesson?" Roy exclaimed. "You know I ought to be getting back again. Christina—"

"All right, just a minute," Mr. Theodore replied.

When the Miss Bannisters' brother came back, Miss Selina came with him. "Come and get tidy for dinner," she said, "and afterwards we'll drive home."

"Oh, but I can't stop for dinner!" Roy cried. "It's much too important to stop for dinner; I'm not really hungry either."

"Dinner will only take a little while," said Miss Selina, "and the horse can be getting ready at the same time; and if you were to walk you wouldn't be home nearly so soon as you will if you drive, dinner time included."

"But the lesson—?" Roy gasped again.

"Oh, we've thought of a better way than the lesson," Miss Selina said. "Mr. Bannister is going with you."

It took a moment for Roy to appreciate this, but when he did he was the happiest boy in Dormstaple.

He never tasted a nicer chicken, he said afterwards.

Certainly not more than three-quarters of an hour had passed before the carriage was on its way to Mapleton—with the Miss Bannisters' brother propped up with cushions (for he could not bear the jolting of carriages) on the back seat, and Miss Selina and Miss Sarah, who had come to look after their brother, on the other. Roy was on the box. You never saw such puzzled faces as the Dormstaple people had when the party went by, for Mr. Theodore had not driven out these twenty years; but their surprise was nothing to that of old Mary, who wandered about the rooms all the rest of the day muttering, "Little imperent boy!"

At the Mapleton gates Roy jumped down and rushed up to the house. His mother came to the door as he reached it. "Oh, mother, mother," he cried, "he's come himself!"

"Who has come?" she asked, forgetting to say anything about Roy's long absence. "I hoped it was the doctor. Christina is worse, I'm afraid; she won't sleep."

"It's all right," Roy assured her. "I've brought the Miss Bannisters' brother, who mends dolls and everything, and he'll put the eyes right in no time, and then Chrissie'll be well again. Here they are!"

At this moment the carriage reached the door; but Mrs. Tiverton's perplexities were not removed by it. On the contrary, they were increased, for she saw before her three total strangers. Miss Selina, however, hastily stepped out and took Mrs. Tiverton's hand and explained the whole story, adding, "We are not coming in; my sister and I have a call to pay a little further on. We shall come back in less than an hour for our brother, carry him off, and be no trouble at all. I know how little you must want even people that you know just now." In spite of Mrs. Tiverton's protest, Miss Selina had her way, and the sisters drove off.

While this conversation had been in progress, Roy had been speaking to the Miss Bannisters' brother. He had been preparing the speech ever since they had started, for it was very important. "Please," he said, "please how much will this visit be, because I want to pay for it myself?"

The Miss Bannisters' brother smiled. "But suppose you haven't enough," he said.

"Oh, but I think I have," Roy told him. "I've got seven-and-six, and when the vet. came to see General Gordon it was only five shillings."

The Miss Bannisters' brother smiled again. "Our infirmary is rather peculiar," he said. "We don't take money at all; we take promises;

different kinds of promises from different people, according to their means. We ask rich parents' friends to promise to give away old toys or story-books, or scrap-books, or something of that kind, to real hospitals—children's hospitals. We find that much better than money. Money's such a nuisance. One is always losing the key to the money-box."

Roy was a little disappointed. "Oh, yes," he said, however, "I'll do that. Won't I just? But, you know," he added, "you can always break open a money-box if it comes to the worst. Pokers aren't bad."

It was just then that the Miss Bannisters drove off, and Mrs. Tiverton asked their brother to come to Christina's room with her. Roy would have given anything to have been allowed upstairs; but as it was forbidden he went to see Jim and tell him the news.

Christina was moaning in the bed with Joan Shoesmith in her arms as the Miss Bannisters' brother sat down beside her. "Come," he said gently, "let me feel your pulse."

Christina pushed her wrist towards him wearily.

"Oh, no, not yours," he said, with a little laugh. "I mean your little lady's. I'm not your doctor. I'm a doll's doctor."

Christina turned her poor flushed face towards him for the first time. A doll's doctor—it was a new idea. And he really seemed to be all right—not anyone dressed up to make her feel foolish or coax her into taking horrid medicine. "Was it your carriage I heard?" she asked.

"Yes," he said. "I have come on purpose. But so many dolls are ill just now that I must be getting away soon. It's quite a bad time for dolls, especially—oddly enough—French ones."

"Mine is French," Christina said, growing really interested.

"Ah, how very curious!" he answered. "And now for the pulse," and he drew out a large gold watch.

Mrs. Tiverton was looking on with tears in her eyes. Christina had not taken this quiet interest in anything or kept so still in bed for many hours. Not even the sleeping draught had had any effect.

The Miss Bannisters' brother held Joan Shoesmith's tiny wrist and looked very grave. "Dear, dear!" he said, "I ought to have been sent for before, and then I could have cured her here in your arms. As it is, I must take her to the light. Won't you have that nice jelly while I am treating Miss ——? Let me see, what was the name?"

"Joan," Christina said: "Joan Shoesmith."

"Ah, yes—Miss Shoesmith. By the time you have finished the jelly I ought to have finished my visit." So saying he rose and carried Joan Shoesmith to the window seat behind the curtains, while Mrs. Tiverton gave Christina the jelly. Christina took it, nurse said afterwards, like a lamb—though I never saw a lamb take jelly.

Meanwhile, the Miss Bannisters' brother had taken some tools and a tube of seccotine from his pocket, and he had lifted up Joan Shoesmith's hair, cut a hole in her head, and was busily readjusting the machinery of her eyes. It was all done in five minutes, just as Christina was eating the last mouthful. "There," he said, returning to the bedside, "that's all right. I think our patient can see now as well as ever."

Christina peered into Joan Shoesmith's face with a cry of joy, and sank back on the pillow in an ecstasy of content.

Neither Mrs. Tiverton nor the Miss Bannisters' brother dared to move for some minutes. While they sat there the doctor tiptoed in. He crossed to the bed and looked at Christina. "She's asleep," he said. "Splendid! She's all right now. It was sleep she wanted more than anything. Don't let her hear a sound, nurse, for hours."

They found Roy waiting for the news. When he heard it he jumped for joy. His mother caught him up and hugged him. "You thoughtful little imp," she cried—and, turning to the doctor, told him the story. He went off, laughing. "I shall take my door-plate down when I get home," he called out as he drove off, "and send it round to you, Bannister. You're the real doctor."

When the Miss Bannisters drove back they found tea all ready, and Mrs. Tiverton would not hear of their leaving without it. And when they did leave, an hour later, they were all fast friends.

Roy and Christina never think of going to Dormstaple now without calling at the red house.

The Idea That Went Astray

By Pauline Carrington Bouvé

It was Danny's idea. Danny always had a great many ideas, and sometimes they were good, sometimes they were not, as is apt to be the case with people who have a great many of anything—especially ideas.

"It will be such fun!" said Amy.

"And something new," agreed Janie.

"Who'll cut the face?" asked Fred, who always wanted to know how things were going to be done.

"Can't you, Milly?" asked all the children at once. "Can't you?" and they all gathered round a little girl who was dressing a doll in an automobile suit.

"What are you talking about?" she asked. "What kind of a face, and what for?" She was fastening the odd lenses from two pairs of Aunt Mildred's spectacles into a wire frame for goggles for the doll.

"Why, a pumpkin face, to scare Uncle Ned! He always laughs at us if we are afraid of anything."

"If you will get the pumpkin—a nice large one—and will lend me your new jack-knife, why, I'll see what I can do," she said.

Fred promised, and the rest of that day and the next the children spent in preparation for Hallowe'en. Uncle Ned was a young lawyer in Boston, but he came home Saturday nights to spend Sundays with Aunt Mildred, and Hallowe'en happened to come on Saturday, which just suited.

Milly succeeded in making a very ugly face making enormous eyes and a monstrous mouth, in which she managed to fasten two rows of corn grains for teeth. Then, when the rest of the children were out playing, she took her pumpkin head up into the attic, and hunted for other things to complete its make-up. In an old trunk she found a heavy wig, and this she fastened firmly on the head with some glue. When at last she showed it, with its great shock of black hair, everybody agreed that it was ugly enough to frighten anybody.

"He'll think it's a goblin," said Milly, who had read a great many fairy-stories.

"There aren't any goblins," said Fred, who was always practical.

In the evening, soon after supper, they all went out and stuck it up on the end of a stray bean-pole, which they leaned up against the post of the garden gate. Dave Peters gave them a candle, which they lighted and thrust inside of the hollow head.

"Ugh, how ugly!" they said, and then went in the house to wait.

After a while Fred proposed going out to see how it looked again, and every one of the children followed him. What if the candle should have burned out or been blown out?

Fred gave a low whistle and stopped before he reached the gate, and all the children called, "What's the matter?"

There the ugly thing hung, the light shining through the big empty eyes and grinning corn teeth, and just behind there was certainly a great white something that looked like wings!

"What's that white thing?" said Milly, in a frightened whisper, as she clutched Fred's arm.

"Let's go back!" begged Amy and Janie.

"There's nothing to be afraid of," said Fred, boldly; but he did not move a step nearer to the gate. "You are always so 'fraid of things!"

"Oh, go see what it is! I'm scared, scared!" wailed Milly, who scarcely recognized her own handiwork in the darkness, so strange it looked.

In the excitement they did not hear the car whistle nor the sound of footsteps on the gravel walk.

Just then a breeze sprang up, flaring the candle, which sent out a long tongue of flame from the pumpkin head's mouth, and the white something behind began to wave. Like a flock of frightened birds the children, Fred, Amy, Janie and Milly, turned and ran as fast as they could, stumbling over each other in their flight.

A man's figure darkened the doorway. "Hello!" said Uncle Ned. "What's happened?"

"Oh, the pumpkin—there's something there behind it—we thought we'd scare you!"

They were all talking together, so Uncle Ned did not understand at first.

"And you scared yourselves?" he said, at last. "Come, let us see what the 'something white' is," and he went straight up to the garden fence and pulled down Aunt Mildred's white crocheted shawl.

"Milly forgot to take it in, as I asked her," remarked Aunt Mildred, "and it's lucky you found it."

Uncle Ned laughed so loud that everybody else laughed, too.

Then he put his hand down into his overcoat pocket and brought forth two big brown parcels of nuts and candy, and Aunt Mildred brought in a basket of big red apples, and after all, it was a jolly Hallowe'en, although, as Milly remarked, the "getting scared part got mixed up."

Gravity Gregg

By Isaac Ogden Rankin

John Paul Gregg had a hobby. Nobody could doubt it who was with him, even though he did not happen to hear one of the other boys call him "Specific Gravity," or "Fic," for short. Gravity Gregg it was and continued to be until it got into the newspapers, and now it is probably settled upon him for life.

When he was a baby he was always investigating the why and the wherefore and more particularly the how of everything he could get his chubby hands on. If he saw anything moving, especially, he always wanted to know why it moved—a curiosity which cost him a finger before he was ten years old.

He was a pretty good all-round student, but it was in the natural philosophy class that he shone. He had picked up somewhere an old copy of a standard book on physics, and his use of the information he had gathered from it caused terror to the good lady who had charge of the department in the village school.

He was apt, for instance, to complicate her mild and innocent experiments by suggesting new applications of the principle involved; and the amount of broken apparatus which went down to his account in the laboratory where the boys were sometimes allowed to work made his mother sigh.

His devotion to physics seemed very unpractical to quiet Mrs. Gregg, who had set her heart on making a minister of her eldest son. She had named him John Paul, by way of having the names of two apostles ready for the future, and she had day-dreams of sitting in the front pew in church to hear him preach, while she looked up to him with wondering delight.

It was a trial to be thinking of the Rev. John Paul Gregg, a tall, dignified and grave man, who was respected by everybody and had, perhaps, published a book of sermons, and then to have a freckled lad, round-faced and brown as a berry, with a scar across his forehead where an exploding crucible had just missed the eye, burst in upon her to beg her best preserving-kettle for an experiment. And to hear the future clergyman called "Fic" Gregg all over her end of the town made her shudder.

Most of the people of Lavenham who knew him thought Specific Gravity mildly insane, but they all liked him. He was so simple and sincere and kind that they could not help it; but they never knew what he would be up to next in the line of dangerous experiment. He was as inventive as a fox, as spry as a cat, and as steady-headed as a monkey.

Old Deacon Podgers looked out at his window one morning when it was blowing half a gale, and on the top of the unfinished steeple of the new Baptist Church saw a strange black object. The deacon, who had been a sea-captain all his active days, turned to the wall for his spy glass, and recognized Gravity Gregg, who had climbed up there to study the vibration of materials, as he told the deacon when he asked him why he risked his life so recklessly.

John Paul acquired his name of Specific Gravity from an early answer in the philosophy class, but it did not become publicly his until one day after an anxious night in the big railroad freight-yards just outside the town.

The Gregg house was on the brow of the hill overlooking the river and the flats where the railroad runs, and Fic knew every landmark visible from his window.

It was a holiday. He had been fishing all day and went to bed early, but woke up about midnight with a start to see a flickering light reflected on the wall. He was at the window in a moment, and after taking an observation said to himself, "That's in the freight-yards! It must be a car on fire!"

It was not a big blaze, like a burning house, but a flickering little blaze, like that of the lamps on the fruit-peddlers' stands at night.

The desire to investigate was strong upon John Paul. His mother had never objected to his going to fires, but would she let him go so late at night? He would not wake her up to ask, and with a sigh went back to bed again and dropped off to sleep—only to be wakened up by the distant sound of a fire-engine rattling through the streets and to see the same flickering light at the same spot on the wall.

He went to the window again and took the field-glass, which was one of his most cherished possessions.

"It's a car, sure enough, and they've got the engines out," he said. "I wish I could go and see."

He went back to bed, but tossed and tossed, while the light still flickered on the wall.

"It's strange they don't put it out," he thought. "They must have been at work at it two or three hours."

He rose again and went to the window, but the air was so cold that he dressed himself, his curiosity all the while growing stronger. Taking his shoes in his hand he went softly down to the door, took the spare latch-key from its hook, let himself quietly out, put on his shoes, and slipped down to the front gate.

It was a windy night, with the moon eating up the clouds, and the streets were very quiet. The first sign of excitement was at the gate of the yards, where another fire-engine was just going in.

Fic slipped in beside it and took a short cut across the tracks, between and under the cars, to the other side next the big freight-house, where a fire-engine was pumping water through long lines of black hose on a big tank-car that was all in a blaze on the under side.

The tracks were flooded. Fic balanced himself on a rail and watched the blazing car with a puzzled look. Every time the stream of water fairly struck the centre of the flame it flew in every direction in sheets and threads of fire, but always settled back at the bottom of the car.

The division superintendent of the road drove up. Fic knew him by sight, for he lived in Lavenham and went to his church.

"What's the matter?" the superintendent said, in a high-keyed voice. "Why don't you put out the fire?"

Three men drew out of the group around the fire-engine and came to the side of the buggy. One was the yardmaster, another the conductor in charge of the train, and the third the fire-chief.

"It's naphtha," said the chief. "There's a leak somewhere in the pipes that lets it down to the fire a little at a time. We can't get at it for the heat, and the water only scatters it."

"The stuff must be pretty well out by this time," said the conductor; "and when it gets low and the fire works up into the tank there will be an explosion. It's awful stuff for fire."

Fic was standing by the front wheel of the buggy and saw the superintendent's face grow pale by the flickering light.

"Can't you move the car?"

"We can't get near enough to couple, and the truck is about burned through. We moved the other cars, but we can't move the buildings."

"Why not bring up the gravel-train from the lower switch and fill up from below until the fire is buried."

"There won't be time. The tank's nearly empty now. It's been burning all night."

"I'm not so sure about that," answered the chief. "Those tanks hold a lot, and it doesn't take much naphtha to make a big blaze. What I'm afraid of is that it will explode while it is half full, and scatter the burning stuff all over the yard. Or else it will burn a week, and stop all the work in the yards while we are waiting for it to burst! That will never do."

Fic had been doing a lot of thinking while this hasty consultation went on. He had not studied his physics for nothing, and he was sure he had the key to the problem.

"Please, Mr. Sanderson, may I speak?"

The four men looked down and saw a boy in a short jacket, with eyes that were burning with excitement, and Mr. Sanderson said, in amazement: "Hello! Who are you, and what are you doing here?"

"If you please," said Fic, drawing himself up to the dashboard in his excitement, "I know how to put out the fire!"

"You do, do you! Well, speak up quick! It'll be worth a good many thousand dollars and perhaps a few lives, if you do."

"Take off the lid of the tank on top and pour water into the tank. The wind blows the fire to one side, and if you can once get a hose in you will do it."

"How will that put the fire out?" cried the superintendent.

"It's the specific gravity. Water is denser than naphtha and will sink to the bottom. If it doesn't explode when you open it, it won't afterward. The water will sink to the bottom and get into the leaky pipes."

"I believe the lad's right," said the fire-chief. "At all events, we'll try it. Who'll help?"

Two or three volunteers came forward and lifted a ladder on the windward side of the car. The chief mounted and pried up the lid. No explosion followed, and on thrusting in his hand he found that the naphtha was still very near the top. If the fire should reach and scatter it there would be no hope of saving the buildings, he knew, and even the vapour was dangerous. He called for a hose, thrust it in at the vent, and pulled down the lid to keep the vapour in. Then he climbed down to watch the result.

Already, as he reached the ground and turned to look, the flame had diminished. In five minutes the fire was out, and water was dripping from the cooled end of the leaky pipe, which was soon tied up and made safe. Not only was the danger over, but almost the whole contents of the tank were saved.

No sooner was the work of repair over by the gleam of hastily lighted lanterns than the superintendent, like a man relieved by miracle, suddenly pulled himself up from the side of the disabled car and looked about him.

Then he shouted, "Where's that boy?"

Nobody knew. For the moment they had forgotten all about the boy in thinking of the escape from peril; and as for John Paul, so soon as he saw that the fire was out and his faith in the principle of specific gravity vindicated, his interest had ceased, and he had turned across the flooded tracks toward home.

He slipped quietly in, got to bed by half past four without disturbing anybody, and was up as usual when his mother called him to help her with the morning work. He never troubled her with his experiments, and it did not occur to him to speak of the night's adventure.

Even the reporter of the Daily Flashlight was too much interested in the success of the experiment to interview the boy, although he made the best of him in his story in the morning paper. He was a stranger in Lavenham, and had never heard of the uncanny doings of Gravity Gregg. It was not until the next day that the whole story got out, and Fic found it necessary to go to school by the back streets to avoid public notice.

When the division superintendent reached home in the early morning, he found his wife waiting for him with a cup of hot coffee, and as he drank it he told her the story.

"I suppose I shall have to advertise for the boy," he said. "I can't let him go. He saved the car and the buildings, and perhaps the lives of some of us."

"You needn't do that," answered Mrs. Sanderson, who knew nothing about physics but had caught two words in the story. "He lives right around the corner in the little brown house. He's the oldest son of the Widow Gregg, and nearly blew our Ralph's head off one day last week with one of his experiments. All the boys call him Gravity Gregg."

While Mrs. Gregg was at breakfast the door-bell rang, and Mr. Sanderson invited himself in. It took a long while to tell the story, for

Mrs. Gregg couldn't understand that John Paul had been anywhere but safe in bed all night, and John Paul couldn't see that there was anything to make a fuss about in so simple an expedient in practical physics.

People said that the railroad ought to make the boy a handsome present, but it did not. What it did do was to see that he got the best kind of an education and then to put him where he could climb high in their employ.

He carries a watch which Mr. Sanderson and the fire-chief gave him as soon as he was considered by them old enough to take care of it, on the case of which is engraved a name and a date. His mother is proud of him, and, luckily for her pet ambition, she is quite as proud of another son who is just such a minister as she hoped to make of John Paul Gregg.

Jonnasen

By Dallas Lore Sharp

It was a half-holiday at the quarries; the schools, the stores and shops all closed at noon. The whole quarry town had turned out to see the great granite shaft hauled to the station.

To avoid the risk and cost of two loadings, the forty-ton stone had been derricked to the road at the edge of the quarry, and there, under a temporary shed, had been cut, polished and crated. It now lay blocked upon a low, powerful dray, ready to be moved to the freight siding in the village, over a mile distant.

The stone was the largest single block of granite ever quarried at the Laston ledges. It had been an expensive job from the start, and a very troublesome one. It had led to a strike, a riot, and almost to murder.

There had been no man among the two hundred in the quarries capable of properly dressing the stone. So the company had brought in

Gunar Gustavesen to do the work. And the men were angry at the intrusion of the outsider.

The company was warned. So was Gustavesen. But the work on the shaft went on—until the strike. Jonnasen, the leader of the men, was as sure he was right and as stubborn as Hendricks, president of the firm. Then the men grew ugly, there was a riot, Gustavesen's furniture was burned in the street, and he himself so brutally attacked that he still lay slowly mending in one of the company's houses.

It was a bitter victory, and Jonnasen was too honest a man to like it. When it was reported to him that Havelok Gustavesen, the sixteen-year-old son of the non-union man, had found some menial work in the company's stables, he made it clear to the men that the boy was to be let alone. That is how it happened that young Gustavesen appeared among the men who were busy with the twenty-four-horse team attached to the heavy dray.

The road from the quarry to the station was down grade except for two steep hills, where the ledges cropped out, and where every ounce of the pulling power of the great team would be required. At the top of the second rise the downward slope stretched away for about half a mile with a sharp curve round the edge of the old quarry. The curve was guarded by heavy stone posts and a wooden rail.

The possibilities of all this had been reckoned with, and in order to keep the forty tons of granite from pushing the horses before it, a pair of heavy steel shoes had been fitted to a brake that might have held a freight-train.

Jonnasen settled himself upon the seat of the dray, gathered up the reins of the pole-team, and, with his foot upon the brake, gave the word to start. The drivers of the forward spans echoed the command, and the dray rolled out upon the road.

There is something inspiring in the work of willing horses. It is a noble enthusiasm, little less than inspiration, that takes possession of the horses themselves. The crowd along the road felt it and cheered, as the twelve pairs, pulling like one, took the great polished shaft to the top of the first hill.

It was a short and gentle descent to the second and steepest ridge. Jonnasen put on the brake, and caught the weight so easily that the horses of the pole moved free in their traces, yet kept them fairly taut.

Near the bottom of the slope he started them forward on the trot, loosed the brake, and sent the long line at a good pace to take the second ridge.

It was a pretty piece of work. So beautifully did the immense stone mount the rise that even the members of the firm in attendance cheered with the rest.

Then a silence fell. No one spoke of danger, but as the great, shining shaft pointed down the slope, its forty tons of dead weight seemed suddenly to have changed into active power. It seemed to poise at the top of the hill. It was a thing alive.

The ridge was a narrow ledge of granite, hardly wide enough to stop the dray upon. Jonnasen had intended to breathe his team here, but by the time the dray was up, the lead horses were already going down, and the load, without a pause, began to descend.

Jonnasen bore down on the brake, drew in his horses, and looked off down the long grade to the turn about the precipitous edge of the old quarry.

He drew a short, hard breath. No cooler man than this tall Swede ever held a rein. He could handle horses as he could handle men.

But he had made a mistake, and he knew it instantly. He should have stopped on the ridge, as he intended. He should have unhooked all the horses ahead of the pole-team here. They were in the way. The horses at the pole could guide the load down. The others were a menace, if anything should happen.

"But nothing should happen!" he muttered to himself, and a half-smile broke over his rugged face as he heard the grind of the brake and saw the slack in the traces taken up. The load was under his foot.

Just then the lead horses broke into a trot. Immediately the whole line started. Jonnasen bore down on the brake, and drew his own team hard back to check the pull, when there was a sharp crack, like the report of a pistol, and one of the steel shoes fell broken to the road.

Instantly a dozen warning voices told him what he too well knew had happened. The big horses knew, too, and settled back to stop the push from behind. Jonnasen put all his weight into the single steel shoe that bit at the back wheel. A stream of sparks flew from the tire, and a wild, shrill scream told that the brake still worked. But the horses were sliding.

Then the pole ran into the team ahead, the horses plunged, and there was confusion.

"Unhook them from the pole!" Jonnasen called to the nearest driver. The man dropped his lines, caught the jangling traces and tried to run in between the teams, but was struck by a hoof and rolled out of the road.

Panic seized the whole line of frightened horses. Some of the drivers still held their teams back, but they were being dragged helplessly.

"Unhook them!" Jonnasen shouted to the crowd shrinking back against the fence. Were he free to let his own team go, they might keep ahead of the load, and take the turn with a possible chance of rounding the edge of the deep quarry.

"Unhook them!" he shouted again, powerless to quit his place and do the thing himself. But no one was able to move.

Then a lithe young figure came bounding down from the ridge. It was young Gustavesen. He sprang upon the dray, ran forward, seized the whip in Jonnasen's hand, and in a cool, deliberate voice, said:

"When I get hold, let 'em jump quick." He dropped between the horses to the pole, and clutching the harness, got quickly out to the end. He was bending to catch the evener when a forward wheel struck a rut, and the long tongue snapped him viciously into the air.

He caught the hames of the nigh horse, and saved himself. Hanging to the hames, he swung back, lay out along the tongue, and reached again for the evener.

Jonnasen was watching, and as the boy laid his hand upon the big hook, he loosed the reins, the horses lunged, and the long, heavy bar was unhooked almost of itself.

Like a flash the boy straightened and swung the lash about the horses ahead, throwing himself an instant later upon the back of the horse he was holding.

The loosened teams were barely dragged to the side as the pole-team went by on the gallop, with its forty-ton stone.

Jonnasen had the horses under perfect control. He could guide them straight ahead. But the mighty stone was gathering momentum with every leap of the team, and powerful as they were Jonnasen began to realise that they would never be able to check or turn the downward plunge at the curve on the edge of the quarry.

Then he saw that young Gustavesen was making no attempt to fling himself from the galloping horse.

"Jump!" he shouted. "Jump, quick!"

Havelok turned. "I can't jump!" he called back. "My leg! Tend your team! I'm safe here!"

The absolute confidence of the boy sent a strange thrill through the big Swede. It steadied him.

They were near to the turn, with the horses running close to the inner side, and still well in hand.

Jonnasen thought quickly. It was a chance—the only chance. One of them—both of them—might escape if he could hit with the long iron hub of the rear wheel the tough young white oak that stood out on the very round of the sharp curve.

Jonnasen drew the horses in a little, spoke to them quietly, then sent the front wheel past the tree with a bite at the bark, pulled the team hard in, and leaped.

There was a dull crash, a ripping of harness, and a grinding crunch as the forty-ton stone slued over the crushed wheel across the broken top of the tree.

Jonnasen was picked up in the road, unconscious, but not seriously hurt. The escape of Gustavesen was more than luck. It was a miracle, but a miracle worked by his own presence of mind, and the coolness, quickness and good judgement of Jonnasen.

As the wheel struck, the traces parted, the pole-chains snapped, and the horses shot ahead free, with the boy clinging to the harness.

When he was helped down, his right leg was found to be broken; but that had happened back along the road, when he was snapped from the pole while trying to unhook the forward teams. And it was this that prevented his trying to fling himself off to the road as his perilous ride began.

No harm had come to the shaft. The dray was a wreck, but the great stone lay unbroken, and almost unscratched, among the débris.

It was a week later, as both Gustavesens, father and son, were convalescing, that they received a letter, concluding as follows:

> Henceforth a man shall be a man here. Some things have been done that the men in this quarry are ashamed of. They believe now that every man has a right to work and live under the law according to the dictates of his own conscience.
>
> For the men,
>
> (Signed) Jonnasen.

In The Oven

By Richard Washburn Child

"I am inclined to think that a girl's wit is quicker than a man's in a tight place, if the place is tight enough."

Mr. Colchester had spoken after we had been silently sitting for several minutes watching the mist that was creeping over the moonlit water and listening to the chirp of the crickets in the grass.

He always began a story by stating the moral. His way was to present some conclusion and then prove it by a personal experience.

"I was thinking of my sister," he explained. "She once saved us both from a fearful death. If it had not been for her ready wit I should have been a biscuit!"

At this every one straightened up perceptibly. Mr. Colchester's stories were always interesting.

"Perhaps all of you do not know that my father was a cracker manufacturer," he continued, "and that he had a shop with machinery and three ovens in it. Of course that would be considered nothing to-day, when there are bakeries that supply thousands of people in every part of the country, but when I was a boy I remember I used to wonder that there were enough mouths to consume all that my father's workmen made.

"I often went down to the shop, for it was really fascinating to watch the mixers turning the great rolls of dough over and over, and see the cutting-machines chopping a long strap of it into little sticky lumps. Then old Carberry, the baker, would toss the pieces which had been patted and moulded by hand on the tiled floor of the oven. Sometimes my sister Margaret used to go with me, for we were great chums, and it was on one of those occasions that we got into trouble.

"The day, I remember, had been rainy, and after a discouraging attempt to amuse ourselves in the house, Margaret said, 'Let's take umbrellas and go down to the bakery.'

"I was so glad of the suggestion that I forgot it was the noon hour, when the men would be gone and the machinery shut down. It wasn't until we saw the deserted room that we remembered it.

"'Well,' said I, 'we are bright, aren't we? But let's look round—I'll tell you, let's look at the cool oven.'

"'Cool oven!' exclaimed Margaret, in surprise.

"I explained to her that in the ordinary course of business only two ovens were used, and that unless there were extra orders there was always one oven which was out of commission, being shut off from the furnaces below by the big sheet-iron dampers.

"I raised the latch of the heavy door and bent down to look across the flat, tiled surface inside.

"'It's just like a cave, isn't it, Bob?' cried my sister; and I laughed at the idea and asked her whether she expected to see a bear or a robber walk out.

"'Of course I don't!' she said, for she always was on her guard against my making fun of her. 'Let's crawl in.'

"'All right,' said I, touching the brick walls to make sure I hadn't made a mistake; and then I followed her inside through the gloomy opening.

"'Will it get my dress dirty?' Margaret asked, out of the darkness.

"'No, indeed,' said I. 'They have to keep these ovens clean as can be. They're fussy about every speck of dust.'

"I had hardly finished when the iron door behind us shut with a resounding clang. One of the workmen who had come back to work had closed it!

"'O Bob,' cried my sister, with a little scream of fright, 'we're shut in!'

"'Like two biscuits,' I laughed. 'Don't you mind. All we have to do is to shout and some one will come.'

"But Margaret was really scared, and groped her way near me to put her hand on my shoulder. I confess the darkness and the close, stuffy air were far from cheerful.

"I began to call as loud as I could, and not getting any answer, I crept over to the solid iron door and began kicking it with my heels. After a moment I stopped, breathing hard from my exercise, and then I heard Margaret's voice behind me, saying:

"'Wait a minute, Bob! Listen!'

"I strained my ears, and from the outside I could hear a rumbling that seemed to come from far, far away.

"'It's the machinery!' I cried. 'It's after one o'clock, and they have begun work again. No wonder they couldn't hear us!'

"By that time I had become really frightened, and I suppose I must have temporarily lost my head. I shouted wildly until my throat was sore, but it seemed only to fill our oven trap with noise. There was no hope whatever that it would penetrate the thick brick walls. Suddenly I was startled into silence by a sound of scraping iron underneath us—a familiar noise to my ears. Some one had pulled open the great damper that shut us off from the fires in the cellar below! They were going to heat our oven!

"'What was that?' exclaimed my sister, touching my hand with her cold fingers. 'What did that noise mean, Bob?' She seemed to know our danger by instinct. I did not answer, for with a sinking heart I felt on my face the first breath of warm air!

"'Tell me, Bob!' demanded Margaret. 'They are heating this oven, aren't they?' She had caught my wrist and pressed it as hard as a girl could squeeze.

"'Yes!' I gasped, trying to speak bravely. I remember I felt that if I were alone I should not care nearly so much, but the idea that my little sister would have to die, too, put me into another panic.

"A second breath of air a good deal hotter than the first fanned my cheek. I jumped up with a scream, and beat and kicked upon the rough brick walls and on the iron door in blind terror. Then, exhausted, I crawled along the floor to the place where Margaret sat. She was crying quietly—I could tell because when I put my arm about her I could feel that she was shaking.

"'They will never, never hear us!' she sobbed.

"'Don't cry, Margy,' said I, patting her wet cheek while I tried to arouse my own courage. 'Perhaps there is another way.'

"I tried to think, but the heat had then become almost unbearable; it stung my nose and seemed to suffocate me. Once when I touched a place on one of the tiles I drew my hand back in real pain. There was no hope of breaking the latch of the iron door, and no one could hear us, though we put our mouths to a little crack at the top of the door and screamed. I was sure we would be baked. My arm was still round my sister, and her hand was still in mine, as if she were seeking the comfort of the touch.

"It was becoming hotter and hotter, but neither of us spoke for several seconds. Then suddenly Margaret started up and cried out, eagerly, 'Tell me, Bob, quick! Have you got a piece of paper?'

"I felt in my pockets. 'Yes, I have an old postal card!' I exclaimed. 'What are you going to do with it?'

"'They can't hear us, but we can make them see!' she cried. 'Hurry! Give it to me—and your jack-knife!'

"I handed them to her, and she began to pick at the hem of her skirt with the point of the knife.

"'We need thread,' she explained, excitedly, 'and if this is a chain-stitch on this hem we can get it!' I lighted a match. 'And it is, Bob, it is!' she cried. I realised that she had caught an end of thread and was carefully ripping it out.

"'Now, Bob,' she commanded, handing me the card, 'punch a hole in the card and tie it through.' Her voice was weak. From my own struggle to keep my senses in the awful heat, I knew that she was nearly at the collapsing point.

"'What are you going to do with it?' I gasped.

"'The door!' she answered, faintly. 'Dangle the card through the crack in the door!' Then I understood her plan at last, and crawling painfully over on my knees, I thrust the postal card down the little crack between the door and the iron jamb.

"'Pull it up and let it down!' cried Margaret, with a final effort, and I jiggled the string so that the paper would dance upon the wall outside. My head swam with the effect of the terrible heat, and it seemed ages before any one came.

"Then suddenly the latch was lifted, the door swung open, and in spite of the blinding daylight which poured in I could see the astonished face of old Carberry, the baker, peering in at us!

"I caught my sister's dress, pulling her toward the opening with all the strength that was left in me, and fell out after her into the old man's arms.

"That is why I say," concluded Mr. Colchester, as he looked round upon us with a smile, "that it was a girl's wit that kept me from being baked like a biscuit. And that is the reason why I say that a girl's wit is the best in a tight place—providing the place is tight enough.

On a Slide-Board

By Robert Barnes

At three o'clock on an August morning the press in the little printing-office on the summit ceased its clatter, and Corey Green brought out a bundle of Stars, wrapped in enamelled cloth, to Bart Collamore.

"Here's your five hundred," said Corey, "hot from the types."

"All right," replied Bart "They'll be on the hotel counters twenty miles away by six."

They walked down the platform before the Summit House. A dim light illumined the office, but the rest of the long building was dark. Only two other persons were awake—Frank Simmons, busy over the printing-press, and Luke Martin, the hotel watchman.

Overhead an occasional star glimmered through the driving wrack, and the low east disclosed the first faint tokens of a cloudy dawn; but in the west frowned a vaporous battlement, black and threatening, from which a strong wind was tearing detached masses and rolling them against the mountainside. Now and then a few flakes of snow flew by on the raw gale.

Lifting his slide-board from the platform, Bart set it on the cog-rail midway of the track.

This rail was bolted to a wooden centrepiece on the ties, and consisted of two parallel strips of wrought angle-iron, connected by steel pins three inches apart, on which the cogs of the engine worked. He turned the nut on the brake-rod until the iron plates by means of which the speed of the board was retarded were in position under the flanges of the rail. Then he pulled on his gloves, jammed his cap down hard, and buttoned his reefer up to his neck.

Corey glanced at the black western sky. "You're liable to hit the storm going down," said he.

"Guess I can beat it out," returned Bart. Seating himself on the slide-board, with the bundle of papers between his knees, he gripped the brake-handles. Almost of itself the board began moving.

"I'll be at the Base House in ten minutes!" he called back, as he sped away down the slope toward the north, while behind him the drone of the wind almost drowned Corey's shout.

"Good luck!"

The slide-board was the conveyance used by employés and trackmen in descending the mountain railroad. Although perilous for a novice, it was easy of management for an experienced hand. It was of seven-eighths-inch spruce, ten inches wide, and something over a yard long. Three cleats screwed across its top kept it from splitting. Underneath were two sets of "shoes," the forward of wood, the rear of iron, parallel strips half an inch thick and four inches apart, just far enough for the top of the cog-rail to slide between them.

As Bart slipped downward, the black buildings on the summit were blotted out by driving clouds. Little by little he swerved westward, turning his back to the dawn, hearing only the hoarse murmur of the rising gale and the rattle of his board.

Guide-books say that the three and one-third miles from summit to base may be covered by slide-board in twenty minutes. Actually, the record is two minutes and forty-seven seconds. This can be appreciated when one remembers that there is a drop of four thousand feet, and that the average grade approximates one in four. Bart had made the trip some hundreds of times in his fourteen years on the road. Every morning that summer he had gone down before daybreak, in order that the little paper printed on the peak might have early distribution among the various hotels.

Faster and faster sped the board. The top of the rack was abundantly lubricated with oil from the cogs of the engine, and the grade was growing steeper. On the left a dim shaft flitted by, memorial of a life lost by exposure on the mountain years before.

Bart put a little more pressure on his brakes. The stout birch handles, somewhat smaller than baseball bats and about as long as the board itself, were connected forward with the brake-rod running across the front in a hollow wooden bar, and with an iron plate under each flange of the rail. To retard his course, the rider simply pulled up on the handles, which were directly under his arms, thus lifting the plates against the flanges and pressing the board down harder on the top of the rack.

The track curved northwest for the next fifteen hundred feet to the Gulf Tank, a water cistern on the left. The grade varied from one in four to one in eight. The wind, keen, strong, and shot with hurrying snowflakes, stung even Bart's seasoned face.

He had worked on the mountain long enough to know what was coming out of that inky bank ahead.

Gulf Tank swept past, a square grey shadow, and the track gradually swung west. And now he caught it in good earnest. The moan of the blast had risen to a furious howling. Bullets of sleet pelted his cheeks. Right before him rose a black wall, the edge of the real storm. It looked almost as if it were solid. Catching his breath, he ducked his head, and bolted straight into the heart of the tempest.

In a second it enveloped him, rain, snow, sleet and hail. His board whizzed faster over the wet, slippery rail.

The grade increased, and he knew he had reached Long Trestle. Beyond lay Jacob's Ladder, the steepest place on the line, pitched considerably over one in three. He must not go too fast there. It was more than a mile and a half still to the bottom. If the board once got away from him—

Bart stiffened himself against the fierce blast, gripped the brake-handles hard, and pulled up on them. A stream of sparks trailed out on each side, as the plates bit at the flanges.

He was leaning well forward now, boring head foremost into the yelling gale. His eyes were closed; he could not keep them open.

Now the Trestle was past, and the Ladder lay just ahead. He could tell where he was by the feel of the track. His head was clear, his nerves steady. All he needed to do was to keep a good hold on those handles, and the board would soon carry him safely to the base.

Suddenly his speed increased. He had struck the Ladder. The grade at its head was not far from one in two. Down he shot, lifting hard on the birch bars.

What was that? It could not be that left brake-handle was buckling! Yes! Something had given way. Up came his hand, higher, higher, higher, yet there was no response of iron grinding against iron.

For just a second Bart felt sick.

The flange was only three-fourths of an inch wide. If that left plate once got out from under it, he knew very well what would happen.

A single brake could never hold the board on the rail. On the next curve, if not before, it would bound from the track with tremendous velocity, and its rider would land somewhere on the rugged mountainside with a broken neck. Somehow, if he cared to live, that plate must never lose its grip on the flange.

The Ladder was four hundred feet long and thirty feet above the rocks at its highest point. Bart was travelling forty miles an hour, so crossing the trestle took less than ten seconds. Before he left it, he saw what he must do.

Instinctively easing up on his right bar, so as to bring an even pressure on both sides, he ran his left hand quickly forward down the birch stick, to locate the break. Not many inches from the socket his fingers found it, where a knurl, imperceptibly weakened by long use, had evidently yielded at last.

Sitting where he did, he could just reach beyond the break by extending his arm full length, and he could exert only a slight upward pull. If he hoped to keep the board on the rail, he must immediately shift his position, so that he might put out his full strength. Several short curves were just ahead.

To change one's place on a narrow board flying down a mountainside at forty miles an hour through a pitch-black hurricane is no fool's task. Very carefully Bart hitched straight forward, until his knees were upright, and he was able to lift strongly on the unbroken portion of the bar. His speed was now simply terrific.

Round a curve he whisked, leaning far inward in the fear that he might ride the rail. Then, as his board settled down on a straightaway, he pulled up with all his might.

To his horror, he found that with so short a leverage he could not press the plate against the flange hard enough to check his speed.

The board was running away with him!

Bart knew every yard of that track, every pitch and curve, from the engine-house at the summit to the Marshfield turntable; and he realised that this was the most critical minute in all his years of railroading. Two courses were open to him—he might stick to the board, or he might roll off.

Which was the less dangerous?

If he rolled off at that speed, the best he could hope for would be a fearful bruising, broken bones and insensibility. It would be hours before rescuers could find him; and hours in that storm meant death.

If he stayed on, he took the chance of being hurled from the rail at some curve; besides, what would happen when he reached the bottom, if he ever did reach it?

He decided to stay on.

The slide-board took the curves at express speed. Time and again Bart thought it was flying off. He wondered to find himself still sitting hunched on the spruce, when Waumbek Tank slipped by. He knew it had passed, although he did not see it.

But little more than a mile due west, and almost thirteen hundred feet lower, lay the terminus. Was this to be his last ride on the line? In a couple of minutes at the most the thing would be decided. Bart manned himself for the finish.

On he shot, straining at the bars, head down through the pitch darkness. He was dashing against a forty-mile gale at an equal speed; that was equivalent to standing still in a hurricane blowing eighty miles. It shrieked round him with indescribable fury, striving to hurl him backward from his seat. His cap was torn away, and the sleet pattered like a sand-blast on his bare skull.

Cold Spring Tank flitted past, and the last steep pitch was near, seventeen hundred to the mile. In a moment Bart was rushing madly down the descent. His head swam with the hideous speed. His board vibrated and trembled as it hurtled along the track. All seemed unreal, uncanny. But although dazed and buffeted, he never for an instant loosed his grip of the bars. A "green" man might have lost his head, and that could have had but one result.

Almost sooner than he could think, he was at the bottom of the pitch, darting over the Ammonoosuc bridge. Only a few hundred feet more. The track, he knew, was clear to its end, for cars and engines were housed for the night. Now for one last, long, hard pull!

Deaf, blind, numb, exhausted, bent almost double, he drained his strength to the dregs for a clutch on the handles; then he lifted, as if he would tear the flange from the centrepiece.

There was a terrific shrieking as the iron surfaces ground together. Fire followed each brake.

A building rushed by on the right—the carpenter-shop. Bart did not actually see it, but he knew it was gone.

Then came the car-barn, the turntable, the engine-house and repair-shop, and the long wood-shed. Less than thirty yards more! His speed was slackening on the level grade, but it was still tremendous.

And now the laundry was past—the last building. Twenty-five feet beyond it the cog-rail ended. Bart threw all that was left of himself into one final, mighty wrench.

A second later he found himself rolling blindly along the ties, head over heels and heels over head, cuffed, punched, battered, as if a dozen flails were beating him at once on every part of his body. At last he came to a stop, a bruised, dizzy heap.

After a little Bart sat up, tried his arms and legs, and found he could get on his feet. He felt himself all over. Luckily his bones were well padded with muscle, so none of them were broken.

The storm was still blowing forty miles an hour, but by contrast it seemed to him to be almost over. He hunted until he found his bundle of papers; it had been tied tightly, and had not burst open. Then he limped up to the Base House.

"Here are your 'Stars,'" said he to the driver of the team, shivering outside. "I've done my part; now see if you can get 'em to Bethlehem before six o'clock."

The Call of the Sea

By Frederick Palmer

The only memory of his father that Franklin Thompson had was the photograph of a young naval officer in uniform which his mother, with tears in her eyes, often showed him. She died when Franklin was six, leaving him, her only cause for living longer, to the care of his father's brother. When he realised how unwelcome he was in his new home, the only solace he had in the world was the photograph. He would look at it for an hour at a time, and read again and again the inscription on the back.

Before he was quite alone in the world he had heard the sea a-calling. On his holidays he would walk to the shore, and watch the ships go and come. Each was a speaking individuality, which he would recognize should he see it again. The salt breath was ever in his nostrils, the tang of salt spray in his veins.

When he was eleven, his cousin Edward, five years his senior, received the appointment to Annapolis. If Franklin felt any envy he stifled it. The inscription on the photograph in his father's own hand forbade that.

"Be honest; envy nobody; strive hard," it ran.

Two years later Franklin knew that his school-days were at an end.

"I'll look for a place for you to learn some business," said his uncle, as if the boy's preferences for an occupation did not count.

Early the next morning Franklin went to the great bay near his home, as he always did when he was heavy of heart. Three men-of-war, one a new battle-ship, their white sides gleaming, rested their enormous weights on the water as gently as swans. On the battle-ship it was visiting day. From her side the monster reached down her big gangway, with holystoned steps and immaculate rope, as a gallant officer offers his hand to a lady.

At the threshold of the deck Franklin paused, as one who suddenly sees his dreams materialise in broad daylight. No one of the knots of sightseers, going here and there with the spectators' "Ahs!" and occasional questions, noticed the boy, who stood immovable, noting every detail of the leviathan. Each gun seemed to him a living thing.

He saw some jackies going about their appointed duties, and others under the shade of the awnings aft, mending their clothes. The officer of the deck must be the happiest man in the world, Franklin thought. He imagined how his father must have looked, pacing back and forth in the same way. Oh, if his father were only alive, then perhaps he, too, might go to Annapolis! He looked up at the bridge and imagined himself in a great storm, with the spray stinging his face and blinding his eyes, and the mountain of steel as obedient to his commands as a bicycle to the turn of the handle-bar.

"Wouldn't you like to look around a bit?" asked a voice at his elbow.

Its owner, Franklin saw, was a boy of about his own age, dressed like the jackies in summer white.

"Would I? Would I?" The way Franklin asked the question was answer enough from any one boy to another.

"I guess you'll do," said his new friend, laughing. "My name's Harry Grimm. I'm a 'prentice."

Harry showed how the ammunition was hoisted for the thirteen-inch gun by touching a button; he slipped a dummy shell into the breech of one of the three-inch rapid fires; but he was quite unable to answer all of his guest's questions.

Franklin did not leave the man-of-war until the last boat was going ashore. That night he told his uncle of his desire to join the navy as an apprentice.

Uncle William was in unusually bad temper. He thought a moment and then said:

"I don't believe you'll ever be any use in business. Probably you'd run away to sea if I got you a place. I'll take you to the navy-yard to-morrow."

At any rate, Uncle William thought, he would be free from any further responsibility or care for the boy. Nevertheless, he knew what Franklin's proud father or his proud mother, were either of them alive, would say. That thought stung him a little.

While his cousin was at the school where officers are made, Franklin was to be trained for a seaman. Edward would begin his career with rank and position just beyond the highest grade that Franklin could ever attain. Franklin must be ever on the forecastle side of the dividing line between officer and man. He might rise to be a chief gunner, while Edward might be an admiral.

But Franklin did not understand this. He was in the period of light-hearted youth when the responsibility for his future rested on his guardian's shoulders. He was entirely under the spell of the call of the sea.

A year later found him bound for South America on a small cruiser, which continued around the Horn and on to Hong Kong to join the Asiatic squadron, which was even then preparing for the conflict with Spain. In all that long voyage he had never once been seasick, and he had grown to love the sea from familiarity as much as he had loved it in anticipation.

On that great morning when the American men-of-war ran into Manila Bay, the executive officer set him to look for torpedo-boats. The story of how he reported, with his hand to his cap in salute, "Torpedo-boat on our starboard bow, sir; she's sinking by the bow, sir; she's sunk," went the round of the messes. After the battle came that long period of waiting until the army took the city. When the sun was not as hot as an oven, the clouds poured torrents that rose from the hot awnings in steam.

By this time Franklin had come to comprehend the separation of officer and man as only actual service can reveal it. Sometimes, with cap in hand, he had to pass through the ward-room and the officers' quarters. These, which had been his father's portion, would be his cousin's, but could never be his.

His fellow apprentices were quite content with the forecastle. They felt more at home aft than they would forward. There was Charley, for example. Charley studied as little as he might; he was always getting into mischief, but was withal a bright, good-hearted fellow, with the makings of a first-class seaman in him.

The boatswain, known as "Pete" in the forecastle and "Deering" forward—and there you have his two names—used to fend off intrusion when Franklin was busy with his books. All his studies had the requirements for admission to Annapolis in view. Not that he expected ever to have his learning put to the test. He knew no one, he had no hope of knowing any one, who could secure for him the coveted appointment. It pleased him to be ready.

One day, as he was bending over the little box which is at once a seaman's work-basket and wardrobe, the captain, who had strolled aft, stopped by his side, and looking over his shoulder, saw a photograph.

"Why, that's Thompson!" he exclaimed. "Is he any relation of yours?"

"My father, sir," Franklin replied, as he sprang to his feet and saluted.

"I did not know that," the captain repeated, thoughtfully.

He picked up the photograph, and scanned the face of his old messmate. Afterward he never passed Franklin without a smiling glance. But that glance, meant so kindly, had a sting. It seemed to say that he was in a position unworthy of his father's name.

When a visiting congressman of the United States came aboard the cruiser as a guest, Pete instantly sought out Franklin, and taking him to one side where he would not be overheard, said:

"Now's your chance, my bully boy. A congressman can do 'most anything, so they say. You go right up to this one and knock your cap smart as you can, and tell him who your father was and that you want to go to Annapolis."

Franklin had not the courage or the presumption, whichever you call it; Pete called it "gall."

"If you won't, sonny, I will."

And when he saw the congressman sitting on the deck after general quarters, he approached him with a eulogy as earnest as it was picturesque. The congressman smiled, and asked to see Franklin.

"Now, sonny," said Pete, "I've cleared the channel; go forward and do your evolutions."

As Franklin stood before the elderly, dignified man sitting beside the captain on the captain's deck, he felt himself to be quite the most insignificant apprentice in the world. The congressman looked him over keenly from head to foot, as if he were examining the texture of the cloth on the back of his jacket.

"Do you want to go to Annapolis?"

Did he want to? Does the tender shoot of spring want the sunlight? Franklin's voice trembled with hope:

"Yes, sir. More than anything else in the world."

"I'm not making any promises," the congressman said, finally. "Congressmen haven't a pocketful of blanks to fill out whenever they see a bright boy. I'll see what I can do."

When, by the rules of the navy, Franklin was supposed to be sound asleep that night, he was wide awake, building air-castles. How long would he have to wait before he heard from the congressman? Would he ever hear?

The statesman did not appear again aboard the cruiser for many days. In the meantime, a new cadet, with his stripe fresh on his arm, came to the cruiser. It was none other than Franklin's own cousin, Edward. When they met at drill there was no look of recognition in Edward's face. Later, in one of the intervals of the day which the forecastle may call its own, the officer came aft and in a patronising manner asked the apprentice how he was getting on. When Franklin told him very well, Edward said it was awkward for an officer to have a cousin in the forecastle, and walked away. Franklin flushed at the remark, and repeated under his breath his father's advice, as the soldier of the old, superstitious days repeated his talisman.

The next day Franklin had shore leave. On his way back to the quay he saw his fellow apprentice, Charley, in bad company. He forgot all else except his friend's plight and his horror over it. When, finally, he had separated Charley from the lounger who wanted to show the sailor boy the town, the cruiser's launch had gone. They had to hire a native to row them out in a banka, which crept at a snail's pace in the gathering darkness.

For the first time in his life Franklin was among the accused who stood at the mast the next morning to hear their sentences from the captain, who acts as judge, and with the captain was the congressman. Franklin saw his look of surprise as their eyes met. The captain spoke of his own grief in delivering sentence of suspension from leave privilege for six months.

Franklin's head swam, and his cheeks were aflame. He could only reply with a hoarse "Yes, sir."

As he turned to go he heard the congressman say sarcastically that he did not think "that boy was so very anxious to go to Annapolis."

Franklin was the only one of the ship's company who did not brighten when they received the electric thrill of an order, which broke their weary vigil in the famous bay by sending the cruiser to patrol duty among the southern islands. But when they were under way Franklin found that the congressman was still aboard, and his hopes revived a little. For a week of coasting from port to port he looked in vain for some event which would set him right.

Then came an order transferring him. He was assigned to the *Marietta*, a tiny gunboat no bigger than a harbour tugboat and with but half the draft. He had only time to get his belongings together, which does not take a sailor long. He found that his cousin had also been transferred, and was to be commander of the cockle-shell.

The *Marietta's* first assignment was to take none other than the congressman up a river to the capital of a province where he had a son, an officer of the army, in command of the garrison. There Franklin would definitely see the last of him. They had no thought of meeting with any delay on their run of the five miles of winding stream, but it is when they are least expected that guerrillas appear.

The congressman was sitting in the bow admiring the scenery, the little engine was "chugging" earnestly, the screw was whirling vigorously through the muddy water, when out of the soft green foliage of the right bank cracked a volley. The congressman, a veteran himself, dropped on the deck and looked about him for a rifle, his old eyes flashing.

The cadet had never been under fire before. He dodged and fell on the deck with the others. Franklin was at the wheel and remained erect, frightened but not forgetting his duty. There had not been a tremor of the rudder.

"Steer for that bank, sharp, sharp!" Edward called, and Franklin obeyed. "I don't want to—to endanger your life," he panted to the congressman, his sentence broken by the ring of a bullet against the hull, and whistle of other bullets over their heads.

"Seems to me I'd put a few shots back at 'em in the meanwhile," said the congressman. "What's that for?" He nodded toward a rapid-fire gun in the bow. "And that?" toward a one-pounder in the stern.

Edward could not fail to take the hint. He sprang up with trembling limbs and ran to the rapid-fire gun, calling for the other to be manned. A bullet struck its support before he could put it in action. That made him forget all his training. He aimed wildly, and jammed the delicate machine almost instantly. Then, in his desperation, he ran toward the wheel.

"Steer in closer, closer!"

"It's too shallow, sir," Franklin replied.

"No, it's not." The ensign could hear the triumphant shouts of the insurgents, who increased their fire. He was wild with exasperation. "It's not!" he repeated, and seized the wheel in his own hands and turned it hard alee. The bow veered sharply. For an instant the boat flew forward, then grounded.

As if they had been waiting on this for a signal, a fire broke out from some bushes which rose above the level of the grassy bank on the left side.

"Both sides!" gasped the ensign. He sprang overboard, as much to avoid the fire as anything. "Push her off!"

Everybody leaped into the water. When the insurgents on the left bank saw the predicament of the Americans, they broke out of their cover with a yell, and came running toward them. Meanwhile, the *Marietta* was still in range of the fire from the other side. It was a question only of minutes, yes, of seconds, before they would be prisoners.

The current swung the *Marietta* partially round and drove her fast into the soft mud, and the misdirected efforts of her crew to free her were as unavailing as if she were a battle-ship.

"Can't somebody fire that gun? Can't somebody fire?" the congressman called, putting the strength of his sixty years against the hull, and feeling his shoes sinking in the soft ooze beneath them.

At this juncture, in face of the fire, Franklin sprang on deck, and ran aft to the jammed instrument of their hope. He felt as cool as his father's son ought to feel under such circumstances. The parts of the mechanism were not a jumble to him as they were to the excited cadet, and he saw the difficulty and how simple it was. His study, his questions, had not been in vain.

"Man the one-pounder! Get the rifles, everybody!" he called, with the instinct of command.

As they tumbled aboard the crew heard the rat-tat-tat of the gun under Franklin's hand, sweeping the field of white-shirted figures pressing forward, and soon a little shell from the one-pounder threw up dirt at their feet. The insurgents were too near their prize to be stopped yet.

"Keep cool, everybody, keep cool!" said the congressman, himself firing with the nice calculation of a man at a range.

The Americans did not realise that shots were still coming from the rear. They knew that the insurgents on the other side of the stream could not cross it, and that was enough. If the gun should jam again, all would be lost.

But it did not jam; and soon the insurgents, no longer able to stand the persistent accuracy of the machine, began to fall back, and finally ran in pell-mell flight, leaving their wounded behind.

Promptly Franklin whirled his gun round and began firing upon the first attacking party, which withdrew when it saw that it was unsupported by the other side.

When excitement no longer made their efforts futile, and one was not pushing against another, and with the screw properly directed to their assistance, the crew was very soon able to force the stranded *Marietta* back into the stream.

After the congressman had emptied the water out of his shoes and was once more seated, with nothing to do but to enjoy the scenery, he said to Franklin, in beaming gratitude:

"Well, young man, you're quite a general!"

Franklin blushed. The remark did not make him think of his ambition. It gave him speech for another cause.

"O sir, I want you not to believe that those charges were true. They weren't. I wouldn't have overstayed leave if it hadn't been—but—but you ask Charley the rest."

"I don't believe them. To prove it, all you've got to do is to pass the examination to Annapolis. I'll see that you get the appointment."

Franklin's manner and his eyes spoke his gratitude better than his tongue. Edward, who had overheard, looked proudly at his cousin, and then said to the congressman:

"I thank you, too, sir! I sha'n't be happy till he wears the uniform his father wore. He saved us all to-day."

His little speech saved Edward from a court of inquiry. He became Franklin's best friend, and if ever he goes into action again there is no doubt that he will behave like a veteran.

On a Tight Rope

By Albert W. Tolman

"My highest ambition at seventeen," said the linotype operator, "was to become a professional acrobat. I then lived with my parents on a farm near the manufacturing town of N. All my spare time was spent in vaulting, jumping, turning handsprings, and practising other feats of strength and agility.

"On the Fourth of July a travelling tight-rope performer, Signor Lupini of Verona, as the posters called him, was to display his skill on a rope above the river that flowed through the town. He arrived with two assistants on the afternoon of July 3d, and a crowd of boys, myself among them, met him at the railroad station. We saw a spare, wiry man, above the ordinary height, light-complexioned, with steely-blue eyes. He looked us over inquiringly.

"'Boys,' said he, 'I need some young fellow to help me to-morrow. Who wants to be wheeled across the rope in a barrow?'

"The others hung back; but I jumped at the chance. 'I do!' I exclaimed, quickly. He seemed pleased as he ran his eyes over me. I was of medium height, with good muscles.

"'All right,' he said. 'Come to the hotel at seven, and I'll tell you what's wanted.'

"At the stroke of the hour I was on hand, and he explained my duties. Then he pulled a ten-dollar bill from his pocket.

"'That's yours at nine to-morrow night if you do your work well,' he said. 'Now go home and sleep soundly.'

"My parents were spending the Fourth with cousins in a neighbouring town, so I was alone in the house. I went to bed early, but until long after midnight excitement kept me from getting a single wink.

"The next day I was on hand bright and early. I helped stretch the rope between two mill roofs, ran errands, and made myself generally useful. When not busy I hung about, watching my employer. He certainly was an artist in his line, a man without bravado, either all nerves or none at all. I could not help thinking, too, that for an Italian he spoke English remarkably well.

"At half past two a carriage took us from the hotel to the western mill. We dressed in the loft. The signor donned his tinsel-spangled tights. I figured as clown in an old stovepipe hat and white cotton suit, liberally besprinkled with stars of red and green. The same colours streaked my face. As we clambered through the scuttle, the crowds lining the bridges and banks set up a shout, and the town band on the other mill began playing 'The Star-Spangled Banner.'

"Sharp at three o'clock the music stopped. The assistant on our roof advanced to the edge, fired six blank cartridges from a self-cocking revolver, and shouted this magniloquent announcement through a megaphone:

"'Ladies and gentlemen, the celebrated Signor Lupini will now illustrate his art, assisted by Rinaldo Nobisco, the famous clown, recently secured from the London hippodrome, ladies and gentlemen, at great trouble and expense.'

"Whistles and catcalls from the boys below greeted this absurd reference to me, and I felt rather foolish. Signor Lupini stepped briskly forward, bowed to his audience and was soon promenading along the spidery line between the two cornices. Aided by a long balancing-pole, he stood on one foot, knelt, lay down, walked across blindfold, and performed many other marvellous feats. His perfect control of nerve and muscle fascinated me. I did not realise that his facility came from years of toilsome practice.

"Here was the calling for me. I resolved to stretch a rope the very next day between the beams over the haymow.

"During the signor's exhibition the crowd was very quiet, and the band did not play. It was only when he was once more safe upon the roof that their long-restrained applause broke forth, and the band struck up 'Hail to the Chief.' He rested a few minutes, and then motioned to me to make ready.

"Among our paraphernalia was a strong, light wheelbarrow with a tire grooved to fit the rope. I began to feel a little shaky; but there was no time to indulge this emotion, for my employer exclaimed: 'All aboard, my boy, and remember, a stiff upper lip!'

"I seated myself, facing forward, my feet dangling on each side of the wheel. Signor Lupini, stooping, gripped the handles.

"'Sit steady,' he said. 'Don't wink one eye unless you wink the other at the same time.'

"He ran me a few turns round the gravelled surface, then flicked the wheel dexterously up on the rope and headed straight for the edge.

"'Keep perfectly still,' he adjured me, 'and you're as safe as you'd be on the street.'

"For all my assumption of coolness, I was frightened half out of my wits. I shut my eyes for a moment, and when I opened them we were fairly out on the tremulous hemp.

"'Don't look down,' cautioned the signor. 'Face straight forward. Sit tight.'

"Hardly daring to breathe, I stiffened myself as if I were in a plaster cast. I could see the narrow line just ahead buckle slightly at the approach of the wheel. How long that two hundred feet seemed!

"Slowly, surely, we drew near the roof. The tire jolted against the cornice. In two or three seconds we were safely on the gravel. Then the band blared out and the crowds set off explosives. My fright was over, and I felt proud as a peacock.

"On the trip back my employer made me sit facing him, and I had a good chance to admire the easy, effortless play of his wiry muscles. He was a thorough gymnast, a man of steel and india-rubber. After several other trips, during which I occupied different positions on the barrow, we went back to the hotel.

"Promptly at eight we emerged again through the scuttle. A crowd bigger than that of the afternoon had gathered, and a roar of applause greeted us. I say 'us,' for by this time I felt myself to be almost as important as Signor Lupini. My head was completely turned.

"The evening performance possessed certain novel features. Tin pans of red fire stood on each cornice, and along the bridge-rails had been stationed a half-dozen boys liberally supplied with rockets and Roman candles.

"The master of ceremonies fired an introductory volley with his revolver.

"'Light up, Jimmy!' he shouted to his associate across the river, at the same time touching a match to the pan beside him. Jimmy obeyed. A deep red glow illuminated the scene, flashing from the mill windows, and revealing the human clusters on bridges and banks.

"As in the afternoon, Signor Lupini began with a few feats performed alone, the blaze of fireworks making his spangled tights glitter. I waited impatiently for our dual performance, thirsting for some of the applause. Finally my turn came, and the signor wheeled me back and forth several times. So great was my confidence in him that I had forgotten my nervousness.

"At last nine o'clock was near.

"'Now, my boy,' said my employer, 'we'll wind up with something I don't try very often. I see you have good grit.'

"He screwed to the barrow sides a light, strong chair of steel, its seat a yard in air. After helping me into this, he passed me a long-handled pan of red fire. We were to close in a blaze of glory. 'Keep cool,' said he, 'and we'll give 'em something to look at.'

"He trundled me up to the cornice, his assistant dropped a lighted lucifer into the pan, and we moved out on the rope amid the crimson glare and the whizzing of rockets. The crowd yelled, and one of the boys setting off fireworks from the lower bridge lost his head.

"*Whi-s-s-sh!* A badly aimed rocket shot not five feet over our heads, showering us with sparks. A little lower, and it would have dashed us from the rope. Signor Lupini drew a quick breath. I cringed in my steel chair, but still kept tight hold of the pan handle. The sudden fright set my teeth chattering. My employer noticed my trepidation.

"'Keep quiet, my boy, and we'll get over all right,' said he, reassuringly, cool as a cucumber.

"On we rolled, smoothly and steadily. We were about half-way across when the unlucky rocketeer on the lower bridge outdid his previous blunder. A warning shriek blended with the swish of a projectile. I dared not turn my head, but a sidelong glance revealed a fiery comet heading straight toward us. Signor Lupini saw it, too, and could not repress a cry of alarm. The next second it was upon us. I shut my eyes, convinced that we were lost. A whir, a rushing of flame, a slight shock! The apparition had passed, and we were still on the rope.

"I was hardly daring to congratulate myself when my heart was chilled by a low groan behind me. The barrow wabbled. The signor was trembling violently, swaying, reeling like a drunken man; every throb of his body came to me through the tight-clutched handles. Something fearful must have happened. I clung to the chair arms in sheer paralysis of horror. An accident would hurl us down seventy-five feet into the river, where drowning or maiming worse than death awaited us.

"We moved a few feet farther, then stopped. The barrow swayed, as if about to overturn. Another groan from the signor. I would have questioned him, but the words died in my throat. Perhaps he had been pierced by the rocket, and might at any instant fall unconscious.

"Cries of horror rose from the spectators. The rockets and Roman candles ceased. The entertainment threatened to become a tragedy.

"Again we started, moving intermittently. Now a few quick steps would fill me with the dread of being flung off; now we almost stopped, and I feared we should never go on. Before and behind us fizzed the red fire. Signor Lupini's feet shuffled on the rope, his breath came hard. Not a word in explanation, but always those terrible groans. My hair bristled.

"With straining eyes I stared ahead into the red glare on the approaching mill. How slowly the distance lessened! On the roof stood Jimmy, gazing at us, pale and open-mouthed. The speechless horror on his face reflected our peril.

"The cornice was only ten feet off. Signor Lupini thrust the barrow suddenly forward. A second later the wheel grated on the gravel; it was none too soon. As a long sigh of relief rose from the spellbound crowds, the gymnast collapsed into a writhing heap. It took three men to get him down through the scuttle and into the carriage that conveyed him to his hotel.

"The rocket had struck his right calf a glancing blow. His skill had enabled him to withstand a shock that would have overthrown a clumsier man; but his muscles, steeled to resist, had cramped violently, and we had been in deadly peril all the way across. Two lives had hung on his ability to resist the agonising pains and preserve his poise.

"That last hundred feet decided me that I didn't care to be a professional acrobat. The tight rope was never stretched between the beams of the haymow."

Down the Incline

By Charles Newton Hood

"All that I had to do to earn my one hundred and twenty-five dollars a week salary was, four times each week-day, to climb to the top of a high tower, mount a bicycle, ride it down a long, narrow incline, pitched at an angle of about forty-five degrees, then up a few feet and out through the air, across a gap of thirty feet to another platform, and so to the ground."

It was John Manser who was speaking, formerly one of the most daring performers in what is called the carnival business.

"No, I am not doing that sort of an act now.

"My mother had been writing to me, begging me to stop, but I was looking forward to getting married, and that one hundred and twenty-five dollars a week was making the nest-egg grow.

"I was one of the 'feature' acts furnished by the Ferari Brothers to street fairs, carnivals and the like, and had stepped from construction boss to performer one day by taking the place of an indisposed athlete at an hour's notice, and leaping the gap successfully on his bicycle without any previous rehearsal. I was at once put on as a regular performer with the company.

"My work did not seem so very terrible to me. With the bands playing and with the thousands of happy spectators looking on, it was rather pleasant than otherwise to climb to the top of the high platform, dressed in my gay costume, and at the word, come hurtling down the steep run, and then up and out through the air like a bird.

"All that seemed to be required was to be absolutely sure that the apparatus was put up strong and perfectly true, and that the gap was of exactly the correct width. Mine was precisely twenty-eight feet and four inches. I always superintended the erection of everything myself, and trued every part up with the utmost care.

"In the act itself, it required only strong hands and arms to keep the bicycle steady and straight down the run, and to lean back a little and give a strong up pull on the handle-bar when we 'took off' for the jump, so that the machine would surely strike on the rear wheel on the other side, to prevent the shock which would throw me headlong if the front wheel should strike first, or even at the same instant.

"All summer long I had enjoyed the work, and I often wondered that they should pay me so much for such a simple thing. Even when the performer who 'looped-the-loop' on a bicycle in another part of the grounds fell and was crippled for life, I ascribed it to the fact that his health was not very good, and that he sometimes resorted to stimulants to help him through his act; and his misfortune did not render me at all nervous regarding my own work.

"It was the last day of the carnival at Grand Creek. We had had a most successful week, and on the closing night it was estimated that not less than fifteen thousand people crowded the grounds. The last of my four rides for the day was scheduled for eleven o'clock at night, and was to be the closing feature.

"Promptly at five minutes of eleven I climbed to the platform, and my bicycle was sent up to me by rope and pulley. It was a heavy, dark night, but the thousands of electric lights made the grounds almost as light as day. Little lamps were strung thickly all down the run, and the skeleton framework of my tower and trestles was outlined with them.

"A fitful, eddying wind had come up, which roared dismally through the timbers. It swayed the big framework somewhat, but not enough to trouble me.

"The people had come crowding to my portion of the grounds, and as I gazed down at their upturned faces, massed so thickly together below me, the sight was a weird one under the electric lights.

"Straight ahead of me lay the narrow run, with its broad stripe of white down the centre, to aid me in steering, then the 'saucer,' as it was called, at the bottom, where the run turned up toward the 'take-off,' then the wide gap and the farther platform, with its even wider guiding stripe of white.

"I gave the bicycle a quick examination, stood up straight and made the little posing flourish which is expected of all athletes, fixed my bicycle on the run, and seated myself firmly. The official announcer below raised his hand. The band stopped playing, and there was that breathless hush of apprehension and expectation which is so carefully worked up for sensational acts.

"'All ready?' shouted the announcer.

"'Right!' I responded.

"'Go!'

"The snare-drummer of the band struck into the long roll with which he always accompanied my flights. Instantly I removed the restraining foot which I had kept upon the platform, placed it upon the locked pedal, and shot rapidly down the incline.

"At that instant every electric light in the city of Grand Creek went out!

"It was a darkness doubly dense and awful after the brilliancy of the moment before. Perfectly helpless, I was plunging down a steep, narrow incline toward probable death. If the wheel swerved but a little to the right or left, I should sweep over the edge and be dashed to pieces on the ground below.

"My bicycle, rushing down the incline, travelled at the rate of fifty miles an hour. Sometimes now I awake at night with a gasp of horror from having lived over those awful moments, but at the time my thoughts were cool and collected.

"'It all depends on you, Jack, my boy,' I told myself. 'You can't be smashed any harder for keeping your head.'

"I knew that the wheel was absolutely straight for the jump when I started, and grasping the handles, I bent every effort toward keeping the wheel perfectly rigid. Down I rushed through the darkness, and so strange was the sensation that it almost seemed as if the wheel had left the run, and was sailing through the air. The speed seemed doubly terrific. Even if I kept the run, could I hold the wheel for the jump and what then?

"The saucer came almost before I expected it. In spite of myself I must have given a spasmodic twist to the handles, for the wheel twisted in my hands and swerved. I threw myself frantically to one side and lost consciousness!

"Yes, I'm alive yet. Entirely uninjured except for the thump which put me to sleep when I struck the platform.

"The great momentum swept both the wheel and myself from the edge of the take-off and hurled us against the yielding bodies of those in the front row of the crowd, backed by the thousands of other spectators, as against a carefully prepared and cushioned buffer. It was learned that not less than eighteen persons received the impact of the wheel and myself at the same instant, and so scattered was the blow that nobody was injured in the slightest.

"One very fat man, who had been standing with his handsome top-hat held behind him, told me that he sat down with fearful suddenness after receiving my head in his stomach, and he showed me his hat; but he wasn't hurt.

"The next day the Ferari Brothers Carnival Company went to Battle Rapids, but my ticket read East Putney, Vermont."

The Cost of Loving

By Frederick Orin Bartlett

With a slight lift of his heavy shoulders, Dr. Schriftman brought to a close his final lecture of the year to the senior medical class. For a moment he faced these young men aggressively. With his shaggy white beard, his wiry grey hair, his bulky body, he looked more like some good-natured Santa Claus than a surgeon who was famous on two continents for his stoicism as well as his skill. It was tradition that he should say what he was about to say to each graduating class.

"Shentlemen," he began in his rough guttural, which still retained the trace of an accent. "Shentlemen, you are about to enter a profession which will be very jealous of you. It demands all—everything. You will be tempted by many false gods—by women, by gold. Peware! Let your work be your religion, your wife, and your reward. So you will be goot surgeons. Shentlemen, I wish you success."

As he turned to leave the platform, he was greeted with noisy and hearty cheering.

"Raus mit der ladies!" shouted some one.

The cry was taken up with a will, but when another voice broke through with: "Hoch Schriftman!" the one hundred throats strained themselves to the utmost in a final effort to give expression to their genuine appreciation of the man.

But Schriftman, indifferent alike to their jests and plaudits, had already jammed his silk hat on the back of his head and was hurrying down stairs to where his machine waited to whisk him to the hospital.

He timed his day as by a stop watch. He rose at seven, gave himself until eight to finish his solitary breakfast, and, hurrying off to the medical school, remained there until eleven. He was at the hospital from eleven-thirty until three. From three-ten until five he kept his office hours. He generally dined alone in his apartments after this and gave up his evenings to consultations, to the preparation of papers, and to study. It was a long evening, for he seldom retired until two. More often than not he was called to the hospital after this and finished his sleep there. The doctors' quarters were as much home to him as the three book-cluttered rooms which led from his office. And yet there were men—young men, too—who envied Schriftman, and when tempted by bright eyes and warm cheeks quoted to themselves his famous epigram:

"It costs too much to love."

As his machine drew up before the big grey building, a young interne hurried out, opened the door, and then fell back respectfully to give to his senior the place of honour by Schriftman's side. In answer to questions which went to their mark like arrows, Burrell covered the progress of every case since the day before and turned to the new patient in Ward 27.

"Female, age eight. Mother an actress, died of pneumonia; father a bicycle rider, killed in an accident. Family history negative."

And so with a dozen other medical details Burrell led up to the result of his preliminary examination and to the laboratory report. He made no diagnosis except in connection with her weak heart. But to Schriftman it was not the faulty heart but the chronic pain in the back which was significant. As he removed his hat and gloves before going to the ward, he pressed his cross-examination deeper. It was evident to Dr. Burrell that it was to be the rare good fortune of this female, age eight, to prove an interesting case to Schriftman.

In the meanwhile the lass in question lay stretched out on her back, watching with hectic interest the hurried movements of the head nurse. There wasn't very much of Gretzel left; just a shrivelled body, a thin mouth, a straight, sensitive nose, a pair of blue eyes, and a wealth of light hair. But the eyes were quite perfect. So deep and clear, so timid and yet so wise were these that as they peered out of the haggardness of their surroundings they gave the effect of a maid within a maid. It was as though some other soul, unrelated to this pain-racked body, were peering through the mask of her gaunt features. The eyes were younger and fresher and stronger than the rest of her. At present they were unusually alert.

In contrast to the isolated boarding-house room from which they had brought her, life here fairly buzzed. The plaints and groanings of her fellow patients, the shadow-like movements of the nurses, the constant coming and going of the young doctors on their unknown errands, the catlike tread of life through the night, the undercurrent of suspense, and her own helplessness in the midst of it kept her on guard. The nurses, drawn to her at once, tried to reassure her, but to little purpose, because Gretzel believed nothing of what they whispered. People had lied to her all her life. When her father had told her she would soon be well and that then he would take her far out into the country, he had lied. When her father was killed, her mother had lied to her, saying that daddy had only gone away for a little while to prepare a home for them both. Then her mother had died and every one had lied about that. They said that she had gone to join daddy and that some day she would send for Gretzel. Finally the landlady had lied when she had been hurried off into the ambulance. This woman had assured Gretzel that she might possibly find her mother at the hospital. She hadn't found her mother—the nurses had never heard of her mother. So now, with her thin lips tight together, she listened, believing nothing, but kept her eyes wide open ready for what might happen next.

Nearer and nearer to her came Fate in the person of Schriftman—Schriftman the silent, who could skirt with his knife the fringe of the soul itself. His progress through the ward was accompanied with more awe than that of a sovereign through his court. To the huddled group of internes at his back he stood for the highest goal in their profession; to those patients who knew him he stood as the literal arbiter of life and death. When those clear eyes—as brilliantly hard as glacial ice—were upon them, when those quick, mobile fingers fluttered over their bruised bodies, they breathed slowly and prayed. For they knew it was given to him to do things possible to no other man. But though many an eye warmed at sight of him, though many an arm pleaded toward him, though many lips trembled gratitude at his approach, he rigidly preserved his impersonality. He had neither smile nor jest. His eyes never warmed; they only lighted.

Gretzel saw him as he entered the ward opposite her. She shrank beneath the clothes with only her eyes showing and studied the man. She liked his size first of all. She had a weakling's reverence for physical strength. The broad shoulders, the long, heavy arms appealed to her at once. Then she liked his whiskers. They reminded her of pictures of Santa Claus. Finally, she liked his deep bass voice. It seemed to her that a man with a voice like that must tell the truth. She wasn't sure of this, but the longer she listened to it and the nearer it came, the less afraid she grew. She ventured the tip of her nose above the bedclothes, then her mouth, and finally her chin. By the time the group reached her side she was facing them all, in the open.

For a moment Schriftman stood over her and met her gaze. He had never felt his soul so searched as it was during the next few seconds. And yet the silent questions asked of him were simple. Gretzel sought only to know if he were a man to tell the truth and if she could trust him with her tender, sensitive body. She had fought the boarding-house doctor tooth and nail from the beginning. Not only had he lied to her but he had hurt her brutally. Now she wished to know if she must be on her guard with this other. So for a moment her excited big eyes rested on his, which were like candles burning in a frosty room. Then quite simply and unafraid she shoved down the bedclothes and, turning over on her face, exposed her throbbing back.

Dr. Burrell caught the nurse's eye. The latter gave a gulpy sort of smile and turned away. With a grunt Schriftman bent over the thin frame. His fingers, which at times seemed endowed with five senses, played up and down her spine, to the right, to the left, then back again up and down. Though at times he stopped to probe deep, he did not hurt her much. It seemed to her that some of the strength of his broad back ran out of his finger tips and for a moment checked the biting ache which had gnawed at her for a twelvemonth. Once, at a certain spot, he made her cringe, but she understood that this was not done intentionally.

Schriftman, his brow knitted, called for Burrell's stethoscope. He placed it over Gretzel's wobbly heart and listened. One of his big hands lay on the coverlet. Suddenly he felt his thumb in the clutch of a warm, tight grip. He found it difficult to listen after this, for the sturdy pound of his own heart became curiously intermingled with this other jerky beat. Extricating his thumb, he glared at Burrell.

"Transfer this patient to a private ward," he ordered.

In the luxurious seclusion of a room to herself, with everything to eat that her fickle palate craved, with bright-coloured German picture books to look at, with a nurse whose sole duty it was to attend to her alone, Gretzel felt like an invalid princess. But all these things were as nothing compared with the joy of the frequent visits of the big doctor himself. Had it not been for him Gretzel would have looked with suspicion on the whole arrangement; she would have lain awake all night worrying about what might grow out of this. She had learned that every sweet was only a mask of something bitter—like her pills. Whenever anyone had been especially nice to her at home, it was sure to be followed by something terrible. When her father died, her mother had brought her a doll, and when her mother died the landlady had brought her an apple.

But this was different. When she felt Schriftman's hand close over hers she knew that now no more harm could come to her. He was big enough to take quick revenge on anyone who should hurt her. The consequent relaxation of her tense nerves brought even some surcease of pain, so that at night she frequently slept two or three hours at a time. But the best thing about these naps was the excitement of waking up and finding this shaggy-bearded Santa Claus by the side of her bed. It might be eleven at night or two in the morning or four in the morning that he came, but always he came between the dusk and the dawn. Always his greeting was the same:

"How it goes, kleine mädchen?"

Always she answered:

"I'm partickly comfy, Mister Santy."

Then he would seat himself by the bed, she would take a tight grip on his thumb, and they were off in a jiffy to some glorious German fairyland.

The wonder was where the Herr Doctor found these stories. They certainly were not in any of his scientific treatises and he had read nothing else for forty years.

If he made them up as he went along, then he must have had more imagination than anyone ever suspected. It was to be noted, however, that in these stories the heroine could trace her beauty, her charm, as well as the success of all her adventures, to the fact that she was very particular to eat as much as possible of whatever was brought to her.

"Und so," as he informed her one night, "if you would be a princess, you must eat und you must sleep. Ach—so you will become gr-ross und r-rosy und peautiful."

"Me?" Gretzel questioned doubtfully.

She had never been ambitious in that direction.

"You are peautiful already inside," answered Schriftman. "It does not need much after that to be peautiful outside—choost some fat und some proteids."

"Sum fat an' sum protydids," murmured Gretzel, as though committing it to memory.

This was a new idea to her—this possibility of being beautiful. For herself she didn't care, but if Santy wished it, then it was worth trying for. She became a little bit jealous of these German princesses. But a new thought disturbed her.

"It's so hard to be beau-ti-ful when your back aches you," she sighed.

"Ach," replied the doctor with a frown, "dot iss true. But when we are gr-ross und are r-rosy—so perhaps the ache will go."

Gretzel quickly searched his eyes. She had been told before that this ache might go. It had always been a lie. Now Santy himself had told her. On the whole, she was sorry he had told her this. With all her confidence in him she could not believe that such a thing was possible. And if it were not possible, then—he must be like the others.

He had risen to go, and was bending over her as tenderly as a mother. She reached up a thin hand and drew down his shaggy head until her lips rested against his ear.

"I'm partickly comfy," she assured him anxiously. "Let the ache be."

He kissed her lips.

"Mein kleine mädchen," he trembled. "Ach, mein kleine mädchen."

It was three o'clock in the morning when he left her, but he routed Burrell out of bed and made him sit up until half-past four, while he discussed everything under the face of the sun except that which was disturbing him. Burrell, dog-tired, listened patiently, but when Schriftman finally explained himself, he gave a start.

"Dot case in Ward A," Schriftman blurted out, dropping into a broad dialect, as he always did when deeply moved. "I t'ink Richards iss der man to do dot—hein?"

"To do Gretzel?" exclaimed Burrell.

Schriftman nodded, looking up at Burrell from beneath his wiry eyebrows.

"Why, doctor," cried Burrell, "there's just one man in the world to do that operation—and that's you!"

Schriftman's head sank.

"Richards is a great operator," admitted Burrell, "but he hasn't your nerve. And, good Lord, it's going to take a man of iron to do that operation without ether."

Schriftman winced. Burrell ran on excitedly.

"Why, you yourself said she didn't have a chance in ten, but without you—why, it wouldn't be a chance in a hundred."

Burrell was pleading. He was pleading with his heart in the plea, for he was pleading for Gretzel's life. The operation had been the talk of the hospital for three weeks. The girl's heart was too weak to stand an anaesthetic, and even with the local application of cocaine the operation was bound to be brutal. Everyone knew there was just one Schriftman—just one man with the brains, the hand, and the nerve to do it. This wasn't a task for an ordinary surgeon; it was a task for a surgical machine. Burrell had been waking up lately in a cold sweat trying to find out how he could avoid assisting. Without ether—good heavens! there was only one Schriftman; only one man who could keep his hand steady with Gretzel's poor body quivering beneath it.

Moreover, there wasn't another man who had the skill to give the lass even a show for her suffering. Speed is what would count, and there was no such nimble fingers in the world as Schriftman's.

Burrell was on his feet.

"Gretzel's life is literally in your hands, doctor," he exclaimed impulsively. "God give her strength to bear the ordeal."

"Amen," muttered Schriftman.

During the next few weeks Gretzel seemed actually to grow slightly plump and rosy, but almost in the same proportion Schriftman grew wan and pale.

He realised that Burrell had told the truth; if the child was to have a fighting chance for life, then he must do the operation. But was it possible to make the kleine mädchen understand that what he did he did for her own dear sake? Could he make her realise that the hand she grasped so confidently would not willingly cause her brutal pain? Ach—the honest trust of those blue eyes!

There came a morning when Gretzel was given no breakfast. She protested to the head nurse.

"Santy will be very mad on me if I don't eat my egg," she declared.

"I think he will forgive you this time, dear," answered the nurse.

"Why?" Gretzel asked pointedly.

"Because—because—"

"I ain't beau-ti-ful yet," Gretzel interrupted with a glance at her thin arm.

The nurse threw herself on her knees by the side of the girl. She kissed that thin arm again and again.

"Yes, you are beautiful and wonderful," she half sobbed. "Don't ask me questions, Gretzel. *Please* don't ask me questions."

Gretzel placed her hand on the nurse's head. She didn't like to see anyone worried. And because, here, she herself seemed always to be the cause of worry she answered reassuringly the only comforting thing she could think of:

"I'm partickly comfy."

Whereupon the nurse rose swiftly and hurried out of the room.

Santy favoured Gretzel with an unexpected visit this same morning. He came in shortly after the nurse had left, and Gretzel explained to him at once that she had not had her egg.

"So?" Schriftman answered nervously.

He seated himself on the edge of the bed. He placed his hand firmly on her shoulder.

"Kleine mädchen," he faltered, "if you were mein own kleine mädchen I could not loff you more."

She put her arms around his neck.

"Dear, dear Santy," she cooed.

"So," he said, "so you must neffer forget dot."

He drew a little away from her. What he had to say he said looking fair into her blue eyes.

"To-day," he said, "we must make der ache go—poof—foreffer!"

He snapped his fingers.

"The ache," she questioned anxiously.

"Foreffer," he assured her. "Und if it hurts you when it iss going—"

She smiled up into his face. She grasped his thumb.

"I ain't skeered of bein' hurted with you, I guess."

He held his breath a moment. He couldn't say any more after that.

So it was Burrell who was forced to prepare the maid for what was to be done. He did it as well as he knew how, but he made a bungling job of it. He left her gasping for breath with all the old fear in her eyes. The thing she could not understand was what had become of Santy. She called for him again and again.

The best Burrell could think of to tell her was that the Herr Doctor had gone to save a little girl from death and that he would come back as soon as he could.

Schriftman was depending upon the disguise of his operating robes to prevent Gretzel from recognizing him. But he had forgotten to reckon with the fact that she might wonder at his apparent desertion of her at this the gravest crisis in her life. Burrell's explanation did not help very much. When they lifted her gently to the stretcher and carried her through the corridors to the high-vaulted amphitheatre, Santy was nowhere to be seen. Pale, dumb, dazed, Gretzel looked everywhere for him in vain.

Burrell in an ante-room assisted Schriftman into his sterilized surplice. He adjusted the mask over the surgeon's beard and the white cap over his hair, leaving only his eyes exposed. Then he helped him into his rubber gloves. He himself was white and loose in all his joints, but Schriftman, though white, was like a marble statue. He was rigid and inhumanly cold. He moved about with the quick certainty of motion of an automaton. He gave his orders in a voice that clicked like an instrument. Burrell could not help admiring such self-control, but at the same time it made him shudder.

When all was ready Schriftman walked noiselessly in to the amphitheatre. Gretzel was lying face down with an interne stationed at either side of her head. A nurse stood ready near the glittering array of instruments. Schriftman scarcely breathed as he approached, but he had no sooner reached the girl's side than she forced up her head. For a heartbeat she stared wildly at the sheeted figure. Then she gave a glad, confident cry:

"Santy! Santy!"

Schriftman without replying nodded a signal, and the internes gently forced Gretzel back again. But Burrell slumped to the floor like an empty grain sack and was of no more use to anyone.

For twenty-four hours after the operation Schriftman sat outside Gretzel's door and received five-minute reports on her condition. Then when he realised that she bade fair to tide over the first terrible shock, he returned to his lonely room and slept. He was exhausted as he had never before been, and when he woke up he was still exhausted. Something seemed to have gone from him. He made his morning hospital visit to everyone except Gretzel, but his mind was loose and vague. So a week passed, and they told him that while the maid was free from pain and was making a good recovery, she shrank from everyone who approached her.

"Und she neffer asks for Santy—hein?" he questioned the nurse.

The nurse lowered her eyes.

"No," she admitted gently.

He waited another week with the success of his wonderful operation his only consolation. There was no doubt now but that in time Gretzel would really be as gross and rosy as any of the princesses he had pictured to her. For a long time yet he must watch that weak heart, to be sure, but with care and patience much might be done even with that. If only she would let him, he would make that his life work. He wanted to make her his legal daughter; he wanted to buy a little house in the country and take her there; he wanted to make her a real fairyland princess.

"Und she neffer asks yet for Santy—hein?"

"No," answered the nurse.

"So," he murmured, turning away his head. He waited a moment. Then he asked:

"You speak sometimes off me?"

"Yes," answered the nurse.

He did not press her further, and so she was saved from telling him that at the mere mention of his name the maid shrank away in terror.

Schriftman waited until Gretzel's temperature was normal—until for the first time in her life she slept soundly through the night. He himself had been sleeping less than one hour in the twenty-four. His clothes hung pitifully loose about his once firm body. As Burrell said, he was proving the truth of his own epigram: his love was costing him much—too much.

There came a day when Schriftman could stand it no longer; when he could fight himself no longer. He stole to the door of Gretzel's room while she was at breakfast. The nurse had seen him coming and was running down the corridor as fast as she could run. She heard the maid's shriek of terror and forced both hands over her ears.

Schriftman clutched at his heart. He grew ten years older in a minute as he saw the girl shrink away. She did not cry out again, but she kept her head hidden beneath the bedclothes.

"Kleine mädchen," he trembled. "Don't do dot. See, I vill go! I vill go und neffer again vill I scare you!"

She did not move.

"Goot-pye, kleine mädchen!" He trembled· "Goot-pye, leedle brincess."

As he backed toward the door there was something in his voice that made Gretzel peek out over the bedclothes. The detail that riveted her attention was his wasted form. He looked to her as though he had been sick. It recalled to her all the misery of her own long sickness—all the ache of those long nights now gone forever. She saw pain written in his eyes, and she who knew so well the horror of pain suddenly forgot in her wider sympathy all her personal fears of the man. Her little mother's heart grew big with pity. With her own ache gone and the ache in him so manifest, she felt the stronger of the two. There was no longer any reason why she should be afraid of him. It was he who looked afraid.

She sat up in bed and studied him a moment as he cowed away from her. Then she reached for her egg.

"Santy," she said, "come here."

Like a blind man, he obeyed.

"Now," she said firmly, "you mus' eat an egg. So you will be gross an' rosy."

Schriftman does not operate any more; he is too busy obeying his daughter's orders for one thing. But he does lecture, and last year he concluded his speech to the senior medical class with these words: "It costs much to love, ach, yet, but—not too much."

Ladybird

By Edith Barnard

It began on a very beautiful morning in early June. The roses in the rectory garden were all a-bloom, great white clouds were floating as near to earth as they dared, songbirds were busy with nests and nestlings, and the very young rector came out of his house to enjoy it all. It had been his house for only a few weeks; he was so young as a rector that this was his first charge, and so young as a man that he longed to lay aside his clerical suit and go swimming or fishing. He was both old enough and young enough, however, to enjoy every cloud and blossom and song; he was far from those monotonous years of middle life when one day is much like another.

His rectory garden was, indeed, a charming one. His parishioners had seen to that. The rectory was new and looked old, the garden was new and looked old; even the hedge that surrounded the garden and churchyard was tall of growth, but had been planted only a year or so. The church was the fashionable house of worship for the fashionable new village—the village just far enough out of town to make a convenient between-season resting place for those favoured townsfolk who could spend their time as they spent their money—pretty much as they willed. They wanted their church and rectory to be as beautiful and Old-World like as possible, and they had made them so.

The rector was not one for whose idle hands his arch-enemy might find mischief; he had come out to his piazza whistling, his hands in his pockets; but he saw at a glance that the roses bordering his front walk would look the better for a little trimming, and straightway he set to work. Still whistling, busy with knife and twine, happy as a school-boy whittling a man-o'-war, he did not notice that some one came through the little gate, and stood quite near, behind him.

A small voice said: "Good-morning!"

The young rector turned quickly, and beheld an amazingly red little figure. Her frock was red, her shoes and stockings were red, and her over-large hat was red. She wore white kid gloves and carried a small red cardcase. But her little face was not red; it was white, very white, and framed in a mass of flying black hair; her eyes were black, too, and large and wide opened. The rector stared at the brilliant little figure; she might have been the picture of an elf-child, were it not for the amusing imitations of grown-up conventionalities, the gloves and cardcase.

"Good-morning!" she said again, in just the same tone.

"Oh! I beg your pardon! Good-morning!" said the rector.

"You are the new rector, I know," said the child. "I am Miss Torrington, and I've come to call on your wife and daughters."

The rector's stare turned into a look of frank amazement, even bewilderment. "My—I beg your pardon; I'm afraid I don't quite understand!"

"I've come to call on your wife and daughters," repeated the little girl. "I'm Miss Virginia Witherspoon Torrington," she declared convincingly, "and I live next door to you—over there, in the big house."

"Oh, yes, I see," replied the rector. He was as punctiliously polite as the occasion demanded, but his mouth twitched just a little. "I'm sure I beg your pardon. I must be very stupid. But I regret to say that I have no wife or daughters."

"Are you sure you haven't" asked Miss Torrington.

"I'm afraid I am," said the rector, humbly and apologetically. "Won't you come in and call on me instead?"

Miss Torrington pondered for a moment. "I think a gentleman ought to pay the *first* call on a lady, don't you?"

The rector bit his lip, but the child went on: "Maggie O'Brien certainly told me there were three ladies in the family here!"

"Oh!" exclaimed the young rector, as if he had found something. "Why, of course, there are! I didn't think of that! There *are* three ladies, and it's very good of you to call on them. They'll be delighted. You see, it was your speaking of my wife and daughters that made me forget."

"What are they, then?" asked the child.

"One is my grandmother, and the others are my aunts."

"Oh, really? I should think you'd like the grandmother one. You know if you don't have a grandmother already you can't ever get one, and you can get a wife and daughters."

"That's very true," acknowledged the rector. "I suppose you haven't a grandmother yourself?"

"No, but I have a father—an only father. You know what *that* is, I suppose; only fathers are a great deal of care. Mine needs a lot of looking after."

"Well, I'll tell you," suggested the rector. "I'll lend you my grandmother once in a while! That is, if you will come over and help me occasionally, I will. I hope you'll have the time to come. You don't have to look after your father every minute, do you?"

"Oh, no," she replied. "He's away a good deal. But I think I ought to see her before I borrow her, don't you?"

"Oh, I beg your pardon," said the rector again. "If you'll come into the house I'll call her, and my aunts, too. I'm so glad you don't mind their not being my wife and daughters."

He held open for her the door of the little parlour, and was starting toward the stairs when Miss Torrington called: "Oh—er—!"

When the rector turned toward her she said: "I'd like to send up my cards, please. I don't often get a chance to use them, you know, and—"

The rector said, gravely: "I quite understand. I ought to have thought of it. I never send my own cards up to them, and I suppose that's why I forgot." He was about to take them in his hand, but Miss Torrington drew them back.

"Maggie O'Brien always takes them on a silver tray. I'm very partic'lar about it at my house."

The rectory owned no silver tray, but there was a silver butter-dish, a valued family heirloom, much too large and fine for every-day use. It was kept on the sideboard in the tiny dining-room. The rector gravely brought it; Miss Torrington seemed quite satisfied, even a little awed at its elegance, and deposited her cards upon it.

That was the way her first visit began; it ended in ginger cookies, and hugs and kisses from the grandmother, and tremulous tears, mixed with laughter, from the aunts. On the second visit she went all over the little place with the rector; together they hunted for eggs—the younger aunt owned four hens and a rooster. They plucked delicious red strawberries, and gathered a bunch of red roses. There were two acres of greenhouses on the grounds of the big house—but these were really, truly roses, roses meant to be gathered.

On her third visit she made herself at home, and from that day she owned the rectory, the grandmother, the aunts, and the rector. In everything but years he was as young as she, and sometimes she was as old as he. All through the summer they played together, for the child blossomed into rosiness, and her father came to rely more and more on the advice of the aunts and the borrowed grandmother concerning her. She flitted between the two houses, and that was the way she won her name. The young rector would say:

"Come, little Ladybird, fly away home"—and home was on either side of the hedge. The name stayed with her always, for it suited her well—the black-eyed little elf-child in her red frocks.

The second summer brought her back early, flying through the gate into the arms of the borrowed grandmother, hugging the aunts while they laughed and exclaimed over her growth, and dancing up and down before the young rector, who was far more glad to get her back than he himself knew. They taught each other many things that summer—to fish and to climb trees, to say rimes which some day might catch fairies, to throw stones straight, and to make dolls into Indians and early Christian martyrs.

One day the rector, while writing a sermon, saw through his study window an unusual movement in the hedge just opposite. His window opened to the floor, so he went out of it, on tiptoe, to investigate. Ladybird was on the ground, trying to manage a very large saw, and scraping away with all her might at the trunk of one of the hedge plants. When the rector stood over her she looked up and laughed.

"I wanted to surprise you, old parson," she said. "I'm going to cut a hole in the hedge; it takes too long to go around by the gates!"

The rector remonstrated, but she had her way, and before long there was a plainly marked path from the gap in the hedge to the study window. It was even more plainly marked during the third summer, for they began to read together, and the study held a new world for her. There were no books at the big house, and the rectory held more of books than of anything else, except peace and gentleness. The next year the borrowed grandmother was not there to welcome her, but the play and the study went on.

When she was twelve she asked him the first question concerning himself. She was sitting on the sill of the long window, her thin little elbows on her knees, her chin in her little claw-like hands; she was looking at the clouds and the sunset, without seeing either. The rector could no longer see to write, and had come to the window to watch the glowing west.

Whenever she scolded him, or was very serious, she would use his name. After a while she asked "Mark, why do you stay in the country?"

"It's a good place to stay in, isn't it?" he answered.

"Yes, of course. But father said that you had been asked to go to St. John's in town. He said you were—you—Why do you stay here, Mark?"

The young rector stood looking over her head at the sunset and made no reply. Ladybird looked up at him, then out toward the west again.

"I know why, Mark! *They* wouldn't like the town."

"They've always had the country, you know," he said simply. "They were so happy to come here, and they love it."

Presently he lifted her up. "Good-night, Ladybird," he said gaily. "Fly away home!" But she walked slowly that night, and the rector went back to his sermon, which was on the simple life; his parishioners loved theories.

When Ladybird was fourteen, the rector found her one day weeping over a novel. That night he talked for hours with her father and when she came the next day she told him, delightedly and proudly, but just a little tearfully, that she was going to boarding-school. For two summers she did not come back, but at sixteen she took him again for her confidant, telling him all about the boys, the flowers and notes they sent, what she said in return, how this one had mournful eyes and that one did dance like a dream. He enjoyed it all, and teased her, and after that there were no further breaks in their friendship. She wrote him from time to time, and he knew all her love affairs by heart, and laughed immoderately over them. When she was eighteen she came back for a few weeks, and they were weeks of delight at the rectory; she made them love her all over again, and after she had left for Europe the rector kept the shade of the long window pulled down, until the grass had grown up again on the little path through the hedge.

A year or two after that her father became governor of his State, and Ladybird became Miss Torrington indeed. She wrote long, infrequent letters to the rector, and to the one old aunt; they heard of her through every one, and when she came back to open the big house for a great house-party they saw for themselves how beautiful and charming and gracious she was, and they guessed how many people beside themselves loved her. Even then, with all the house full, she would sometimes steal off, toward sunset time, and flit through the gap in the hedge to the rectory.

Then, after a year or two more, she came back to stay longer, not in red now, but in black. The elderly cousin who lived with her took the care of the house, and Ladybird, in her first loneliness, sought out her oldest friend. She made him drive with her, walk with her, read with her, and he obeyed her will by day and lay wakeful at night, with aching heart and stricken conscience. They read over the old books together, and almost all of their talks began with: "Oh, do you remember?" They went together very often to the grave of the dear borrowed grandmother; Ladybird tried to make some ginger cookies by the old recipe, but they were not very good. They got up at dawn one day, and went fishing again, and as in the old days Ladybird caught all the fish, and wouldn't take them off the hook. Their favourite walk was along the crest of the hill; there they could look down on the church and the big house, and all the other houses and their beautiful parks. From there they could watch the sunset best, and there it was even cooler and quieter than in the rectory garden.

One day they sat on the rock ledge until the red glow of the setting sun had nearly faded. Their talk had ceased. The man was sitting below the girl, and she looked down at his head; there were grey hairs here and there. Her lips trembled a little, and she leaned over farther. The rector looked up; he found her face close to his.

"Mark," she began, but he sprang up quickly and held out his hands: "Come, little Ladybird, fly away home!" The girl did not move.

"No," she said. "Sit down. I want to say something to you."

He said again imperatively: "No. Come, Ladybird! It is damp here. It is too near the clouds!" She saw how white his face had grown, and her own flushed; they went down without speaking.

After that day the rector became very busy with parish work, and resolutely refused to take any more walks or drives. Guests came to the big house, and after that more guests and more. There was one who came more often than the others, and at the end of the summer the rector watched him drive away with Ladybird. She had come to bid him good-by, but he had basely hidden himself upstairs!

During the winter that followed the rectory heard from her but seldom. Rumours came of her engagement; the rumours were denied, then re-affirmed. The old aunt declared that the child would have written at once if they were true; the rector made no comment. In the spring he made some changes in his garden, and when the roses bloomed he busied himself there more than he had ever done before. One warm June day, while he way tying up the swaying branches that bordered his front walk, and thinking of the quaint little red-frocked elf-child who had come to him there years before, she came through the gate and up the walk toward him, her hands outstretched, her face all gladness and youth and beauty. "I've come here first," she cried. "I've come to call!"

They both laughed, and went in to see the old aunt, the lapse of all the years bridged over between them. She begged to be allowed to stay to tea, and declared the biscuits the most delicious that even the rectory oven had ever baked, and the gooseberry jam as good as ever. After tea she went, uninvited, to the rector's study. She stood for an instant in the doorway, looking around the familiar room; then she looked up at the man standing beside her, and moved toward the long window. "Come with me to the hedge, old parson," she called, and before he could answer she flitted through the window and toward the familiar gap.

When he reached her side he found her standing with tightly clasped hands. She heard him come, and cried: "Oh, Mark, Mark, what is it? Who put it there?"

The rector had no voice to answer her, and after a moment of waiting she turned to him. "Did you put that there? Did you, did you put that there?" Still he made no answer, and with a sob she moved off toward the gate. Then he spoke.

"Oh, Ladybird, Ladybird, I *had* to! Don't go away like that! Ladybird—see—it is a rosebush, a red rose, Ladybird. I tell you I had to! Virginia!"

But she had run through the rectory gate, and was already on her way to the big house. For weeks after that he did not see her. She came to the rectory only when he was away, and again there were guests at the big house, and again one guest who came more frequently than all the others. The rector came upon this young man one day, down by the river. He was looking very unhappy indeed, so evidently unhappy that the rector, accustomed as he was to respond to all appeals for pity and mercy, involuntarily stopped. The young man held out his hand.

"Thank you, sir," he said, and laughed a little. "I see you know what's up with me. I didn't know I was such a fool as to show it."

"I ought not to have stopped," said the rector. "I beg your pardon." He would have gone on, but the boy touched his arm.

"Please don't say that, sir. I'd rather have seen you than any one else I know. In fact, I was coming to the rectory—later. I thought perhaps I could get you to help me out, sir."

The rector winced a little at the boy's deference, but asked: "What is it?"

Again the other laughed, somewhat ruefully. "Oh, I'm sure you know," he said. "I've loved her ever since my freshman year, when she was at boarding-school. She's never done anything else but turn me down, but she says this has got to be the last time. I thought if you could be persuaded to say a word to her, sir, she might look at it differently. She cares more for you than for any one else, and you've always been like a father to her, sir!"

The rector looked at the honest, boyish face, and said: "I'll do as you ask."

Therefore, an hour later, Ladybird was standing before him, in her own drawing-room, her cheeks flaming with anger. "Did he ask you to come here, or did you come of your own accord?" she demanded.

"Both, Virginia," answered the truthful rector meekly.

"Don't you dare to call me Virginia," she commanded. "You know I hate it! If you came of your own accord you are an interfering person, and if you came because he told you to, you're a—you're a—"

"The boy loves you very much, Virginia, and I think he'd make you a good husband."

"Do you want me to marry him? Are you tired of looking at me?"

"I think he would make you a good husband."

"Do you want to see me married?"

The rector got up, and started for the door, but she stood in front of him. "Was that why you planted the rosebush in the hedge?" she asked. He bowed before her, and she watched him grow pale. Then she laughed, a little low, tender laugh, and—kissed him. The rector was dimly aware of her swift rush from the room, and of his own going home blindly.

The next day he left his house early, to walk over the hills to the home of a distant poor parishioner; coming home late in the afternoon he came upon her, seated on the ledge of rock upon the hillcrest. She walked calmly to meet him, and standing bravely before him she asked him the question. It was then that the rector discovered that the Angel with which he had been struggling was not, as he had believed, the Angel of Temptation, but, indeed, the Angel of Life. As they walked down later, in the red glow, hand in hand, he asked:

"Do you remember, Ladybird, the cards on the silver butter-dish?"

She laughed and said: "And those first ginger cookies?"

"Do you remember the day you were up in the apple tree, Ladybird, and hit me with an apple?"

"And that was before I learned to 'throw straight,' too!"

"You were very repentant, so we went fishing the next day. You leaned over the brook to see yourself, and your hair fell into the water."

"It wasn't very long," she laughed.

"How long is it now, Ladybird?" he asked.

She pursed up her lips. "Oh, longer," she said.

At the edge of the woods they stood for a last look at the churchyard below. "Can you give up the other life, Ladybird?" he asked seriously.

"There is no other," she replied softly.

"Oh, Ladybird, Ladybird, when will you come home?" he cried.

She shook her head at him, laughing. "Oh, parson, old parson, you couldn't ask one great, important question, but you're a genius at asking silly ones!"

The Drasnoe Pipe-Line

By Arthur Stanwood Pier

On a windy and sullen morning in May, 1864, a caravan of fifty wagons, each piled high with barrels, crawled down the muddy road from the Drasnoe oil-field. Beside the leading team of the procession walked a one-armed man and a fifteen-year-old boy. The faces of the two were not cheerful. That of the man was sad; the boy's was anxious.

Behind trooped the other teamsters, shouting, cracking their long blacksnake whips, swearing at the horses, the mud, the threatening sky. They were always boisterous and blasphemous during the long daily haul.

The one-armed man and the boy walked together silently by preference.

"Do you suppose General Grant is done fighting by this time?" the boy asked, at last.

His companion smiled sadly.

"I guess he won't be done fighting for a good many months yet. But I shouldn't wonder if he was out of the Wilderness by now."

"It must be a big battle," said the boy. "Most as big as Gettysburg, don't you think, John?"

"Pretty nigh."

"How long do you suppose before we hear about father—whether he's all right?"

"Depends on how long the battle lasts. I guess in a week."

"That's an awful time to wait. Your folks didn't hear about you till ten days after it happened, did they?" He glanced at the empty sleeve.

"I believe not. But there was a good deal to 'tend to after Gettysburg. Maybe there won't be so much in this battle."

"I wish I was down there instead of hauling oil every day," said the boy.

"You're making more money hauling oil," replied the teamster. The boy glanced at him, hurt and scornful. "Yes," continued the man, in his quiet voice, "you're making quite a heap of money. And as long as you're doing that, what's the good of running off to fight? That's what all that gang behind us would tell you—and there's mighty few of them that are staying away from the war to support their mothers." In his quiet voice there brimmed suddenly the full bitterness of contempt: "Floaters—and stay-at-homes!"

The boy thought that perhaps John Denny was hard on the men. At least it was not cowardice that kept them hauling oil when they might be shouldering rifles. The boy had seen too many evidences of their courage and recklessness to believe that; he had seen also too many rough-and-tumble fights among them to believe that a distaste for fighting kept them in the paths of peace. Nor was it altogether greed for the dollars that were being so lavishly squandered in the oil country in those days that detained them; among them all there was hardly one who was laying money by.

The boy himself, with his small farm wagon, had earned as much as seventy dollars in a week. But what the men earned so rapidly they spent as royally; it was the excitement of a sudden prosperity, greater than any they had ever expected or foreseen and the joy of indulging it had made them heedless of the call to arms.

The boy was aware that whether they liked John Denny or not—and in view of his ill-concealed contempt it was hard for them to like him—they yielded him position and respect.

The summer before, while the armies of North and South were battling in one corner of Pennsylvania, in another there had sprung up excitement over oil. John Denny had returned from Gettysburg with his right arm shot off at the shoulder, and had found this excitement at its height.

He could make a living, one-armed as he was, on the farm. But instead, he mortgaged the place and drilled for oil. The hole was a dry one; and Denny faced the world in debt as well as crippled.

Fortunately, the great Drasnoe wells began to flow at about that time, and teamsters were needed to transport the oil to the railroad eight miles away. The prices of oil and labour were high; and after six months of hard teaming, Denny had paid off his debt. And his fellow teamsters, who had mostly drifted in from "outside," yielded him grudgingly a certain admiration. It was not diminished by the fact that he held them all at a distance—all but the boy, Elmer Todd, who was the youngest of the teamsters, and whom he took under his protection.

At a turn in the road they saw a wagon backed up into a field. Two men were unloading sections of pipe. A third, a young man in high boots, such as the teamsters wore, stood by, giving directions. He looked up at Denny and the boy, and his face brightened pleasantly.

"Morning!" he said. "We'll get the last of our pipe laid to-day."

Denny stopped his team. "That so?" he said, grimly. "You expect when it's laid it will stay, Mr. Ross?"

The young man's eyes narrowed together into a frown; his clean-cut face assumed a more determined expression. "That's what I expect," he said.

"There's some talk to indicate it won't," said Denny. He was in a black mood, and this young superintendent, who was making his fortune instead of hearing arms, came in for a share of his contempt.

"When you hear any such talk, Mr. Denny, discourage it," said Ross. "The men won't gain by fighting with us over this matter."

"I guess," observed Denny, brutally, "that if you were any good for fighting you would be elsewhere, Mr. Ross. Get up, boys!" He cracked his whip and walked on beside his horses.

"That brought the blood to his face, didn't it?" he said to the boy, with a laugh.

Beside the road and up over the rising meadows ran a ridge of freshly turned earth. "It looks," said the boy, after a silence, "as if we wouldn't make many more trips."

"Yes. Once they begin pumping oil through that pipe-line, it's back to the farm for you and me. Well—teaming has been a lift for me, anyway, this winter."

"I've got three hundred dollars all my own," said the boy, proudly. "It will start me in at college some time—when father comes home."

"It's more, I guess, than a good many have saved up." Denny glanced back along the line of wagons. "And when they're cut off from their day's work—I expect there will be trouble."

The teamsters observed no great secrecy in expressing their emotions and in making threats. In consequence of specific declarations which he had heard, at nine o'clock that night Denny was crossing the Drasnoe oil-field, following the ridge that denoted the pipe-line.

As he walked, he kept his eyes on the ridge, intent for any sign that it had been tampered with. After he had gone a mile he came to a strip of woods, through which the pipe-line was laid, although at this point the road diverged and made a circuit.

The woods were not more than half a mile in area, and except for another clump of forest six miles distant, near the railway station, made the only secluded spot through which the pipe-line passed. The teamsters all lived in the vicinity of the Drasnoe field.

"They won't go six miles to cut pipe," Denny thought. "Right here's the place to catch 'em."

The sky had cleared during the afternoon; it was a mild, clear night, with a moon that showed the road from the edge of the woods for some distance.

Denny sat down on a log, lighted the lantern he had brought, and taking a book from his pocket, began to read.

Presently he looked up, and made out a figure approaching across the fields, following the pipe-line. He shielded the lantern and waited. When the approaching man entered the woods he stepped out to meet him.

"Mr. Ross!" Denny ejaculated, contemptuously.

"What are you doing here?" The superintendent's voice was menacing.

"I'm constable of this borough, Mr. Ross, and I'm here to prevent mischief."

"Then we're on the same errand."

"Are we?" Denny asked. "You'd better go home to bed, Mr. Ross. You don't want to get mixed up in this. You wouldn't be any good—and it mightn't be good for you."

"Look here, John Denny!" Ross stepped up close; his eyes flashed in the light of the lantern that Denny held aloft. "You the same as called me a coward to-day, and because you've got only one arm I can't resent it! You told me that if I was any good for fighting I'd be somewhere else than here. Now I want you to know one thing—my plans were laid last week to leave for the front next Monday. You think I haven't wanted to go! I don't tell my private affairs to you or any other man, but I'll say this much: over in Oil City I'm leaving a family provided for if anything happens to me."

"If that's the case," Denny said, slowly, "I take it back, Mr. Ross. I take everything back."

They sat down together on the log and talked amicably. Denny's thoughts were turned back to his war experience. He told the new recruit stories of campaigning and battle. Ross listened with a respect of which his maimed subordinate became somehow conscious. That tribute of respect from one whom he had both envied and despised, and whom he had come so suddenly to like, swept the bitterness from Denny's soul.

"You're giving up a good bit to go," he said, at last. "Old man Drasnoe likes you; you've got a start toward being a millionaire. You throw it all up and go off to the war—and you can't tell what you may come back to."

"I'll have to run my chance," Ross answered.

"Mr. Drasnoe satisfied to have you leave?"

"Yes," replied Mr. Ross, quietly, "Mr. Drasnoe is quite satisfied. He likes the man I've picked to take my place." Denny's interest was at once awakened.

"And who might that be?"

Ross hesitated. "It's hardly time to talk about it yet."

"Oh, all right. I wasn't meaning to pry."

They arranged to divide the night into watches Denny was to sleep until twelve, then Ross would rouse him and sleep till four.

At about one o'clock, while Ross, lying at the foot of a tree, was sleeping, the marauders came. Denny saw them as they climbed over the fence by the roadside. He awakened Ross, and said:

"They're coming. You'd better leave this to me—as constable. If they see you, they'll get ugly. You go in behind that thicket and wait."

Ross protested. "You can come out if you're needed," Denny said; and the superintendent reluctantly withdrew. Denny put out his lantern, and stepping behind a great oak, awaited the approach.

There were a dozen men, carrying lanterns, mattocks and spades; they passed close by where Denny stood.

"Spread out, now—and rip it up all along!" cried one; and he lifted his mattock and brought it down upon the earth.

Denny stepped forward.

"Boys," he said, "hold on!"

They faced him, startled. The one who had spoken caught up a lantern and turned it on him.

"Denny!" he exclaimed. "Spyin' on us!"

"I'm borough constable," said Denny. "Destroying property has a penalty attached." The men crowded round him, disturbed, angry, threatening.

"Well, here we are!" said the leader, scornfully. "Arrest us."

"There won't be any arrests if there's no damage done, O'Brien," Denny answered.

O'Brien turned and struck his mattock into the earth. "Show him a little damage, boys," he urged. "Yank up the pipe."

The others set to work, cursing at Denny meanwhile. The dirt flew; they flung it jeeringly at him.

"All right," said Denny. "You are twelve men against one. Maybe I can't arrest you to-night, but I've got your names."

In a few moments they had exposed the pipe, which was not buried deep. Then O'Brien knelt and sawed it through in two places, and cast the section at Denny's feet.

"There!" he said. "How d'ye like the looks of that, Mr. Constable? And now, so's you won't follow us and see where else we operate, we'll just tie you up for a while."

"You fellows will be piling up trouble for yourselves," Denny warned them. "Murphy and Conway, there—you ought to have more sense."

One of these two men, Murphy, spoke in a low voice, unwillingly:

"I guess maybe we'd better quit. If he reports us—"

"He ain't going to report us!" interrupted O'Brien. "He don't dare. Come, boys, get a-hold of him, and we'll tie him up—"

He advanced a step toward Denny, and in the same instant Denny drew a revolver and levelled it at O'Brien's head.

"Don't lay a hand on me," he said, quietly.

"Get behind him and grab him, somebody!" shouted O'Brien. "Spread out and get round him."

But the men hesitated. "I said we'd ought to have wore masks!" muttered one. "He's seen us all now."

O'Brien made a quick dash, trying to circle Denny, who whirled and held the revolver pointed at O'Brien's face.

"Jump on him now!" shouted O'Brien; and then one, bolder than the others, sprang upon Denny's shoulders and bore him to the ground. O'Brien was instantly upon him also, got possession of his revolver, and then with breathless imprecations began winding a rope about his ankles.

"All right!" muttered Denny. "You've got me—but you fellows will pay for this."

Then Ross walked into the midst of the group. The leader of the gang looked up from where he knelt. "It's you, is it?" he said, defiantly.

Ross turned from him to the others.

"Will you give me five minutes?" he asked. "I'm in your power; I'm all alone. Will you let me have five minutes to talk?"

"Go on," said one of the men.

"Just five minutes, mind," said O'Brien, truculently. He tightened the rope that bound Denny's arm behind his back and stood up.

"When I came here to-night," Ross began, persuasively, "it was with the idea that there might be some trouble over this pipe-line. But though I was expecting trouble, there was only one man that I looked on as my personal enemy, and that was John Denny. He called me a coward to my face this morning; and when I came here a couple of hours ago, and found him on duty as constable, I felt I'd found more trouble than I was looking for. Well, we talked the whole matter out—and came to an understanding. And maybe, after talking this other matter out, you and I can come to an understanding.

"Here's the situation. A pump and a pipe together are going to do for almost nothing more than all you men have been in the habit of doing for a good deal of money. They're going to put you out of business. So you get together and decide to put the pipe out of business. And you mean to keep putting it out of business just as often as it resumes. Isn't that stating the case."

Two or three of the men laughed uneasily; there was no dissent.

"Now you can do that to-night; you can keep on doing it for a while. But you must see—your common sense must tell you—that when an economical way of doing a thing is discovered, the expensive way has got to be abandoned. They are to have a pipe-line over in the Deepwater valley, and the teamsters will have to quit; they are to have another up at Anderson, and the teamsters will have to quit; they're putting pipe-lines in everywhere. It's a fact you've got to face; the day of the teamster in the oil regions is over.

"Just to make it practical—to demonstrate it, not to make threats—listen. You cut this pipe to-night. What happens? There are two witnesses against you—John Denny and myself. All that the law requires is two witnesses. It's true you have us in your power to-night—but I hardly think any of you mean to do murder in cold blood.

You may think of keeping us out of the way for a while—maybe using force on us to make us hold our tongues. But some time you'll have to let us go free—and I expect we will go free without making any promises."

He spoke these words with slow distinctness and emphasis; there was an uneasy stirring in the crowd.

"Moreover," Ross continued, "before I started out to-night I left a note at home, saying where I was going and why. If I should mysteriously disappear, that note will afford a clue. You may all feel that you're strong enough to defy the law and destroy property and commit violence. But even supposing this is true—what can you gain by it? Do you think the company whose pipe you cut will ever again employ you to drive its wagons? Drasnoe would rather let his oil forever run to waste than be coerced into letting you handle it. And you can't so easily carry matters with a high hand—"

"You begin to threaten us!" cried O'Brien. "We've had enough—"

"I don't mean to threaten," Ross replied. "I'm just trying to make a complete statement of the case. In a moment I'll talk in a way that you can't regard as threatening. But as to your being able to override the law—you know, of course, what will happen. The company will spend its last cent fighting for its rights. It will hire men to protect its property. The community will be roused against you. You'll have to fight with the company's watchmen; you can't go on cutting its pipe with impunity. And meanwhile you'll be blacklisted by the company, whereas, if you accept this overturn in a peaceful spirit, the company will try to give work of some kind to as many of you as want it. Now I've come to the end of everything that may sound threatening. Are you willing I should go on for a few moments longer?"

"No," shouted O'Brien. But "Yes!" cried the others; and some of them turned to O'Brien and bade him be still.

"I want you to know that last week I tendered my resignation as superintendent, to take effect next Monday. Next Monday I start for Virginia, to join Grant's army. It's just occurred to me that that would be a pretty good thing for those of you to do who are out of a job and so have a hankering to fight somebody." He spoke the words with a smile; by the lantern-light he could see the smile reflected on the face of some of the men. "I hope you'll think better of fighting the company—for if you don't, I'll have to stay here and deprive General Grant of my services." This time the smile on his face was echoed by a murmur of laughter. "I'd be mighty glad if those of you who feel bound to fight somebody would join me next Monday and start for the Wilderness. I don't know that it would be any more of a fight than you'd get by staying here and tackling the company—but I guess it would be enough. That's all I have to say; and now if you think the only thing is to string me up on one of those trees, I can't help myself."

"I guess there won't be any lynching!" muttered one of the men; from the others there issued only sheepish, uncomfortable laughter. O'Brien was silent.

"Well," remarked Murphy, at last. "I don't know but I may join your soldier squad on Monday, captain. Looks like things will be kind of quiet round here for a full-grown fightin' man."

At this there was loud laughter, and Ross knew that he had won.

"You think, Mr. Ross," said a man, hesitatingly, "if a fellow was to stay, the company might find him a job?"

"I think so. That will be one of the problems for my successor—who, by the way, is lying there with his feet tied."

The men gazed at one another; Denny lay speechless and amazed. Then one of the men turned to O'Brien.

"O'Brien," he said, gravely, "if you and me are looking for jobs, suppose we untie his feet."

At eight o'clock on Monday morning there waited at the railway station a group of ten men, who were starting South to join Grant's army. Among them was one whom the others half jestingly, yet half-seriously also, called "Captain." He stepped apart from the rest to speak to a one-armed man and a boy who had just driven up to the platform. The sound of the approaching train made itself heard.

"You'll be sure to see father for me, won't you, Mr. Ross?" said the boy.

"Sure. I'm glad you had word he was all right. I'll send you a letter as soon as I see him—and I'll tell him all about you. Good-by, Elmer!"

He turned to the one-armed man.

"Good-by, Denny!"

The train rushed along the platform as Denny gripped Ross's hand.

"Good-by, Mr. Ross—thank you—" His voice broke, but he regained it. "Come back to us—and come back—*whole!*"

Then, amid the cheers of the few who had gathered to see the departure, the recruits boarded the train, and the train pulled away.

"He *will* come back!" said Denny to Elmer, with conviction. "Even if the whole of Lee's army lays a trap for him, he'll come back."

Manuk Del Monte

By Rowland Thomas

Early one morning, just before the dawn, three of us were riding wearily down the slope of one of the great grassy hills—some people call them mountains—which lie between the provinces of Isabella and Nueva Vizcaya.

We had been travelling all night by moonlight, and now as the east was growing rosy we were winding down to a little wood in the valley, where we hoped to find a mountain stream to give us water for our breakfast, and a thing of far more importance, grazing for the horses, for it was the dry season, and the grass on the hills was parched and dead. The breakfast swung with mocking lightness behind Justin's saddle, merely a few handfuls of cold rice rolled in the butt of a banana leaf. It was also tiffin and dinner, for we were travelling light and fast, and carried not even chocolate, nothing but the rice.

I was watching the gyrations of the breakfast moodily, for I was sleepy and hungry and sore, when suddenly from the wood below us the crow of a cock rang out, shrill and triumphant. I was surprised, for few people live along a trail used mostly by bandits and head-hunters.

Suddenly from the slope of a farther hill the call rang out again, and then the whole wood echoed with the sounds of the farmyard.

"What town is this?" I asked the boys, although we were at least a day's journey from any settlement which I knew.

Justin laughed, and even Tranquid smiled stiffly.

"It is no town, señor," said Justin. "It is the *manuk del monte*—the wild chicken—which you hear."

After saddles were off and the horses' backs were washed, the animals rolled and grazed luxuriously by the swift, clear stream, and Tranquid, prince of servants, dexterously unrolled the breakfast.

He laid stones on the corners of the leaf, and patted the snowy mass of rice out smoothly, and filled a bamboo drinking-cup from the brook, while I pretended not to see. At meal-times Tranquid has a solemn and important air worthy of the most autocratic of London butlers, and I am a babe in his hands.

"Breakfast is served, señor," said Tranquid, gravely.

"I come," I replied, with equal gravity, and rolled over twice and came up on my knees, Japanese fashion, beside my lowly table.

Just as I was going to plunge my fingers into the rice, a cock crowed loud and clear among the trees close at hand. A great ferocity of meat hunger swept over me.

"Give me the boom-boom, Justin!" I commanded. "We will have manuk del monte for breakfast."

The cock crowed often while I stole through the undergrowth, as softly as the ferns and bristly creepers would let me.

As I drew near, the crowing ceased, and I was peering about the brush and shrub for a sight of the cock when—*whir*! From the lower branches of a tree, fifty feet above my head, a splendid bird shot out with a boom like a partridge and sailed away between the tree trunks, a dazzling vision of white and green and gold.

I was too startled to shoot, for I had never before seen chickens that roost like eagles and flew like pheasants and were as brilliant as humming-birds.

In a moment I heard his strong wings beating on the other side of the valley, and I went back and ate my rice quietly.

That incident began my acquaintance with the wild chickens, and they soon grew to be a very dear part of the forest life, bringing me an odd mixture of pleasant memory and homesickness as I listened to them.

We heard them always when we made and left our one-night homes along the trail. The cocks proved to be just as exacting husbands as their domesticated cousins, crowing their families home and abroad with fussy punctuality.

If a gay young cockerel or a giddy pullet lingered too long afield, the lord of the flock grew noisy with anxiety as the sunset faded. With the dawn he woke, brisk and important, and woe betide the sleepyhead of the family.

There was no "Rouse up, sweet slugabed" for him, but an ear-splitting call, and we often chuckled at thought of the sheepish haste of the laggard when that sound penetrated to his sleepy brain.

A tropical forest is a thing of awe and mystery, with its eternal dim twilight and tangled creepers, and innumerable dark vistas which hide inhabitants one seldom hears and never sees. Most of the creatures seem to feel the silent immensity and vagueness as a man does, and seek safety in unobtrusiveness.

These brave, cheery birds alone were unaffected by it, and they crowed and cackled and clucked about their business of living as carelessly as if there were no such thing as fear in the world.

Yet with all their independence they showed a baffling shyness, and many weeks went by before I caught more than a distant glimpse of one.

Tranquid hunted them with painful devotion. But he was a child of the cities, lost in the mountains as a puppy would have been. When a cock crowed near a camping-place, his face would brighten hopefully, and he would go creeping off with the noiselessness of a young elephant. Back and forth he crashed in the brush, pulling branches aside with excessive caution and peeping behind them.

At last the bird would flush from a tree and shoot away in a blur of coloured light. Then Tranquid would straighten up with a nervous jerk, and cry triumphantly:

"There, señor, I have found him! There he goes. Look! Look!" pointing up to the tree where he had been.

On these occasions Justin always lay on the grass and laughed.

Justin was a woodland philosopher, and had discovered that town-bred folk and wild chickens had been sent into the world for his amusement. He never deigned to take any further part in the pursuit.

When it came to stalking a deer or running down a pig he was all eagerness and skill, and would lead me for hours without a thought of rest, but chickens were beneath him. Occasionally, however, as we rode along, a crow would caw somewhere above us. Then Justin was full of excitement.

"Look, señor!" he would shout, pointing up to the empty sky. "I have found him. There! There!"

In spite of Justin's jesting, my desire to see a wild cock face to face only increased with repeated failure.

I never tried to shoot one after that first experience. I would as soon have thought of shooting at a monkey. But I wanted to have one for my own, to look at, and draw pictures of, and show to my poor friends who lived down in the plains through the hot season, and complained of prickly heat. I even dreamed of presenting one to my friend, the captain, and letting him create a new and lusty race of fowls, a breed which would meet the hawk in his own element, and laugh at woven-wire fences.

At last, up in a little mountain village, my opportunity came. Tranquid announced, with the respectful elation he sometimes permitted himself, that a man had a wild rooster. Would the señor like to come to see it?

The señor was willing, so we went down the narrow grass-grown street together, stepping carefully over the babies and pigs that were basking in the sun.

In the yard of a little tumble-down shack we found a rusty brown bird tied to a post by a bit of twine about his leg. The old man, his owner, scattered a few kernels of corn, and the poor dingy thing pecked at them in a half-hearted way. A hen came bustling up and he pecked peevishly at her once or twice, and then hopped back to his post and stood there, dull and round-shouldered, like a sulky boy who had decided that the corn was not of much importance, anyway, and had put his hands in his pockets.

I was slow to believe that this could be a brother of the swift, bright bird which had boomed out of a treetop that first morning, but I presently discovered that it was. The long, slender body, the powerful wings, the sharp, heavy bill, were the product of generations of wild life. And under the dust and rustiness of the feathers there were still traces of the green and gold of the forest. The changes were due only to a changed mode of life.

"The man says," explained Tranquid, "that he has had this rooster for a long time, and it is dirty. He says he will catch a clean one for the señor, if he pleases."

Of course the señor pleased; and one bright morning we set out. The old man, our guide, marched in front, most importantly, for it is not every day that one has a chance to show a señor what a clever man one is at catching wild chickens, and the old man knew that his grandchildren would tell their children about this expedition.

Under his arm he carried a red fighting cock. It struck me as a bit odd to carry such an animal on a hunting trip, but I asked no questions. One feels no surprise in the Philippines in meeting people with roosters under their arms; it is quite the usual thing. Tranquid followed the old man, respectfully hopeful. Then came Justin, smiling, and I brought up the rear.

A mile or so from the village the wall of the forest rose, dark and impenetrable. But at one point a stream came down from the hills, and there the field extended into the woods for a little way, making a sort of room, cool and shadowy, and carpeted with short, thick turf.

Here the old man halted, and waited till we all stood about him. Then he drew from the pocket of his blouse a bundle of twine, wound on four pointed sticks. Justin stopped smiling. Anything in the nature of a trap, anything which matched man's wits against the instinct of the wild creatures, interested Justin.

The old man chose a spot of level ground and set to work. He drove one of the little stakes into the ground, uncoiled the twine, drove another, and so on, until he had marked out a square, about a yard on a side. On three sides the twine was carried on the stakes a few inches above the ground, and from this fence, every hand's breadth or so, hung a little noose of fibre.

The fourth side of the square was a wall of brush, and at the centre of this the old man now drove a fifth stake, and tied his fighting cock to it by a very short tether. Then he opened all the little nooses and spread them carefully on the ground within the square. Justin inspected the work.

"It is very good," he announced at last. "One would not believe that this old man could be so wise. The wild rooster hears this one. He wishes to fight. All roosters wish to fight always. He comes from the wood, dancing, so! This one crows and fluffs out his feathers, so! The wild rooster comes to the little fence and they look at each other, so!" said Justin, using Tranquid for illustration. "He cannot pass under the little fence; it is too low. He cannot step over it; it is too high. He hops, so! His foot falls in the noose, and—so!" said Justin, dancing on one foot and cackling shrilly. "*Abáa.* It is very good. The old man is much wiser than one would think to look at him."

The old man listened to this monologue with disgust.

"Now we shall go and be very quiet. The manuk del monte does not like noisy ones," he said, glancing at Justin.

So we went and sat down where some bushes screened us and yet left us a view of the trap. After half an hour Justin curled up and went to sleep. The breeze was cool and the grass was soft, and soon I followed his example.

I was awakened by a bell-like call from the forest. The captive rooster was dancing at his stake. Presently he flapped his wings and stood on tiptoe and answered scornfully. They challenged back and forth till at last, with a boom of wings, the wild cock, the very one I had been dreaming of, dropped on the grass.

As he caught sight of the traitor he spread all his splendid plumage and crowed again. And the red bird answered bravely. After all, it was not his fault that he was a traitor.

The wild bird ran forward with a swift, steady gait very unlike the awkward stride of his tame cousins, and lowered his head, and spread his ruff. Then he stood up straight and scratched sticks and grass into the air with a sturdy leg and crowed. The traitor kicked furiously at his tether, but it held, and the wild cock advanced to the fence.

For a moment the two looked at each other with lowered heads, and then they sprang. The traitor, of course, collapsed in an ignominious heap. As the wild cock landed inside the fence, his foot barely touched the ground. But the touch was enough. One of the little nooses tightened about his legs, and as he sprang again he, too, came down with a jerk.

The birds were rising to face each other when we ran forward, and he turned toward us at the noise. I expected to see him struggle madly to escape. But the brave little fellow faced us, and flapped his wings and stretched his neck, challenging us fearlessly. In a moment the old man had tossed a handkerchief over his head and loosened the noose, and I held him between my hands.

I could feel the little muscles taut as steel wires beneath my fingers, and the heart beating furiously, but he made no sound and did not struggle. I looked at the lustrous markings of his back and wings, and the long, drooping tail-feathers, and then all at once came a picture of the draggled, spiritless captive back in the old man's yard. I plucked away the handkerchief and tossed him into the air.

His wings beat very loud in the stillness, and we all started. Then I looked round sheepishly. Tranquid was staring up stupidly, with his mouth in a big, round O. Justin was laughing, but suddenly he pointed excitedly to Tranquid's mouth and shouted:

"Look, señor! I have found him. There he goes. Look! Look!" And it would be hard to say whether the old man gazed at Justin or at me with the deeper disgust.

"THREE OF US WERE RIDING DOWN THE SLOPE OF
THE GREAT, GRASSY HILLS"

- Manuk Del Monte

From the painting by by W. H. D. Koerner

The Man Without a Country

By Edward Everett Hale

I suppose that very few casual readers of the New York Herald of August 18th observed in an obscure corner among the "Deaths," the announcement—

"Nolan. Died, on board U. S. Corvette Levant, Lat. 2° 11′ S., Long. 131° W., on the 11th of May, Philip Nolan."

I happened to observe it, because I was stranded at the old Mission-House in Makinaw, waiting for a Lake Superior steamer which did not choose to come, and I was devouring to the very stubble all the current literature I could get hold of, even down to the deaths and marriages in the Herald. My memory for names and people is good, and the reader will see, as he goes on, that I had reason enough to remember Philip Nolan. There are hundreds of readers who would have paused at that announcement, if the officer of the *Levant* who reported it had chosen to make it thus:—"Died, May 11th, The Man without a Country." For it was as "The Man without a Country" that poor Philip Nolan had generally been known by the officers who had him in charge during some fifty years, as, indeed, by all men who sailed under them. I dare say there is many a man who has taken wine with him once a fortnight, in a three years' cruise, who never knew that his name was "Nolan," or whether the poor wretch had any name at all.

There can now be no possible harm in telling this poor creature's story. Reason enough there has been till now, ever since Madison's administration went out in 1817, for very strict secrecy, the secrecy of honour itself, among the gentlemen of the navy who have had Nolan in successive charge. And certainly it speaks well for the *esprit de corps* of the profession, and the personal honour of its members, that to the press this man's story has been wholly unknown—and, I think, to the country at large also. I have reason to think, from some investigations I made in the Naval Archives when I was attached to the Bureau of Construction, that every official report relating to him was burned when Ross burned the public buildings at Washington. One of the Tuckers, or possibly one of the Watsons, had Nolan in charge at the end of the war; and when, on returning from his cruise, he reported at Washington to one of the Crowninshields—who was in the Navy Department when he came home—he found that the Department ignored the whole business. Whether they really knew nothing about it or whether it was a "*Non mi ricordo*" determined on as a piece of policy, I do not know.

But this I do know, that since 1817, and possibly before, no naval officer has mentioned Nolan in his report of a cruise.

But, as I say, there is no need for secrecy any longer. And now the poor creature is dead, it seems to me worth while to tell a little of his story, by way of showing young Americans of to-day what it is to be A MAN WITHOUT A COUNTRY.

Philip Nolan was as fine a young officer as there was in the "Legion of the West," as the Western division of our army was then called. When Aaron Burr made his first dashing expedition down to New Orleans in 1805, at Fort Massac, or somewhere above on the river, he met, as the Devil would have it, this gay, dashing, bright young fellow, at some dinner-party, I think. Burr marked him, talked to him, walked with him, took him a day or two's voyage in his flat-boat, and, in short, fascinated him. For the next year, barrack-life was very tame to poor Nolan. He occasionally availed himself of the permission the great man had given him to write to him. Long, high-worded, stilted letters the poor boy wrote and rewrote and copied. But never a line did he have in reply from the gay deceiver. The other boys in the garrison sneered at him, because he sacrificed in this unrequited affection for a politician the time which they devoted to Monongahela, hazard, and high-low-jack. Bourbon, euchre, and poker were still unknown. But one day Nolan had his revenge. This time Burr came down the river not as an attorney seeking a place for his office, but as a disguised conqueror. He had defeated I know not how many district-attorneys; he had dined at I know not how many public dinners; he had been heralded in I know not how many

Weekly Arguses, and it was rumoured that he had an army behind him and an empire before him. It was a great day—his arrival—to poor Nolan. Burr had not been at the fort an hour before he sent for him. That evening he asked Nolan to take him out in his skiff, to show him a canebrake or a cottonwood tree, as he said,—really to seduce him; and by the time the sail was over, Nolan was enlisted body and soul. From that time, though he did not yet know it, he lived as A MAN WITHOUT A COUNTRY.

What Burr meant to do I know no more than you, dear reader. It is none of our business just now. Only, when the grand catastrophe came, and Jefferson and the House of Virginia of that day undertook to break on the wheel all the possible Clarences of the then House of York, by the great treason-trial at Richmond, some of the lesser fry in that distant Mississippi Valley, which was farther from us than Puget's Sound is to-day, introduced the like novelty on their provincial stage, and, to while away the monotony of the summer at Fort Adams, got up, for *spectacles*, a string of court-martials on the officers there. One and another of the colonels and majors were tried, and, to fill out the list, little Nolan, against whom, Heaven knows, there was evidence enough,—that he was sick of the service, had been willing to be false to it, and would have obeyed any order to march any-whither with any one who would follow him had the order been signed, "By command of His Exc. A. Burr." The courts dragged on. The big flies escaped,—rightly for all I know. Nolan was proved guilty enough, as I say; yet you and I would never have heard of him, reader, but that, when the president of the court asked him at the close, whether he wished to say anything to show that he had always been faithful to the United States, he cried out, in, a fit of frenzy,—

"D—n the United States! I wish I may never hear of the United States again!"

I suppose he did not know how the words shocked old Colonel Morgan, who was holding the court. Half the officers who sat in it had served through the Revolution, and their lives, not to say their necks, had been risked for the very idea which he so cavalierly cursed in his madness. He, on his part, had grown up in the West of those days, in the midst of "Spanish plot," "Orleans plot," and all the rest. He had been educated on a plantation where the finest company was a Spanish officer or a French merchant from Orleans. His education, such as it was, had been perfected in commercial expeditions to Vera Cruz, and I think he told me his father once hired an Englishman to be a private tutor for a winter on the plantation. He had spent half his youth with an older brother, hunting horses in Texas; and, in a word, to him "United States" was scarcely a reality. Yet he had been fed by "United States" for all the years since he had been in the army. He had sworn on his faith as a Christian to be true to "United States." It was "United States" which gave him the uniform he wore, and the sword by his side. Nay, my poor Nolan, it was only because "United States" had picked you out first as one of her own confidential men of honour that "A. Burr" cared for you a straw more than for the flat-boat men who sailed his ark for him. I do not excuse Nolan; I only explain to the reader why he damned his country, and wished he might never hear her name again.

He never did hear her name but once again.

From that moment, September 23, 1807, till the day he died, May 11, 1863, he never heard the name again. For that half century and more he was a man without a country.

Old Morgan, as I said, was terribly shocked. If Nolan had compared George Washington to Benedict Arnold, or had cried, "God save King George," Morgan would not have felt worse.

He called the court into his private room, and returned in fifteen minutes, with a face like a sheet, to say,—

"Prisoner, hear the sentence of the court! The court decides, subject to the approval of the President, that you never hear the name of the United States again."

Nolan laughed. But nobody else laughed. Old Morgan was too solemn, and the whole room was hushed dead as night for a minute. Even Nolan lost his swagger in a moment. Then Morgan added,—

"Mr. Marshal, take the prisoner to Orleans in an armed boat, and deliver him to the naval commander there."

The marshal gave his orders and the prisoner was taken out of court.

"Mr. Marshal," continued old Morgan, "see that no one mentions the United States to the prisoner. Mr. Marshal, make my respects to Lieutenant Mitchell at Orleans, and request him to order that no one shall mention the United States to the prisoner while he is on board ship. You will receive your written orders from the officer on duty here this evening. The court is adjourned without day."

I have always supposed that Colonel Morgan himself took the proceedings of the court to Washington City, and explained them to Mr. Jefferson. Certain it is that the President approved them—certain, that is, if I may believe the men who say they have seen his signature. Before the *Nautilus* got round from New Orleans to the Northern Atlantic coast with the prisoner on board the sentence had been approved, and he was a man without a country.

The plan then adopted was substantially the same which was necessarily followed ever after. Perhaps it was suggested by the necessity of sending him by water from Fort Adams and Orleans. The Secretary of the Navy—it must have been the first Crowninshield, though he is a man I do not remember—was requested to put Nolan on board a government vessel bound on a long cruise, and to direct that he should be only so far confined there as to make it certain that he never saw or heard of the country. We had few long cruises then, and the navy was very much out of favour; and as almost all of this story is traditional, as I have explained, I do not know certainly what his first cruise was. But the commander to whom he was intrusted—perhaps it was Tingey or Shaw, though I think it was one of the younger men—we are all old enough now—regulated the etiquette and the precautions of the affair, and according to his scheme they were carried out, I suppose, till Nolan died.

When I was second officer of the *Intrepid*, some thirty years after, I saw the original paper of instructions. I have been sorry ever since that I did not copy the whole of it. It ran, however, much in this way:—

"WASHINGTON (with a date, which must have been late in 1807).

"SIR—You will receive from Lieutenant Neale the person of Philip Nolan, late a Lieutenant in the United States Army.

"This person on his trial by court-martial 'expressed with an oath the wish that he might never hear of the United States again.'

"The court sentenced him to have his wish fulfilled.

"For the present, the execution of the order is intrusted by the President to this Department.

"You will take the prisoner on board your ship and keep him there with such precautions as shall prevent his escape.

"You will provide him with such quarters, rations, and clothing as would be proper for an officer of his late rank, if he were a passenger on your vessel on the business of his government.

"The gentlemen on board will make any arrangements agreeable to themselves regarding his society. He is to be exposed to no indignity of any kind, nor is he ever unnecessarily to be reminded that he is a prisoner.

"But under no circumstances is he ever to hear of his country or to see any information regarding it; and you will specially caution all the officers under your command to take care, that, in the various indulgences which may be granted, this rule, in which his punishment is involved, shall not be broken.

"It is the intention of the government that he shall never again see the country which he has disowned. Before the end of your cruise you will receive orders which will give effect to this intention.

"Respectfully yours,

"W. Southward,
"For the Secretary of the Navy."

If I had only preserved the whole of this paper, there would be no break in the beginning of my sketch of this story. For Captain Shaw, if it were he, handed it to his successor in the charge, and he to his, and I suppose the commander of the *Levant* has it to-day as his authority for keeping this man in this mild custody.

The rule adopted on board the ships on which I have met "the man without a country" was, I think, transmitted from the beginning. No mess liked to have him permanently, because his presence cut off all talk of home or of the prospect of return, of politics or letters, of peace or of war,—cut off more than half the talk men liked to have at sea. But it was always thought too hard that he should never meet the rest of us, except to touch hats, and we finally sank into one system. He was not permitted to talk with the men, unless an officer was by. With officers he had unrestrained intercourse, as far as they and he chose. But he grew shy, though he had favourites: I was one. Then the captain always asked him to dinner on Monday. Every mess in succession took up the invitation in its turn. According to the size of the ship, you had him at your mess more or less often at dinner. His breakfast he ate in his own state-room—he always had a state-room,—which was where a sentinel or somebody on the watch could see the door. And whatever else he ate or drank, he ate or drank alone. Sometimes, when the marines or sailors had any special jollification, they were permitted to invite "Plain Buttons," as they called him. Then Nolan was sent with some officer, and the men were forbidden to speak of home while he was there. I believe the theory was that the sight of his punishment did them good. They called him "Plain Buttons," because while he always chose to wear a regulation army-uniform, he was not permitted to wear the army-button, for the reason that it bore either the initials or the insignia of the country he had disowned.

I remember, soon after I joined the navy, I was on shore with some of the older officers from our ship and from the *Brandywine*, which we had met at Alexandria. We had leave to make a party and go up to Cairo and the Pyramids. As we jogged along (you went on donkeys then), some of the gentlemen (we boys called them "Dons," but the phrase was long since changed) fell to talking about Nolan, and some one told the system which was adopted from the first about his books and other reading. As he was almost never permitted to go on shore, even though the vessel lay in port for months, his time at the best hung heavy; and everybody was permitted to lend him books, if they were not published in America and made no allusion to it. These were common enough in the old days, when people in the other hemisphere talked of the United States as little as we do of Paraguay. He had almost all the foreign papers that came into the ship, sooner or later; only somebody must go over them first, and cut out any advertisement or stray paragraph that alluded to America. This was a little cruel sometimes, when the back of what was cut out might be as innocent as Hesiod. Right in the midst of one of Napoleon's battles, or one of Canning's speeches, poor Nolan would find a great hole, because on the back of the page of that paper there had been an advertisement of a packet for New York, or a scrap from the President's message. I say this was the first time I ever heard of this plan, which afterwards I had enough and more than enough to do with. I remember it, because poor Phillips, who was of the party, as soon as the allusion to reading was made, told a story of something which happened at the Cape of Good Hope on Nolan's first voyage; and it is the only thing I ever knew of that voyage. They had touched at the Cape, and had done the civil thing with the English Admiral and the fleet, and then, leaving for a long cruise up the Indian Ocean, Phillips had borrowed a lot of English books from an officer, which, in those days, as indeed in these, was quite a windfall. Among them, as the Devil would order, was the "Lay of the Last Minstrel," which they had all of them heard of, but which most of them had never seen. I think it could not have been published long. Well, nobody thought there could be any risk of anything national in that, though Phillips swore old Shaw had cut out the "Tempest" from Shakespeare before he let Nolan have it, because he said "the Bermudas ought to be ours, and, by Jove, should be one day." So Nolan was permitted to join the circle one afternoon when a lot of them sat on deck smoking and reading aloud. People do not do such things so often now; but when I was young we got rid of a great deal of time so. Well, so it happened that in his turn Nolan took the book and read to the others; and he read very well, as I know. Nobody in the circle knew a line of the poem, only it was all magic and Border chivalry, and was ten thousand years ago. Poor Nolan read steadily through the fifth canto, stopped a minute and drank something, and then began, without a thought of what was coming,—

> "Breathes there the man, with soul so dead,
> Who never to himself hath said,"—

It seems impossible to us that anybody ever heard this for the first time; but all these fellows did then, and poor Nolan himself went on, still unconsciously or mechanically,—

> "This is my own, my native land!"—

Then they all saw something was to pay; but he expected to get through, I suppose, turned a little pale, but plunged on,—

> "Whose heart hath ne'er within him burned,
> As home his footsteps he hath turned
> From wandering on a foreign strand?—
> If such there breathe, go, mark him well,"—

By this time the men were all beside themselves, wishing there was any way to make him turn over two pages; but he had not quite presence of mind for that; he gagged a little, coloured crimson, and staggered on,—

> "For him no minstrel raptures swell;
> High though his titles, proud his name,
> Boundless his wealth as wish can claim,
> Despite these titles, power, and pelf,
> The wretch, concentred all in self,"—

and here the poor fellow choked, could not go on, but started up, swung the book into the sea, vanished into his state-room, "And by Jove," said Phillips, "we did not see him for two months again. And I had to make up some beggarly story to that English surgeon why I did not return his Walter Scott to him."

That story shows about the time when Nolan's braggadocio must have broken down. At first, they said he took a very high tone, considered his imprisonment a mere farce, affected to enjoy the voyage, and all that; but Phillips said that after he came out of his state-room he never was the same man again. He never read aloud again, unless it was the Bible or Shakespeare or something else he was sure of. But it was not that merely. He never entered in with the other young men exactly as a companion again. He was always shy afterwards, when I knew him—very seldom spoke, unless he was spoken to, except to a very few friends. He lighted up occasionally—I remember late in his life hearing him fairly eloquent on something which had been suggested to him by one of Fléchier's sermons—but generally he had the nervous, tired look of a heart-wounded man.

When Captain Shaw was coming home—if as I say, it was Shaw—rather to the surprise of everybody, they made one of the Windward Islands, and lay off and on for nearly a week. The boys said the officers were sick of salt-junk, and meant to have turtle-soup before they came home. But after several days the *Warren* came to the same rendezvous; they exchanged signals; she sent to Phillips and these homeward bound men, letters and papers and told them she was outward-bound, perhaps to the Mediterranean, and took poor Nolan and his traps on the boat back to try his second cruise. He looked very blank when he was told to get ready to join her. He had known enough of the signs of the sky to know that till that moment he was going "home." But this was a distinct evidence of something he had not thought of, perhaps—that there was no going home for him, even to a prison. And this was the first of some twenty such transfers, which brought him sooner or later into half our best vessels, but which kept him all his life at least some hundred miles from the country he had hoped he might never hear of again.

It may have been on that second cruise—it was once when he was up the Mediterranean—that Mrs. Graff, the celebrated Southern beauty of those days, danced with him. They had been lying a long time in the Bay of Naples, and the officers were very intimate in the English fleet, and there had been great festivities, and our men thought they must give a great ball on board the ship. How they ever did it on board the *Warren* I am sure I do not know. Perhaps it was not the *Warren*, or perhaps ladies did not take up so much room as they do now.

They wanted to use Nolan's state-room for something, and they hated to do it without asking him to the ball; so the captain said they might ask him, if they would be responsible that he did not talk with the wrong people, "who would give him intelligence." So the dance went on, the finest party that had ever been known, I dare say; for I never heard of a man-of-war ball that was not. For ladies they had the family of the American consul, one or two travellers, who had adventured so far, and a nice bevy of English girls and matrons, perhaps Lady Hamilton herself.

Well, different officers relieved each other in standing and talking with Nolan in a friendly way, so as to be sure that nobody else spoke to him. The dancing went on with spirit, and after a while even the fellows who took this honorary guard of Nolan ceased to fear any *contretemps*. Only when some English lady—Lady Hamilton, as I said, perhaps—called for a set of "American dances," an odd thing happened. Everybody then danced contra-dances. The black band, nothing loath, conferred as to what "American dances" were, and started off with "Virginia Reel," which they followed with "Money Musk," which, in its turn in those days, should have been followed by "The Old Thirteen." But just as Dick, the leader, tapped for his fiddles to begin, and bent forward, about to say, in true negro state, "'The Old Thirteen,' gentlemen and ladies!" as he had said "'Virginny Reel,' if you please!" and "'Money-Musk,' if you please!" the captain's boy tapped him on the shoulder, whispered to him, and he did not announce the name of the dance; he merely bowed, began on the air, and they all fell to—the officers teaching the English girls the figure, but not telling them why it had no name.

But that is not the story I started to tell. As the dancing went on, Nolan and our fellows all got at ease, as I said—so much so, that it seemed quite natural for him to bow to that splendid Mrs. Graff, and say—

"I hope you have not forgotten me, Miss Rutledge. Shall I have the honour of dancing?"

He did it so quickly, that Fellows, who was by him, could not hinder him. She laughed and said—

"I am not Miss Rutledge any longer, Mr. Nolan; but I will dance all the same," just nodded to Fellows, as if to say he must leave Mr. Nolan to her, and led him off to the place where the dance was forming.

Nolan thought he had got his chance. He had known her at Philadelphia, and at other places had met her, and this was a Godsend. You could not talk in contra-dances as you do in cotillions, or even in the pauses of waltzing; but there were chances for tongues and sounds, as well as for eyes and blushes. He began with her travels, and Europe, and Vesuvius, and the French; and then, when they had worked down, and had that long talking-time at the bottom of the set, he said, boldly—a little pale, she said, as she told me the story, years after—

"And what do you hear from home, Mrs. Graff?"

And that splendid creature looked through him. Jove! how she must have looked through him!

"Home!! Mr. Nolan!!! I thought you were the man who never wanted to hear of home again!"—and she walked directly up the deck to her husband, and left poor Nolan alone, as he always was. He did not dance again.

I cannot give any history of him in order; nobody can now; and, indeed, I am not trying to. These are the traditions, which I sort out, as I believe them, from the myths which have been told about this man for forty years. The lies that have been told about him are legion. The fellows used to say he was the "Iron Mask"; and poor George Pons went to his grave in the belief that this was the author of "Junius," who was being punished for his celebrated libel on Thomas Jefferson. Pons was not very strong in the historical line. A happier story than either of these I have told is of the war. That came along soon after. I have heard this affair told in three or four ways—and, indeed, it may have happened more than once. But which ship it was on I cannot tell. However, in one, at least, of the great frigate-duels with the English, in which the navy was really baptised, it happened that a round-shot from the enemy entered one of our ports square, and took right down the officer of the gun himself, and almost every man of the gun's crew. Now you may say what you choose about courage, but that is not a nice thing to see. But, as the men who were not killed picked themselves up, and as they and the surgeon's people were carrying off the bodies, there appeared Nolan, in his shirt sleeves, with the rammer in his hand, and, just as if he had been an officer, told them off with authority—who should go to the cock-pit with the wounded men, who should stay with him—perfectly cheery, and with that way which makes men feel sure all is right and is going to be right. And he finished loading his gun with his own hands, aimed it, and bade the men fire. And there he stayed, captain of that gun, keeping those fellows in spirits, till the enemy struck—sitting on the carriage while the gun was cooling, though he was exposed all the time—showing them easier ways to handle heavy shot—making the raw hands laugh at their own blunders—and when the gun cooled again, getting it loaded and fired twice as often as any other gun on the ship. The captain walked forward by way of encouraging the men, and Nolan touched his hat, and said—

"I am showing them how we do this in the artillery, sir."

And this is the part of the story where all the legends agree; and the commodore said—

"I see you do, and I thank you, sir; and I shall never forget this day, sir; and you never shall, sir."

And after the whole thing was over, and he had the Englishman's sword, in the midst of the state and ceremony of the quarter-deck, he said—

"Where is Mr. Nolan? Ask Mr. Nolan to come here."

And when Nolan came, the captain said—

"Mr. Nolan, we are all very grateful to you to-day; you are one of us to-day; you will be named in the despatches."

And then the old man took off his own sword of ceremony, and gave it to Nolan, and made him put it on. The man told me this who saw it. Nolan cried like a baby, and well he might. He had not worn a sword since that infernal day at Fort Adams. But always afterwards, on occasions of ceremony, he wore that quaint old French sword of the commodore's.

The captain did mention him in the despatches. It was always said he asked that he might be pardoned. He wrote a special letter to the Secretary of War. But nothing ever came of it. As I said, that was about the time when they began to ignore the whole transaction at Washington, and when Nolan's imprisonment began to carry itself on because there was nobody to stop it without any new orders from home.

I have heard it said that he was with Porter when he took possession of the Nukahiwa Islands. Not this Porter, you know, but old Porter, his father, Essex Porter—that is, the old Essex Porter, not this Essex. As an artillery officer, who had seen service in the west, Nolan knew more about fortifications, embrasures, ravelins, stockades, and all that, than any of them did; and he worked with a right good-will in fixing that battery all right. I have always thought it was a pity Porter did not leave him in command there with Gamble. That would have settled all the question about his punishment. We should have kept the islands, and at this moment we should have one station in the Pacific Ocean. Our French friends, too, when they wanted this little watering-place, would have found it was preoccupied. But Madison and the Virginians, of course flung all that away.

All that was near fifty years go. If Nolan was thirty then, he must have been near eighty when he died. He looked sixty when he was forty. But he never seemed to me to change a hair afterwards. As I imagine his life, from what I have seen and heard of it, he must have been in every sea, and yet almost never on land. He must have known, in a formal way, more officers in our service than any man living knows. He told me once, with a grave smile, that no man in the world lived so methodical a life as he. "You know the boys say I am the Iron Mask, and you know how busy he was." He said it did not do for any one to try to read all the time, more than to do anything else all the time; but that he read just five hours a day. "Then," he said, "I keep up my note-books, writing in them at such and such hours from what I have been reading; and I include in these my scrap-books." These were very curious indeed. He had six or eight, of different subjects. There was one of History, one of Natural Science, one which he called "Odds and Ends." But they were not merely books of extracts from newspapers. They had bits of plants and ribbons, shells tied on, and carved scraps of bone and wood which he had taught the men to cut for him, and they were beautifully illustrated. He drew admirably. He had some of the funniest drawings there, and some of the most pathetic, that I have ever seen in my life. I wonder who will have Nolan's scrap-books.

Well, he said his reading and his notes were his profession, and that they took five hours and two hours respectively of each day. "Then," said he, "every man should have a diversion as well as a profession. My Natural History is my diversion." That took two hours a day more. The men used to bring him birds and fish, but on a long cruise he had to satisfy himself with centipedes and cockroaches and such small game. He was the only naturalist I ever met who knew anything about the habits of the house-fly and the mosquito. All those people can tell you whether they are *Lepidoptera* or *Steptopotera*; but as for telling how you can get rid of them, or how they get away from you when you strike them—why Linnæus knew as little of that as John Fox the idiot did. These nine hours made Nolan's regular daily "occupation." The rest of the time he talked or walked. Till he grew very old, he went aloft a great deal. He always kept up his exercise; and I never heard that he was ill. If any other man was ill, he was the kindest nurse in the world; and he knew more than half the surgeons do. Then if anybody was sick or died, or if the captain wanted him to, on any other occasion, he was always ready to read prayers. I have said that he read beautifully.

My own acquaintance with Philip Nolan began six or eight years after the war, on my first voyage after I was appointed a midshipman. It was in the first days after our Slave Trade treaty, while the Reigning House, which was still the House of Virginia, had still a sort of sentimentalism about the suppression of the horrors of the Middle Passage, and something was sometimes done that way. We were in the South Atlantic on that business. From the time I joined, I believe I thought Nolan was a sort of lay chaplain—a chaplain with a blue coat.

I never asked about him. Everything in the ship was strange to me. I knew it was green to ask questions, and I suppose I thought there was a "Plain-Buttons" on every ship. We had him to dine in our mess once a week, and the caution was given that on that day nothing was to be said about home. But if they had told us not to say anything about the planet Mars or the Book of Deuteronomy, I should not have asked why; there were a great many things which seemed to me to have as little reason. I first came to understand anything about "the man without a country" one day when we overhauled a dirty little schooner which had slaves on board. An officer was sent to take charge of her, and, after a few minutes, he sent back his boat to ask that some one might be sent him who could speak Portuguese. We were all looking over the rail when the message came, and we all wished we could interpret, when the captain asked who spoke Portuguese. But none of the officers did; and just as the captain was sending forward to ask if any of the people could, Nolan stepped out and said he should be glad to interpret, if the captain wished, as he understood the language. The captain thanked him, fitted out another boat with him, and in this boat it was my luck to go.

When we got there, it was such a scene as you seldom see, and never want to. Nastiness beyond account, and chaos run loose in the midst of the nastiness. There were not a great many of the negroes; but by way of making what there were understand that they were free, Vaughan had had their hand-cuffs and ankle-cuffs knocked off, and, for convenience sake, was putting them upon the rascals of the schooner's crew. The negroes were, most of them, out of the hold, and swarming all round the dirty deck, with a central throng surrounding Vaughan and addressing him in every dialect, and *patois* of a dialect, from the Zulu click up to the Parisian of Beledeljereed.

As we came on deck, Vaughan looked down from a hogshead, on which he had mounted in desperation, and said:

"For God's love, is there anybody who can make these wretches understand something? The men gave them rum, and that did not quiet them. I knocked that big fellow down twice, and that did not soothe him. And then I talked Choctaw to all of them together; and I'll be hanged if they understand that as well as they understand the English."

Nolan said he could speak Portuguese, and one or two fine-looking Kroomen were dragged out, who, as it had been found already, had worked for the Portuguese on the coast at Fernando Po.

"Tell them they are free," said Vaughan; "and tell them that these rascals are to be hanged as soon as we can get rope enough."

Nolan "put them into Spanish"—that is, he explained it in such Portuguese as the Kroomen could understand, and they in turn to such of the negroes as could understand them. Then there was such a yell of delight, clinching of fists, leaping and dancing, kissing of Nolan's feet, and a general rush made to the hogshead by way of spontaneous worship of Vaughan, as the *deus ex machina* of the occasion."Tell them," said Vaughan, well pleased, "that I will take them all to Cape Palmas."

This did not answer so well. Cape Palmas was practically as far from the homes of most of them as New Orleans or Rio Janeiro was; that is, they would be eternally separated from home there. And their interpreters, as we could understand, instantly said: "*Ah, non Palmas,*" and began to propose infinite other expedients in most voluble language. Vaughan was rather disappointed at this result of his liberality, and asked Nolan eagerly what they said. The drops stood on poor Nolan's white forehead, as he hushed the men down, and said:

"He says, 'Not Palmas.' He says, 'Take us home, take us to our own country, take us to our own house, take us to our own pickaninnies and our own women.' He says he has an old father and mother who will die if they do not see him. And this one says he left his people all sick, and paddled down to Fernando to beg the white doctor to come and help them, and that these devils caught him in the bay just in sight of home, and that he had never seen anybody from home since then. And this one says," choked out Nolan, "that he has not heard a word from his home in six months, while he has been locked up in an infernal barracoon."

Vaughan always said he grew grey himself while Nolan struggled through this interpretation. I, who did not understand anything of the passion involved in it, saw that the very elements were melting with fervent heat, and that something was to pay somewhere. Even the negroes themselves stopped howling, as they saw Nolan's agony, and Vaughan's almost equal agony of sympathy. As quick as he could get words, he said:

"Tell them yes, yes, yes; tell them they shall go to the Mountains of the Moon if they will. If I sail the schooner through the Great White Desert they shall go home!"

And after some fashion Nolan said so. And then they all fell to kissing him again, and wanted to rub his nose with theirs.

But he could not stand it long; and getting Vaughan to say he might go back, he beckoned me down into our boat. As we lay back in the stern-sheets and the men gave way, he said to me: "Youngster, let that show you what it is to be without a family, without a home, and without a country. And if you are ever tempted to say a word or to do a thing that shall put a bar between you and your family, your home, and your country, pray God in His mercy to take you that instant home to His own heaven. Stick by your family, boy; forget you have a self, while you do everything for them. Think of your home, boy; write and send, and talk about it. Let it be nearer and nearer to your thought, the farther you have to travel from it; and rush back to it, when you are free, as that poor black slave is doing now. And for your country, boy," and the words rattled in his throat, "and for that flag," and he pointed to the ship, "never dream a dream but of serving her as she bids you, though the service carry you through a thousand hells. No matter what happens to you, no matter who flatters you or who abuses you, never look at another flag, never let a night pass but you pray God to bless that flag. Remember, boy, that behind all these men you have to do with, behind officers, and government, and people even, there is the Country Herself, your Country, and that you belong to Her as you belong to your own mother. Stand by Her, boy, as you would stand by your mother, if those devils there had got hold of her to-day!"

I was frightened to death by his calm, hard passion; but I blundered out, that I would, by all that was holy, and that I had never thought of doing anything else. He hardly seemed to hear me; but he did, almost in a whisper, say: "O, if anybody had said so to me when I was of your age!"

I think it was this half-confidence of his, which I never abused, for I never told this story till now, which afterward made us great friends. He was very kind to me. Often he sat up, or even got up, at night, to walk the deck with me, when it was my watch. He explained to me a great deal of my mathematics, and I owe to him my taste for mathematics. He lent me books, and helped me about my reading. He never alluded so directly to his story again; but from one and another officer I have learned, in thirty years, what I am telling. When we parted from him in St. Thomas harbour, at the end of our cruise, I was more sorry than I can tell. I was very glad to meet him again in 1830; and later in life, when I thought I had some influence in Washington, I moved heaven and earth to have him discharged. But it was like getting a ghost out of prison. They pretended there was no such man, and never was such a man. They will say so at the Department now! Perhaps they do not know. It will not be the first thing in the service of which the Department appears to know nothing!

There is a story that Nolan met Burr once on one of our vessels, when a party of Americans came on board in the Mediterranean. But this I believe to be a lie; or, rather it is a myth, *ben trovato*, involving a tremendous blowing-up with which he sunk Burr—asking him how he liked to be "without a country." But it is clear from Burr's life that nothing of the sort could have happened; and I mention this only as an illustration of the stories which get a-going where there is the least mystery at the bottom.

So poor Philip Nolan had his wish fulfilled. I know but one fate more dreadful; it is the fate reserved for those men who shall have one day to exile themselves from their country because they have attempted her ruin, and shall have at the same time to see the prosperity and honour to which she rises when she has rid herself of them and their iniquities. The wish of poor Nolan, as we all learned to call him, not because his punishment was too great, but because his repentance was so clear, was precisely the wish of every Bragg and Beauregard who broke a soldier's oath two years ago, and of every Maury and Barron who broke a sailor's. I do not know how often they have repented. I do know that they have done all that in them lay that they might have no country—that all the honours, associations, memories, and hopes which belong to "country" might be broken up into little shreds and distributed to the winds. I know, too, that their punishment, as they vegetate through what is left of life to them in wretched Boulognes and Leicester Squares, where they are destined to upbraid each other till they die, will have all the agony of Nolan's, with the added pang that every one who sees them will see them to despise and to execrate them. They will have their wish, like him.

For him, poor fellow, he repented of his folly, and then, like a man, submitted to the fate he had asked for. He never intentionally added to the difficulty or delicacy of the charge of those who had him in hold.

Accidents would happen; but they never happened from his fault. Lieutenant Truxton told me that, when Texas was annexed, there was a careful discussion among the officers, whether they should get hold of Nolan's handsome set of maps, and cut Texas out of it—from the map of the world and the map of Mexico. The United States had been cut out when the atlas was bought for him. But it was voted, rightly enough, that to do this would be virtually to reveal to him what had happened, or, as Harry Cole said, to make him think Old Burr had succeeded. So it was from no fault of Nolan's that a great botch happened at my own table, when, for a short time, I was in command of the *George Washington* corvette, on the South American station. We were lying in the La Plata, and some of the officers, who had been on shore, and had just joined again, were entertaining us with accounts of their misadventures in riding the half-wild horses of Buenos Ayres.

Nolan was at table, and was in an unusually bright and talkative mood. Some story of a tumble reminded him of an adventure of his own, when he was catching wild horses in Texas with his adventurous cousin at a time when he must have been quite a boy. He told the story with a good deal of spirit—so much so, that the silence which often follows a good story hung over the table for an instant, to be broken by Nolan himself. For he asked perfectly unconsciously:

"Pray, what has become of Texas? After the Mexicans got their independence, I thought that province of Texas would come forward very fast. It is really one of the finest regions on earth; it is the Italy of this continent. But I have not seen or heard a word of Texas for near twenty years."

There were two Texan officers at the table. The reason he had never heard of Texas was that Texas and her affairs had been painfully cut out of his newspapers since Austin began his settlements; so that, while he read of Honduras and Tamaulipas, and, till quite lately, of California—this virgin province, in which his brother had travelled so far, and, I believe, had died, had ceased to be to him. Waters and Williams, the two Texas men, looked grimly at each other, and tried not to laugh. Edward Morris had his attention attracted by the third link in the chain of the chaplain's chandelier. Waters was seized with a convulsion of sneezing. Nolan himself saw that something was to pay, he did not know what. And I, as master of the feast, had to say—

"Texas is out of the map, Mr. Nolan. Have you seen Captain Back's curious account of Sir Thomas Roe's Welcome?"

After that cruise I never saw Nolan again. I wrote to him at least twice a year, for in that voyage we became even confidentially intimate; but he never wrote to me. The other men tell me that in those fifteen years he *aged* very fast, as well he might indeed, but that he was still the same gentle, uncomplaining, silent sufferer that he ever was, bearing as best he could his self-appointed punishment—rather less social, perhaps, with new men whom he did not know, but more anxious, apparently, than ever to serve and befriend and teach the boys, some of whom fairly seemed to worship him. And now it seems the dear old fellow is dead. He has found a home at last, and a country.

Since writing this, and while considering whether or no I would print it, as a warning to the young Nolans and Vallandighams and Tatnalls of to-day of what it is to throw away a country, I have received from Danforth, who is on board the *Levant*, a letter which gives an account of Nolan's last hours. It removes all my doubts about telling this story.

To understand the first words of the letter, the non-professional reader should remember that after 1817, the position of every officer who had Nolan in charge was one of the greatest delicacy. The government had failed to renew the order of 1807 regarding him. What was a man to do? Should he let him go? What, then, if he were called to account by the Department for violating the order of 1807? Should he keep him? What, then, if Nolan should be liberated some day, and should bring an action for false imprisonment or kidnapping against every man who had had him in charge? I urged and pressed this upon Southward, and I have reason to think that other officers did the same thing. But the Secretary always said, as they so often do at Washington, that there were no special orders to give, and that we must act on our own judgement. That means, "If you succeed, you will be sustained; if you fail, you will be disavowed." Well, as Danforth says, all that is over now, though I do not know but I expose myself to a criminal prosecution on the evidence of the very revelation I am making.

Here is the letter:—

"*Levant*, 2° 2´ S. at 131° W.

"Dear Fred:—I try to find heart and life to tell you that it is all over with dear old Nolan. I have been with him on this voyage more than I ever was, and I can understand wholly now the way in which you used to speak of the dear old fellow. I could see that he was not strong, but I had no idea the end was so near. The doctor has been watching him very carefully, and yesterday morning came to me and told me that Nolan was not so well, and had not left his state-room—a thing I never remember before. He had let the doctor come and see him as he lay there—the first time the doctor had been in the state-room—and he said he should like to see me. O dear! do you remember the mysteries we boys used to invent about his room, in the old *Intrepid* days? Well, I went in, and there, to be sure, the poor fellow lay in his berth, smiling pleasantly as he gave me his hand, but looking very frail. I could not help a glance round, which showed me what a little shrine he had made of the box he was lying in. The stars and stripes were triced up above and around a picture of Washington, and he had painted a majestic eagle, with lightnings blazing from his beak and his foot just clasping the whole globe, which his wings overshadowed. The dear old boy saw my glance, and said, with a sad smile, 'Here, you see, I have a country!' And then he pointed to the foot of his bed, where I had not seen before a great map of the United States, as he had drawn it from memory, and which he had there to look upon as he lay. Quaint, queer old names were on it, in large letters: 'Indiana Territory,' 'Mississippi Territory,' and 'Louisiana Territory,' as I suppose our fathers learned such things; but the old fellow had patched in Texas, too; he had carried his western boundary all the way to the Pacific, but on that shore he had defined nothing.

"'O Danforth,' he said, 'I know I am dying. I cannot get home. Surely you will tell me something now?—Stop! stop! Do not speak till I say what I am sure you know, that there is not in this ship, that there is not in America—God bless her!—A more loyal man than I. There cannot be a man who loves the old flag as I do, or prays for it as I do, or hopes for it as I do. There are thirty-four stars in it now, Danforth. I thank God for that, though I do not know what their names are. There has never been one taken away: I thank God for that. I know by that that there has never been any successful Burr. O Danforth, Danforth,' he sighed out, 'how like a wretched night's dream a boy's idea of personal fame or of separate sovereignty seems, when one looks back on it after such a life as mine! But tell me—tell me something—tell me everything, Danforth, before I die!'

"Ingham, I swear to you that I felt like a monster that I had not told him everything before. Danger or no danger, delicacy or no delicacy, who was I, that I should have been acting the tyrant all this time over this dear, sainted old man, who had years ago expiated, in his whole manhood's life, the madness of a boy's treason? 'Mr. Nolan,' said I, 'I will tell you everything you ask about. Only, where shall I begin?'

"O the blessed smile that crept over his white face! and he pressed my hand and said, 'God bless you!' 'Tell me their names,' he said, and he pointed to the stars on the flag. The last I know is Ohio. My father lived in Kentucky. But I have guessed Michigan and Indiana and Mississippi—that was where Fort Adams is—they make twenty. But where are your other fourteen? You have not cut up any of the old ones, I hope?'

"Well, that was not a bad text, and I told him the names in as good order as I could, and he bade me take down his beautiful map and draw them in as best I could with my pencil. He was wild with delight about Texas, told me how his cousin died there; he had marked a gold cross near where he supposed his grave was; and he had guessed at Texas. Then he was delighted as he saw California and Oregon;—that, he said, he had suspected partly, because he had never been permitted to land on that shore, though the ships were there so much. 'And the men,' said he, laughing, 'brought off a good deal besides furs.' Then he went back—heavens, how far!—to ask about the *Chesapeake*, and what was done to Barron for surrendering her to the *Leopard*, and whether Burr ever tried again—and he ground his teeth with the only passion he showed. But in a moment that was over, and he said, 'God forgive me, for I am sure I forgive him.' Then he asked about the old war—told me the true story of his serving the gun the day we took the *Java*—asked about dear old David Porter, as he called him. Then he settled down more quietly, and very happily, to hear me tell in an hour the history of fifty years.

"How I wished it had been somebody who knew something! But I did as well as I could. I told him of the English war. I told him about Fulton and the steamboat beginning. I told him about old Scott, and Jackson; told him all I could think of about the Mississippi, and New Orleans, and Texas, and his own old Kentucky. And do you think, he asked who was in command of the 'Legion of the West.' I told him it was a very gallant officer named Grant, and that, by our last news, he was about to establish his headquarters at Vicksburg. Then, 'Where is Vicksburg?' I worked that out on the map; it was about a hundred miles, more or less, above his old Fort Adams; and I thought Fort Adams must be a ruin now. 'It must be at old Vick's plantation, at Walnut Hills,' said he: 'well, that is a change!'

"I tell you, Ingham, it was a hard thing to condense the history of half a century into that talk with a sick man. And I do not now know what I told him—of emigration, and the means of it—of steamboats, and railroads, and telegraphs—of inventions, and books, and literature—of the colleges, and West Point, and the Naval School—but with the queerest interruptions that ever you heard. You see it was Robinson Crusoe asking all the accumulated questions of fifty-six years!

"I remember he asked, all of a sudden, who was President now; and when I told him, he asked if Old Abe was General Benjamin Lincoln's son. He said he met old General Lincoln, when he was quite a boy himself, at some Indian treaty. I said no, that Old Abe was a Kentuckian like himself, but I could not tell him of what family; he had worked up from the ranks. 'Good for him!' cried Nolan; 'I'm glad of that. As I have brooded and wondered, I have thought our danger was in keeping up those regular successions in the first families.'

"Then I got talking about my visit to Washington. I told him of meeting the Oregon congressman, Harding; I told him about the Smithsonian, and the Exploring Expedition; I told him about the Capitol, and the statues for the pediment, and Crawford's Liberty, and Greenough's Washington: Ingham, I told him everything I could think of that would show the grandeur of his country and its prosperity; but I could not make up my mouth to tell him a word about this infernal Rebellion!

"And he drank it in, and enjoyed it as I cannot tell you. He grew more and more silent, yet I never thought he was tired or faint. I gave him a glass of water, but he just wet his lips, and told me not to go away. Then he asked me to bring the Presbyterian 'Book of Public Prayer,' which lay there, and said, with a smile that it would open at the right place—and so it did.

"There was his double red mark down the page; and I knelt down and read, and he repeated with me, 'For ourselves and our country, O gracious God, we thank Thee, that, notwithstanding our manifold transgressions for Thy holy laws, Thou hast continued to us Thy marvellous kindness,'—and so to the end of that thanksgiving.

"Then he turned to the end of the same book, and I read the words more familiar to me: 'Most heartily we beseech

Thee with Thy favour to behold and bless Thy servant, the President of the United States, and all others in authority,'—and the rest of the Episcopal collect. 'Danforth,' said he, 'I have repeated those prayers night and morning, it is now fifty-five years.' And then he said he would go to sleep.

"He bent me down over him and kissed me; and he said, 'Look in my Bible, Danforth, when I am gone.' And I went away.

"But I had no thought it was the end. I thought he was tired and would sleep. I knew he was happy and I wanted him to be alone.

"But in an hour, when the doctor went in gently, he found Nolan had breathed his life away with a smile. He had something pressed close to his lips. It was his father's badge of the Order of the Cincinnati.

"We looked in his Bible, and there was a slip of paper at the place where he had marked the text:—

"'They desire a country, even a heavenly: wherefore God is not ashamed to be called their God: for he hath prepared for them a city.'

"On this slip of paper he had written:—

"'Bury me in the sea; it has been my home, and I love it. But will not some one set up a stone for my memory at Fort Adams or at Orleans, that my disgrace may not be more than I ought to bear? Say on it:—

"'*In Memory of*
"'PHILIP NOLAN,
"'*Lieutenant in the Army of the United States.*
"'He loved his country as no other man has loved her, but no man deserved less at her hands.'"

The Foreman

By Stewart Edward White

A man is one thing; a man *plus* his work is another, entirely different. You can learn this anywhere, but in the lumber woods best of all.

Especially is it true of the camp boss, the foreman. A firm that knows its business knows this and so never considers merely what sort of a character a candidate may bear in town. He may drink or abstain, may exhibit bravery or cowardice, strength or weakness—it is all one to the lumbermen who employ him. In the woods his quality must appear. So often the man most efficient and trusted in the especial environment of his work is the most disreputable outside it. The mere dignifying quality of labour raises his value to the nth power. In it he discovers the self-respect which, in one form or another, is absolutely necessary to the man who counts. His resolution to succeed has back of it this necessity of self-respect, and so is invincible. A good boss gives back before nothing which will further his job.

Most people in the North Country understand this double standard; but occasionally someone, either stupid or inexperienced or unobservant, makes the mistake of concluding that the town-character and the woods-character are necessarily the same. If he acts in accordance with that erroneous idea, he gets into trouble. Take the case of Silver Jack and the walking boss of Morrison & Daly, for instance. Silver Jack imagined his first encounter with Richard Darrell in Bay City indicated the certainty of like results to his second encounter with that individual in Camp Thirty. His mistake was costly; but almost anybody could have told him better. To understand the case, you must first meet Richard Darrell.

The latter was a man about five feet six inches in height, slenderly built, yet with broad, hanging shoulders. His face was an exact triangle, beginning with a mop of red-brown hair, and ending with a pointed chin. Two level quadrilaterals served him as eyebrows, beneath which a strong hooked nose separated his round, brown, chipmunk's eyes. When he walked, he threw his heavy shoulders slightly forward. This, in turn, projected his eager, nervous countenance. The fact that he was accustomed to hold his hands half open, with the palms square to the rear, lent him a peculiarly ready and truculent air. His name, as has been said, was Richard Darrell; but men called him Roaring Dick.

For upward of fifteen years he had been woods foreman for Morrison & Daly, the great lumber firm of the Beeson Lake district. That would make him about thirty-eight years old. He did not look it. His firm thought everything of him in spite of the fact that his reputation made it exceedingly difficult to hire men for his camps. He had the name of a "driver." But this little man, in some mysterious way of his own, could get in the logs. There was none like him. About once in three months he would suddenly appear, worn and haggard, at Beeson Lake, where he would drop into an iron bed, which the Company maintained for that especial purpose. Tim Brady, the care-taker, would bring him food at stated intervals. After four days of this, he would as suddenly disappear into the forest, again charged with the vital, restless energy which kept him on his feet fourteen hours a day until the next break down. When he looked directly at you, this nerve-force seemed to communicate itself to you with the physical shock of an impact.

Richard Darrell usually finished banking his season's cut a month earlier than anybody else. Then he drew his pay at Beeson Lake, took the train for Bay City, and set out to have a good time. Whiskey was its main element. On his intensely nervous organisation it acted like poison. He would do the wildest things. After his money was all spent, he started up river for the log-drive, hollow-eyed, shaking. In twenty-four hours he was himself again, dominant, truculent, fixing his brown chipmunk eyes on the delinquents with the physical shock of an impact, coolly balancing beneath the imminent ruin of a jam.

Silver Jack, on the other hand, was not nervous at all, but very tall and strong, with bronze-red skin, and flaxen white hair, moustache and eyebrows. The latter peculiarity earned him his nickname. He was at all times absolutely fearless and self-reliant in regard to material conditions, but singularly unobservant and stupid when it was a question of psychology. He had been a sawyer in his early experience, but later became a bartender in Muskegon.

He was in general a good-humoured animal enough, but fond of a swagger, given to showing off, and exceedingly ugly when his passions were aroused.

His first hard work, after arriving in Bay City, was, of course, to visit the saloons. In one of these he came upon Richard Darrell. The latter was enjoying himself noisily by throwing wine-glasses at a beer advertisement. As he always paid liberally for the glasses, no one thought of objecting.

"Who's th' bucko?" inquired Silver Jack of a man near the stove.

"That's Roaring Dick Darrell, walkin' boss for M. & D.," replied the other.

Silver Jack drew his flax-white eyebrows together.

"Roaring Dick, eh? Roaring Dick? Fine name fer a bad man. I s'pose he thinks he's perticular reckless, don't he?"

"I do'no. Guess he is. He's got th' name fer it."

"Well," said Silver Jack, drawing his powerful back into a bow, "I ain't much; but I don't like noise—'specially roaring."

With the words he walked directly across the saloon to the foreman.

"My name is Silver Jack," said he, "I come from Muskegon way. I don't like noise. Quit it."

"All right," replied Dick.

The other was astonished. Then he recovered his swagger and went on:

"They tell me you're the old he-coon of this neck of th' woods. P'r'aps you *were*. But I'm here now. Ketch on? I'm th' boss of this shebang now."

Dick smiled amiably. "All right," he repeated.

This second acquiescence nonplussed the newcomer. But he insisted on his fight.

"You're a bluff," said he, insultingly.

"Ah! get out!" replied Dick with disgust.

"What's that?" shouted the stranger, towering with threatening bulk over the smaller man.

And then to his surprise Dick Darrell began to beg.

"Don't you hit me!" he cried, "I ain't done nothing to you. You let me alone! Don't you let him touch me!" he called beseechingly to the barkeeper. "I don't want to get hurt. Stop it! Let me be!"

Silver Jack took Richard Darrell by the collar and propelled him rapidly to the door. The foreman hung back like a small boy in the grasp of a schoolmaster, whining, beseeching, squirming, appealing for help to the barkeeper and the bystanders. When finally he was energetically kicked into the gutter, he wept a little with nervous rage.

"Roaring Dick! Rats!" said Silver Jack. "Anybody can do him proper. If that's your 'knocker,' you're a gang of high bankers."

The other men merely smiled in the manner of those who know. Incidentally Silver Jack was desperately pounded by Big Dan, later in the evening, on account of that "high-banker" remark.

Richard Darrell, soon after, went into the woods with his crew, and began the tremendous struggle against the wilderness. Silver Jack and Big Dan took up the saloon business at Beeson Lake, and set themselves to gathering a clientèle which should do them credit.

The winter was a bad one for everybody. Deep snows put the job behind; frequent storms undid the work of an infinitely slow patience. When the logging roads were cut through, the ground failed to freeze because of the thick white covering that overlaid it. Darrell in his mysterious compelling fashion managed somehow. Everywhere his thin eager triangle of a face with the brown chipmunk eyes was seen, bullying the men into titanic exertions by the mere shock of his nervous force. Over the thin crust of ice cautious loads of a few thousand feet were drawn to the banks of the river. The road-bed held. Gradually it hardened and thickened. The size of the loads increased. Finally Billy O'Brien drew up triumphantly at the rollway.

"There's a rim-racker!" he exclaimed. "Give her all she'll stand, Jimmy."

Jimmy Hall, the scaler, laid his flexible rule over the face of each log. The men gathered, interested in this record load.

"Thirteen thousand two hundred and forty," announced the scaler at last.

"Whoopee!" crowed Billy O'Brien, "that'll lay out Rollway Charley by two thousand feet!"

The men congratulated him on his victory over the other teamster, Rollway Charley. Suddenly Darrell was among them, eager, menacing, thrusting his nervous face and heavy shoulders here and there in the crowd, bullying them back to the work which they were neglecting. When his back was turned they grumbled at him savagely, threatening to disobey, resolving to quit. Some of them did quit: but none of them disobeyed.

Now the big loads were coming in regularly, and the rollways became choked with the logs dumped down on them from the sleighs. There were not enough men to roll them down to the river, nor to "deck" them there in piles. Work accumulated. The cant-hook men became discouraged. What was the use of trying? They might as well take it easy. They did take it easy. As a consequence the teamsters had often to wait two, three hours to be unloaded. They were out until long after dark, feeling their way homeward through hunger and cold.

Dick Darrell, walking boss of all the camps, did the best he could. He sent message after message to Beeson Lake demanding more men. If the rollways could be definitely cleared once, the work would lighten all along the line. Then the men would regain their content. More help was promised, but it was slow in coming. The balance hung trembling. At any moment the foreman expected the crisis, when the men, discouraged by the accumulation of work, would begin to "jump," would ask for their "time" and quit, leaving the job half finished in the woods. This catastrophe must not happen. Darrell himself worked like a demon until dark, and then, ten to one, while the other men rested, would strike feverishly across to Camp Twenty-eight or Camp Forty, where he would consult with Morgan or Scotty Parsons until far into the night. His pale, triangular face showed the white lines of exhaustion, but his chipmunk eyes and his eager movements told of a determination stronger than any protest of a mere nature.

Now fate ordained that Silver Jack for the purposes of his enlightenment should select just this moment to drum up trade. He was, in his way, as anxious to induce the men to come out of the woods as Richard Darrell was to keep them in. Beeson Lake at this time of year was very dull. Only a few chronic loafers, without money, ornamented the saloon walls. On the other hand, at the four camps of Morrison & Daly were three hundred men each with four months' pay coming to him. In the ordinary course of events these men would not be out for sixty days yet, but Silver Jack and Big Dan perfectly well knew that it only needed the suggestion, the temptation, to arouse the spirit of restlessness. That a taste or so of whiskey will shiver the patience of men oppressed by long monotony is as A B C to the North Country saloon-keeper. Silver Jack resolved to make the rounds of the camps sure that the investment of a few jugs of whiskey would bring down to Beeson Lake at least thirty or forty woods-wearied men.

Accordingly he donned many clothes, and drove out into the wilderness a cutter containing three jugs and some cigars in boxes. He anticipated trouble. Perhaps he would even have to lurk in the woods, awaiting his opportunity to smuggle his liquor to the men.

However, luck favoured him. At Camp Twenty-eight he was able to dodge unseen into the men's camp. When Morgan, the camp foreman, finally discovered his presence, the mischief had been done. Everybody was smoking cigars, everybody was happily conscious of a warm glow at the pit of the stomach, everybody was firmly convinced that Silver Jack was the best fellow on earth. Morgan could do nothing. An attempt to eject Silver Jack, an expostulation even, would, he knew, lose him his entire crew. The men, their heads whirling with the anticipated delights of a spree, would indignantly champion their new friend. Morgan retired grimly to the "office." There, the next morning, he silently made out the "time" of six men, who had decided to quit. He wondered what would become of the rollways.

Silver Jack, for the sake of companionship, took one of the "jumpers" in the cutter with him. He was pleased over his success, and intended now to try Camp Thirty, Darrell's headquarters. In regard to Morgan he had been somewhat uneasy, for he had never encountered that individual; but Darrell he thought he knew. The trouble at Bay City had inspired him with a great contempt for the walking boss. That is where his mistake came in.

It was very cold. The snow was up to the horses' bellies, so Silver Jack had to drive at a plunging walk. Occasionally one or the other of the two stood up and thrashed his arms about. At noon they ate sandwiches of cold fried bacon, which the frost rendered brittle as soon as it left the warmth of their inside pockets. Underfoot the runners of the cutter shrieked loudly. They saw the tracks of deer and wolves and partridge, and encountered a few jays, chickadees, and woodpeckers. Otherwise the forest seemed quite empty. By half-past two they had made nine miles, and the sun, in this high latitude, was swinging lower. Silver Jack spoke angrily to his struggling animals. The other had fallen into silence of numbness.

They did not know that across the reaches of the forest a man was hurrying to intercept them, a man who hastened to cope with this new complication as readily as he would have coped with the emergency of a lack of flour or the sickness of horses. They drove confidently.

Suddenly from nowhere a figure appeared in the trail before them. It stood, silent and impassive, with forward-drooping, heavy shoulders, watching the approaching cutter through inscrutable chipmunk eyes. When the strangers had approached to within a few feet of this man, the horses stopped of their own accord.

"Hello, Darrell," greeted Silver Jack, tugging at one of the stone jugs beneath the seat, "you're just the man I wanted to see."

The figure made no reply.

"Have a drink," offered the big man, finally extricating the whiskey.

"You can't take that whiskey into camp," said Darrell.

"Oh, I guess so," replied Silver Jack, easily, hoping for the peaceful solution. "There ain't enough to get anybody full. Have a taster, Darrell; it's pretty good stuff."

"I mean it," repeated Darrell. "You got to go back." He seized the horses' bits and began to lead them in the reversing circle.

"Hold on there!" cried Silver Jack. "You let them horses alone! You old little runt! Let them alone I say!" The robe was kicked aside, and Silver Jack prepared to descend.

Richard Darrell twisted his feet out of his snow-shoe straps. "You can't take that whiskey into camp," he repeated simply.

"Now look here, Darrell," said the other in even tones, "don't you make no mistake. I ain't selling this whiskey; I'm *giving* it away. The law can't touch me. You ain't any right to say where I'll go, and I'm going where I please!"

"You got to go back with that whiskey," replied Darrell.

Silver Jack threw aside his coat, and advanced. "You get out of my way, or I'll kick you out, like I done at Bay City."

In an instant two blows were exchanged. The first marked Silver Jack's bronze-red face just to the left of his white eyebrow. The second sent Richard Darrell gasping and sobbing into the snow-bank ten feet away. He arose with the blood streaming from beneath his moustache. His eager, nervous face was white; his chipmunk eyes narrowed; his great hands, held palm backward, clutched spasmodically. With the stealthy motion of a cat he approached his antagonist, and sprang. Silver Jack stood straight and confident, awaiting him. Three times the aggressor was knocked entirely off his feet. The fourth he hit against the cutter body, and his fingers closed on the axe which all voyagers through the forest carry as a matter of course.

"He's gettin' ugly. Come on, Hank!" cried Silver Jack.

The other man, with a long score to pay the walking boss, seized the iron starting-bar, and descended. Out from the inscrutable white forest murder breathed like a pestilential air. The two men talked about it easily, confidently.

"You ketch him on one side, and I'll come in on the other," said the man named Hank, gripping his short, heavy bar.

The forest lay behind; the forest, easily penetrable to a man in moccasins. Richard Darrell could at any moment have fled beyond the possibility of pursuit. This had become no mere question of a bar-room fisticuff, but of life and death. He had begged abjectly from the pain of a cuff on the ear; now he merely glanced over his shoulder toward the safety that lay beyond. Then, with a cry, he whirled the axe about his head and threw it directly at the second of his antagonists. The flat of the implement struck heavily, full on the man's forehead. He fell, stunned. Immediately the other two precipitated themselves on the weapons. This time Silver Jack secured the axe, while Darrell had to content himself with the short, heavy bar. The strange duel recommenced, while the horses, mildly curious, gazed through the steam of their nostrils at their warring masters.

Overhead the ravens of the far north idled to and fro. When the three men lay still on the trampled snow, they stooped, nearer and nearer. Then they towered. One of the men had stirred.

Richard Darrell painfully cleared his eyes and dragged himself to a sitting position, sweeping the blood of his shallow wound from his forehead. He searched out the axe. With it he first smashed in the whiskey jugs. Then he wrecked the cutter, chopping it savagely until it was reduced to splinters and twisted iron. By the time this was done, his antagonists were in the throes of returning consciousness. He stood over them, dominant, menacing.

"You hit th' back trail," said he, "very quick! Don't you let me see you 'round these diggings again."

Silver Jack, bewildered, half stunned, not understanding this little cowardly man who had permitted himself to be kicked from the saloon, rose slowly.

"You stand there!" commanded Darrell. He opened a pocket-knife, and cut the harness to bits, leaving only the necessary head-stalls intact.

"Now git!" said he. "Pike out!—fer Beeson Lake. Don't you stop at no Camp Twenty-eight!"

Appalled at the prospect of the long journey through the frozen forest, Silver Jack and his companion silently led the horses away. As they reached the bend in the trail, they looked back. The sun was just setting through the trees, throwing the illusion of them gigantic across the eye. And he stood there huge, menacing, against the light—the dominant spirit, Roaring Dick of the woods, the incarnation of Necessity, the Man defending his Work, the Foreman!

The Gray Collie

By Georgia Wood Pangborn

The steam had retired, clanking, from the radiator, withdrawing to the cellar like the dragging chain of Marley's ghost. The blue flame of a Bunsen burner was the only light and heat left. Now and then the wind flung handfuls of spiteful sleet at the window.

"I don't know anything about ghosts," said Henrietta, plaintively. "I'm as bad in psychology as mathematics. I might tell about the grey collie, but he was real. Don't let that chocolate boil over, Isabel."

Isabel poured out three steaming cups, thick and sweet, for in the young twenties and late teens the appetite is still bizarre.

"I'll tell it as it happened," sighed Henrietta. "I don't believe I could make anything up to save my neck."

She was small and sad-eyed, with a timid manner, and sat on a wolf-skin, leaning one elbow on its head, which had green eyes of sinister slant, and bristling ears.

"You know who Artaxerxes was?"

"Artaxerxes," they recited, "was your old wolf-hound who was really benevolent, but everybody was afraid of him, and when he wagged his tail it waved like a cat's, sinuously, instead of swinging in a clubby, careless way, as a dog's should."

"He was white with grey spots," mused Henrietta; "I suppose his family in Siberia looked like that to match the snow when they went out hunting, and he was shaggy and soft.

"We chained him the night the circus came to town. He heard a lion roar as the train went by at three o'clock, and, at first, I thought we had another lion in the barn. Gracious! If he hadn't been chained he would have been over the wall and chased that lion to the station.

"I went down to soothe him and see if his chain had given in any of its links. I never saw him so out of temper. Finally he consented to lie down, though he grumbled about it, and the tip of his tail kept twitching, not wagging. He hardly ever wagged it.

"He worried all that day. 'Don't you know there are bears and lions and tigers and wolves out there?' he'd say—'Isn't it my business to protect you from such things? Do let me go and kill a few. I'll come right back!'

"We supposed he would stop worrying when the circus went, but instead, he got worse. He explained how it was his business to find out what had become of all those animals. In the evenings, as soon as he was unchained, he would march up and down inside the wall, holding his nose to the wind and every now and then making a low impatient sound in his throat, as if he were worried about something and making plans.

"One morning Farmer Grosman came to our house, very fierce: 'Your dog's been killing my sheep.' We explained that he never got over the six-foot wall, but nothing would do. If he hadn't done it, who had? If we did not shoot him, he would, and so on.

"Papa was very polite. He said he regretted that he could allow no shooting on the place except what he did himself. 'You are certainly entitled to shoot any dog or dogs which you may discover molesting your sheep, and I shall exercise the same prerogative in protecting my dog.'

"He said it with that deprecating smile of his—I believe he smiled deprecatingly when he got cut off from his men at Antietam, and fought his way out of a lot of rebels who tried to make him prisoner. He hated Grosman, who was the meanest man in town and starved his horses.

"The man went off growling, and said he'd see the Mayor. We chained Artie up that night. In the morning we found his cat, dead, with a half-eaten piece of poisoned meat beside it. Artie thought everything of that cat. He had carried it around in his mouth ever since it was a little kitten. He always had to have his cat, the way a child has to have a doll. Any other cat he'd have sighted half a mile away and chased. But that one was his own, and anything it did was all right. It's all in being acquainted. Papa sat up all the next night with a shotgun. We heard that the people from the French quarter of the village insisted that Artie got over the wall at night and roamed around and got into mischief. They said they heard him howling up on Mount Phelim, and talked a great deal about what they were going to do to him and us. Those Canucks would have it that he was a man-wolf, and could change about from one thing to another. You can't argue with them, when they get a notion like that.

"One morning Pete Lancto, who mows the lawn, said he had seen the devil, and that he was like a shaggy dog.

"'Probably it *was* a dog!' I said. But he told a lot of lies about smelling brimstone and flames coming out of its eyes.

"I said: 'I guess you were *tenet*' (that's their word for 'tight').

"But he hadn't touched a drop, and had only been to get a new salt codfish at the store.

"'Well, anyway, if it smelt of brimstone, it wasn't Artie.'

"But that idiot said: 'The devil, he can smell brimstone when he wants to—*je pense que oui!*'

"So I let him alone. You can't argue with a man who hasn't any premises to argue from.

"It was my work to go to the village for the mail. I went after supper, about sunset, or a little later.

"The road curves along the side of Mount Phelim, which is not much of a mountain, but rather too big for a hill. When you look south it is as if the trees stood on each others' heads, and there are wide, open spaces, like a park, so that you can see between the trunks, only by the road the underbrush is thick like a hedge. But on the north side of the road you don't want to tumble off, for the Powasket runs below, hidden under the tops of trees, so that you only know it's there from the sound. When I was little, I used to be afraid of that road, because a Canuck nurse-girl had scared me with stories of bears and catamounts and Indians.

"That was why papa had me go for the mail. He never could stand cowards. At first he used to sneak along behind me, and when I got hysterical would saunter up as if he were just out for a walk, and show me how pretty the sunset was over toward Canada, or cluck for squirrels to come out and see what we wanted, or take me up into the woods a little to find Indian pipes like caryatides holding up dead leaves. So it wasn't very long before I grew to love the walk, and the sound of the wind in the trees, even when it was dark. I got quite friendly with the squirrels, and used to leave little piles of nuts as I went to the village, and when I came back they would be all gone. There aren't many squirrels up there that can afford pecans and Brazil-nuts. I suppose they wondered till their heads ached why I left them around so carelessly.

"But when I grew to like it at night, papa began to object. A good many times when I've been sitting on the edge of the road swinging my feet over the Powasket, watching the last colour going out beyond Canada, and listening to the owls and frogs and things, he has come to meet me and grumbled about 'going to extremes.' But I had him, you see, and only laughed. Hadn't he trained me to do it?

"So about that time he got me Artaxerxes for a chaperone, and he was a good deal of a nuisance, for the village folk disliked him from the first. When they whistled to their own dogs to get them out of his way, how could he tell they weren't calling to him? And when he'd turn to see what they wanted, they'd think he was coming after them and run, which was nonsense.

"We were keeping Artie chained that week of the sheep-killing fuss. How he hated it! When I stepped upon the horse-block to mount Pixie—I rode most of that week, and he knew I never took him when I took Pixie, because he had a nasty way of snapping at her nose, not meaning anything, but it got on her nerves dreadfully—and when I mounted Pixie and shook my crop at him, he would stand up at the end of his chain, his fore paws beating the air and his tongue hanging out, because he was choking himself so hard; and I've often thought he looked more unattractive that way with his one head than any picture of Cerberus with three.

"It was particularly hard on him now that his cat was dead. We had got him a new kitten, but it wasn't broken in yet, and couldn't understand that he didn't mean anything when he carried it around in his mouth.

"It was that evening that I saw the grey collie the first time. There were long streaks of late sunlight reaching up into the mountain and he was so mixed up in the light and shadow that it was only by chance I saw him at all, he was so like the tree trunks and bowlders; but he happened to be in a place that I knew all about, because it was where papa and I had often sat, and I knew no grey patch of anything belonged just there. It was like finding an animal in one of those old puzzle-pictures, where they're all mixed up in the branches.

"I reined up and whistled, and called him every name I could think of, but he did not stir, so that I almost thought my eyes were wrong after all; but there was no mistaking those pointed ears cocked toward me. I thought he might be the sheep-killer, though he was such an aristocratic creature, for what can you expect of a dog that's lost and hungry and unhappy? I'd probably steal something myself if I felt that way. I knew that nobody in our part of the country owned such a dog as that, and I wondered if his master were dead up there on the mountain. There are so many queer accidents—but it was the closed season. The more I wondered, the queerer it seemed.

"All of a sudden, Pixie snorted and plunged so that I was almost thrown, for I wasn't expecting it, and was leaning over with a loose rein and my arm out toward the collie. I had trusted that mare like my own sister, and had believed her a sensible soul, but she never stopped until she reached the barn, sweating and trembling like anything.

"I was so out of patience that I left her at home with Artie the next time I went for the mail. I planned as I went through the woods how I would make the collie's acquaintance and bring him home, and how he and Artie would strike up a friendship. They were both such splendid fellows and so lonely. I thought a good deal about it, how I'd manage, for I knew that if I wasn't careful they'd be more likely to kill each other first—like Balin and Balan, you know—and make up afterward.

"I didn't meet the collie until I was coming back. It was twilight, and the moon was rather narrow to see by. There was a rustle and snapping in the bushes at the side of the road.

"'Nice fellow!' I said, and stopped. I could make out the silhouette of his ears cocked toward me, and a little glimmer where his eyes were. 'Poor old chap,' I said, 'did you lose your folks?' But he wouldn't say a word, and backed off when I went toward him, so finally I went on, hoping he would follow, and he did, but slyly, so I could hardly be sure it was he, keeping beside me in the underbrush.

"When I reached the open, and looked back, he was standing in a faint patch of moonlight, in the middle of the road, looking after me with his head down a little, something the way people look at you under their eyebrows when they're trying to understand.

"I whistled and called, but it was no use. He stood there as long as I did, and I finally went on without him. But I couldn't get him off my mind. It seemed such a wild, lonesome life for a dog that must have been brought up in a pleasant home, with regular meals and a fireplace to lie in front of, and probably a girl like me to take him walking. And it seemed as if it must be something queer and tragic to send him off that way by himself. I thought more and more how some young fellow might be lying dead up there on the mountain. I made up a whole story about it that evening. And that night I dreamed I had the collie and found a collar hidden in his ruff, and was trying to read his name on it—but you know how hard it is to read anything in a dream; you look at a letter and it changes to something else, or dances off to one side. Then he seemed to be telling me a long story, the way animals do in dreams, but when I woke up it turned into nonsense.

"I knew he would meet me the next evening, and so I took some of Artie's dog-biscuit with me, and while the collie padded along the other side of the bushes, tried to reach some through to him, but he wouldn't touch it, though once he sniffed a little very daintily, and then blew out his breath, as dogs do when they've found out all they want to know about a smell. He kept right beside me. As we neared the opening he grew bolder, frisked across the road in front and came up from the other side.

As I pretended to pay no attention, he came close behind and touched my elbow, hardly enough to say so, but I felt his breath warm through my sleeve.

"When I came out into the open moonlight he stood as he had before at the edge of the woods, and watched me out of sight. I couldn't believe that he was the sheep-killer, he seemed so gentle and timid, but I didn't dare speak of him to any one—it would have seemed like betraying a trust—for I knew that in other people's minds, if they found out that he was there, it would lie between him and Artie, and as Artie was out of the question, they would take it out in killing the collie anyhow. I felt something the way Southern girls do in novels, when they're hiding a handsome Union soldier.

"The next evening I started as usual, but just as I got to the woods, Artie came tearing after me, dragging a yard of chain and pretending he thought I wanted him! I could have slapped him, but took it out in being sarcastic, with words he couldn't understand, and hitched his chain to my belt, so that if he started to be impolite to the other fellow, I could have something to say about it.

"We reached the post-office safely enough, but I was glad he was tight to my belt, for some rough men looked at us in that ugly, suspicious way and said 'sheep-killer' once or twice, and 'loup-garou.' So I really felt safer when we reached the woods, in spite of dreading the meeting between Artie and the collie.

"But I didn't hear or see anything of him until we were half-way through, and then, so far off it might have been on top of the mountain, I heard him howl—not exactly a howl, but a queer cry, as if he were calling to something at a distance, kind of sorrowful, but fierce, too. It went down my back like a chip of ice—but I'd hardly heard it when Artie roared in answer, and I was being carried up that mountain at the end of his chain like a cart after a runaway horse.

"And I had thought I could hold him! Gracious! I tried to catch at the branches, but they broke. We went through a patch of blackberries, and there was a mucky little spring, where I fell in the mud and scared the frogs, and I think it must have been half-way up Phelim, where I finally caught tight hold of a tree trunk and my belt broke and Artie went on as if he didn't know the difference. I don't know how long it was before I got my breath and began to think. Then I heard them—away off at the top, the frogs singing between as peaceful as could be—but I heard that wicked snarling and knew they were at it—Balin and Balan—and that they were so well matched it was likely to be the death of both, unless I could stop it. I followed the sound and climbed after, though I was all weak and trembling. You can see on my hands now how the thorns had scratched, and my clothes were heavy and sticky with mud. It seemed ages before I got there. I think I was crying.

"I knew I couldn't do anything, but I picked up the heaviest stick I could find, though all the sticks you can pick up in the woods are as rotten and light as powder. They didn't seem to know I was there. They were in a little open space, and the moonlight lit up their eyes now and then. I could see that the collie was a more tremendous fellow than I had thought—and then—all of a sudden—I knew!

"And because I knew I didn't even try to pull Artie away when he got the other fellow by the throat, and held him down, while he got weaker and weaker. I looked at him there in the moonlight, and cried, and wondered how I'd been so stupid.

"While I sat there wringing my hands and waiting for Artie to let go, some men came up and turned a bull's-eye lantern on me, and seemed so astonished they couldn't do anything but swear, though each would try to shut the other up, now and then, saying there 'was a lady present.'

"One of them seemed to think it was funny, and explained what they had said to each other, the way people always do for animals or babies. 'Siberian wolf and Siberian wolf-hound! Must 'a seemed kin' o' natural for them fellers to meet up. 'Beg pardon,' says the wolf, 'ain't I seen you before?'—and says the pup, 'I don't know, but you're certainly the chap my mammy told me to lick if ever I come acrost you, and, by thunder, I'll do it!' Which he did. 'Will you be so kind, Miss, when your little terrier there has quite finished, to call him off? It'd be rayther indelicate for a stranger to interfere.'

"The other man seemed sorry. 'Nothing left but his pelt, which is some chewed, but could be mended up into a real elegant rug, which the young lady might be pleased to accept.'"

Henrietta thoughtfully scratched the ears of the rug, and ran her fingers over the rows of beautiful teeth. "This is the collie."

"But sometimes I wonder just what he had in mind when I felt his breath on my elbow. Most people would say that he was thinking how convenient I would be some evening when no sheep was handy, but I'm not sure. At the time I supposed he was sad and lonesome, and glad of my company. A wolf, after all, is a good deal of a person. He was so frightfully solitary, you see—nobody to answer his gathering cry—half a world away from his own people."

The Fore-Room Rug

By Kate Douglas Wiggin

Diadema, wife of Jot Bascom, was sitting at the window of the village watch-tower, so called because it commanded a view of nearly everything that happened in Pleasant River; those details escaping the physical eye being supplied by faith and imagination working in the light of past experience. She sat in the chair of honour, the chair of choice, the high-backed rocker by the southern window, in which her husband's mother, old Mrs. Bascom, had sat for thirty years, applying a still more powerful intellectual telescope to the doings of her neighbours. Diadema's seat had formerly been on the less desirable side of the little light-stand, where Priscilla Hollis was now installed.

Mrs. Bascom was at work on a new fore-room rug, the former one having been transferred to Miss Hollis's chamber; for, as the teacher at the brick schoolhouse, a graduate of a Massachusetts normal school and the daughter of a deceased judge, she was a boarder of considerable consequence. It was a rainy Saturday afternoon, and the two women were alone. It was a pleasant, peaceful sitting-room, as neat as wax in every part. The floor was covered by a cheerful patriotic rag carpet woven entirely of red, white, and blue rags, and protected in various exposed localities by button rugs—red, white, and blue disks superimposed one on the other.

Diadema Bascom was a person of some sentiment. When her old father, Captain Dennett, was dying, he drew a wallet from under his pillow, and handed her a twenty-dollar bill to get something to remember him by. This unwonted occurrence burned itself into the daughter's imagination, and when she came as a bride to the Bascom house she refurnished the sitting-room as a kind of monument to the departed soldier, whose sword and musket were now tied to the wall with neatly hemmed bows of bright red cotton.

The chair cushions were of red-and-white glazed patch, the turkey wings that served as hearth brushes were hung against the white-painted chimney-piece with blue skirt braid, and the white shades were finished with home-made scarlet "tossels." A little whatnot in one corner was laden with the trophies of battle. The warrior's brass buttons were strung on a red picture cord and hung over his daguerreotype on the upper shelf; there was a tarnished shoulder strap, and a flattened bullet that the captain's jealous contemporaries swore *he* never stopped, unless he got it in the rear when he was flying from the foe. There was also a little tin canister in which a charge of powder had been sacredly preserved. The scoffers, again, said that "the cap'n put it in his musket when he went into the war, and kep' it there till he come out." These objects were tastefully decorated with the national colours. In fact, no modern æsthete could have arranged a symbolic symphony of grief and glory with any more fidelity to an ideal than Diadema Bascom, in working out her scheme of red, white, and blue.

Rows of ripening tomatoes lay along the ledges of the windows, and a tortoiseshell cat snoozed on one of the broad sills. The tall clock in the corner ticked peacefully. Priscilla Hollis never tired of looking at the jolly red-cheeked moon, the group of stars on a blue ground, the trig little ship, the old house, and the jolly moon again, creeping one after another across the open space at the top.

Jot Bascom was out, as usual, gathering statistics of the last horse trade; little Jot was building "stickin'" houses in the barn; Priscilla was sewing long strips for braiding; while Diadema sat at the drawing-in frame, hook in hand, and a large basket of cut rags by her side.

Not many weeks before she had paid one of her periodical visits to the attic. No housekeeper in Pleasant River save Mrs. Jonathan Bascom would have thought of dusting a garret, washing the window and sweeping down the cobwebs once a month, and renewing the camphor bags in the chests twice a year; but notwithstanding this zealous care the moths had made their way into one of her treasure-houses, the most precious of all—the old hair trunk that had belonged to her sister Lovice.

Once ensconced there, they had eaten through its hoarded relics, and reduced the faded finery to a state best described by Diadema as "reg'lar riddlin' sieves." She had brought the tattered pile down into the kitchen, and had spent a tearful afternoon in cutting the good pieces from the perforated garments. Three heaped-up baskets and a full dish-pan were the result; and as she had snipped and cut and sorted, one of her sentimental projects had entered her mind and taken complete possession there.

"I declare," she said, as she drew her hooking-needle in and out, "I wouldn't set in the room with some folks and work on these pieces; for every time I draw in a scrap of cloth Lovice comes up to me for all the world as if she was settin' on the sofy there. I ain't told you my plan, Miss Hollis, and there ain't many I shall tell; but this rug is going to be a kind of a hist'ry of my life and Lovey's wrought in together, just as we was bound up in one another when she was alive. Her things and mine was laid in one trunk, and the moths sha'n't cheat me out of 'em altogether. If I can't look at 'em wet Sundays, and shake 'em out, and have a good cry over 'em, I'll make 'em up into a kind of dumb show that will mean something to me, if it don't to anybody else.

"We was the youngest of thirteen, Lovey and I, and we was twins. There's never been more'n half o' me left sence she died. We was born together, played and went to school together, got engaged and married together, and we all but died together, yet we wa'n't a mite alike. There was an old lady come to our house once that used to say, 'There's sister Nabby, now: she'n' I ain't no more alike 'n if we wa'n't two; she's jest as dif'rent as I am t'other way.' Well, I know what I want to put into my rag story, Miss Hollis, but I don't hardly know how to begin."

Priscilla dropped her needle, and bent over the frame with interest.

"A spray of two roses in the centre—there's the beginning; why, don't you see, dear Mrs. Bascom?"

"Course I do," said Diadema, diving to the bottom of the dish-pan. "I've got my start now, and don't you say a word for a minute. The two roses grow out of one stalk; they'll be Lovey and me, though I'm consid'able more like a potato blossom. The stalk's got to be green, and here is the very green silk mother walked bride in, and Lovey and I had roundabouts of it afterwards. She had the chicken-pox when we was about four years old, and one of the first things I can remember is climbing up and looking over mother's footboard at Lovey, all speckled. Mother had let her slip on her new green roundabout over her nightgown, just to pacify her, and there she set playing with the kitten Reuben Granger had brought her. He was only ten years old then, but he'd begun courting Lovice. The Grangers' farm joined ours. They had eleven children, and mother and father had thirteen, and we was always playing together. Mother used to tell a funny story about that. We were all little young ones and looked pretty much alike, so she didn't take much notice of us in the daytime when we was running out 'n' in; but at night, when the turn-up bedstead in the kitchen was taken down and the trundle-beds were full, she used to count us over, to see if we were all there. One night, when she'd counted thirteen and set down to her sewing, father come in and asked if Moses was all right, for one of the neighbours had seen him playing side of the river about supper-time. Mother knew she'd counted us straight, but she went round with a candle to make sure. Now, Mr. Granger had a head as red as a sumac bush; and when she carried the candle close to the beds to take another tally, there was thirteen children, sure enough, but if there wa'n't a red-headed Granger right in amongst our boys in the turn-up bedstead! While father set out on a hunt for our Moses, mother yanked the sleepy little red-headed Granger out o' the middle and took him home, and father found Moses asleep on a pile of shavings under the joiner's bench.

"They don't have such families nowadays. One time when measles went all over the village, they never came to us, and Jabe Slocum said there wa'n't enough measles to go through the Dennett family, so they didn't start in on 'em. There, I ain't going to finish the stalk; I'm going to draw in a little here and there all over the rug, while I'm in the sperit of plannin' it, and then it will be plain work of matching colours and filling out.

"You see the stalk is mother's dress, and the outside green of the moss roses is the same goods, only it's our roundabouts. I meant to make 'em red, when I marked the pattern, and then fill out round 'em with a light colour; but now I ain't satisfied with anything but white, for nothing will do in the middle of the rug but our white wedding dresses. I shall have to fill in dark, then, or mixed. Well, that won't be out of the way, if it's going to be a true rag story; for Lovey's life went out altogether, and mine hasn't been any too gay.

"I'll begin Lovey's rose first. She was the prettiest and the liveliest girl in the village, and she had more beaux than you could shake a stick at. I generally had to take what she left over. Reuben Granger was crazy about her from the time she was knee-high; but when he went away to Bangor to study for the ministry, the others had it all their own way. She was only seventeen; she hadn't ever experienced religion, and she was mischievous as a kitten.

"You remember you laughed, this morning, when Mr. Bascom told about Hogshead Jowett? Well, he used to want to keep company with Lovey; but she couldn't abide him, and whenever he come to court her she clim' into a hogshead, and hid till after he'd gone. The boys found it out, and used to call him 'Hogshead Jowett.' He was the biggest fool in Foxboro' Four Corners; and that's saying consid'able, for Foxboro' is famous for its fools, and always has been. There was thirteen of 'em there one year. They say a man come out from Portland, and when he got as fur as Foxboro' he kep' inquiring the way to Dunstan; and I declare if he didn't meet them thirteen fools, one after another, standing in their front dooryards ready to answer questions. When he got to Dunstan, says he, 'For the Lord's sake, what kind of a village is it that I've just went through? Be they *all* fools there?'

"Hogshead was scairt to death whenever he come to see Lovice. One night, when he'd been there once, and she'd hid, as she always done, he come back a second time, and she went to the door, not mistrusting it was him. 'Did you forget anything?' says she, sparkling out at him through a little crack. He was all taken aback by seeing her, and he stammered out, 'Yes, I forgot my han'k'chief; but it don't make no odds, for I didn't pay out but fifteen cents for it two year ago, and I don't make no use of it 'ceptins to wipe my nose on.' How we did laugh over that! Well, he had a conviction of sin pretty soon afterwards, and p'r'aps it helped his head some; at any rate, he quit farming, and become a Bullockite preacher.

"It seems odd, when Lovice wa'n't a perfessor herself, she should have drawed the most pious young men in the village, but she did; she had good Orthodox beaux, Free and Close Baptists, Millerites and Adventists, all on her string together; she even had one Cochranite, though the sect had mostly died out. But when Reuben Granger come home, a full-feathered-out minister, he seemed to strike her fancy as he never had before, though they were always good friends from children. He had light hair and blue eyes and fair skin (his business being under cover kep' him bleached out), and he and Lovey made the prettiest couple you ever see; for she was dark complexioned, and her cheeks no otherways than scarlit the whole durin' time. She had a change of heart that winter; in fact, she had two of 'em, for she changed hers for Reuben's, and found a hope at the same time. 'Twas a good, honest conversion, too, though she did say to me she was afraid that if Reuben hadn't taught her what love was or might be, she'd never have found out enough about it to love God as she'd ought to.

"There, I've begun both roses, and hers is 'bout finished. I sha'n't have more'n enough white alapaca. It's lucky the moths spared one breadth of the wedding dresses; we was married on the same day, you know, and dressed just alike. Jot wa'n't quite ready to be married, for he wa'n't any more forehanded 'bout that than he was 'bout other things; but I told him Lovey and I had kept up with each other from the start, and he'd got to fall into line or drop out of the percession. Now what next?"

"Wasn't there anybody at the wedding but you and Lovice?" asked Priscilla, with an amused smile.

"Land, yes! The meeting-house was cram jam full. Oh, to be sure! I know what you're driving at! Well, I have to laugh to think I should have forgot the husbands! They'll have to be worked into the story, certain; but it'll be consid'able of a chore, for I can't make flowers out of coat and pants stuff, and there ain't any more flowers on this branch, anyway."

Diadema sat for a few minutes in rapt thought, and then made a sudden inspired dash upstairs, where Miss Hollis presently heard her rummaging in an old chest. She soon came down, triumphant.

"Wa'n't it a providence I saved Jot's and Reuben's wedding ties! And here they are—one yellow and green mixed, and one brown. Do you know what I'm going to do? I'm going to draw in a butterfly hovering over them two roses, and make it out of the neckties—green with brown spots. That'll bring in the husbands; and land! I wouldn't have either of 'em know it for the world. I'll take a pattern of that lunar moth you pinned on the curtain yesterday."

Miss Hollis smiled in spite of herself. "You have some very ingenious ideas and some very pretty thoughts, Mrs. Bascom, do you know it?"

"It's the first time I ever heard tell of it," said Diadema cheerfully. "Lovey was the pretty-spoken, pretty-appearing one; I was always plain and practical. While I think of it, I'll draw in a little mite of this red into my carnation pink. It was a red scarf Reuben brought Lovey from Portland. It was the first thing he ever give her, and aunt Hitty said if one of the Abel Grangers give away anything that cost money, it meant business. That was all fol-de-rol, for there never was a more liberal husband, though he was a poor minister; but then they always *are* poor, without they're rich; there don't seem to be any half-way in ministers.

"We was both lucky that way. There ain't a stingy bone in Jot Bascom's body. He don't make much money, but what he does make goes into the bureau drawer, and the one that needs it most takes it out. He never asks me what I done with the last five cents he give me. You've never been married, Miss Hollis, and you ain't engaged, so you don't know much about it; but I tell you there's a heap o' foolishness talked about husbands. If you get the one you like yourself, I don't know as it matters if all the other women folks in town don't happen to like him as well as you do; they ain't called on to do that. They see the face he turns to them, not the one he turns to you. Jot ain't a very good provider, nor he ain't a man that's much use round a farm, but he's such a fav'rite I can't blame him. There's one thing: when he does come home he's got something to say, and he's always as lively as a cricket, and smiling as a basket of chips. I like a man that's good comp'ny, even if he ain't so forehanded. There ain't anything specially lovable about forehandedness, when you come to that. I shouldn't ever feel drawed to a man because he was on time with his work. He's got such pleasant ways, Jot has! The other afternoon he didn't get home early enough to milk; and after I done the two cows, I split the kindling and brought in the wood, for I knew he'd want to go to the tavern and tell the boys 'bout the robbery up to Boylston. There ain't anybody but Jot in this village that has wit enough to find out what's going on, and tell it in an int'resting way round the tavern fire. And he can do it without being full of cider, too; he don't need any apple juice to limber *his* tongue!

"Well, when he come in, he sees the pails of milk, and the full wood-box, and the supper laid out under the screen cloth on the kitchen table, and he come up to me at the sink, and says he, 'Diademy, you're the best wife in this county, and the brightest jewel in my crown—that's what *you* are!' (He got that idee out of a duet he sings with Almiry Berry.) Now I'd like to know whether that ain't pleasanter than 'tis to have a man do all the shed 'n' barn work up smart, and then set round the stove looking as doleful as a last year's bird's-nest? Take my advice, Miss Hollis: get a good provider if you can, but anyhow try to find you a husband that'll keep on courting a little now and then, when he ain't too busy; it smooths things consid'able round the house.

"There, I got so int'rested in what I was saying, I've went on and finished the carnation, and some of the stem, too. Now what comes next? Why, the thing that happened next, of course, and that was little Jot.

"I'll work in a bud on my rose and one on Lovey's, and my bud'll be made of Jot's first trousers. The goods ain't very appropriate for a rosebud, but it'll be mostly covered with green on the outside, and it'll have to do, for the idee is the most important thing in this rug. When I put him into pants, I hadn't any cloth in the house, and it was such bad going Jot couldn't get to Wareham to buy me anything; so I made 'em out of an old grey cashmere skirt, and lined 'em with flannel."

"Buds are generally the same colour as the roses, aren't they?" ventured Priscilla.

"I don't care if they be," said Diadema obstinately. "What's to hender this bud's bein' grafted on? Mrs. Granger was as black as an Injun, but the little Granger children were all red-headed, for they took after their father. But I don't know; you've kind o' got me out o' conceit with it. I s'pose I could have taken a piece of his baby blanket; but the moths never et a mite o' that, and it's too good to cut up. There's one thing I can do: I can make the bud with a long stem, and have it growing right up alongside of mine—would you?"

"No, it must be stalk of your stalk, bone of your bone, flesh of your flesh, so to speak. I agree with you, the idea is the first thing. Besides, the grey is a very light shade, and I dare say it will look like a bluish white."

"I'll try it and see; but I wish to the land the moths *had* eat the pinning-blanket, and then I could have used it. Lovey worked the scallops on the aidge for me. My grief! what int'rest she took in my baby clothes! Little Jot was born at Thanksgiving time, and she come over from Skowhegan, where Reuben was settled pastor of his first church. I shall never forget them two weeks to the last day of my life. There was deep snow on the ground. I had that chamber there, with the door opening into this setting-room. Mother and father Bascom kep' out in the dining-room and kitchen, where the work was going on, and Lovey and the baby and me had the front part of the house to ourselves, with Jot coming in on tiptoe, heaping up wood in the fireplaces so 't he 'most roasted us out. He don't forget his chores in time o' sickness.

"I never took so much comfort in all my days. Jot got one of the Billings girls to come over and help in the housework so 't I could lay easy 's long as I wanted to; and I never had such a rest before nor since. There ain't any heaven in the book o' Revelations that's any better than them two weeks was. I used to lay quiet in my good feather bed, fingering the pattern of my best crochet quilt, and looking at the fire-light shining on Lovey and the baby. She'd hardly leave him in the cradle a minute. When I didn't want him in bed with me, she'd have him in her lap. Babies are common enough to most folks, but Lovey was diff'rent. She'd never had any experience with children, either, for we was the youngest in our family; and it wa'n't long before we come near being the oldest, too, for mother buried seven of us before she went herself. Anyway, I never saw nobody else look as she done when she held my baby. I don't mean nothing blasphemious when I say 'twas for all the world like your photograph of Mary, the mother of Jesus.

"The nights come in early, so it was 'most dark at four o'clock. The little chamber was so peaceful! I could hear Jot rattling the milk-pails, but I'd draw a deep breath o' comfort, for I knew the milk would be strained and set away without my stepping foot to the floor. Lovey used to set by the fire, with a tall candle on the light-stand behind her, and a little white knit cape over her shoulders. She had the pinkest cheeks, and the longest eyelashes, and a mouth like a little red buttonhole; and when she bent over the baby, and sung to him—though his ears wa'n't open, I guess, for his eyes wa'n't—the tears o' joy used to rain down my cheeks. It was pennyrial hymns she used to sing mostly, and the one I remember best was:

"'Daniel's wisdom may I know,
Stephen's faith and spirit show;
John's divine communion feel,
Moses' meekness, Joshua's zeal,
Run like the unwearied Paul,
Win the day and conquer all.
"'Mary's love may I possess,
Lydia's tender-heartedness,
Peter's fervent spirit feel,
James's faith by works reveal,
Like young Timothy may I
Every sinful passion fly.'

"'Oh, Diademy,' she'd say, 'you was always the best, and it's nothing more'n right the baby should have come to you. P'r'aps God will think I'm good enough some time; and if he does, Diademy, I'll offer up a sacrifice every morning and every evening. But I'm afraid,' says she, 'He thinks I can't stand any more happiness, and be a faithful follower of the cross. The Bible says we've got to wade through fiery floods before we can enter the kingdom. I don't hardly know how Reuben and I are going to find any to wade through; we're both so happy, they'd have to be consid'able hot before we took notice, says she, with the dimples all breaking out in her cheek.

"And that was true as gospel. She thought everything Reuben done was just right, and he thought everything she done was just right. There wa'n't nobody else; the world was all Reuben 'n' all Lovey to them. If you could have seen her when she was looking for him to come from Skowhegan! She used to watch at the attic window; and when she seen him at the foot of the hill, she'd up like a squirrel, and run down the road without stopping for anything but to throw a shawl over her head. And Reuben would ketch her up as if she was a child, and scold her for not putting a hat on, and take her under his coat coming up the hill. They was a sight for the neighbours, I must confess, but it wa'n't one you could hardly disapprove of neither. Aunt Hitty said it was tempting Providence and couldn't last, and God would visit his wrath on 'em for making idols of sinful human flesh.

"She was right one way—it didn't last; but nobody can tell me God was punishing of 'em for being too happy. I guess he ain't got no objection to folks being happy here below, if they don't forget it ain't the whole story.

"Well, I must mark in a bud on Lovey's stalk now, and I'm going to make it of her baby's long white cloak. I earned the money for it myself, making coats, and put four yards of the finest cashmere into it; for three years after little Jot was born I went over to Skowhegan to help Lovey through her time o' trial. Time o' trial! I thought I was happy, but I didn't know how to be as happy as Lovey did; I wa'n't made on that pattern.

"When I first showed her the baby (it was a boy, same as mine), her eyes shone like two evening stars. She held up her weak arms, and gathered the little bundle o' warm flannel into 'em; and when she got it close she shut her eyes and moved her lips, and I knew she was taking her lamb to the altar and off'ring it up as a sacrifice. Then Reuben come in. I seen him give one look at the two dark heads laying close together on the white piller, and then go down on his knees by the side of the bed. 'Twa'n't no place for me; I went off, and left 'em together. We didn't mistrust it then, but they only had three days more of happiness, and I'm glad I give 'em every minute."

The room grew dusky as twilight stole gently over the hills of Pleasant River. Priscilla's lip trembled; Diadema's tears fell thick and fast on the white rosebud, and she had to keep wiping her eyes as she followed the pattern.

"I ain't said as much as this about it for five years," she went on, with a tell-tale quiver in her voice, "but now I've got going, I can't stop. I'll have to get the weight out o' my heart somehow.

"Three days after I put Lovey's baby into her arms the Lord called her home. 'When I prayed so hard for this little new life, Reuben,' says she, holding the baby as if she could never let it go, 'I didn't think I'd got to give up my own in place of it; but it's the first fiery flood we've had, dear, and though it burns to my feet I'll tread it as brave as I know how.'

"She didn't speak a word after that; she just faded away like a snowdrop, hour by hour. And Reuben and I stared one another in the face as if we was dead instead of her, and we went about that house o' mourning like sleep-walkers for days and days, not knowing whether we et or slept, or what we done.

"As for the baby, the poor little mite didn't live many hours after its mother, and we buried 'em together. Reuben and I knew what Lovey would have liked. She gave her life for the baby's, and it was a useless sacrifice, after all. No, it wa'n't neither; it *couldn't* have been! You needn't tell me God'll let such sacrifices as that come out useless! But anyhow, we had one coffin for 'em both, and I opened Lovey's arms and laid the baby in 'em. When Reuben and I took our last look, we thought she seemed more'n ever like Mary, the mother of Jesus. There never was another like her, and there never will be. 'Nonesuch,' Reuben used to call her."

There was silence in the room, broken only by the ticking of the old clock and the tinkle of a distant cowbell. Priscilla made an impetuous movement, flung herself down by the basket of rags, and buried her head in Diadema's gingham apron.

"Dear Mrs. Bascom, don't cry. I'm sorry, as the children say."

"No, I won't more'n a minute. Jot can't stand it to see me give way. You go and touch a match to the kitchen fire, so 't the kettle will be boiling, and I'll have a minute to myself. I don't know what the neighbours would think to ketch me crying over my drawing-in frame; but the spell's over now, or 'bout over, and when I can muster up courage I'll take the rest of the baby's cloak and put a border of white everlastings round the outside of the rug. It'll always mean the baby's birth and Lovey's death to me; but the flowers will remind me it's life everlasting for both of 'em, and so it's the most comforting end I can think of."

It was indeed a beautiful rug when it was finished and laid in front of the sofa in the fore-room. Diadema was very choice of it. When company was expected, she removed it from its accustomed place, and spread it in a corner of the room where no profane foot could possibly tread on it. Unexpected callers were managed by a different method. If they seated themselves on the sofa, she would fear they did not "set easy" or "rest comfortable" there, and suggest their moving to the stuffed chair by the window. The neighbours thought this solicitude merely another sign of Diadema's "p'ison neatness," excusable in this case, as there was so much white in the new rug.

The fore-room blinds were ordinarily closed, and the chillness of death pervaded the sacred apartment; but on great occasions, when the sun was allowed to penetrate the thirty-two tiny panes of glass in each window, and a blaze was lighted in the fireplace, Miss Hollis would look in as she went upstairs, and muse a moment over the pathetic little romance of rags, the story of two lives worked into a bouquet of old-fashioned posies, whose gay tints were brought out by a setting of sombre threads. Existence had gone so quietly in this remote corner of the world that all its important events, babyhood, childhood, betrothal, marriage, motherhood, with all their mysteries of love and life and death, were chronicled in this narrow space not two yards square.

Diadema came in behind the little school-teacher one afternoon.

"I cal'late," she said, "that being kep' in a dark room, and never being tread on, it will last longer 'n I do. If it does, Priscilla, you know that white crape shawl of mine I wear to meetings hot Sundays: that would make a second row of everlastings round the border. You could piece out the linings good and smooth on the under side, draw in the white flowers, and fill 'em round with black to set 'em off. The rug would be han'somer than ever then, and the story—would be finished."

Cressey's New-Year's Rent

By Albert Lee

Fred Hallowell was sitting at his desk in the Gazette office, looking listlessly out into the City Hall Park, where the biting wind was making the snowflakes dance madly around the leafless trees and in the empty fountain, and he was almost wishing that there would be so few assignments to cover as to allow him an afternoon indoors to write "specials." The storm was the worst of the season, and as this was the last day of December, it looked as if the old year were going out with a tumultuous train of sleet and snow. But if he had seriously entertained any hopes of enjoying a quiet day, these were dispelled by an office-boy who summoned him to the city desk.

"Good-morning, Mr. Hallowell," said the city editor, cheerfully. "Here is a clipping from an afternoon paper which says that a French family in Houston Street has been dispossessed and is in want. Mr. Wilson called my attention to it because he thinks, from the number given, the house belongs to old Q. C. Baggold. We don't like Baggold, you know, and if you find he is treating his tenants unfairly we can let you have all the space you want to show him up. At any rate, go over there and see what the trouble is; there is not much going on to-day."

Fred took the clipping and read it as he walked back to his desk. It was very short—five or six lines only—and the facts stated were about as the city editor had said. The young man got into his overcoat and wrapped himself up warmly, and in a few moments was himself battling against the little blizzard with the other pedestrians whom he had been watching in the City Hall Park from the office windows.

When he reached Houston Street he travelled westward for several blocks, until he came into a very poor district crowded with dingy tenement-houses that leaned against one another in an uneven sort of way, as if they were tired of the sad kind of life they had been witnessing for so many years. The snow that had piled up on the window-sills and over the copings seemed to brighten up the general aspect of the quarter, because it filled in the cracks and chinks of material misery, and made the buildings look at least temporarily picturesque, just as paint and powder for a time may hide the traces of old age and sorrow. Fred found the number 179 painted on a piece of tin that had become bent and rusty from long service over a narrow doorway, and as he stood there comparing it with the number given in his clipping, a little girl with a shawl drawn tightly over her head and around her thin little shoulders came out of the dark entrance and stopped on the door-sill for a moment, surprised, no doubt, at the sight of the tall rosy-cheeked young man so warmly clad in a big woollen overcoat that you could have wrapped her up in several times, with goods left over to spare.

"Hello! little girl," said Fred, quickly. "Does Mr. Cressy live here?"

The child stared for a few seconds at the stranger, and then she answered, bashfully: "Yes, sir. But he has got to go away."

"But he hasn't gone yet?" continued Fred; and then noticing that the child, in her short calico skirt, was shivering from the cold, and that her feet were getting wet with the snow, he added, "Come inside a minute and tell me where I can find Mr. Cressy."

The two stepped into the dark narrow hallway that ran through the house to the stairway in the rear, where a narrow window with a broken pane let in just enough light to prove there was day outside. The little girl leaned against the wall, and looked up at the reporter as if she suspected him of having no good intentions toward the man for whom he was inquiring. Very few strangers ever came into that house to do good, she knew. Most of them came for money—rent money—and sometimes they came, as a man had come for Mr. Cressy, to tell him he must go.

"What floor does he live on?" asked Fred.

"On the fifth floor, sir," answered the child. "In the back, sir. But I think he is really going away, sir."

"Well, no matter about that," said Fred, smiling. "I will go up and see him. I hope he won't have to go out in the storm. It is not good for little girls to go out in the storm, either," he added. "Does your mamma know you are going out?"

"Oh, yes, sir! She has sent me to the Sisters to try to get some medicine."

"Is she sick?" asked Fred, quickly.

"Yes, sir," continued the child.

"What floor does she live on? I will stop in and see her."

"Oh, you'll see her! She's in the room, too."

"Then you are Mr. Cressy's little girl?"

"Yes, sir."

So Fred patted her on the head and told her to hurry over to the Sisters in Eleventh Street, and gave her ten cents to ride in the horse-cars; and then he opened the door for her, and as soon as she had left he felt his way back to the staircase and climbed to the fifth floor.

There he knocked upon a door, which was soon opened by a man apparently forty years of age, a man of slightly foreign appearance, with a careworn look, but with as honest a face as you could find anywhere.

"Is this Mr. Cressy?" asked Fred.

"Yes, my name's Cressy," replied the man. He spoke with so slight an accent that it was hardly noticeable.

"I am a reporter from the Gazette," continued Fred.

"Oh!" said the man. "Come in," and as he spoke he looked somewhat embarrassed and anxious, for this was doubtless the first time he had had any dealings with a newspaper. Lying on a bed in an alcove was a woman who looked very ill, and piled in a corner near the door were a couple of boxes and a few pieces of furniture. The stove had not yet been taken down, and some pale embers in it only just kept the chill off the atmosphere. Fred took off his hat, and led the man across the room toward the window.

"Have you been dispossessed?" he asked.

"Yes," said the man; "we must leave to-night."

"Why?" asked the reporter.

Cressy smiled in a ghastly sort of way.

"Because," he replied—"because I have not a cent to my name, sir, and the landlord has got it in for me—and I must go."

"Who is your landlord?" asked the reporter.

"Baggold—Q. C. Baggold, the shoe-man."

"How much do you owe?"

"Twenty dollars—two months' rent."

"Were you ever in arrears before?"

"Never."

"What's the trouble? Out of work?"

"Yes, sir, I have been. But I've got a job now, and I'll have money on the tenth of the month. But that is not it."

"What is 'it,' then?" continued Fred.

"Well, I'll tell you. I don't want this in the paper, but I'll tell you. Baggold hates me. He knows the woman's sick, and he takes advantage of my owing him to drive me out. Do you want to know why? Well, I'll tell you. I worked for him for five years, sir, in his shoe-factory. He brought me over from France to do the fine work. He had a lawsuit about six months ago, and he offered me $500 to lie for him on the stand. I would not do it, sir, and when they called me as a witness I told the truth, and that settled the case, and Baggold had to pay $10,000, sir, for a sly game on a contract. Then he sent me off, and I've been looking for a job, and I've got behind, and I'm just getting up again, and here he is sending me out into the snow! To-morrow is what we call at home, in France, the *jour de l'an*—the day of the New Year, sir, and it is a fête. And the little one, here, always looked forward to that day, sir, for a doll or a few sweetmeats; but this time—I don't think she'll have a roof for her little head! I have not a place in the world to go to, sir, but to the police station, and there's the woman on her back!"

Two big tears rolled down the man's cheeks. Fred felt a lump rising in his throat, and he knew that if he had had twenty dollars in his pocket he would have given it to Cressy. But he did not have twenty dollars, so he coughed vigorously, and put on his hat quickly, and said:

"Well, this is hard, Mr. Cressy. I'll see what we can do. I must go up town for a while, and then I'll come back and see you. Don't move out in this storm till the last minute."

As he rushed down the stairs he met the little girl coming back with a big blue bottle of something with a yellow label on it. He stopped and pulled a quarter out of his pocket, thrust it into the child's hand, and leaped on down the stairs, leaving the little girl more frightened than surprised, as he dashed out into the snow.

He entered the first drug-store he came to and looked up Q. C. Baggold's address in the directory. It was nearly four o'clock, and he argued the rich shoe-manufacturer would be at his home. The address given in the directory was in a broad street in the fashionable quarter of the city. Half an hour later Fred was pulling at Mr. Baggold's door-bell. The butler who answered the summons thought Mr. Baggold was in, and took Fred's card after showing the young man into the parlour. This was a large elegantly furnished room filled with costly ornaments, almost any one of which, if offered for sale, would have brought the amount of Cressy's debt, or much more.

Presently Mr. Baggold came into the room. He was a short man with a bald head and a sharp nose, and his small eyes were fixed very close to one another under a not very high forehead.

"I am a reporter from the Gazette," began Fred at once. "I have called to see you, Mr. Baggold, about this man Cressy whom you have ordered to be dispossessed."

"Ah, yes," said Mr. Baggold, smiling. "My agent has told me something about this matter, but I hardly think it is of sufficient importance to be of interest to the readers of the Gazette."

"The readers of the Gazette," continued Fred "are always interested in good deeds, Mr. Baggold, and especially when these are performed by rich men. I came here hoping you would disavow the action of your agent, and say that the Cressy's might remain in the room."

"Nonsense!" replied Mr. Baggold. "I cannot interfere with my agent. I pay him to take care of my rents, and I can't be looking after fellows who won't pay. This man Cressy is in arrears, and he must get out."

"But his wife is sick," argued Fred.

"Bah!" retorted the other. "That is an old excuse. These scoundrels try all sorts of dodges to cheat a man whom they think has money."

"This woman is actually sick, Mr. Baggold," said Fred, severely, "and to drive her out in a storm like this is positive cruelty."

"Cressy has had two weeks to find other quarters, and to-morrow is the first of the month. I can't keep him any longer."

"Yes, to-morrow is the great French fête-day, and you put Cressy in the street."

"My dear sir," returned the rich man, "I cannot allow sentiment to interfere with my business. If I did I should never collect rents in Houston Street. And, as I told you before, I do not see that this question is one to interest the public. It is purely a matter of my private business."

"Very true," replied Fred; "but I don't think it would look well in print."

This statement seemed to startle Mr. Baggold a little, and Fred thought it made him feel uncomfortable. There was a brief silence, after which the rich man said:

"It would depend entirely upon how you put it in print. To tell you the truth, I am not at all in favour of these sensational articles that so many newspapers publish nowadays. Reporters often jump at conclusions before they are familiar with the facts of a case, and it makes things disagreeable for all concerned. Now, if you will only listen to me, sir, I think we can come to an understanding about this Cressy matter. I don't want anything about it to get into the papers—especially now. I have many reasons, but I cannot give them to you. Yet I think we can come to an understanding," he repeated, as he looked at Fred and smiled.

"How?" asked the reporter.

"Well," drawled Mr. Baggold, "there are some points that I may be able to explain to you. Of course I don't want to put you to any trouble for nothing. If it is worth something to me not to have notoriety thrust upon me, of course, on the other hand, it might be worth something to you to cause the notoriety. But just excuse me a moment."

Mr. Baggold arose hastily and stepped into a rear room, apparently his library or study.

"H'm," thought Fred to himself. "This old chap talks as though he were going to offer me money. I'd just like to see him try! I'd give him such a roasting as he has never had before! Some of these crooked old millionaires think that sort of thing works with reporters, but I'll show him that it does not. I have never known a newspaper man yet that would accept a bribe."

And as Fred mused in this fashion, Mr. Baggold returned. He bore a long yellow envelope in his hand.

"Here," he said, "are some papers and other things that I should like to have you look over before you write the article. I think they will influence you in your opinion of the matter. I am sorry I cannot tell you any more just now, but I have an appointment which I must keep. Take these papers and look them over at your leisure, and if you find later this evening that they are not satisfactory, I will talk with you further. Good-afternoon, sir. I hope you will excuse me for the present."

And so saying he handed the envelope to Fred, bowed pleasantly, and left the room. Fred had been standing near the door, and so he put the envelope in his pocket and went out. He walked a few blocks down the street, and went into the large hotel on the corner in order to get out of the storm and to find some quiet place where he might look over Mr. Baggold's documents. He was very curious to see what they could be. He found a seat in a secluded corner of the office, and there tore open the envelope. To his disgust, it contained three ten-dollar bills, and a brief note, unsigned, which read,

> "The accompanying papers will show you that the matter we spoke of is not of sufficient importance to be published."

Fred Hallowell was furious. This was the first time in his brief career as a newspaper man that anything like this had happened to him. He grew red in the face, his fingers twitched, and he felt as if he had never before been so grossly insulted. As he sat in his chair, fuming and wondering what he should do, Griggs, the fat and jolly political reporter of the Gazette, came up to him and said, laughing,

"Well, you look as if you were plotting murder!"

"I am—almost!" exclaimed Fred, and then he told Griggs all about what had happened.

Griggs listened patiently, and at the end he chuckled to himself, and said: "Well, Hallowell, don't waste any righteous wrath on any such stuff as that Baggold. I'll tell you how to get even with him." And then he talked for twenty minutes to the younger man.

At the end of the conference Fred smiled and buttoned his coat, and hastened back to Cressy's room in Houston Street. He found a Sister of Charity there nursing the sick woman. Cressy came to the door, pale and eager.

"Well?" he said nervously.

"Oh, it's all right," returned Fred, laughing. "I have just seen Mr. Baggold. He said his agent was perfectly right in having you dispossessed, because that was business; but when he heard what I had to say, he gave me this money." And here Fred handed out the thirty dollars. "It is for you to pay the agent with, and then you can keep your room, and you will have ten dollars besides."

Cressy was speechless. The sick woman wept softly. The Sister said something in Latin, and the little girl just looked; she did not understand what it was all about.

"You see," said Fred to Cressy, "I suppose Mr. Baggold does not want his business to be interfered with by his sentiment." And before Cressy could reply the reporter had slipped out of the door, and in a moment was hurrying down town to his office.

The next morning—New-Year's morning—the Gazette contained a pretty little story of how a rich man, who had heard of the distress of a tenant, put his hand in his own pocket and paid his tenant's rent to himself, so that the new year would begin well for him by having rents coming in at the very opening of the twelvemonth.

"I'll bet Baggold was surprised this morning when he read that," gurgled the genial Griggs; "but it will do him more good than ten columns of abuse and exposure. So here's a Happy New Year to him!"

"DOES MR. CRESSY LIVE HERE?"

- Cressy's New-Year's Rent

From the drawing by Edwin J. Meeker

Mr. O'Leary's Second Love

By Charles Lever

The play over, O'Leary charged himself with the protection of madam, while I enveloped Emily in her cashmere, and drew her arm within my own. What my hand had to do with hers I know not; it remains one of the unexplained difficulties of that eventful evening. I have, it is true, a hazy recollection of pressing some very taper and delicately formed fingers; and remember, too, the pain I felt next morning on awaking, by the pressure of a too tight ring, which had, by some strange accident, found its way to my finger, for which its size was but ill adapted.

"You will join us at supper, I hope," said Mrs. Bingham, as Trevanion handed her to her carriage. "Mr. Lorrequer, Mr. O'Leary, we shall expect you."

I was about to promise to do so, when Trevanion suddenly interrupted me, saying that he had already accepted an invitation, which would, unfortunately, prevent us; and having hastily wished the ladies good-night, hurried me away so abruptly, that I had not a moment given for even one parting look at the fair Emily.

"Why, Trevanion," said I, "what invitation are you dreaming of? I, for one, should have been delighted to have gone home with the Binghams."

"So I perceive," said Trevanion, gravely; "and it was for that precise reason I so firmly refused what, individually, I should have been most happy to accept."

"Then pray have the goodness to explain."

"It is easily done. You have already, in recounting your manifold embarrassments, told me enough of these people, to let me see that they intend you should marry among them; and, indeed, you have gone quite far enough to encourage such an expectation. Your present excited state has led you sufficiently far this evening, and I could not answer for your not proposing in all form before the supper was over; therefore, I had no other course open to me than positively to refuse Mrs. Bingham's invitation. But here we are now at the 'Cadran rouge;' we shall have our lobster and a glass of Moselle, and then to bed, for we must not forget that we are to be at St. Cloud by seven."

"Ah! that is a good thought of yours about the lobsters," said O'Leary; "and now, as you understand these matters, just order supper, and let us enjoy ourselves."

With all the accustomed dispatch of a *restaurant*, a most appetising *petit souper* made its speedy appearance; and although now perfectly divested of the high excitement which had hitherto possessed me, my spirits were excellent, and I never more relished our good fare and good fellowship.

After a toast to the health of the fair Emily had been proposed and drained by all three, Trevanion again explained how much more serious difficulty would result from any false step in that quarter than from all my other scrapes collectively.

This he represented so strongly, that for the first time I began to perceive the train of ill consequences that must inevitably result, and promised most faithfully to be guided by any counsel he might feel disposed to give me.

"Ah! what a pity," said O'Leary, "it is not my case. It's very little trouble it would cost any one to break off a match for me. I had always a most peculiar talent for those things."

"Indeed!" said Trevanion. "Pray, may we know your secret? for perhaps, ere long, we may have occasion for its employment."

"Tell it, by all means," said I.

"If I do," said O'Leary, "it will cost you a patient hearing; for my experiences are connected with an episode in my early life, which, although not very amusing, is certainly instructive."

"Oh! by all means, let us hear it," said Trevanion.

"Well, agreed," said O'Leary; "only once for all, as what I am about to confide is strictly confidential, you must promise never even to allude to it hereafter in even the most remote manner, much less indulge in any unseemly mirth at what I shall relate."

Having pledged ourselves to secrecy and a becoming seriousness, O'Leary began his story as follows:

"You may easily suppose," began Mr. O'Leary, "that the unhappy termination of my first passion served as a shield to me for a long time against my unfortunate tendencies toward the fair, and such was really the case. I never spoke to a young lady for three years after, without a reeling in my head, so associated in my mind was love and sea-sickness. However, at last, what will not time do? It was about four years from the date of this adventure, when I became so oblivious of my former failure, as again to tempt my fortune. My present choice, in every way unlike the last, was a gay, lively girl, of great animal spirits, and a considerable turn for raillery, that spared no one; the members of her own family were not even sacred in her eyes; and her father, a reverend dean, as frequently figured among the ludicrous as his neighbours.

"The Evershams had been very old friends of a rich aunt of mine, who never, by the by, had condescended to notice me till I made their acquaintance; but no sooner had I done so, than she sent for me, and gave me to understand that in the event of my succeeding to the hand of Fanny Eversham, I should be her heir and the possessor of about sixty thousand pounds. She did not stop here; but by canvassing the dean in my favour, speedily put the matter on a most favourable footing, and in less than two months I was received as the accepted suitor of the fair Fanny, then one of the reigning belles of Dublin.

"They lived at this time, about three miles from town, in a very pretty country, where I used to pass all my mornings, and many of my evenings, too, in a state of happiness that I should have considered perfect, if it were not for two unhappy blots—one, the taste of my betrothed for laughing at her friends; another, the diabolical propensity of my intended father-in-law to talk politics; to the former I could submit; but with the latter submission only made bad worse; for he invariably drew up as I receded, dryly observing that with men who had no avowed opinions, it was ill-agreeing; or that, with persons who kept their politics as a school-boy does his pocket-money, never to spend, and always ready to change, it was unpleasant to dispute. Such taunts as these I submitted to, as well I might; secretly resolving, that as I now knew the meaning of Whig and Tory, I'd contrive to spend my life, after marriage, out of the worthy dean's diocese.

"Time wore on, and at length, to my most pressing solicitations it was conceded that a day for our marriage should be appointed. Not even the unlucky termination of this my second love affair can deprive me of the happy souvenir of the few weeks which were to intervene before our destined union.

"The mornings were passed in ransacking all the shops where wedding finery could be procured—laces, blondes, velvets, and satins, littered every corner of the deanery—and there was scarcely a carriage in a coach-maker's yard in the city that I had not sat and jumped in, to try the springs, by the special direction of Mrs. Eversham, who never ceased to impress me with the awful responsibility I was about to take upon me, in marrying so great a prize as her daughter—a feeling I found very general among many of my friends at the Kildare Street club.

"Among the many indispensable purchases which I was to make, and about which Fanny expressed herself more than commonly anxious, was a saddle-horse for me. She was a great horse-woman, and hated riding with only a servant; and had given me to understand as much about half-a-dozen times each day for the last five weeks. How shall I acknowledge it—equestrianism was never my forte. I had all my life considerable respect for the horse as an animal, pretty much as I dreaded a lion or a tiger; but as to any intention of mounting upon the back of one, and taking a ride, I should as soon have dreamed of taking an airing upon a giraffe; and as to the thought of buying, feeding, and maintaining such a beast at my own proper cost, I should just as soon have determined to purchase a pillory or a ducking-stool, by way of amusing my leisure hours.

"However, Fanny was obstinate—whether she suspected anything or not I cannot say—but nothing seemed to turn her from her purpose; and although I pleaded a thousand things in delay, yet she grew each day more impatient, and at last I saw there was nothing for it but to submit.

"When I arrived at this last bold resolve, I could not help feeling that to possess a horse, and not be able to mount him, was only deferring the ridicule; and as I had so often expressed the difficulty I felt in suiting myself as a cause of my delay, I could not possibly come forward with anything very objectionable, or I should be only the more laughed at. There was, then, but one course to take; a fortnight still intervened before the day which was to make me happy, and I accordingly resolved to take lessons in riding during the interval, and by every endeavour in my power become, if possible, able to pass muster on the saddle before my bride.

"Poor old Lalouette understood but little of the urgency of the case, when I requested his leave to take my lessons each morning at six o'clock, for I dared not absent myself during the day without exciting suspicion; and never, I will venture to assert, did knight-errant of old strive harder for the hand of his lady-love than did I during that weary fortnight; if a hippogriff had been the animal I bestrode, instead of being, as it was, an old wall-eyed grey, I could not have felt more misgivings at my temerity, or more proud of my achievement. In the first three days the unaccustomed exercise proved so severe, that when I reached the deanery I could hardly move, and crossed the floor pretty much as a pair of compasses might be supposed to do if performing that exploit. Nothing, however, could equal the kindness of my poor dear mother-in-law in embryo, and even the dean too. Fanny indeed, said nothing; but I rather think she was disposed to giggle a little; but my rheumatism, as it was called, was daily inquired after, and I was compelled to take some infernal stuff in my port wine, at dinner, that nearly made me sick at table.

"'I am sure you walk too much,' said Fanny, with one of her knowing looks. 'Papa, don't you think he ought to ride? it would be much better for him.'

"'I do, my dear,' said the dean. 'But then you see he is so hard to be pleased in a horse. Your old hunting days have spoiled you; but you must forget Melton and Grantham, and condescend to keep a hack.'

"I must have looked confoundedly foolish here, for Fanny never took her eyes off me, and continued to laugh in her own wicked way.

"It was now about the ninth or tenth day of my purgatorial performances; and certainly, if there be any merit in fleshly mortifications, these religious exercises of mine should stand my part hereafter. A review had been announced in the Phœnix park, which Fanny had expressed herself most desirous to witness; and as the dean would not permit her to go without a chaperon, I had no means of escape, and promised to escort her. No sooner had I made this rash pledge than I hastened to my confidential friend, Lalouette, and having imparted to him my entire secret, asked him in a solemn and imposing manner, 'Can I do it?' The old man shook his head dubiously, looked grave, and muttered at length, 'Mosch depend on de horse.' 'I know it—I know it—I feel it,' said I, eagerly—'then where are we to find an animal that will carry me peaceably through this awful day? I care not for his price.'

"'Votre affaire ne sera pas trop chère,' said he.

"'Why, how do you mean?' said I.

"He then proceeded to inform me that, by a singularly fortunate chance, there took place that day an auction of 'cast horses,' as they are termed, which had been used in the horse police force; and that from long riding and training to stand fire, nothing could be more suitable than one of these, being both easy to ride and not given to start at noise.

"I could have almost hugged the old fellow for his happy suggestion, and waited with impatience for three o'clock to come, when we repaired together to Essexbridge, at that time the place selected for these sales.

"I was at first a little shocked at the look of the animals drawn up; they were most miserably thin, most of them swelled in the legs, few without sore backs, and not one eye on an average in every three; but still they were all high-steppers, and carried a great tail. 'There's your affaire,' said the old Frenchman, as a long-legged, fiddle-headed beast was led out; turning out his forelegs so as to endanger the man who walked beside him.

"'Yes, there's blood for you,' said Charley Dycer, seeing my eye fixed on the wretched beast; 'equal to fifteen stone with any fox-hounds; safe in all his paces, and warranted sound; except,' added he, in a whisper, 'a slight spavin in both hind legs, ring-bone, and a little touch in the wind.' Here the animal gave an approving cough. 'Will any gentleman say fifty pounds to begin?' But no gentleman did. A hackney-coachman, however, said five, and the sale was opened; the beast trotting up and down nearly over the bidders at every moment, and plunging on so that it was impossible to know what was doing.

"'Five ten—fifteen—six pounds—thank you, sir—guineas—seven pounds,' said I, bidding against myself, not perceiving that I had spoken last. 'Thank you, Mr. Moriarty,' said Dycer, turning toward an invisible purchaser supposed to be in the crowd. 'Thank you, sir, you'll not let a good one go that way.' Every one here turned to find out the very knowing gentleman; but he could nowhere be seen.

"Dycer resumed, 'Seven ten, for Mr. Moriarty. Going for seven ten—a cruel sacrifice—there's action for you—playful beast.' Here the devil had stumbled and nearly killed a basket-woman with two children.

"'Eight,' said I, with a loud voice.

"'Eight pounds, quite absurd,' said Dycer, almost rudely; 'a charger like that for eight pounds—going for eight pounds—going—nothing above eight pounds—no reserve, gentlemen, you are aware of that. They are all, as it were, his Majesty's stud—no reserve whatever—last time, eight pounds—gone.'

"Amid a very hearty cheer from the mob, God knows why, but a Dublin mob always cheers—I returned accompanied by a ragged fellow, leading my new purchase after me with a hay halter.

"'What is the meaning of those letters?' said I, pointing to a very conspicuous G. R., with sundry other enigmatical signs, burned upon the animal's hind quarter.

"'That's to show he was a po-lis,' said the fellow with a grin; 'and when ye ride with ladies, ye must turn the decoy side.'"

"The auspicious morning at last arrived; and, strange to say, that the first waking thought was of the unlucky day that ushered in my yachting excursion, four years before. Why this was so I cannot pretend to guess: there was but little analogy in the circumstances, at least so far as anything had then gone. 'How is Marius?' said I to my servant, as he opened my shutters. Here let me mention that a friend of the Kildare Street club had suggested this name from the remarkably classic character of my steed's countenance; his nose, he assured me, was perfectly Roman.

"'Marius is doing finely, sir, barring his cough, and the trifle that ails his hind legs.'

"'He'll carry me quietly, Simon; eh?'

"'Quietly! I'll warrant he'll carry you quietly, if that's all.'

"Here was comfort, certainly. Simon had lived forty years as pantry boy with my mother, and knew a great deal about horses. I dressed myself, therefore, in high spirits; and if my pilot jacket and oil-skin cap in former days had half persuaded me that I was born for marine achievements, certainly my cords and tops, that morning, went far to convince me that I must have once been a very keen sportsman somewhere, without knowing it. It was a delightful July day that I set out to join my friends, who, having recruited a large party, were to rendezvous at the corner of Stephen's Green; thither I proceeded in a certain rambling trot, which I have often observed is a very favourite pace with timid horsemen and gentlemen of the medical profession. I was hailed with a most hearty welcome by a large party as I turned out of Grafton Street, among whom I perceived several friends of Miss Eversham, and some young dragoon officers, not of my acquaintance, but who appeared to know Fanny intimately, and were laughing heartily with her as I rode up.

"I don't know if other men have experienced what I am about to mention or not; but certainly to me there is no more painful sensation than to find yourself among a number of well-mounted, well-equipped people, while the animal you yourself bestride seems only fit for the kennel. Every look that is cast at your unlucky steed—every whispered observation about you are so many thorns in your flesh, till at last you begin to feel that your appearance is for very little else than the amusement and mirth of the assembly; and every time you rise in your stirrups you excite a laugh.

"'Where, for mercy's sake, did you find that creature?' said Fanny, surveying Marius through her glass.

"'Oh, him, eh? Why, he is a handsome horse, if in condition—a charger, you know—that's his style.'

"'Indeed,' lisped a young lancer, 'I should be devilish sorry to charge, or be charged with him.' And here they all chuckled at this puppy's silly joke, and I drew up to repress further liberties.

"'Is he anything of a fencer?' said a young country gentleman.

"'To judge from his near eye, I should say much more of a boxer,' said another.

"Here commenced a running fire of pleasantry at the expense of my poor steed; which, not content with attacking his physical, extended to his moral qualities. An old gentleman near me observing, 'that I ought not to have mounted him at all, seeing he was so deuced groggy;' to which I replied, by insinuating, that if others present were as free from the influence of ardent spirits, society would not be a sufferer; an observation that, I flatter myself, turned the mirth against the old fellow, for they all laughed for a quarter of an hour after.

"Well, at last we set out in a brisk trot, and, placed near Fanny, I speedily forgot all my annoyances in the prospect of figuring to advantage before her. When we reached the College Green the leaders of the cortège suddenly drew up, and we soon found that the entire street opposite the Bank was filled with a dense mob of people, who appeared to be swayed hither and thither, like some mighty beast, as the individuals composing it were engaged in close conflict. It was nothing more nor less than one of those almost weekly rows which then took place between the students of the University and the town's-people, and which rarely ended without serious consequences. The numbers of people pressing on to the scene of action soon blocked up our retreat, and we found ourselves most unwilling spectators of the conflict. Political watch-words were loudly shouted by each party; and at last the students, who appeared to be yielding to superior numbers, called out for the intervention of the police. The aid was nearer than they expected; for at the same instant a body of mounted policemen, whose high helmets rendered them sufficiently conspicuous, were seen trotting at sharp pace down Dame Street. On they came with drawn sabres, led by a well-looking, gentleman-like personage in plain clothes, who dashed at once into the middle of the fray, issuing his orders, and pointing out to his followers to secure the ring-leaders. Up to this moment I had been a most patient and rather amused spectator of what was doing. Now, however, my part was to commence, for at the word 'Charge,' given in a harsh, deep voice by the sergeant of the party, Marius, remembering his ancient instinct, pricked up his ears, cocked his tail, flung up both his hind legs till they nearly broke the Provost's windows, and plunged into the thickest of the fray like a devil incarnate.

"Self-preservation must be a strong instinct, for I well remember how little pain it cost me to see the people tumbling and rolling beneath me, while I continued to keep my seat. It was only a moment before, and that immense mass were a man-to-man encounter, now all the indignation of both parties seemed turned upon me; brick-bats were loudly implored and paving-stones begged to throw at my devoted head; the Wild Huntsman of the German romance never created half the terror nor one-tenth of the mischief that I did in less than fifteen minutes, for the ill-starred beast continued twining and twisting like a serpent, plunging and kicking the entire time, and occasionally biting too; all which accomplishments, I afterwards learned, however little in request in civil life, are highly prized in the horse police.

"Every new order of the sergeant was followed in his own fashion by Marius, who very soon contrived to concentrate in my unhappy person all the interest of about fifteen hundred people.

"'Secure that scoundrel,' said the magistrate, pointing with his finger towards me, as I rode over a respectable-looking old lady with a grey muff. 'Secure him. Cut him down.'

"'Ah, devil's luck to him, if ye do,' said a newsmonger with a broken shin.

"On I went, however; and now, as the Fates would have it, instead of bearing me out of further danger, the confounded brute dashed onward to where the magistrate was standing, surrounded by policemen. I thought I saw him change colour as I came on. I suppose my own looks were none of the pleasantest, for the worthy man evidently liked them not. Into the midst of them we plunged, upsetting a corporal, horse and all, and appearing as if bent upon reaching the alderman.

"'Cut him down, for Heaven's sake. Will nobody shoot him?' said he, with a voice trembling with fear and anger.

"At these words a wretch lifted up his sabre, and made a cut at my head. I stooped suddenly, and throwing myself from the saddle, seized the poor alderman round the neck, and both came rolling to the ground together. So completely was he possessed with the notion that I meant to assassinate him, that while I was endeavouring to extricate myself from his grasp, he continued to beg his life in the most heart-rending manner.

"My story is now soon told. So effectually did they rescue the alderman from his danger that they left me insensible, and I only came to myself some days after by finding myself in the dock in Green Street, charged with an indictment of nineteen counts; the only word of truth is what lay in the preamble, for the 'devil inciting' me only would ever have made me the owner of that infernal beast, the cause of all my misfortunes. I was so stupefied from my beating that I know little of the course of the proceedings. My friends told me afterward that I had a narrow escape from transportation; but for the greatest influence exerted in my behalf, I should certainly have passed the autumn in the agreeable recreation of pounding oyster-shells or carding wool; and it certainly must have gone hard with me, for, stupefied as I was, I remember the sensation in court when the alderman made his appearance with a patch over his eye. The affecting admonition of the little judge—who, when passing sentence upon me, adverted to the former respectability of my life and the rank of my relatives—actually made the galleries weep.

"Four months in Newgate and a fine to the king, then, rewarded my taste for horse exercise; and it's no wonder if I prefer going on foot.

"As to Miss Eversham, the following short note from the dean concluded my hopes in that quarter:

> "'Deanery, Wednesday morning.
>
> "'Sir—After the very distressing publicity to which your late conduct has exposed you—the so open avowal of political opinions, at variance with those (I will say) of every gentleman—and the recorded sentence of a judge on the verdict of

twelve of your countrymen—I should hope that you will not feel my present admonition necessary to inform you that your visits to my house shall cease.

"'The presents you made my daughter, when under our unfortunate ignorance of your real character, have been addressed to your hotel, and I am your most obedient, humble servant,

"'Oliver Eversham.'

"Here ended my second affair 'par amour;' and I freely confess to you that if I can only obtain a wife in a sea voyage, or a steeple-chase, I am likely to fulfil one great condition in modern advertising—'as having no incumbrance, nor any objection to travel.'"

Note

Thackeray's only book for children, "The Rose and the Ring," has given him a place among writers for children that is the equal of that which he enjoys as one of the world's greatest novelists. His fondness for children was proverbial and it appears over and over again in his writings.

This story was written of Christmas time in the year 1854 while the author was living at Rome. Thackeray wrote it to entertain a little young friend, a girl who had been ill. As he finished a chapter to read to her he would illustrate it with these droll pictures hastily sketched with his pen.

The Rose and the Ring

Or

The History of Prince Giglio and Prince Bulbo
A Fireside Pantomime for Great and Small Children
By Mr. M. A. Titmarsh

Prelude

It happened that the undersigned spent the last Christmas season in a foreign city where there were many English children.

In that city, if you wanted to give a child's party, you could not even get a magic-lantern or buy Twelfth-Night characters—those funny painted pictures of the King, the Queen, the Lover, the Lady, the Dandy, the Captain, and so on—with which our young ones are wont to recreate themselves at this festive time.

My friend Miss Bunch, who was governess of a large family that lived in the *Piano Nobile* of the house inhabited by myself and my young charges (it was the Palazzo Poniatowski at Rome, and Messrs. Spillmann, two of the best pastrycooks in Christendom, have their shop on the ground floor): Miss Bunch, I say, begged me to draw a set of Twelfth-Night characters for the amusement of our young people.

She is a lady of great fancy and droll imagination, and having looked at the characters, she and I composed a history about them, which was recited to the little folks at night, and served as our fireside pantomime.

Our juvenile audience was amused by the adventures of Giglio and Bulbo, Rosalba and Angelica. I am bound to say the fate of the Hall Porter created a considerable sensation; and the wrath of Countess Gruffanuff was received with extreme pleasure.

If these children are pleased, thought I, why should not others be amused also? In a few days Dr. Birch's young friends will be expected to re-assemble at Rodwell Regis, where they will learn everything that is useful, and under the eyes of careful ushers continue the business of their little lives.

But, in the meanwhile, and for a brief holiday, let us laugh and be as pleasant as we can. And you elder folk—a little joking, and dancing, and fooling will do even you no harm. The author wishes you a merry Christmas, and welcomes you to the Fireside Pantomime.

M. A. TITMARSH.

December, 1854.

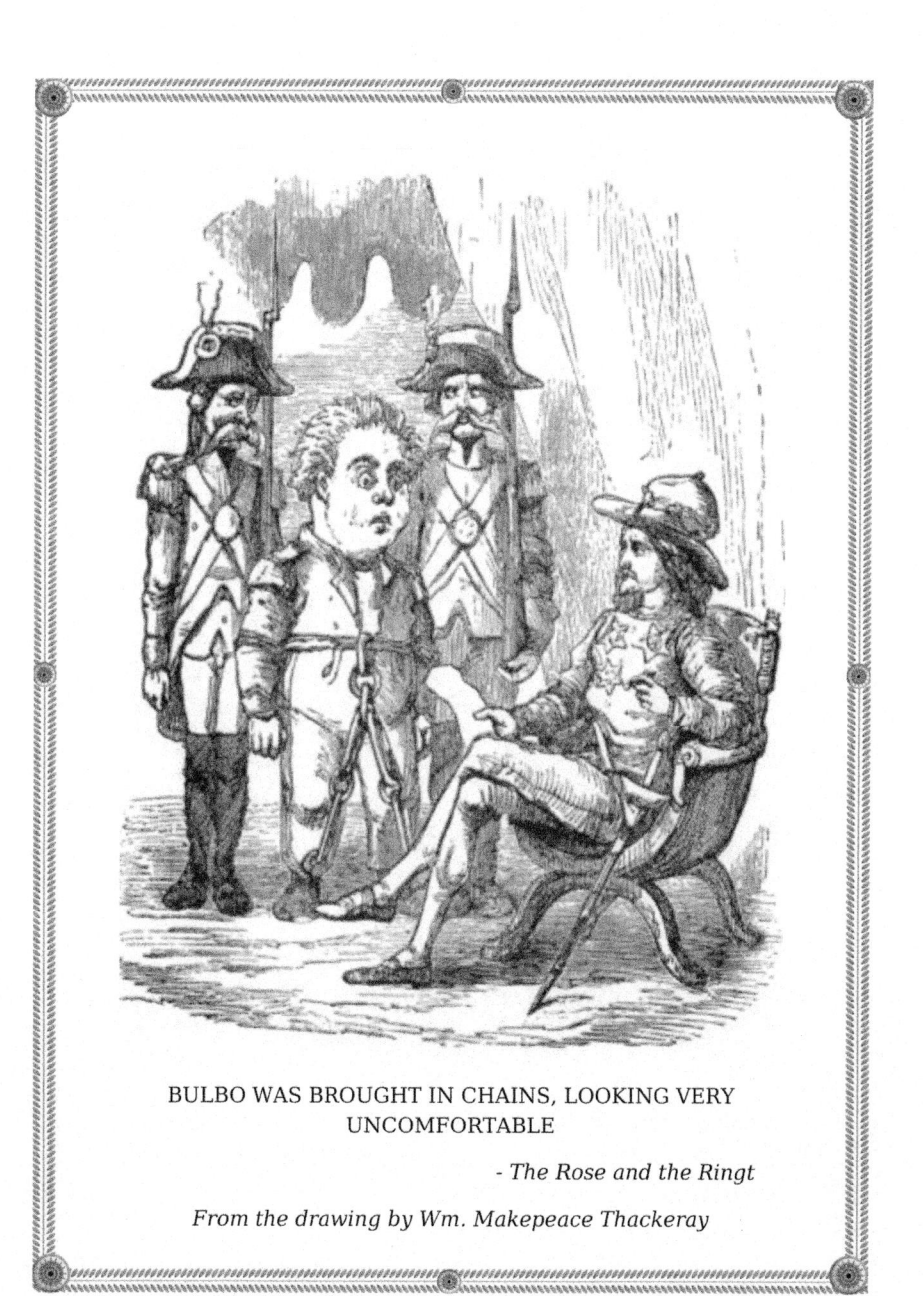

BULBO WAS BROUGHT IN CHAINS, LOOKING VERY
UNCOMFORTABLE

- *The Rose and the Ringt*

From the drawing by Wm. Makepeace Thackeray

The Rose and the Ring

By William Makepeace Thackeray

With illustrations by the Author

I

Shows How The Royal Family Sate Down for Breakfast

This is Valoroso XXIV., King of Paflagonia, seated with his Queen and only child at their royal breakfast-table, and receiving the letter which announces to His Majesty a proposed visit from Prince Bulbo, heir of Padella, reigning King of Crim Tartary. Remark the delight upon the monarch's royal features. He is so absorbed in the perusal of the King of Crim Tartary's letter that he allows his eggs to get cold, and leaves his august muffins untasted.

"What! that wicked, brave, delightful Prince Bulbo!" cries Princess Angelica; "so handsome, so accomplished, so witty—the conqueror of Rimbombamento, where he slew ten thousand giants!"

"Who told you of him, my dear?" asks His Majesty.

"A little bird," says Angelica.

"Poor Giglio!" says mamma, pouring out the tea.

"Bother Giglio!" cries Angelica, tossing up her head, which rustled with a thousand curl-papers.

"I wish," growls the King—"I wish Giglio was...."

"Was better? Yes, dear, he is better," says the Queen. "Angelica's little maid, Betsinda, told me so when she came to my room this morning with my early tea."

"You are always drinking tea," said the monarch, with a scowl.

"It is better than drinking port or brandy and water," replies Her Majesty.

"Well, well, my dear, I only said you were fond of drinking tea," said the King of Paflagonia, with an effort as if to command his temper. "Angelica! I hope you have plenty of new dresses; your milliner's bills are long enough. My dear Queen, you must see and have some parties. I prefer dinners, but of course you will be for balls. Your everlasting blue velvet quite tires me: and, my love, I should like you to have a new necklace. Order one. Not more than a hundred or a hundred and fifty thousand pounds."

"And Giglio, dear?" says the Queen.

"Giglio may go to the—"

"Oh, sir," screams Her Majesty. "Your own nephew! our late King's only son."

"Giglio may go to the tailor's, and order the bills to be sent in to Glumboso to pay. Confound him! I mean bless his dear heart. He need want for nothing; give him a couple of guineas for pocket-money, my dear; and you may as well order yourself bracelets while you are about the necklace, Mrs. V."

Her Majesty, or *Mrs. V.*, as the monarch facetiously called her (for even royalty will have its sport, and this august family were very much attached), embraced her husband, and, twining her arm round her daughter's waist, they quitted the breakfast-room in order to make all things ready for the princely stranger.

When they were gone, the smile that had lighted up the eyes of the *husband* and *father* fled—the pride of the *King* fled—the MAN was alone. Had I the pen of a G. P. R. James, I would describe Valoroso's torments in the choicest language; in which I would also depict his flashing eye, his distended nostril—his dressing-gown, pocket-handkerchief, and boots. But I need not say I have *not* the pen of that novelist; suffice it to say, Valoroso was alone.

He rushed to the cupboard, seizing from the table one of the many egg-cups with which his princely board was served for the matin meal, drew out a bottle of right Nantz or Cognac, filled and emptied the cup several times, and laid it down with a hoarse "Ha, ha, ha! now Valoroso is a man again!"

"But oh!" he went on (still sipping, I am sorry to say), "ere I was a king, I needed not this intoxicating draught; once I detested the hot brandy wine, and quaffed no other fount but nature's rill. It dashes not more quickly o'er the rocks than I did, as, with blunderbuss in hand, I brushed away the early morning dew, and shot the partridge, snipe, or antlered deer! Ah! well may England's dramatist remark, 'Uneasy lies the head that wears a crown!' Why did I steal my nephew's, my young Giglio's—? Steal! said I? no, no, no, not steal, not steal. Let me withdraw that odious expression. I took, and on my manly head I set, the royal crown of Paflagonia; I took, and with my royal arm I wield, the sceptral rod of Paflagonia; I took, and in my outstretched hand I hold, the royal orb of Paflagonia! Could a poor boy, a snivelling, drivelling boy—was in his nurse's arms but yesterday, and cried for sugar-plums and puled for pap—bear up the awful weight of crown, orb, scepter? gird on the sword my royal fathers wore, and meet in fight the tough Crimean foe?"

And then the monarch went on to argue in his own mind (though we need not say that blank verse is not argument) that what he had got it was his duty to keep, and that, if at one time he had entertained ideas of a certain restitution, which shall be nameless, the prospect by a *certain marriage* of uniting two crowns and two nations which had been engaged in bloody and expensive wars, as the Paflagonians and the Crimeans had been, put the idea of Giglio's restoration to the throne out of the question: nay, were his own brother, King Savio, alive, he would certainly will away the crown from his own son in order to bring about such a desirable union.

Thus easily do we deceive ourselves! Thus do we fancy what we wish is right! The King took courage, read the papers, finished his muffins and eggs, and rang the bell for his Prime Minister. The Queen, after thinking whether she should go up and see Giglio, who had been sick, thought, "Not now. Business first; pleasure afterwards. I will go and see dear Giglio this afternoon; and now I will drive to the jeweller's, to look for the necklace and bracelets." The Princess went up into her own room, and made Betsinda, her maid, bring out all her dresses; and as for Giglio, they forgot him as much as I forget what I had for dinner last Tuesday twelvemonth.

II

How King Valoroso Got the Crown, and How Prince Giglio Went Without It

Paflagonia, ten or twenty thousand years ago, appears to have been one of those kingdoms where the laws of succession were not settled; for when King Savio died, leaving his brother Regent of the kingdom, and guardian of Savio's orphan infant, this unfaithful regent took no sort of regard of the late monarch's will; had himself proclaimed sovereign of Paflagonia under the title of King Valoroso XXIV., had a most splendid coronation, and ordered all the nobles of the kingdom to pay him homage. So long as Valoroso gave them plenty of balls at Court, plenty of money and lucrative places, the Paflagonian nobility did not care who was king; and as for the people, in those early times, they were equally indifferent. The Prince Giglio, by reason of his tender age at his royal father's death, did not feel the loss of his crown and empire. As long as he had plenty of toys and sweetmeats, a holiday five times a week, and a horse and gun to go out shooting when he grew a little older, and, above all, the company of his darling cousin, the King's only child, poor Giglio was perfectly contented; nor did he envy his uncle the royal robes and sceptre, the great hot uncomfortable throne of state, and the enormous cumbersome crown in which that monarch appeared from morning till night. King Valoroso's portrait has been left to us; and I think you will agree with me that he must have been sometimes *rather tired* of his velvet, and his diamonds, and his ermine, and his grandeur. I shouldn't like to sit in that stifling robe with such a thing as that on my head.

No doubt, the Queen must have been lovely in her youth, for though she grew rather stout in after life, yet her features, as shown in her portrait, are certainly *pleasing*. If she was fond of flattery, scandal, cards, and fine clothes, let us deal gently with her infirmities, which, after all, may be no greater than our own. She was kind to her nephew; and if she had any scruples of conscience about her husband's taking the young Prince's crown, consoled herself by thinking that the King, though a usurper, was a most respectable man, and that at his death Prince Giglio would be restored to his throne, and share it with his cousin, whom he loved so fondly.

The Prime Minister was Glumboso, an old statesman, who most cheerfully swore fidelity to King Valoroso, and in whose hands the monarch left all the affairs of his kingdom. All Valoroso wanted was plenty of money, plenty of hunting, plenty of flattery, and as little trouble as possible. As long as he had his sport, this monarch cared little how his people paid for it: he engaged in some wars, and of course the Paflagonian newspapers announced that he gained prodigious victories: he had statues erected to himself in every city of the empire; and of course his pictures placed everywhere, and in all the print-shops: he was Valoroso the Magnanimous, Valoroso the Victorious, Valoroso the Great, and so forth—for even in these early times courtiers and people knew how to flatter.

This royal pair had one only child, the Princess Angelica, who, you may be sure, was a paragon in the courtiers' eyes, in her parents', and in her own. It was said she had the longest hair, the largest eyes, the slimmest waist, the smallest foot, and the most lovely complexion of any young lady in the Paflagonian dominions. Her accomplishments were announced to be even superior to her beauty; and governesses used to shame their idle pupils by telling them what Princess Angelica could do. She could play the most difficult pieces of music at sight. She could answer any one of "Mangnall's Questions." She knew every date in the history of Paflagonia, and every other country. She knew French, English, Italian, German, Spanish, Hebrew, Greek, Latin, Cappadocian, Samothracian, Ægean and Crim Tartar. In a word, she was a most accomplished young creature; and her governess and lady-in-waiting was the severe Countess Gruffanuff.

Would you not fancy, from this picture, that Gruffanuff must have been a person of the highest birth? She looks so haughty that I should have thought her a Princess at the very least, with a pedigree reaching as far back as the Deluge. But this lady was no better born than many other ladies who give themselves airs; and all sensible people laughed at her absurd pretensions. The fact is, she had been maid-servant to the Queen when Her Majesty was only Princess and her husband had been head footman; but after his death or *disappearance*, of which you shall hear presently, this Mrs. Gruffanuff, by flattering, toadying, and wheedling her royal mistress, became a favourite with the Queen (who was rather a weak woman), and Her Majesty gave her a title, and made her nursery governess to the Princess.

And now I must tell you about the Princess's learning and accomplishments, for which she had such a wonderful character. Clever Angelica certainly was, but as *idle as possible*. Play at sight, indeed! she could play one or two pieces, and pretend that she had never seen them before; she could answer half a dozen "Mangnall's Questions"; but then you must take care to ask the *right* ones. As for her languages, she had masters in plenty, but I doubt whether she knew more than a few phrases in each, for all her pretence; and as for her embroidery and her drawing, she showed beautiful specimens, it is true, but *who did them?*

This obliges me to tell the truth, and to do so I must go back ever so far, and tell you about the Fairy Blackstick.

III

Tells Who the Fairy Blackstick Was, And Who Were Ever So Many Grand Personages Besides

Between the kingdoms of Paflagonia and Crim Tartary, there lived a mysterious personage, who was known in those countries as the Fairy Blackstick, from the ebony wand or crutch which she carried; on which she rode to the moon sometimes, or upon other excursions of business or pleasure, and with which she performed her wonders.

When she was young, and had been first taught the art of conjuring by the necromancer, her father, she was always practising her skill, whizzing about from one kingdom to another upon her black stick, and conferring her fairy favours upon this Prince or that. She had scores of royal godchildren; turned numberless wicked people into beasts, birds, millstones, clocks, pumps, bootjacks, umbrellas, or other absurd shapes; and, in a word, was one of the most active and officious of the whole College of fairies.

But after two or three thousand years of this sport, I suppose Blackstick grew tired of it. Or perhaps she thought, "What good am I doing by sending this Princess to sleep for a hundred years? by fixing a black pudding on to that booby's nose? by causing diamonds and pearls to drop from one little girl's mouth, and vipers and toads from another's? I begin to think I do as much harm as good by my performances. I might as well shut my incantations up, and allow things to take their natural course.

"There were my two young goddaughters, King Savio's wife, and Duke Padella's wife, I gave them each a present, which was to render them charming in the eyes of their husbands, and secure the affection of those gentlemen as long as they lived. What good did my Rose and my Ring do these two women? None on earth. From having all their whims indulged by their husbands, they became capricious, lazy, ill-humoured, absurdly vain, and leered and languished, and fancied themselves irresistibly beautiful, when they were really quite old and hideous, the ridiculous creatures! They used actually to patronise me when I went to pay them a visit—*me*, the Fairy Blackstick, who knows all the wisdom of the necromancers, and who could have turned them into baboons, and all their diamonds into strings of onions, by a single wave of my rod!" So she locked up her books in her cupboard, declined further magical performances, and scarcely used her wand at all except as a cane to walk about with.

So when Duke Padella's lady had a little son (the Duke was at that time only one of the principal noblemen in Crim Tartary), Blackstick, although invited to the christening, would not so much as attend; but merely sent her compliments and a silver papboat for the baby, which was really not worth a couple of guineas. About the same time the Queen of Paflagonia presented His Majesty with a son and heir; and guns were fired, the capital illuminated, and no end of feasts ordained to celebrate the young Prince's birth. It was thought the Fairy, who was asked to be his godmother, would at least have presented him with an invisible jacket, a flying horse, a Fortunatus's purse, or some other valuable token of her favour; but instead, Blackstick went up to the cradle of the child Giglio, when everybody was admiring him and complimenting his royal papa and mamma, and said, "My poor child, the best thing I can send you is a little *misfortune*"; and this was all she would utter, to the disgust of Giglio's parents, who died very soon after, when Giglio's uncle took the throne, as we read in Chapter I.

In like manner, when Cavolfiore, King of Crim Tartary, had a christening of his only child, Rosalba, the Fairy Blackstick, who had been invited, was not more gracious than in Prince Giglio's case. Whilst everybody was expatiating over the beauty of the darling child, and congratulating its parents, the Fairy Blackstick looked very sadly at the baby and its mother, and said, "My good woman (for the Fairy was very familiar, and no more minded a Queen than a washerwoman)—my good woman, these people who are following you will be the first to turn against you; and as for this little lady, the best thing I can wish her is a *little misfortune.*"

So she touched Rosalba with her black wand, looked severely at the courtiers, motioned the Queen an adieu with her hand, and sailed slowly up into the air out of the window.

When she was gone, the Court people, who had been awed and silent in her presence, began to speak. "What an odious Fairy she is (they said)—a pretty Fairy, indeed! Why, she went to the King of Paflagonia's christening, and pretended to do all sorts of things for that family; and what has happened—the Prince, her godson, has been turned off his throne by his uncle. Would we allow our sweet Princess to be deprived of her rights by any enemy? Never, never, never, never!"

And they all shouted in a chorus, "Never, never, never, never!"

Now, I should like to know, and how did these fine courtiers show their fidelity? One of King Cavolfiore's vassals, the Duke Padella just mentioned, rebelled against the King, who went out to chastise his rebellious subject. "Any one rebel against our beloved and august Monarch!" cried the courtiers; "any one resist *him*? Pooh! He is invincible, irresistible. He will bring home Padella a prisoner, and tie him to a donkey's tail, and drive him round the town, saying, 'This is the way the Great Cavolfiore treats rebels.'"

The King went forth to vanquish Padella; and the poor Queen, who was a very timid, anxious creature, grew so frightened and ill, that I am sorry to say she died; leaving injunctions with her ladies to take care of the dear little Rosalba. Of course they said they would. Of course they vowed they would die rather than any harm should happen to the Princess. At first the Crim Tartar Court Journal stated that the King was obtaining great victories over the audacious rebel: then it was announced that the troops of the infamous Padella were in flight: then it was said that the royal army would soon come up with the enemy, and then—then the news came that King Cavolfiore was vanquished and slain by His Majesty, King Padella the First!

At this news, half the courtiers ran off to pay their duty to the conquering chief, and the other half ran away, laying hands on all the best articles in the palace; and poor little Rosalba was left there quite alone—quite alone; and she toddled from one room to another, crying, "Countess! Duchess!" (only she said "Tountess, Duttess," not being able to speak plain) "bring me my mutton sop; my Royal Highness hungry! Tountess! Duttess!" And she went from the private apartments into the throne room and nobody was there—and thence into the ball-room and nobody was there—and thence into the pages' room and nobody was there—and she toddled down the great staircase into the hall and nobody was there—and the door was open, and she went into the court, and into the garden, and thence into the wilderness, and thence into the forest where the wild beasts live and was never heard of any more!

A piece of her torn mantle and one of her shoes were found in the wood in the mouths of two lionesses' cubs, whom King Padella and a royal hunting party shot—for he was King now, and reigned over Crim Tartary. "So the poor little Princess is done for," said he; "well, what's done can't be helped. Gentlemen, let us go to luncheon!" And one of the courtiers took up the shoe and put it in his pocket. And there was an end of Rosalba!

IV

How Blackstick Was Not Asked to The Princess Angelica's Christening

When the Princess Angelica was born, her parents not only did not ask the Fairy Blackstick to the christening party, but gave orders to their porter absolutely to refuse her if she called. This porter's name was Gruffanuff, and he had been selected for the post by their Royal Highnesses because he was a very tall fierce man, who could say "Not at home" to a tradesman or an unwelcome visitor with a rudeness which frightened most such persons away. He was the husband of that Countess whose picture we have just seen, and as long as they were together they quarrelled from morning till night. Now this fellow tried his rudeness once too often, as you shall hear. For the Fairy Blackstick coming to call upon the Prince and Princess, who were actually sitting at the open drawing-room window, Gruffanuff not only denied them, but made the most *odious vulgar sign* as he was going to slam the door in the Fairy's face! "Git away, hold Blackstick!" said he. "I tell you, Master and Missis ain't at home to you;" and he was, as we have said, *going* to slam the door.

But the Fairy, with her wand, prevented the door being shut; and Gruffanuff came out again in a fury, swearing in the most abominable way, and asking the Fairy "whether she thought he was a going to stay at that there door hall day?"

"You *are* going to stay at that door all day and all night, and for many a long year," the Fairy said, very majestically; and Gruffanuff, coming out of the door, straddling before it with his great calves, burst out laughing, and cried "Ha, ha, ha! this *is* a good un! Ha—ah—what's this? Let me down—O—o—H'm!" and then he was dumb!

For, as the Fairy waved her wand over him, he felt himself rising off the ground, and fluttering up against the door, and then, as if a screw ran into his stomach, he felt a dreadful pain there, and was pinned to the door; and then his arms flew up over his head; and his legs, after writhing about wildly, twisted under his body; and he felt cold, cold, growing over him, as if he was turning into metal; and he said, "O—o—H'm!" and could say no more, because he was dumb.

He *was* turned into metal! He was, from being *brazen*, *brass*! He was neither more nor less than a knocker! And there he was, nailed to the door in the blazing summer day, till he burned almost red-hot; and there he was, nailed to the door all the bitter winter nights, till his brass nose was dropping with icicles. And the postman came and rapped at him, and the vulgarest boy with a letter came and hit him up against the door. And the King and Queen (Princess and Prince they were then) coming home from a walk that evening, the King said, "Hullo, my dear! you have had a new knocker put on the door. Why, it's rather like our porter in the face! What has become of that boozy vagabond?" And the housemaid came and scrubbed his nose with sand-paper; and once, when the Princess Angelica's little sister was born, he was tied up in an old kid glove; and, another night, some *larking* young men tried to wrench him off, and put him to the most excruciating agony with a turnscrew. And then the Queen had a fancy to have the colour of the door altered; and the painters dabbed him over the mouth and eyes, and nearly choked him, as they painted him pea-green. I warrant he had leisure to repent of having been rude to the Fairy Blackstick!

As for his wife, she did not miss him; and as he was always guzzling beer at the public-house, and notoriously quarrelling with his wife, and in debt to the tradesmen, it was supposed he had run away from all these evils, and emigrated to Australia or America. And when the Prince and Princess chose to become King and Queen, they left their old house, and nobody thought of the porter any more.

V

How Princess Angelica Took a Little Maid

One day, when the Princess Angelica was quite a little girl, she was walking in the garden of the palace, with Mrs. Gruffanuff, the governess, holding a parasol over her head, to keep her sweet complexion from the freckles, and Angelica was carrying a bun, to feed the swans and ducks in the royal pond.

They had not reached the duck-pond, when there came toddling up to them such a funny little girl! She had a great quantity of hair blowing about her chubby little cheeks, and looked as if she had not been washed or combed for ever so long. She wore a ragged bit of a cloak, and had only one shoe on.

"You little wretch, who let you in here?" asked Gruffanuff.

"Div me dat bun," said the little girl, "me vely hungry."

"Hungry! what is that?" asked Princess Angelica, and gave the child the bun.

"Oh, Princess!" says Gruffanuff, "how good, how kind, how truly angelical you are! See, your Majesties," she said to the King and Queen, who now came up, along with their nephew, Prince Giglio, "how kind the Princess is! She met this little dirty wretch in the garden—I can't tell how she came in here, or why the guards did not shoot her dead at the gate!—and the dear darling of a Princess has given her the whole of her bun!"

"I didn't want it," said Angelica.

"But you are a darling little angel all the same," says the governess.

"Yes; I know I am," said Angelica. "Dirty little girl, don't you think I am very pretty?" Indeed, she had on the finest of little dresses and hats; and, as her hair was carefully curled, she really looked very well.

"Oh, pooty, pooty!" says the little girl, capering about, laughing, and dancing, and munching her bun; and as she ate it she began to sing, "Oh, what fun to have a plum bun! how I wis it never was done!" At which, and her funny accent, Angelica, Giglio, and the King and Queen began to laugh very merrily.

"I can dance as well as sing," says the little girl. "I can dance, and I can sing, and I can do all sorts of ting."

And she ran to a flower-bed, and pulling a few polyanthuses, rhododendrons, and other flowers, made herself a little wreath, and danced before the King and Queen so drolly and prettily, that everybody was delighted.

"Who was your mother—who were your relations, little girl?" said the Queen.

The little girl said, "Little lion was my brudder; great big lioness my mudder; neber heard of any udder." And she capered away on her one shoe, and everybody was exceedingly diverted.

So Angelica said to the Queen, "Mamma, my parrot flew away yesterday out of its cage, and I don't care any more for any of my toys; and I think this funny little dirty child will amuse me. I will take her home, and give her some of my old frocks."

"Oh, the generous darling!" says Gruffanuff.

"Which I have worn ever so many times, and am quite tired of," Angelica went on; "and she shall be my little maid. Will you come home with me, little dirty girl?" The child clapped her hands, and said, "Go home with you—yes! You pooty Princess!—Have a nice dinner, and wear a new dress!" And they all laughed again, and took home the child to the palace, where, when she was washed and combed, and had one of the Princess's frocks given to her, she looked as handsome as Angelica, almost. Not that Angelica ever thought so; for this little lady never imagined that anybody in the world could be as pretty, as good, or as clever as herself. In order that the little girl should not become too proud and conceited, Mrs. Gruffanuff took her old ragged mantle and one shoe, and put them into a glass box, with a card laid upon them, upon which was written, "These were the old clothes in which little Betsinda was found when the great goodness and admirable kindness of her Royal Highness the Princess Angelica received this little outcast." And the date was added, and the box locked up.

For a while little Betsinda was a great favourite with the Princess, and she danced, and sang, and made her little rhymes, to amuse her mistress. But then the Princess got a monkey, and afterwards a little dog, and afterwards a doll, and did not care for Betsinda any more, who became very melancholy and quiet, and sang no more funny songs, because nobody cared to hear her. And then, as she grew older, she was made a little lady's-maid to the Princess; and though she had no wages, she worked and mended, and put Angelica's hair in papers, and was never cross when scolded, and was always eager to please her mistress, and was always up early and to bed late, and at hand when wanted, and in fact became a perfect little maid. So the two girls grew up, and, when the Princess came out, Betsinda was never tired of waiting on her; and made her dresses better than the best milliner, and was useful in a hundred ways. Whilst the Princess was having her masters, Betsinda would sit and watch them; and in this way she picked up a great deal of learning; for she was always awake, though her mistress was not, and listened to the wise professors when Angelica was yawning or thinking of the next ball. And when the dancing-master came, Betsinda learned along with Angelica; and when the music-master came, she watched him, and practised the Princess's pieces when Angelica was away at balls and parties; and when the drawing-master came, she took note of all he said and did; and the same with French, Italian, and all other languages—she learned them from the teacher who came to Angelica. When the Princess was going out of an evening she would say, "My good Betsinda, you may as well finish what I have begun." "Yes, miss," Betsinda would say, and sit down very cheerful, not to *finish* what Angelica begun, but to *do* it. For instance, the Princess would begin a head of a warrior, let us say, and when it was begun it was something like this—

But when it was done, the warrior was like this—

(only handsomer still if possible), and the Princess put her name to the drawing; and the Court and King and Queen, and above all poor Giglio, admired the picture of all things, and said, "Was there ever a genius like Angelica?" So, I am sorry to say, was it with the Princess's embroidery and other accomplishments; and Angelica actually believed that she did these things herself, and received all the flattery of the Court as if every word of it was true. Thus she began to think that there was no young woman in all the world equal to herself, and that no young man was good enough for her. As for Betsinda, as she heard none of these praises, she was not puffed up by them, and being a most grateful, good-natured girl, she was only too anxious to do everything which might give her mistress pleasure. Now you begin to perceive that Angelica had faults of her own, and was by no means such a wonder of wonders as people represented Her Royal Highness to be.

VI

How Prince Giglio Behaved Himself

And now let us speak about Prince Giglio, the nephew of the reigning monarch of Paflagonia. It has already been stated, in page 398??, that as long as he had a smart coat to wear, a good horse to ride, and money in his pocket, or rather to take out of his pocket, for he was very good-natured, my young Prince did not care for the loss of his crown and sceptre, being a thoughtless youth, not much inclined to politics or any kind of learning. So his tutor had a sinecure. Giglio would not learn classics or mathematics, and the Lord Chancellor of Paflagonia, Squaretoso, pulled a very long face because the Prince could not be got to study the Paflagonian laws and constitution; but, on the other hand, the King's gamekeepers and huntsmen found the Prince an apt pupil; the dancing-master pronounced that he was a most elegant and assiduous scholar; the First Lord of the Billiard Table gave the most flattering reports of the Prince's skill; so did the Groom of the Tennis Court; and as for the Captain of the Guard and Fencing Master, the *valiant* and *veteran* Count Kutasoff Hedzoff, he avowed that since he ran the General of Crim Tartary, the dreadful Grumbuskin, through the body, he never had encountered so expert a swordsman as Prince Giglio.

I hope you do not imagine that there was any impropriety in the Prince and Princess walking together in the palace garden, and because Giglio kissed Angelica's hand in a polite manner. In the first place they are cousins; next, the Queen is walking in the garden too (you cannot see her, for she happens to be behind that tree), and Her Majesty always wished that Angelica and Giglio should marry; so did Giglio: so did Angelica sometimes, for she thought her cousin very handsome, brave, and good-natured: but then you know she was so clever and knew so many things, and poor Giglio knew nothing, and had no conversation. When they looked at the stars, what did Giglio know of the heavenly bodies? Once, when on a sweet night in a balcony where they were standing, Angelica said, "There is the Bear." "Where?" says Giglio. "Don't be afraid, Angelica! if a dozen bears come, I will kill them rather than they shall hurt you." "Oh, you silly creature!" says she; "you are very good, but you are not very wise." When they looked at the flowers, Giglio was utterly unacquainted with botany, and had never heard of Linnæus. When the butterflies passed, Giglio knew nothing about them, being as ignorant of entomology as I am of algebra. So you see, Angelica, though she liked Giglio pretty well, despised him on account of his ignorance. I think she probably valued *her own learning* rather too much; but to think too well of one's self is the fault of people of all ages and both sexes. Finally, when nobody else was there, Angelica liked her cousin well enough.

    King Valoroso was very delicate in health, and withal so fond of good dinners (which were prepared for him by his French cook Marmitonio), that is was supposed he could not live long. Now the idea of anything happening to the King struck the artful Prime Minister and the designing old lady-in-waiting with terror. For, thought Glumboso and the Countess, "when Prince Giglio marries his cousin and comes to the throne, what a pretty position we shall be in, whom he dislikes, and who have always been unkind to him. We shall lose our places in a trice; Gruffanuff will have to give up all the jewels, laces, snuffboxes, rings, and watches which belonged to the Queen, Giglio's mother, and Glumboso will be forced to refund two hundred and seventeen thousand millions nine hundred and eighty-seven thousand four hundred and thirty-nine pounds, thirteen shillings, and sixpence halfpenny, money left to Prince Giglio by his poor dear father." So the Lady of Honor and the Prime Minister hated Giglio because they had done him a wrong; and these unprincipled people invented a hundred cruel stories about poor Giglio, in order to influence the King, Queen, and Princess against him; how he was so ignorant that he could not spell the commonest words, and actually wrote Valoroso Valloroso, and spelt Angelica with two l's; how he drank a great deal too much wine at dinner, and was always idling in the stables with the grooms; how he owed ever so much money at the pastrycook's and haberdasher's; how he used to go to sleep at church; how he was fond of playing cards with the pages. So did the Queen like playing cards; so did the King go to sleep at church, and eat and drink too much; and, if Giglio owed a trifle for tarts, who owed him two hundred and seventeen thousand millions nine hundred and eighty-seven thousand four hundred and thirty-nine pounds, thirteen shillings, and sixpence halfpenny, I should like to know? Detractors and tale-bearers (in my humble opinion) had much better look at home. All this backbiting and slandering had effect upon Princess Angelica, who began to look coldly on her cousin, then to laugh at him and scorn him for being so stupid, then to sneer at him for having vulgar associates; and at Court balls, dinners, and so forth, to treat him so unkindly that poor Giglio became quite ill, took to his bed, and sent for the doctor.

His Majesty King Valoroso, as we have seen, had his own reasons for disliking his nephew; and as for those innocent readers who ask why?—I beg (with the permission of their dear parents) to refer them to Shakespeare's pages, where they will read why King John disliked Prince Arthur. With the Queen, his royal but weak-minded aunt, when Giglio was out of sight he was out of mind. While she had her whist and her evening parties, she cared for little else.

I dare say *two villains*, who shall be nameless, wished Doctor Pildrafto, the Court Physician, had killed Giglio right out, but he only bled and physicked him so severely that the Prince was kept to his room for several months, and grew as thin as a post.

Whilst he was lying sick in this way, there came to the Court of Paflagonia a famous painter, whose name was Tomaso Lorenzo, and who was Painter in Ordinary to the King of Crim Tartary, Paflagonia's neighbour. Tomaso Lorenzo painted all the Court, who were delighted with his works; for even Countess Gruffanuff looked young and Glumboso good-humoured in his pictures. "He flatters very much," some people said. "Nay!" says Princess Angelica, "I am above flattery, and I think he did not make my picture handsome enough. I can't bear to hear a man of genius unjustly cried down, and I hope my dear papa will make Lorenzo a knight of his Order of the Cucumber."

The Princess Angelica, although the courtiers vowed Her Royal Highness could draw so *beautifully* that the idea of her taking lessons was absurd, yet chose to have Lorenzo for a teacher, and it was wonderful, *as long as she painted in his studio*, what beautiful pictures she made! Some of the performances were engraved for the Book of Beauty; others were sold for enormous sums at Charity Bazaars. She wrote the *signatures* under the drawings, no doubt, but I think I know who did the pictures—this artful painter, who had come with other designs on Angelica than merely to teach her to draw.

One day, Lorenzo showed the Princess a portrait of a young man in armour, with fair hair and the loveliest blue eyes, and an expression at once melancholy and interesting.

"Dear Signor Lorenzo, who is this?" asked the Princess.

"I never saw any one so handsome," says Countess Gruffanuff (the old humbug).

"That," said the painter, "that, madam, is the portrait of my august young master, His Royal Highness Bulbo, Crown Prince of Crim Tartary, Duke of Acroceraunia, Marquis of Poluphloisboio, and Knight Grand Cross of the Order of the Pumpkin. That is the Order of the Pumpkin glittering on his manly breast, and received by His Royal Highness from his august father, His Majesty King Padella I., for his gallantry at the battle of Rimbombamento, when he slew with his own princely hand the King of Ograria and two hundred and eleven giants of the two hundred and eighteen who formed the King's bodyguard. The remainder were destroyed by the brave Crim Tartar army after an obstinate combat, in which the Crim Tartars suffered severely."

What a Prince! thought Angelica: so brave—so calm-looking—so young—what a hero!

"He is as accomplished as he is brave," continued the Court Painter. "He knows all languages perfectly: sings deliciously: plays every instrument: composes operas which have been acted a thousand nights running at the Imperial Theatre of Crim Tartary, and danced in a ballet there before the King and Queen; in which he looked so beautiful, that his cousin, the lovely daughter of the King of Circassia, died for love of him."

"Why did he not marry the poor Princess?" asked Angelica, with a sigh.

"Because they were *first cousins*, madam, and the clergy forbid these unions," said the Painter.

"And, besides, the young Prince had given his royal heart *elsewhere*."

"And to whom?" asked Her Royal Highness.

"I am not at liberty to mention the Princess's name," answered the Painter.

"But you may tell me the first letter of it," gasped out the Princess.

"That your Royal Highness is at liberty to guess," says Lorenzo.

"Does it begin with a Z?" asked Angelica.

The Painter said it wasn't a Z; then she tried a Y; then an X; then a W, and went so backwards through almost the whole alphabet.

When she came to D, and it wasn't D, she grew very much excited; when she came to C, and it wasn't C, she was still more nervous; when she came to B, *and it wasn't B*, "O dearest Gruffanuff," she said, "lend me your smelling-bottle!" and, hiding her head in the Countess's shoulder, she faintly whispered, "Ah, Signor, can it be A?"

"It was A; and though I may not, by my Royal Master's orders, tell your Royal Highness the Princess's name, whom he fondly, madly, devotedly, rapturously loves, I may show you her portrait," says this slyboots: and leading the Princess up to a gilt frame, he drew a curtain which was before it.

O goodness! the frame contained a LOOKING-GLASS! and Angelica saw her own face!

VII

How Giglio and Angelica Had a Quarrel

The Court Painter of His Majesty the King of Crim Tartary returned to that monarch's dominions, carrying away a number of sketches which he had made in the Paflagonian capital (you know, of course, my dears, that the name of that capital is Blombodinga); but the most charming of all his pieces was a portrait of the Princess Angelica, which all the Crim Tartar nobles came to see. With this work the King was so delighted, that he decorated the Painter with his Order of the Pumpkin (sixth class), and the artist became Sir Tomaso Lorenzo, K. P., thenceforth.

King Valoroso also sent Sir Tomaso his Order of the Cucumber, besides a handsome order for money, for he painted the King, Queen, and principal nobility while at Blombodinga, and became all the fashion, to the perfect rage of all the artists in Paflagonia, where the King used to point to the portrait of Prince Bulbo, which Sir Tomaso had left behind him, and say, "Which among you can paint a picture like that?"

It hung in the royal parlour over the royal sideboard, and Princess Angelica could always look at it as she sat making the tea. Each day it seemed to grow handsomer and handsomer, and the Princess grew so fond of looking at it, that she would often spill the tea over the cloth, at which her father and mother would wink and wag their heads, and say to each other, "Aha! we see how things are going."

In the meanwhile poor Giglio lay upstairs very sick in his chamber, though he took all the doctor's horrible medicines like a good young lad; as I hope *you* do, my dears, when you are ill and mamma sends for the medical man. And the only person who visited Giglio (besides his friend the captain of the guard, who was almost always busy or on parade), was little Betsinda the housemaid, who used to do his bedroom and sitting-room out, bring him his gruel, and warm his bed.

When the little housemaid came to him in the morning and evening, Prince Giglio used to say, "Betsinda, Betsinda, how is the Princess Angelica?"

And Betsinda used to answer, "The Princess is very well, thank you, my Lord." And Giglio would heave a sigh, and think, if Angelica were sick, I am sure *I* should not be very well.

Then Giglio would say, "Betsinda, has the Princess Angelica asked for me to-day?" And Betsinda would answer, "No, my Lord, not to-day"; or, "She was very busy practising the piano when I saw her"; or, "She was writing invitations for an evening party, and did not speak to me"; or make some excuse or other, not strictly consonant with truth; for Betsinda was such a good-natured creature, that she strove to do everything to prevent annoyance to Prince Giglio, and even brought him up roast chicken and jellies from the kitchen (when the Doctor allowed them, and Giglio was getting better), saying, "that the Princess had made the jelly, or the bread-sauce, with her own hands, on purpose for Giglio."

When Giglio heard this he took heart and began to mend immediately; and gobbled up the jelly, and picked the last bone of the chicken-drumsticks, merry-thought, sides'-bones, back, pope's nose, and all—thanking his dear Angelica; and he felt so much better the next day, that he dressed and went downstairs, where, whom should he meet but Angelica going into the drawing-room! All the covers were off the chairs, the chandeliers taken out of the bags, the damask curtains uncovered, the work and things carried away, and the handsomest albums on the table. Angelica had her hair in papers: in a word, it was evident there was going to be a party.

"Heavens, Giglio!" cries Angelica: "*you* here in such a dress! What a figure you are!"

"Yes, dear Angelica, I am come downstairs, and feel so well to-day, thanks to the *fowl* and the *jelly*."

"What do I know about fowls and jellies, that you allude to them in that rude way?" says Angelica.

"Why, didn't—didn't you send them, Angelica dear?" says Giglio.

"I send them indeed! Angelica dear! No, Giglio dear," says she, mocking him, "*I* was engaged in getting the rooms ready for His Royal Highness the Prince of Crim Tartary, who is coming to pay my papa's Court a visit."

"The—Prince—of—Crim—Tartary!" Giglio said, aghast.

"Yes, the Prince of Crim Tartary," says Angelica, mocking him. "I dare say you never heard of such a country. What *did* you ever hear of? You don't know whether Crim Tartary is on the Red Sea or on the Black Sea, I dare say."

"Yes, I do, it's on the Red Sea," says Giglio, at which the Princess burst out laughing at him, and said, "Oh, you ninny! You are so ignorant, you are really not fit for society! You know nothing but about horses and dogs, and are only fit to dine in a mess-room with my Royal father's heaviest dragoons. Don't look so surprised at me, sir: go and put your best clothes on to receive the Prince, and let me get the drawing-room ready."

Giglio said, "Oh, Angelica, I didn't think this of you. *This* wasn't your language to me when you gave me this ring, and I gave you mine in the garden, and you gave me that k—"

But what k was we never shall know, for Angelica, in a rage, cried, "Get out, you saucy, rude creature! How dare you to remind me of your rudeness? As for your little trumpery twopenny ring, there, sir, there!" And she flung it out of the window.

"It was my mother's marriage-ring," cried Giglio.

"*I* don't care whose marriage-ring it was," cries Angelica. "Marry the person who picks it up if she's a woman; you shan't marry *me*. And give me back *my* ring. I've no patience with people who boast about the things they give away. *I* know who'll give me much finer things than you ever gave me. A beggarly ring indeed, not worth five shillings!"

Now Angelica little knew that the ring which Giglio had given her was a fairy ring: if a man wore it, it made all the women in love with him; if a woman, all the gentlemen. The Queen, Giglio's mother, quite an ordinary-looking person, was admired immensely whilst she wore this ring, and her husband was frantic when she was ill. But when she called her little Giglio to her, and put the ring on his finger, King Savio did not seem to care for his wife so much any more, but transferred all his love to little Giglio.

So did everybody love him as long as he had the ring; but when, as quite a child, he gave it to Angelica people began to love and admire *her*; and Giglio, as the saying is, played only second fiddle.

"Yes," says Angelica, going on in her foolish ungrateful way. "*I* know who'll give me much finer things than your beggarly little pearl nonsense." "Very good, miss! You may take back your ring too!" says Giglio, his eyes flashing fire at her and then, as if his eyes had been suddenly opened, he cried out, "Ha! what does this mean? Is *this* the woman I have been in love with all my life? Have I been such a ninny as to throw away my regard upon *you*? Why—actually—yes—you are a little crooked!"

"Oh, you wretch!" cries Angelica.

"And, upon my conscience, you—you squint a little."

"Eh!" cries Angelica.

"And your hair is red—and you are marked with the smallpox—and what? you have three false teeth—and one leg shorter than the other!"

"You brute, you brute, you!" Angelica screamed out; and as she seized the ring with one hand, she dealt Giglio one, two, three smacks on the face, and would have pulled the hair off his head had he not started laughing, and crying—

"Oh dear me, Angelica, don't pull out *my* hair, it hurts! You might remove a great deal of *your own*, as I perceive, without scissors or pulling at all. Oh, ho, ho! ha, ha, ha! he, he, he!"

And he nearly choked himself with laughing, and she with rage; when, with a low bow, and dressed in his Court habit, Count Gambabella, the first lord-in-waiting, entered and said, "Royal Highnesses! Their Majesties expect you in the Pink Throne-room, where they await the arrival of the Prince of Crim Tartary."

VIII

How Gruffanuff Picked the Fairy Ring Up, and Prince Bulbo Came to Court

Prince Bulbo's arrival had set all the Court in a flutter: everybody was ordered to put his or her best clothes on: the footmen had their gala liveries; the Lord Chancellor his new wig; the Guards their last new tunics; and Countess Gruffanuff, you may be sure, was glad of an opportunity of decorating *her* old person with her finest things. She was walking through the court of the Palace on her way to wait upon their Majesties, when she spied something glittering on the pavement, and bade the boy in buttons who was holding up her train, to go and pick up the article shining yonder. He was an ugly little wretch, in some of the late groom-porter's old clothes cut down, and much too tight for him; and yet, when he had taken up the ring (as it turned out to be), and was carrying it to his mistress, she thought he looked like a little Cupid. He gave the ring to her; it was a trumpery little thing enough, but too small for any of her old knuckles, so she put it into her pocket.

"Oh, mum!" says the boy, looking at her, "how—how beyoutiful you do look, mum, to-day, mum!"

"And you, too, Jacky," she was going to say; but, looking down at him—no, he was no longer good-looking at all—but only the carroty-haired little Jacky of the morning. However, praise is welcome from the ugliest of men or boys, and Gruffanuff, bidding the boy hold up her train, walked on in high good-humour. The guards saluted her with peculiar respect. Captain Hedzoff, in the ante-room, said, "My dear madam, you look like an angel to-day." And so, bowing and smirking, Gruffanuff went in and took her place behind her Royal Master and Mistress, who were in the throne-room, awaiting the Prince of Crim Tartary. Princess Angelica sat at their feet, and behind the King's chair stood Prince Giglio, looking very savage.

The Prince of Crim Tartary made his appearance, attended by Baron Sleibootz, his chamberlain, and followed by a black page carrying the most beautiful crown you ever saw! He was dressed in his travelling costume, and his hair, as you see, was a little in disorder. "I have ridden three hundred miles since breakfast," said he, "so eager was I to behold the Prin—the Court and august family of Paflagonia, and I could not wait one minute before appearing in your Majesties' presences."

Giglio, from behind the throne, burst out into a roar of contemptuous laughter; but all the Royal party, in fact, were so flurried, that they did not hear this little outbreak. "Your R. H. is welcome in any dress," says the King. "Glumboso, a chair for His Royal Highness."

"Any dress His Royal Highness wears *is* a Court dress," says Princess Angelica, smiling graciously.

"Ah! but you should see my other clothes," said the Prince. "I should have had them on, but that stupid carrier has not brought them. Who's that laughing?"

It was Giglio laughing. "I was laughing," he said, "because you said just now that you were in such a hurry to see the Princess, that you could not wait to change your dress; and now you say you come in those clothes because you have no others."

"And who are you?" says Prince Bulbo, very fiercely.

"My father was King of this country, and I am his only son, Prince!" replies Giglio, with equal haughtiness.

"Ha!" said the King and Glumboso, looking very flurried; but the former, collecting himself, said, "Dear Prince Bulbo, I forgot to introduce to your Royal Highness my dear nephew, His Royal Highness Prince Giglio! Know each other! Embrace each other! Giglio, give His Royal Highness your hand!" and Giglio, giving his hand, squeezed poor Bulbo's until the tears ran out of his eyes. Glumboso now brought a chair for the royal visitor, and placed it on the platform on which the King, Queen, and Prince were seated; but the chair was on the edge of the platform, and as Bulbo sat down, it toppled over, and he with it, rolling over and over, and bellowing like a bull. Giglio roared still louder at this disaster, but it was with laughter; so did all the Court when Prince Bulbo got up; for though when he entered the room he appeared not very ridiculous, as he stood up from his fall for a moment he looked so exceedingly plain and foolish, that nobody could help laughing at him. When he had entered the room, he was observed to carry a rose in his hand, which fell out of it as he tumbled.

"My rose! my rose!" cried Bulbo; and his chamberlain dashed forwards and picked it up; and gave it to the Prince, who put it in his waistcoat. Then people wondered why they had laughed; there was nothing particularly ridiculous in him. He was rather short, rather stout, rather red-haired, but, in fine, for a Prince, not so bad.

So they sat and talked, the royal personages together, the Crim Tartar officers with those of Paflagonia—Giglio very comfortable with Gruffanuff behind the throne. He looked at her with such tender eyes, that her heart was all in a flutter. "Oh, dear Prince," she said, "how could you speak so haughtily in presence of their Majesties? I protest I thought I should have fainted."

"I should have caught you in my arms," said Giglio, looking raptures.

"Why were you so cruel to Prince Bulbo, dear Prince?" says Gruff.

"Because I hate him," says Gil.

"You are jealous of him, and still love poor Angelica," cries Gruffanuff, putting her handkerchief to her eyes.

"I did, but I love her no more!" Giglio cried. "I despise her! Were she heiress to twenty thousand thrones I would despise her and scorn her. But why speak of thrones? I have lost mine. I am too weak to recover it—I am alone, and have no friend."

"Oh, say not so, dear Prince!" says Gruffanuff.

"Besides," says he, "I am so happy here *behind the throne* that I would not change my place, no, not for the throne of the world!"

"What are you two people chattering about there?" says the Queen, who was rather good-natured, though not overburthened with wisdom. "It is time to dress for dinner. Giglio, show Prince Bulbo to his room. Prince, if your clothes have not come, we shall be very happy to see you as you are." But when Prince Bulbo got to his bedroom, his luggage was there and unpacked; and the hairdresser coming in, cut and curled him entirely to his own satisfaction; and when the dinner-bell rang, the royal company had not to wait above five-and-twenty minutes until Bulbo appeared, during which time the King, who could not bear to wait, grew as sulky as possible. As for Giglio, he never left Madam Gruffanuff all this time, but stood with her in the embrasure of a window, paying her compliments. At length the Groom of the Chambers announced His Royal Highness the Prince of Crim Tartary! and the noble company went into the royal dining-room. It was quite a small party; only the King and Queen, the Princess, whom Bulbo took out, the two Princes, Countess Gruffanuff, Glumboso the Prime Minister, and Prince Bulbo's chamberlain. You may be sure they had a very good dinner—let every boy and girl think of what he or she likes best, and fancy it on the table.

The Princess talked incessantly all dinner-time to the Prince of Crimea, who ate an immense deal too much, and never took his eyes off his plate, except when Giglio, who was carving a goose, sent a quantity of stuffing and onion sauce into one of them. Giglio only burst out a-laughing as the Crimean Prince wiped his shirt-front and face with his scented pocket-handkerchief. He did not make Prince Bulbo any apology. When the Prince looked at him, Giglio would not look that way. When Prince Bulbo said, "Prince Giglio, may I have the honour of taking a glass of wine with you?" Giglio *wouldn't* answer. All his talk and his eyes were for Countess Gruffanuff, who you may be sure was pleased with Giglio's attentions—the vain old creature! When he was not complimenting her, he was making fun of Prince Bulbo, so loud that Gruffanuff was always tapping him with her fan, and saying—"Oh, you satirical Prince! Oh, fie, the Prince will hear!" "Well, I don't mind," says Giglio, louder still. The King and Queen luckily did not hear; for Her Majesty was a little deaf, and the King thought so much about his own dinner, and, besides, made such a dreadful noise, hobgobbling in eating it, that he heard nothing else. After dinner, His Majesty and the Queen went to sleep in their arm-chairs.

This was the time when Giglio began his tricks with Prince Bulbo, plying that young gentleman with port, sherry, madeira, champagne, marsala, cherry-brandy, and pale ale, of all of which Master Bulbo drank without stint. But in plying his guest, Giglio was obliged to drink himself, and, I am sorry to say, took more than was good for him, so that the young men were very noisy, rude, and foolish when they joined the ladies after dinner; and dearly did they pay for that imprudence, as now, my darlings, you shall hear!

Bulbo went and sat by the piano, where Angelica was playing and singing, and he sang out of tune, and he upset the coffee when the footman brought it, and he laughed out of place, and talked absurdly, and fell asleep and snored horridly. Booh, the nasty pig! But as he lay there stretched on the pink satin sofa, Angelica still persisted in thinking him the most beautiful of human beings. No doubt the magic rose which Bulbo wore caused this infatuation on Angelica's part; but is she the first young woman who has thought a silly fellow charming?

Giglio must go and sit by Gruffanuff, whose old face he too every moment began to find more lovely. He paid the most outrageous compliments to her:—There never was such a darling—Older than he was?—Fiddle-de-dee! He would marry her—he would have nothing but her!

To marry the heir to the throne! Here was a chance! The artful hussy actually got a sheet of paper, and wrote upon it, "This is to give notice that I, Giglio, only son of Savio, King of Paflagonia, hereby promise to marry the charming and virtuous Barbara Griselda, Countess Gruffanuff, and widow of the late Jenkins Gruffanuff, Esq."

"What is it you are writing, you charming Gruffy?" says Giglio, who was lolling on the sofa, by the writing-table.

"Only an order for you to sign, dear Prince, for giving coals and blankets to the poor, this cold weather. Look! the King and Queen are both asleep, and your Royal Highness's order will do."

So Giglio, who was very good-natured, as Gruffy well knew, signed the order immediately; and, when she had it in her pocket, you may fancy what airs she gave herself. She was ready to flounce out of the room before the Queen herself, as now she was the wife of the *rightful* King of Paflagonia! She would not speak to Glumboso, whom she thought a brute, for depriving her *dear husband* of the crown! And when candles came, and she had helped to undress the Queen and Princess, she went into her own room, and actually practised on a sheet of paper, "Griselda Paflagonia," "Barbara Regina," "Griselda Barbara, Paf. Reg.," and I don't know what signatures besides, against the day when she should be Queen, forsooth!

IX

How Betsinda Got the Warming-Pan

Little Betsinda came in to put Gruffanuff's hair in papers; and the Countess was so pleased, that, for a wonder, she complimented Betsinda. "Betsinda!" she said, "you dressed my hair very nicely to-day; I promised you a little present. Here are five sh—no, here is a pretty little ring, that I picked—that I have had some time." And she gave Betsinda the ring she had picked up in the court. It fitted Betsinda exactly.

"It's like the ring the Princess used to wear," says the maid.

"No such thing," says Gruffanuff, "I have had it this ever so long. There, tuck me up quite comfortable; and now, as it's a very cold night (the snow was beating in at the window), you may go and warm dear Prince Giglio's bed, like a good girl, and then you may unrip my green silk, and then you can just do me up a little cap for the morning, and then you can mend that hole in my silk stocking, and then you can go to bed, Betsinda. Mind I shall want my cup of tea at five o'clock in the morning."

"I suppose I had best warm both the young gentlemen's beds, ma'am," says Betsinda.

Gruffanuff, for reply, said, "Hau-au-ho!—Grau-haw-hoo!-Hong-hrho!" In fact, she was snoring sound asleep.

Her room, you know, is next to the King and Queen, and the Princess is next to them. So pretty Betsinda went away for the coals to the kitchen, and filled the royal warming-pan.

Now, she was a very kind, merry, civil, pretty girl; but there must have been something very captivating about her this evening, for all the women in the servants' hall began to scold and abuse her. The housekeeper said she was a pert, stuck-up thing: the upper-housemaid asked how dare she wear such ringlets and ribbons, it was quite improper! The cook (for there was a woman-cook as well as a man-cook) said to the kitchen-maid that *she* never could see anything in that creetur: but as for the men, every one of them, Coachman, John, Buttons the page, and Monsieur, the Prince of Crim Tartary's valet, started up, and said:

"My eyes!"
"O mussey!"
"O jemmany!" } "What a pretty girl Betsinda is!"
"O ciel!"

"Hands off; none of your impertinence, you vulgar, low people!" says Betsinda, walking off with her pan of coals. She heard the young gentlemen playing at billiards as she went upstairs: first to Prince Giglio's bed, which she warmed, and then to Prince Bulbo's room.

He came in just as she had done; and as soon as he saw her, "O! O! O! O! O! O! what a beyou—oo—ootiful creature you are! You angel—you

peri—you rosebud, let me be thy bulbul—thy Bulbo, too! Fly to the desert, fly with me! I never saw a young gazelle to glad me with its dark blue eye that had eyes like thine. Thou nymph of beauty, take, take this young heart. A truer never did itself sustain within a soldier's waistcoat. Be mine! Be mine! Be Princess of Crim Tartary! My Royal father will approve our union; and, as for that little carroty-haired Angelica, I do not care a fig for her any more."

"Go away, your Royal Highness, and go to bed, please," said Betsinda, with the warming-pan.

But Bulbo said, "No, never, till thou swearest to be mine, thou lovely, blushing, chambermaid divine! Here, at thy feet, the Royal Bulbo lies, the trembling captive of Betsinda's eyes."

And he went on, making himself so *absurd and ridiculous*, that Betsinda, who was full of fun, gave him a touch with the warming-pan, which, I promise you, made him cry "O-o-o-o!" in a very different manner.

Prince Bulbo made such a noise that Prince Giglio, who heard him from the next room, came in to see what was the matter. As soon as he saw what was taking place, Giglio, in a fury, rushed on Bulbo, kicked him in the rudest manner up to the ceiling, and went on kicking him till his hair was quite out of curl.

Poor Betsinda did not know whether to laugh or to cry; and kicking certainly must hurt the Prince, but then he looked so droll! When Giglio had done knocking him up and down to the ground, and whilst he went into a corner rubbing himself, what do you think Giglio does? He goes down on his own knees to Betsinda, takes her hand, begs her to accept his heart, and offers to marry her that moment.

Fancy Betsinda's condition, who had been in love with the Prince ever since she first saw him in the palace garden, when she was quite a little child.

"Oh, divine Betsinda!" says the Prince, "how have I lived fifteen years in thy company without seeing thy perfections? What woman in all Europe, Asia, Africa, and America, nay, in Australia, only it is not yet discovered, can presume to be thy equal? Angelica? Pish! Gruffanuff?

Phoo! The Queen? Ha, ha! Thou art my Queen. Thou art the real Angelica, because thou art really angelic."

"O, Prince! I am but a poor chambermaid," says Betsinda, looking, however, very much pleased.

"Didst thou not tend me in my sickness, when all forsook me?" continues Giglio. "Did not thy gentle hand smooth my pillow, and bring me jelly and roast chicken?"

"Yes, dear Prince, I did," says Betsinda, "and I sewed your Royal Highness's shirt-buttons on too, if you please, your Royal Highness," cries this artless maiden.

When poor Prince Bulbo, who was now madly in love with Betsinda, heard this declaration, when he saw the unmistakable glances which she flung upon Giglio, Bulbo began to cry bitterly, and tore quantities of hair out of his head, till it all covered the room like so much tow.

Betsinda had left the warming-pan on the floor while the Princes were going on with their conversation, and as they began now to quarrel and be very fierce with one another, she thought proper to run away.

"You great big blubbering booby, tearing your hair in the corner there; of course you will give me satisfaction for insulting Betsinda. You dare to kneel down at Princess Giglio's knees and kiss her hand!"

"She's not Princess Giglio!" roars out Bulbo. "She shall be Princess Bulbo, no other shall be Princess Bulbo."

"You are engaged to my cousin!" bellows out Giglio.

"I hate your cousin," says Bulbo.

"You shall give me satisfaction for insulting her!" cries Giglio in a fury.

"I'll have your life."

"I'll run you through."

"I'll cut your throat."

"I'll blow your brains out."

"I'll knock your head off."

"I'll send a friend to you in the morning."

"I'll send a bullet into you in the afternoon."

"We'll meet again," says Giglio, shaking his fist in Bulbo's face; and seizing up the warming-pan, he kissed it, because, forsooth, Betsinda had carried it, and rushed downstairs. What should he see on the landing but His Majesty talking to Betsinda, whom he called by all sorts of fond names. His Majesty had heard a row in the building, so he stated, and smelling something burning, had come out to see what the matter was.

"It's the young gentlemen smoking, perhaps, sir," says Betsinda.

"Charming chambermaid," says the King (like all the rest of them), "never mind the young men! Turn thy eyes on a middle-aged autocrat, who has been considered not ill-looking in his time."

"Oh, sir! what will Her Majesty say?" cries Betsinda.

"Her Majesty!" laughs the monarch. "Her Majesty be hanged. Am I not Autocrat of Paflagonia? Have I not blocks, ropes, axes, hangmen—ha? Runs not a river by my palace wall? Have I not sacks to sew up wives withal? Say but the word, that thou wilt be mine own—your mistress straightway in a sack is sewn, and thou the sharer of my heart and throne."

When Giglio heard these atrocious sentiments, he forgot the respect usually paid to Royalty, lifted up the warming-pan, and knocked down the King as flat as a pancake; after which, Master Giglio took to his heels and ran away, and Betsinda went off screaming, and the Queen, Gruffanuff, and the Princess, all came out of their rooms. Fancy their feelings on beholding their husband, father, sovereign, in this posture!

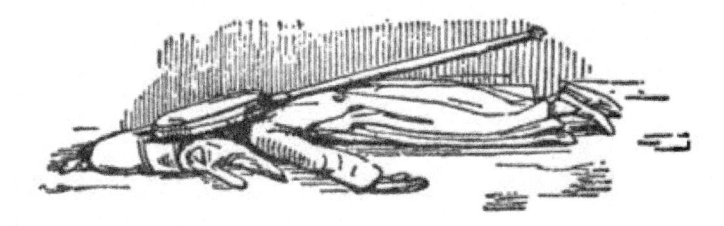

X

How King Valoroso Was In a Dreadful Passion

As soon as the coals began to burn him, the King came to himself and stood up. "Ho! my captain of the guards!" His Majesty exclaimed, stamping his royal feet with rage. O piteous spectacle! the King's nose was bent quite crooked by the blow of Prince Giglio! His Majesty ground his teeth with rage. "Hedzoff," he said, taking a death-warrant out of his dressing-gown pocket, "Hedzoff, good Hedzoff, seize upon the Prince. Thou'lt find him in his chamber two pair up. But now he dared, with sacrilegious hand, to strike the sacred night-cap of a king—Hedzoff, and floor me with a warming-pan! Away, no more demur, the villain dies! See it be done, or else—h'm—ha!—h'm! mind thine own eyes!" and followed by the ladies, and lifting up the tails of his dressing-gown, the King entered his own apartment.

Captain Hedzoff was very much affected, having a sincere love for Giglio. "Poor, poor Giglio!" he said, the tears rolling over his manly face, and dripping down his moustachios; "my noble young Prince, is it my hand must lead thee to death?"

"Lead him to fiddlestick, Hedzoff," said a female voice. It was Gruffanuff, who had come out in her dressing-gown when she heard the noise. "The King said you were to hang the Prince. Well, hang the Prince."

"I don't understand you," says Hedzoff, who was not a very clever man.

"You Gaby! he didn't say *which* Prince," says Gruffanuff.

"No; he didn't say which, certainly," said Hedzoff.

"Well, then, take Bulbo, and hang *him*!"

When Captain Hedzoff heard this, he began to dance about for joy. "Obedience is a soldier's honour," says he. "Prince Bulbo's head will do capitally," and he went to arrest the Prince the very first thing next morning.

He knocked at the door. "Who's there?" says Bulbo. "Captain Hedzoff? Step in, pray, my good Captain; I'm delighted to see you; I have been expecting you."

"Have you?" says Hedzoff.

"Sleibootz, my Chamberlain, will act for me," says the Prince.

"I beg your Royal Highness's pardon, but you will have to act for yourself, and it's a pity to wake Baron Sleibootz."

The Prince Bulbo still seemed to take the matter very coolly. "Of course, Captain," says he, "you are come about that affair with Prince Giglio?"

"Precisely," says Hedzoff, "that affair of Prince Giglio."

"Is it to be pistols, or swords, Captain?" asks Bulbo. "I'm a mighty good hand with both, and I'll do for Prince Giglio as sure as my name is my Royal Highness Prince Bulbo."

"There's some mistake, my Lord," says the Captain. "The business is done with *axes* among us."

"Axes? That's sharp work," says Bulbo. "Call my Chamberlain, he'll he my second, and in ten minutes, I flatter myself, you'll see Master

Giglio's head off his impertinent shoulders. I'm hungry for his blood. Hoo-oo, aw!" and he looked as savage as an ogre.

"I beg your pardon, sir, but by this warrant I am to take you prisoner, and hand you over to—to the executioner."

"Pooh, pooh, my good man!—Stop, I say—ho!—hulloa!" was all that this luckless Prince was enabled to say, for Hedzoff's guards seizing him, tied a handkerchief over his mouth and face, and carried him to the place of execution.

The King, who happened to be talking to Glumboso, saw him pass, and took a pinch of snuff and said, "So much for Giglio. Now let's go to breakfast."

The Captain of the Guard handed over his prisoner to the Sheriff, with the fatal order,

"At sight cut off the bearer's head.
"Valoroso XXIV."

"It's a mistake," says Bulbo, who did not seem to understand the business in the least.

"Poo—poo—pooh," says the Sheriff. "Fetch Jack Ketch instantly. Jack Ketch!"

And poor Bulbo was led to the scaffold, where an executioner with a block and a tremendous axe was always ready in case he should be wanted.

But we must now revert to Giglio and Betsinda.

XI

What Gruffanuff Did to Giglio and Betsinda

Gruffanuff, who had seen what had happened with the King, and knew that Giglio must come to grief, got up very early the next morning, and went to devise some plans for rescuing her darling husband, as the silly old thing insisted on calling him. She found him walking up and down the garden, thinking of a rhyme for Betsinda (*tinder* and *winda* were all he could find), and indeed having forgotten all about the past evening, except that Betsinda was the most lovely of beings.

"Well, dear Giglio," says Gruff.

"Well, dear Gruffy," says Giglio, only *he* was quite satirical.

"I have been thinking, darling, what you must do in this scrape. You must fly the country for a while."

"What scrape?—fly the country? Never without her I love, Countess," says Giglio.

"No, she will accompany you, dear Prince," she says, in her most coaxing accents. "First, we must get the jewels belonging to our royal parents, and those of her and his present Majesty. Here is the key, duck; they are all yours, you know, by right, for you are the rightful King of Paflagonia, and your wife will be the rightful Queen."

"Will she?" says Giglio.

"Yes; and having got the jewels, go to Glumboso's apartment, where, under his bed, you will find sacks containing money to the amount of £217,000,000,987,439 13s. 6½d., all belonging to you, for he took it out of your royal father's room on the day of his death. With this we will fly."

"*We* will fly?" says Giglio.

"Yes, you and your bride—your affianced love—your Gruffy!" says the Countess, with a languishing leer.

"*You* my bride!" says Giglio. "You, you hideous old woman!"

"Oh, you—you wretch! didn't you give me this paper promising marriage?" cries Gruff.

"Get away, you old goose! I love Betsinda, and Betsinda only!" And in a fit of terror he ran from her as quickly as he could.

"He! he! he!" shrieks out Gruff; "a promise is a promise if there are laws in Paflagonia! And as for that monster, that wretch, that fiend, that ugly little vixen—as for that upstart, that ingrate, that beast, Betsinda, Master Giglio will have no little difficulty in discovering her whereabouts. He may look very long before finding *her*, I warrant. He little knows that Miss Betsinda is—"

Is—what? Now, you shall hear. Poor Betsinda got up at five in winter's morning to bring her cruel mistress her tea; and instead of finding her in a good humor, found Gruffy as cross as two sticks. The Countess boxed Betsinda's ears half a dozen times whilst she was dressing; but as poor little Betsinda was used to this kind of treatment, she did not feel any special alarm. "And now," says she, "when Her Majesty rings her bell twice, I'll trouble you, miss, to attend."

So when the Queen's bell rang twice, Betsinda came to Her Majesty and made a pretty little curtsey. The Queen, the Princess, and Gruffanuff were all three in the room. As soon as they saw her they began.

"You wretch!" says the Queen.

"You little vulgar thing!" says the Princess.

"You beast!" says Gruffanuff.

"Get out of my sight!" says the Queen.

"Go away with you, do!" says the Princess.

"Quit the premises!" says Gruffanuff.

Alas! and woe is me! very lamentable events had occurred to Betsinda that morning, and all in consequence of that fatal warming-pan business of the previous night. The King had offered to marry her; of course Her Majesty the Queen was jealous; Bulbo had fallen in love with her; of course Angelica was furious: Giglio was in love with her, and oh, what a fury Gruffy was in!

"Take off that { cap / petticoat / gown } I gave you," they said, all at once,

and began tearing the clothes off poor Betsinda.

"How dare you flirt with { the King?" / Prince Bulbo?" / Prince Giglio?" } cried the Queen, the Princess, and Countess.

"Give her the rags she wore when she came into the house and turn her out of it!" cries the Queen. "Mind she does not go with *my* shoes on, which I lent her so kindly," says the Princess; and indeed the Princess's shoes were a great deal too big for Betsinda.

"Come with me, you filthy hussy!" and taking up the Queen's poker, the cruel Gruffanuff drove Betsinda into her room.

The Countess went to the glass box in which she had kept Betsinda's old cloak and shoe this ever so long, and said, "Take those rags, you little beggar creature, and strip off everything belonging to honest people, and go about your business"; and she actually tore off the poor little delicate thing's back almost all her things, and told her to be off out of the house.

Poor Betsinda huddled the cloak round her back, on which were embroidered the letters PRIN... ROSAL... and then came a great rent.

As for the shoe, what was she to do with one poor little tootsey sandal? the string was still to it, so she hung it round her neck.

"Won't you give me a pair of shoes to go out in the snow, mum, if you please, mum?" cried the poor child.

"No, you wicked beast!" says Gruffanuff, driving her along with the poker—driving her down the cold stairs—driving her through the cold hall—flinging her out into the cold street, so that the knocker itself shed tears to see her!

But a kind fairy made the soft snow warm for her little feet, and she wrapped herself up in the ermine of her mantle, and was gone!

"And now let us think about breakfast," says the greedy Queen.

"What dress shall I put on, mamma? the pink or the pea-green?" says Angelica. "Which do you think the dear Prince will like best?"

"Mrs. V.!" sings out the King from his dressing-room, "let us have sausages for breakfast! Remember we have Prince Bulbo staying with us!"

And they all went to get ready.

Nine o'clock came, and they were all in the breakfast-room, and no Prince Bulbo as yet. The urn was hissing and humming: the muffins were smoking—such a heap of muffins! the eggs were done, there was a pot of raspberry jam, and coffee, and a beautiful chicken and tongue on the side-table. Marmitonio the cook brought in the sausages. Oh, how nice they smelt!

"Where is Bulbo?" said the King. "John, where is His Royal Highness?"

John said he had a took hup His Roilighnessesses shaving-water, and his clothes and things, and he wasn't in his room, which he sposed His Royliness was just stepped hout.

"Stepped out before breakfast in the snow! Impossible!" says the King, sticking his fork into a sausage. "My dear, take one. Angelica, won't you have a saveloy?"

The Princess took one, being very fond of them; and at this moment Glumboso entered with Captain Hedzoff, both looking very much disturbed.

"I am afraid your Majesty—" cries Glumboso.

"No business before breakfast, Glum!" says the King. "Breakfast first, business next. Mrs. V., some more sugar!"

"Sire, I am afraid if we wait till after breakfast it will be too late," says Glumboso. "He—he—he'll be hanged at half-past nine."

"Don't talk about hanging and spoil my breakfast, you unkind vulgar man you," cries the Princess. "John, some mustard. Pray who is to be hanged?"

"Sire, it is the Prince," whispers Glumboso to the King.

"Talk about business after breakfast, I tell you!" says His Majesty, quite sulky.

"We shall have a war, Sire, depend on it," says the Minister. "His father, King Padella...."

"His father, King *who*?" says the King. "King Padella is not Giglio's father. My brother, King Savio, was Giglio's father."

"It's Prince Bulbo they are hanging, Sire, not Prince Giglio," says the Prime Minister.

"You told me to hang the Prince, and I took the ugly one," says Hedzoff. "I didn't, of course, think Your Majesty intended to murder your own flesh and blood!"

The King for all reply flung the plate of sausages at Hedzoff's head. The Princess cried out "Hee-karee-karee!" and fell down in a fainting fit.

"Turn the cock of the urn upon Her Royal Highness," said the King, and the boiling water gradually revived her. His Majesty looked at his watch, compared it by the clock in the parlour, and by that of the church in the square opposite; then he wound it up; then he looked at it again. "The great question is," says he, "am I fast or am I slow? If I'm slow, we may as well go on with breakfast. If I'm fast, why, there is just the possibility of saving Prince Bulbo. It's a doosid awkward mistake, and upon my word, Hedzoff, I have the greatest mind to have you hanged too."

"Sire, I did but my duty; a soldier has but his orders. I didn't expect after forty-seven years of faithful service that my sovereign would think of putting me to a felon's death!"

"A hundred thousand plagues upon you! Can't you see that while you are talking my Bulbo is being hung?" screamed the Princess.

"By Jove! she's always right, that girl, and I'm so absent," says the King, looking at his watch again. "Ha! there go the drums! What a doosid awkward thing though!"

"Oh, papa, you goose! Write the reprieve, and let me run with it," cries the Princess—and she got a sheet of paper, and pen and ink, and laid them before the King.

"Confound it! where are my spectacles?" the Monarch exclaimed. "Angelica! go up into my bedroom, look under my pillow, not your mamma's; there you'll see my keys. Bring them down to me, and—Well, well! what impetuous things these girls are!" Angelica was gone, and had run up panting to the bedroom, and found the keys, and was back again before the King had finished a muffin. "Now, love," says he, "you must go all the way back for my desk, in which my spectacles are. If you would but have heard me out.... Be hanged to her! There she is off again. Angelica! ANGELICA!" When His Majesty called in his *loud* voice, she knew she must obey, and came back.

"My dear, when you go out of a room, how often have I told you, *shut the door*. That's a darling. That's all." At last the keys and the desk and the spectacles were got, and the King mended his pen, and signed his name to a reprieve, and Angelica ran with it as swift as the wind. "You'd better stay, my love, and finish the muffins. There's no use going. Be sure it's too late. Hand me over that raspberry jam, please," said the Monarch. "Bong! Bawong! There goes the half-hour. I knew it was."

Angelica ran, and ran, and ran, and ran. She ran up Fore Street, and down High Street, and through the Market-place, and down to the left, and over the bridge, and up the blind alley, and back again, and round by the Castle, and so along by the Haberdasher's on the right, opposite the lamppost, and round the square, and she came—she came to the

Execution place, where she saw Bulbo laying his head on the block!!! The executioner raised his axe, but at that moment the Princess came panting up and cried "Reprieve!" "Reprieve!" screamed the Princess. "Reprieve!" shouted all the people. Up the scaffold stairs she sprang, with the agility of a lighter of lamps; and flinging herself in Bulbo's arms, regardless of all ceremony, she cried out, "Oh, my Prince! my lord! my love! my Bulbo! Thine Angelica has been in time to save thy precious existence, sweet rosebud; to prevent thy being nipped in thy young bloom! Had aught befallen thee, Angelica too had died, and welcomed death that joined her to her Bulbo."

"H'm! there's no accounting for tastes," said Bulbo, looking so very much puzzled and uncomfortable that the Princess, in tones of tenderest strain, asked the cause of his disquiet.

"I tell you what it is, Angelica," said he, "since I came here yesterday, there has been such a row, and disturbance, and quarrelling, and fighting, and chopping of heads off, and the deuce to pay, that I am inclined to go back to Crim Tartary."

"But with me as thy bride, my Bulbo! Though wherever thou art is Crim Tartary to me, my bold, my beautiful, my Bulbo!"

"Well, well, I suppose we must be married," says Bulbo. "Doctor, you came to read the Funeral Service—read the Marriage Service, will you? What must be, must. That will satisfy Angelica, and then, in the name of peace and quietness, do let us go back to breakfast."

Bulbo had carried a rose in his mouth all the time of the dismal ceremony. It was a fairy rose, and he was told by his mother that he ought never to part with it. So he had kept it between his teeth, even when he laid his poor head upon the block, hoping vaguely that some chance would turn up in his favour. As he began to speak to Angelica, he forgot about the rose, and of course it dropped out of his mouth. The romantic Princess instantly stooped and seized it. "Sweet rose!" she exclaimed, "that bloomed upon my Bulbo's lip, never, never will I part from thee!" and she placed it in her bosom. And you know Bulbo *couldn't* ask her to give the rose back again. And they went to breakfast; and as they walked, it appeared to Bulbo that Angelica became more exquisitely lovely every moment.

He was frantic until they were married; and now, strange to say, it was Angelica who didn't care about him! He knelt down, he kissed her hand, he prayed and begged; he cried with admiration; while she for her part said she really thought they might wait; it seemed to her he was not handsome any more—no, not at all, quite the reverse; and not clever, no, very stupid; and not well bred, like Giglio; no, on the contrary, dreadfully vul—

What, I cannot say, for King Valoroso roared out "*Pooh*, stuff!" in a terrible voice. "We will have no more of this shilly-shallying! Call the Archbishop, and let the Prince and Princess be married offhand!"

So, married they were, and I am sure for my part I trust they will be happy.

XII

How Betsinda Fled, and What Became of Her

Betsinda wandered on and on, till she passed through the town gates, and so on the great Crim Tartary road, the very way on which Giglio too was going. "Ah!" thought she, as the diligence passed her, of which the conductor was blowing a delightful tune on his horn, "how I should like to be on that coach!" But the coach and the jingling horses were very soon gone. She little knew who was in it, though very likely she was thinking of him all the time. Then came an empty cart, returning from market; and the driver being a kind man, and seeing such a very pretty girl trudging along the road with bare feet, most good-naturedly gave her a seat. He said he lived on the confines of the forest, where his old father was a woodman, and, if she liked, he would take her so far on her road. All roads were the same to little Betsinda, so she very thankfully took this one.

And the carter put a cloth round her bare feet, and gave her some bread and cold bacon, and was very kind to her. For all that she was very cold and melancholy. When after travelling on and on, evening came, and all the black pines were bending with snow, and there, at last, was the comfortable light beaming in the woodman's windows; and so they arrived, and went into his cottage. He was an old man, and had a number of children, who were just at supper, with nice hot bread-and-milk, when their elder brother arrived with the cart. And they jumped and clapped their hands; for they were good children; and he had brought them toys from the town. And when they saw the pretty stranger, they ran to her, and brought her to the fire, and rubbed her poor little feet, and brought her bread-and-milk.

"Look, father!" they said to the old woodman, "look at this poor girl, and see what pretty cold feet she has. They are as white as our milk! And look and see what an odd cloak she has, just like the bit of velvet that hangs up in our cupboard, and which you found that day the little cubs were killed by King Padella, in the forest! And look, why, bless us all! she has got round her neck just such another little shoe as that you brought home, and have shown us so often—a little blue velvet shoe!"

"What," said the old woodman, "what is all this about a shoe and a cloak?"

And Betsinda explained that she had been left, when quite a little child, at the town with this cloak and this shoe. And the persons who had taken care of her had—had been angry with her, for no fault, she hoped, of her own. And they sent her away with her old clothes—and here, in fact, she was. She remembered having been in a forest—and perhaps it was a dream—it was so very odd and strange—having lived in a cave with lions there; and, before that, having lived in a very, very fine house, as fine as the King's, in the town.

When the woodman heard this, he was so astonished, it was quite curious to see how astonished he was. He went to his cupboard, and took out of a stocking a five-shilling piece of King Cavolfiore, and vowed it was exactly like the young woman. And then he produced the shoe and piece of velvet which he had kept so long, and compared them with the things which Betsinda wore. In Betsinda's little shoe was written, "Hopkins, maker to the Royal Family"; so in the other shoe was written, "Hopkins, maker to the Royal Family." In the inside of Betsinda's piece of cloak was embroidered, "Prin Rosal"; in the other piece of cloak was embroidered "cess Ba. No. 246." So that when put together you read, "Princess Rosalba. No. 246."

On seeing this, the dear old woodman fell down on his knee, saying, "O my Princess, O my gracious royal lady, O my rightful Queen of Crim Tartary,—I hail thee—I acknowledge thee—I do thee homage!" And in token of his fealty, he rubbed his venerable nose three times on the ground, and put the Princess's foot on his head.

"Why," said she, "my good woodman, you must be a nobleman of my royal father's Court!" For in her lowly retreat, and under the name of Betsinda, Her Majesty, Rosalba, Queen of Crim Tartary, had read of the customs of all foreign courts and nations.

"Marry, indeed, am I, my gracious liege—the poor Lord Spinachi once—the humble woodman these fifteen years syne. Ever since the tyrant Padella (may ruin overtake the treacherous knave!) dismissed me from my post of First Lord."

"First Lord of the Toothpick and Joint Keeper of the Snuffbox? I mind me! Thou heldest these posts under our royal Sire. They are restored to thee, Lord Spinachi! I make thee knight of the second class of our Order of the Pumpkin (the first class being reserved for crowned heads alone). Rise, Marquis of Spinachi!" And with indescribable majesty, the Queen, who had no sword handy, waved the pewter spoon with which she had been taking her bread-and-milk, over the bald head of the old nobleman, whose tears absolutely made a puddle on the ground, and whose dear children went to bed that night Lords and Ladies Bartolomeo, Ubaldo, Catarina, and Ottavia degli Spinachi!

The acquaintance Her Majesty showed with the history, and *noble families* of her empire, was wonderful. "The House of Broccoli should remain faithful to us," she said; "they were ever welcome at our Court.

AND THE GLOOMY PROCESSION MARCHED ON

- The Rose and the Ringt

From the drawing by J. H. Tinker

Have the Articiocchi, as was their wont, turned to the Rising Sun? The family of Sauerkraut must sure be with us—they were ever welcome in the halls of King Cavolfiore." And so she went on enumerating quite a list of the nobility and gentry of Crim Tartary, so admirably had Her Majesty profited by her studies while in exile.

The old Marquis of Spinachi said he could answer for them all; that the whole country groaned under Padella's tyranny, and longed to return to its rightful sovereign; and late as it was, he sent his children, who knew the forest well, to summon this nobleman and that; and when his eldest son, who had been rubbing the horse down and giving him his supper, came into the house for his own, the Marquis told him to put his boots on, and a saddle on the mare, and ride hither and thither to such and such people.

When the young man heard who his companion in the cart had been, he too knelt down and put her royal foot on his head; he too bedewed the ground with his tears; he was frantically in love with her, as everybody now was who saw her; so were the young Lords Bartolomeo and Ubaldo, who punched each other's little heads out of jealousy; and so, when they came from east and west at the summons of the Marquis degli Spinachi, were the Crim Tartar Lords who still remained faithful to the House of Cavolfiore. They were such very old gentlemen for the most part that Her Majesty never suspected their absurd passion, and went among them quite unaware of the havoc her beauty was causing, until an old blind Lord who had joined her party told her what the truth was; after which, for fear of making the people too much in love with her, she always wore a veil. She went about privately, from one nobleman's castle to another; and they visited among themselves again, and had meetings, and composed proclamations and counter-proclamations, and distributed all the best places of the kingdom amongst one another, and selected who of the opposition party should be executed when the Queen came to her own. And so in about a year they were ready to move.

The party of Fidelity was in truth composed of very feeble old fogies for the most part; they went about the country waving their old swords and flags, and calling "God save the Queen!" and King Padella happening to be absent upon an invasion, they had their own way for a little, and to be sure the people were very enthusiastic whenever they saw the Queen; otherwise the vulgar took matters very quietly, for they said, as far as they could recollect, they were pretty well as much taxed in Cavolfiore's time, as now in Padella's.

XIII

How Queen Rosalba Came to the Castle of the Bold Count Hogginamaro

Her Majesty, having indeed nothing else to give, made all her followers Knights of the Pumpkin, and Marquises, Earls, and Baronets; and they had a little court for her, and made her a little crown of gilt paper, and a robe of cotton velvet; and they quarrelled about the places to be given away in her court, and about rank and precedence and dignities—you can't think how they quarrelled! The poor Queen was very tired of her honours before she had had them a month, and I dare say sighed sometimes even to be a lady's-maid again. But we must all do our duty in our respective stations, so the Queen resigned herself to perform hers.

We have said how it happened that none of the Usurper's troops came out to oppose this Army of Fidelity; it pottered along as nimbly as the gout of the principal commanders allowed: it consisted of twice as many officers as soldiers: and at length passed near the estates of one of the most powerful noblemen of the country, who had not declared for the Queen, but of whom her party had hopes, as he was always quarrelling with King Padella.

When they came close to his park gates, this nobleman sent to say he would wait upon Her Majesty: he was a most powerful warrior, and his name was Count Hogginarmo, whose helmet it took two strong negroes to carry. He knelt down before her and said, "Madam and liege lady! it becomes the great nobles of the Crimean realm to show every outward sign of respect to the wearer of the Crown, whoever that may be. We testify to our own nobility in acknowledging yours. The bold Hogginarmo bends the knee to the first of the aristocracy of his country."

Rosalba said, "The bold Count of Hogginarmo was uncommonly kind." But she felt afraid of him, even while he was kneeling, and his eyes scowled at her from between his whiskers, which grew up to them.

"The first Count of the Empire, madam," he went on, "salutes the Sovereign. The Prince addresses himself to the not more noble lady! Madam, my hand is free, and I offer it, and my heart and my sword to your service! My three wives lie buried in my ancestral vaults. The third perished but a year since; and this heart pines for a consort! Deign to be mine, and I swear to bring to your bridal table the head of King Padella, the eyes and nose of his son Prince Bulbo, the right hand and ears of the usurping Sovereign of Paflagonia, which country shall thenceforth be an appanage to your—to *our* Crown! Say yes; Hogginarmo is not accustomed to be denied. Indeed I cannot contemplate the possibility of a refusal: for frightful will be the result; dreadful the murders; furious the devastations; horrible the tyranny; tremendous the tortures, misery, taxation, which the people of this realm will endure, if Hogginarmo's wrath be aroused! I see consent in your Majesty's lovely eyes—their glances fill my soul with rapture!"

"Oh, sir!" Rosalba said, withdrawing her hand in great fright. "Your Lordship is exceedingly kind; but I am sorry to tell you that I have a prior attachment to a young gentleman by the name of—Prince—Giglio—and never—never can marry any one but him."

Who can describe Hogginarmo's wrath at this remark? Rising up from the ground, he ground his teeth so that fire flashed out of his mouth, from which at the same time issued remarks and language, so *loud, violent, and improper*, that this pen shall never repeat them! "R-r-r-r-r-r—Rejected! Fiends and perdition! The bold Hogginarmo rejected! All the world shall hear of my rage; and you, madam, you above all shall rue it!" And kicking the two negroes before him, he rushed away, his whiskers streaming in the wind.

Her Majesty's Privy Council was in a dreadful panic when they saw Hogginarmo issue from the royal presence in such a towering rage, making footballs of the poor negroes—a panic which the events justified. They marched off from Hogginarmo's park very crestfallen; and in another half-hour they were met by that rapacious chieftain with a few of his followers, who cut, slashed, charged, whacked, banged, and pommelled amongst them, took the Queen prisoner, and drove the Army of Fidelity to I don't know where.

Poor Queen! Hogginarmo, her conqueror, would not condescend to see her. "Get a horse-van!" he said to his grooms, "clap the hussy into it, and send her, with my compliments, to His Majesty King Padella."

Along with his lovely prisoner, Hogginarmo sent a letter full of servile compliments and loathsome flatteries to King Padella, for whose life, and that of his royal family, the *hypocritical humbug* pretended to offer the most fulsome prayers. And Hogginarmo promised speedily to pay his humble homage at his august master's throne, of which he begged leave to be counted the most loyal and constant defender. Such a *wary* old *bird* as King Padella was not to be caught by Master Hogginarmo's *chaff*, and we shall hear presently how the tyrant treated his upstart vassal. No, no; depend on't, two such rogues do not trust one another.

So this poor Queen was laid in the straw like Margery Daw, and driven along in the dark ever so many miles to the Court, where King

Padella had now arrived, having vanquished all his enemies, murdered most of them, and brought some of the richest into captivity with him for the purpose of torturing them and finding out where they had hidden their money.

Rosalba heard their shrieks and groans in the dungeon in which she was thrust; a most awful black hole, full of bats, rats, mice, toads, frogs, mosquitoes, bugs, fleas, serpents, and every kind of horror. No light was let into it, otherwise the gaolers might have seen her and fallen in love with her, as an owl that lived up in the roof of the tower did, and a cat, you know, who can see in the dark, and having set its green eyes on Rosalba, never would be got to go back to the turnkey's wife to whom it belonged. And the toads in the dungeon came and kissed her feet, and the vipers wound round her neck and arms, and never hurt her, so charming was this poor Princess in the midst of her misfortunes.

At last, after she had been kept in this place *ever so long*, the door of the dungeon opened, and the terrible King Padella came in.

But what he said and did must be reserved for another chapter, as we must now go back to Prince Giglio.

XIV

What Became of Giglio

The idea of marrying such an old creature as Gruffanuff frightened Prince Giglio so, that he ran up to his room, packed his trunks, fetched in a couple of porters, and was off to the diligence office in a twinkling.

It was well that he was so quick in his operations, did not dawdle over his luggage, and took the early coach, for as soon as the mistake about Prince Bulbo was found out, that cruel Glumboso sent up a couple of policemen to Prince Giglio's room, with orders that he should be carried to Newgate, and his head taken off before twelve o'clock. But the coach was out of the Paflagonian dominions before two o'clock; and I dare say the express that was sent after Prince Giglio did not ride very quick, for many people in Paflagonia had a regard for Giglio, as the son of their old sovereign; a Prince who, with all his weaknesses, was very much better than his brother, the usurping, lazy, careless, passionate, tyrannical, reigning monarch. That Prince busied himself with the balls, fêtes, masquerades, hunting-parties, and so forth, which he thought proper to give on the occasion of his daughter's marriage to Prince Bulbo; and let us trust was not sorry in his own heart that his brother's son had escaped the scaffold.

It was very cold weather, and the snow was on the ground, and Giglio, who gave his name as simple Mr. Giles, was very glad to get a comfortable place in the coupé of the diligence, where he sat with the conductor and another gentleman. At the first stage from Blombodinga, as they stopped to change horses, there came up to the diligence a very ordinary, vulgar-looking woman, with a bag under her arm, who asked for a place. All the inside places were taken, and the young woman was informed that if she wished to travel, she must go upon the roof; and the passenger inside with Giglio (a rude person, I should think), put his head out of the window, and said, "Nice weather for travelling outside! I wish you a pleasant journey, my dear." The poor woman coughed very much, and Giglio pitied her. "I will give up my place to her," says he, "rather than she should travel in the cold air with that horrid cough." On which the vulgar traveller said, "*You'd* keep her warm, I am sure, if it's a *muff* she wants." On which Giglio pulled his nose, boxed his ears, hit him in the eye, and gave this vulgar person a warning never to call him *muff* again.

Then he sprang up gaily on to the roof of the diligence, and made himself very comfortable in the straw. The vulgar traveller got down only at the next station, and Giglio took his place again, and talked to the person next to him. She appeared to be a most agreeable, well-informed, and entertaining female. They travelled together till night, and she gave Giglio all sorts of things out of the bag which she carried, and which indeed seemed to contain the most wonderful collection of articles. He was thirsty—out there came a pint bottle of Bass's pale ale, and a silver mug! Hungry—she took out a cold fowl, some slices of ham, bread, salt, and a most delicious piece of cold plum-pudding, and a little glass of brandy afterwards.

As they travelled, this plain-looking, queer woman talked to Giglio on a variety of subjects, in which the poor Prince showed his ignorance as much as she did her capacity. He owned, with many blushes, how ignorant he was; on which the lady said, "My dear Gigl—my good Mr. Giles, you are a young man, and have plenty of time before you. You have nothing to do but to improve yourself. Who knows but that you may find use for your knowledge some day? When—when you may be wanted at home, as some people may be." "Good heavens, madam!" says he, "do you know me?"

"I know a number of funny things," says the lady, "I have been at some people's christenings, and turned away from other folks' doors. I have seen some people spoilt by good fortune, and others, as I hope, improved by hardship. I advise you to stay at the town where the coach stops for the night. Stay there and study, and remember your old friend to whom you were kind."

"And who is my old friend?" asked Giglio. "When you want anything," says the lady, "look in this bag, which I leave to you as a present, and be grateful to—"

"To whom, madam?" says he.

"To the Fairy Blackstick," says the lady, flying out of the window. And when Giglio asked the conductor if he knew where the lady was?

"What lady?" says the man; "there has been no lady in this coach, except the old woman, who got out at the last stage." And Giglio thought he had been dreaming. But there was the bag which Blackstick had given him lying on his lap; and when he came to the town he took it in his hand and went into the inn.

They gave him a very bad bedroom, and Giglio, when he woke in the morning, fancying himself in the Royal Palace at home, called, "John, Charles, Thomas! My chocolate—my dressing-gown—my slippers"; but nobody came. There was no bell, so he went and bawled out for waiter on the top of the stairs.

The landlady came up, looking—looking like this—

"What are you a hollaring and a bellaring for here, young man?" says she.

"There's no warm water—no servants; my boots are not even cleaned."

"He, he! Clean 'em yourself," says the landlady. "You young students give yourselves pretty airs. I never heard such impudence."

"I'll quit the house this instant," says Giglio.

"The sooner the better, young man. Pay your bill and be off. All my rooms is wanted for gentlefolks, and not for such as you."

"You may well keep the Bear Inn," said Giglio. "You should have yourself painted as the sign."

The landlady of the Bear went away *growling*. And Giglio returned to his room, where the first thing he saw was the fairy bag lying on the table, which seemed to give a little hop as he came in. "I hope it has some breakfast in it," says Giglio, "for I have only a very little money left." But on opening the bag, what do you think was there? A blacking-brush and a pot of Warren's jet, and on the pot was written—

Poor young men their boots must black:
Use me and cork me and put me back.

So Giglio laughed and blacked his boots, and put back the brush and the bottle into the bag.

When he had done dressing himself, the bag gave another little hop, and he went to it and took out—

1. A tablecloth and a napkin.

2. A sugar-basin full of the best loaf-sugar.

4, 6, 8, 10. Two forks, two teaspoons, two knives, and a pair of sugar-tongs, and a butter-knife, all marked G.

11, 12, 13. A teacup, saucer, and slop-basin.

14. A jug full of delicious cream.

15. A canister with black tea and green.

16. A large tea-urn and boiling water.

17. A saucepan, containing three eggs nicely done.

18. A quarter of a pound of best Epping butter.

19. A brown loaf.

And if he hadn't enough now for a good breakfast, I should like to know who ever had one?

Giglio, having had his breakfast, popped all the things back into the bag, and went out looking for lodgings. I forgot to say that this celebrated university town was called Bosforo.

He took a modest lodging opposite the Schools, paid his bill at the inn, and went to his apartment with his trunk, carpet-bag, and not forgetting, we may be sure, his *other* bag.

When he opened his trunk, which the day before he had filled with his best clothes, he found it contained only books. And in the first of them which he opened there was written—

Clothes for the back, books for the head:

Read and remember them when they are read.

And in his bag, when Giglio looked in it, he found a student's cap and gown, a writing-book full of paper, an inkstand, pens, and a Johnson's dictionary, which was very useful to him, as his spelling had been sadly neglected.

So he sat down and worked away, very, very hard for a whole year, during which "Mr. Giles" was quite an example to all the students in the University of Bosforo. He never got into any riots or disturbances. The Professors all spoke well of him, and the students liked him too; so that, when at examination, he took all the prizes, viz.—

The Spelling Prize

The Writing Prize

The History Prize
The Catechism Prize
The French Prize
The Arithmetic Prize
The Latin Prize
The Good Conduct Prize,

all his fellow-students said, "Hurray! Hurray for Giles! Giles is the boy—the student's joy! Hurray for Giles!" And he brought quite a quantity of medals, crowns, books, and tokens of distinction home to his lodgings.

One day after the Examinations, as he was diverting himself at a coffee-house with two friends—(Did I tell you that in his bag, every Saturday night, he found just enough to pay his bills, with a guinea over, for pocket-money? Didn't I tell you? Well, he did, as sure as twice twenty makes forty-five)—he chanced to look in the Bosforo Chronicle, and read off, quite easily (for he could spell, read, and write the longest words now), the following;—

> "ROMANTIC CIRCUMSTANCE.—One of the most extraordinary adventures that we have ever heard has set the neighbouring country of Crim Tartary in a state of great excitement.
>
> "It will be remembered that when the present revered sovereign of Crim Tartary, His Majesty King *Padella*, took possession of the throne, after having vanquished, in the terrific battle of Blunderbusco, the late King *Cavolfiore*, that Prince's only child, the Princess Rosalba, was not found in the royal palace, of which King Padella took possession, and, it was said, had strayed into the forest (being abandoned by all her attendants), where she had been eaten up by those ferocious lions, the last pair of which were captured some time since, and brought to the Tower, after killing several hundred persons.

"His Majesty King Padella, who has the kindest heart in the world, was grieved at the accident which had occurred to the harmless little Princess, for whom His Majesty's known benevolence would certainly have provided a fitting establishment. But her death seemed to be certain. The mangled remains of a cloak, and a little shoe, were found in the forest, during a hunting-party, in which the intrepid sovereign of Crim Tartary slew two of the lion's cubs with his own spear. And these interesting relics of an innocent little creature were carried home and kept by their finder, the Baron Spinachi, formerly an officer in Cavolfiore's household. The Baron was disgraced in consequence of his known legitimist opinions, and has lived for some time in the humble capacity of a woodcutter, in a forest on the outskirts of the Kingdom of Crim Tartary.

"Last Tuesday week Baron Spinachi and a number of gentlemen, attached to the former dynasty, appeared in arms, crying, 'God save Rosalba, the first Queen of Crim Tartary!' and surrounding a lady whom report describes as *'beautiful exceedingly.'* Her history *may* be authentic, is certainly most romantic.

"The personage calling herself Rosalba states that she was brought out of the forest, fifteen years since, by a lady in a car drawn by dragons (this account is certainly *improbable*), that she was left in the Palace Garden of Blombodinga, where Her Royal Highness the Princess Angelica, now married to His Royal Highness Bulbo, Crown Prince of Crim Tartary, found the child, and, with *that elegant benevolence* which has always distinguished the heiress of the throne of

Paflagonia, gave the little outcast a *shelter and a home*! Her parentage not being known, and her garb very humble, the foundling was educated in the Palace in a menial capacity, under the name of *Betsinda*.

"She did not give satisfaction, and was dismissed carrying with her, certainly, part of a mantle and a shoe, which she had on when first found. According to her statement she quitted Blombodinga about a year ago, since which time she has been with the Spinachi family. On the very same morning the Prince Giglio, nephew to the King of Paflagonia, a young Prince whose character for *talent* and *order* were, to say truth, *none of the highest*, also quitted Blombodinga, and has not been since heard of!"

"What an extraordinary story!" said Smith and Jones, two young students, Giglio's especial friends.

"Ha! what is this?" Giglio went on, reading—

"SECOND EDITION, EXPRESS.—We hear that the troop under Baron Spinachi has been surrounded, and utterly routed, by General Hogginarmo, and the *soi-disant* Princess is sent a prisoner to the capital.

"UNIVERSITY NEWS.—Yesterday, at the Schools, the distinguished young student, Mr. Giles, read a Latin oration, and was complimented by the Chancellor of Bosforo, Dr. Prugnaro, with the highest University honour—the wooden spoon."

"Never mind that stuff," says Giles, greatly disturbed. "Come home with me, my friends. Gallant Smith! intrepid Jones! friends of my studies—partakers of my academic toils—I have that to tell shall astonish your honest minds."

"Go it, old boy!" cried the impetuous Smith.

"Talk away, my buck!" says Jones, a lively fellow.

With an air of indescribable dignity, Giglio checked their natural, but no more seemly, familiarity. "Jones, Smith, my good friends," said the Prince, "disguise is henceforth useless; I am no more the humble student Giles, I am the descendant of a royal line."

"*Atavis edite regibus*, I know, old co—," cried Jones. He was going to say old cock, but a flash from THE ROYAL EYE again awed him.

"Friends," continued the Prince, "I am that Giglio, I am, in fact, Paflagonia. Rise, Smith, and kneel not in the public street. Jones, thou true heart! My faithless uncle, when I was a baby filched from me that brave crown my father left me, bred me, all young and careless of my rights, like unto hapless Hamlet, Prince of Denmark; and had I any thoughts about my wrongs, soothed me with promises of near redress. I should espouse his daughter, young Angelica; we two indeed should reign in Paflagonia. His words were false—false as Angelica's heart!—false as Angelica's hair, colour, front teeth! She looked with her skew eyes upon young Bulbo, Crim Tartary's stupid heir, and she preferred him. 'Twas then I turned my eyes upon Betsinda—Rosalba, as she now is. And I saw in her the blushing sum of all perfection; the pink of maiden modesty; the nymph that my fond heart had ever woo'd in dreams," etc., etc.

(I don't give this speech, which was very fine, but very long; and though Smith and Jones knew nothing about the circumstances, my dear reader does, so I go on.)

The Prince and his young friends hastened home to his apartment, highly excited by the intelligence, as no doubt by the *royal narrator's* admirable manner of recounting it, and they ran up to his room where he had worked so hard at his books.

On his writing-table was his bag, grown so long that the Prince could not help remarking it. He went to it, opened it, and what do you think he found in it?

A splendid long, gold-handled, red-velvet-scabbarded, cut-and-thrust sword, and on the sheath was embroidered "Rosalba for Ever!"

He drew out the sword, which flashed and illuminated the whole room, and called out "Rosalba for ever!" Smith and Jones following him, but quite respectfully this time, and taking the time from His Royal Highness.

And now his trunk opened with a sudden pong, and out there came three ostrich feathers in a gold crown, surrounding a beautiful shining steel helmet, a cuirass, a pair of spurs, finally a complete suit of armour.

The books on Giglio's shelves were all gone. Where there had been some great dictionaries, Giglio's friends found two pairs of jack-boots labelled, "Lieutenant Smith," "—Jones, Esq.," which fitted them to a nicety. Besides, there were helmets, back and breast plates, swords, etc., just like in Mr. G. P. R. James's novels; and that evening three cavaliers might have been seen issuing from the gates of Bosforo, in whom the porters, proctors, etc., never thought of recognizing the young Prince and his friends.

They got horses at a livery stable-keeper's, and never drew bridle until they reached the last town on the frontier before you come to Crim Tartary. Here, as their animals were tired, and the cavaliers hungry, they stopped and refreshed at an hostel. I could make a chapter of this if I were like some writers, but I like to cram my measure tight down, you see, and give you a great deal for your money, and, in a word, they had some bread and cheese and ale upstairs on the balcony of the inn. As they were drinking, drums and trumpets sounded nearer and nearer, the market-place was filled with soldiers, and His Royal Highness looking forth, recognized the Paflagonian banners, and the Paflagonian national air which the bands were playing.

The troops all made for the tavern at once, and as they came up Giglio exclaimed, on beholding their leader, "Whom do I see? Yes! No! It is, it is! Phoo! No, it can't be! Yes! It is my friend, my gallant faithful veteran, Captain Hedzoff! Ho! Hedzoff! Knowest thou not thy Prince, thy Giglio? Good Corporal, methinks we once were friends. Ha, Sergeant, an my memory serves me right, we have had many a bout at singlestick."

"I' faith, we have a many, good my Lord," says the Sergeant.

"Tell me, what means this mighty armament," continued His Royal Highness from the balcony, "and whither march my Paflagonians?"

Hedzoff's head fell. "My Lord," he said, "we march as the allies of great Padella, Crim Tartary's monarch."

"Crim Tartary's usurper, gallant Hedzoff? Crim Tartary's grim tyrant, honest Hedzoff!" said the Prince, on the balcony, quite sarcastically.

"A soldier, Prince, must needs obey his orders: mine are to help His Majesty Padella. And also (though alack that I should say it!) to seize wherever I should light upon him—"

"First catch your hare! ha, Hedzoff!" exclaimed His Royal Highness.

"—On the body of *Giglio*, whilome Prince of Paflagonia," Hedzoff went on, with indescribable emotion. "My Prince, give up your sword without ado. Look! we are thirty thousand men to one!"

"Give up my sword! Giglio give up his sword!" cried the Prince; and stepping well forward on to the balcony, the royal youth, *without preparation*, delivered a speech so magnificent that no report can do justice to it. It was all in blank verse (in which, from this time, he invariably spoke, as more becoming his majestic station). It lasted for three days and three nights, during which not a single person who heard him was tired, or remarked the difference between daylight and dark. The soldiers only cheering tremendously, when occasionally, once in nine hours, the Prince paused to suck an orange, which Jones took out of the bag. He explained, in terms which we say we shall not attempt to convey, the whole history of the previous transaction, and his determination not only not to give up his sword, but to assume his rightful crown; and at the end of this extraordinary, this truly *gigantic* effort, Captain Hedzoff flung up his helmet, and cried, "Hurray! Hurray! Long live King Giglio!"

Such were the consequences of having employed his time well at College.

When the excitement had ceased, beer was ordered out for the army, and their Sovereign himself did not disdain a little! And now it was with some alarm that Captain Hedzoff told him his division was only the advanced guard of the Paflagonian contingent, hastening to King

Padella's aid; the main force being a day's march in the rear under His Royal Highness Prince Bulbo.

"We will wait here, good friend, to beat the Prince," His Majesty said, "and *then* will make his royal father wince."

XV

We Return to Rosalba

King Padella made very similar proposals to Rosalba to those which she had received from the various princes who, as we have seen, had fallen in love with her. His Majesty was a widower, and offered to marry his fair captive that instant, but she declined his invitation in her usual polite gentle manner, stating that Prince Giglio was her love, and that any other union was out of the question. Having tried tears and supplications in vain, this violent-tempered monarch menaced her with threats and tortures; but she declared she would rather suffer all these than accept the hand of her father's murderer, who left her finally, uttering the most awful imprecations, and bidding her prepare for death on the following morning.

All night long the King spent in advising how he should get rid of this obdurate young creature. Cutting off her head was much too easy a death for her; hanging was so common in His Majesty's dominions that it no longer afforded him any sport; finally, he bethought himself of a pair of fierce lions which had lately been sent to him as presents, and he determined, with these ferocious brutes, to hunt poor Rosalba down. Adjoining his castle was an amphitheatre where the Prince indulged in bull-baiting, rat-hunting, and other ferocious sports. The two lions were kept in a cage under this place; their roaring might be heard over the whole city, the inhabitants of which, I am sorry to say, thronged in numbers to see a poor young lady gobbled up by two wild beasts.

The King took his place in the royal box, having the officers of his Court around and the Count Hogginarmo by his side, upon whom His Majesty was observed to look very fiercely; the fact is, royal spies had told the monarch of Hogginarmo's behaviour, his proposals to Rosalba, and his offer to fight for the crown. Black as thunder looked King Padella at this proud noble, as they sat in the front seats of the theatre waiting to see the tragedy whereof poor Rosalba was to be the heroine.

At length that Princess was brought out in her nightgown, with all her beautiful hair falling down her back, and looking so pretty that even the beef-eaters and keepers of the wild animals wept plentifully at seeing her. And she walked with her poor little feet (only luckily the arena was covered with sawdust), and went and leaned up against a great stone in the centre of the amphitheatre, round which the Court and the people were seated in boxes, with bars before them, for fear of the great, fierce, red-maned, black-throated, long-tailed, roaring, bellowing, rushing lions. And now the gates were opened, and with a *wurrawarrurawarar* two great lean, hungry, roaring lions rushed out of their den, where they had been kept for three weeks on nothing but a little toast-and-water and dashed straight up to the stone where poor Rosalba was waiting. Commend her to your patron saints, all you kind people, for she is in a dreadful state!

There was a hum and a buzz all through the circus, and the fierce King Padella even felt a little compassion. But Count Hogginarmo, seated by His Majesty, roared out "Hurray! Now for it! Soo-soo-soo!" that nobleman being uncommonly angry still at Rosalba's refusal of him.

But O strange event! O remarkable circumstance! O extraordinary coincidence, which I am sure none of you could *by any possibility* have divined! When the lions came to Rosalba, instead of devouring her with their great teeth, it was with kisses they gobbled her up! They licked her pretty feet, they nuzzled their noses in her lap, they moo'd, they seemed to say, "Dear, dear sister, don't you recollect your brothers in the forest?" And she put her pretty white arms round their tawny necks, and kissed them.

King Padella was immensely astonished. The Count Hogginarmo was extremely disgusted. "Pooh!" the Count cried. "Gammon!" exclaimed his Lordship. "These lions are tame beasts come from Wombwell's or Astley's. It is a shame to put people off in this way. I believe they are little boys dressed up in doormats. They are no lions at all."

"Ha!" said the King, "you dare to say 'gammon' to your Sovereign, do you? These lions are no lions at all, aren't they? Ho! my beef-eaters! Ho! my bodyguard! Take this Count Hogginarmo and fling him into the circus! Give him a sword and buckler, let him keep his armour on, and his weather-eye out and fight these lions."

The haughty Hogginarmo laid down his opera-glass, and looked scowling round at the King and his attendants. "Touch me not, dogs!" he said, "or by St. Nicholas the Elder, I will gore you! Your Majesty thinks Hogginarmo is afraid? No, not of a hundred thousand lions! Follow me down into the circus, King Padella, and match thyself against one of yon brutes. Thou darest not. Let them both come on, then!" And opening a grating of the box, he jumped lightly down into the circus.

Wurra wurra wurra wur-aw-aw-aw!!!
In about two minutes
The Count Hogginarmo was
GOBBLED UP
by
those lions,
bones, boots, and all,
and
There was an
End of him

At this, the King said, "Serve him right, the rebellious ruffian! And now, as those lions won't eat that young woman—"

"Let her off!—let her off!" cried the crowd.

"NO!" roared the King. "Let the beef-eaters go down and chop her into small pieces. If the lions defend her, let the archers shoot them to death. That hussy shall die in tortures!"

"A-a-ah!" cried the crowd. "Shame! shame!"

"Who dares cry out shame?" cried the furious potentate (so little can tyrants command their passions). "Fling any scoundrel who says a word down among the lions!"

I warrant you there was a dead silence then, which was broken by a Pang arang pang pangkarangpang, and a Knight and a Herald rode in at the further end of the circus: the Knight, in full armour, with his vizor up, and bearing a letter on the point of his lance.

"Ha!" exclaimed the King, "by my fay, 'tis Elephant and Castle, pursuivant of my brother of Paflagonia; and the Knight, an my memory serves me, is the gallant Captain Hedzoff! What news from Paflagonia, gallant Hedzoff? Elephant and Castle, beshrew me, thy trumpeting must have made thee thirsty. What will my trusty herald like to drink?"

"Bespeaking first safe conduct from your Lordship," said Captain Hedzoff, "before we take a drink of anything, permit us to deliver our King's message."

"My Lordship, ha!" said Crim Tartary, frowning terrifically. "That title soundeth strange in the anointed ears of a crowned King. Straightway speak out your message, Knight and Herald!"

Reining up his charger in a most elegant manner close under the King's balcony, Hedzoff turned to the Herald, and bade him begin.

Elephant and Castle, dropping his trumpet over his shoulder, took a large sheet of paper out of his hat, and began to read:

"O Yes! O Yes! O Yes! Know all men by these presents, that we, Giglio, King of Paflagonia, Grand Duke of Cappadocia, Sovereign Prince of Turkey and the Sausage Islands, having assumed our rightful throne and title, long time falsely borne by our usurping Uncle, styling himself King of Paflagonia—"

"Ha!" growled Padella.

"Hereby summon the false traitor, Padella, calling himself King of Crim Tartary—"

The King's curses were dreadful. "Go on, Elephant and Castle!" said the intrepid Hedzoff.

"—To release from cowardly imprisonment his liege lady and rightful Sovereign, Rosalba, Queen of Crim Tartary, and restore her to her royal throne: in default of which I, Giglio, proclaim the said Padella sneak, traitor, humbug, usurper, and coward. I challenge him to meet me, with fists or with pistols, with battle-axe or sword, with blunderbuss or singlestick, alone or at the head of his army, on foot or on horseback; and will prove my words upon his wicked ugly body!"

"God save the King!" said Captain Hedzoff, executing a demivolte, two semilunes, and three caracols.

"Is that all?" said Padella, with the terrific calm of concentrated fury.

"That, sir, is all my royal master's message. Here is His Majesty's letter in autograph, and here is his glove, and if any gentleman of Crim Tartary chooses to find fault with His Majesty's expressions, I, Tuffskin

Hedzoff, Captain of the Guard, am very much at his service," and he waved his lance, and looked at the assembly all round.

"And what says my good brother of Paflagonia, my dear son's father-in-law, to this rubbish?" asked the King.

"The King's uncle hath been deprived of the crown he unjustly wore," said Hedzoff gravely. "He and his ex-minister, Glumboso, are now in prison waiting the sentence of my royal master. After the battle of Bombardaro—"

"Of what?" asked the surprised Padella.

"Of Bombardaro, where my liege, his present Majesty, would have performed prodigies of valour, but that the whole of his uncle's army came over to our side, with the exception of Prince Bulbo."

"Ah! my boy, my boy, my Bulbo was no traitor!" cried Padella.

"Prince Bulbo, far from coming over to us, ran away, sir; but I caught him. The Prince is a prisoner in our army, and the most terrific tortures await him if a hair of the Princess Rosalba's head is injured."

"Do they?" exclaimed the furious Padella, who was now perfectly *livid* with rage. "Do they indeed? So much the worse for Bulbo. I've twenty sons as lovely each as Bulbo. Not one but is as fit to reign as Bulbo. Whip, whack, flog, starve, rack, punish, torture Bulbo—break all his bones—roast him or flay him alive—pull all his pretty teeth out one by one! But justly dear as Bulbo is to me—joy of my eyes, fond treasure of my soul!—Ha, ha, ha, ha! revenge is dearer still. Ho! torturers, rackmen, executioners—light up the fires and make the pincers hot! get lots of boiling lead!—Bring out Rosalba!"

XVI

How Hedzoff Rode Back Again to King Giglio

aptain Hedzoff rode away when King Padella uttered this cruel command, having done his duty in delivering the message with which his royal master had entrusted him. Of course he was very sorry for Rosalba, but what could he do?

So he returned to King Giglio's camp, and found the young monarch in a disturbed state of mind, smoking cigars in the royal tent. His Majesty's agitation was not appeased by the news that was brought by his ambassador. "The brutal ruthless ruffian royal wretch!" Giglio exclaimed. "As England's poesy has well remarked, 'The man that lays his hand upon a woman, save in the way of kindness, is a villain.' Ha, Hedzoff!"

"That he is, your Majesty," said the attendant.

"And didst thou see her flung into the oil? and didn't the soothing oil—the emollient oil, refuse to boil, good Hedzoff—and to spoil the fairest lady ever eyes did look on?"

"Faith, good my liege, I had no heart to look and see a beauteous lady boiling down; I took your royal message to Padella, and bore his back to you. I told him you would hold Prince Bulbo answerable. He only said that he had twenty sons as good as Bulbo, and forthwith he bade the ruthless executioners proceed."

"O cruel father—O unhappy son!" cried the King. "Go, some of you, and bring Prince Bulbo hither."

Bulbo was brought in chains, looking very uncomfortable. Though a prisoner, he had been tolerably happy, perhaps because his mind was at rest, and all the fighting was over, and he was playing at marbles with his guards when the King sent for him.

"Oh, my poor Bulbo," said His Majesty, with looks of infinite compassion, "hast thou heard the news?" (for you see Giglio wanted to break the thing gently to the Prince), "thy brutal father has condemned Rosalba-p-p-p-ut her to death, P-p-p-prince Bulbo!"

"What, killed Betsinda! Boo-hoo-hoo," cried out Bulbo. "Betsinda! pretty Betsinda! dear Betsinda! She was the dearest little girl in the world. I love her better twenty thousand times even than Angelica," and he went on expressing his grief in so hearty and unaffected a manner that the King was quite touched by it, and said, shaking Bulbo's hand, that he wished he had known Bulbo sooner.

Bulbo, quite unconsciously, and meaning for the best, offered to come and sit with his Majesty, and smoke a cigar with him, and console him. The *royal kindness* supplied Bulbo with a cigar; he had not had one, he said, since he was taken prisoner.

And now think what must have been the feelings of the most *merciful of monarchs*, when he informed his prisoner that, in consequence of King Padella's *cruel and dastardly behaviour* to Rosalba, Prince Bulbo must instantly be executed! The noble Giglio could not restrain his tears, nor could the Grenadiers, nor the officers, nor could Bulbo himself, when the matter was explained to him, and he was brought to understand that His Majesty's promise, of course, was *above every* thing, and Bulbo must submit. So poor Bulbo was led out, Hedzoff trying to console him, by pointing out that if he had won the battle of Bombardaro, he might have hanged Prince Giglio. "Yes! But that is no comfort to me now!" said poor Bulbo; nor indeed was it, poor fellow!

He was told the business would be done the next morning at eight, and was taken back to his dungeon, where every attention was paid to him. The gaoler's wife sent him tea, and the turnkey's daughter begged him to write his name in her album, where a many gentlemen had wrote it on like occasions! "Bother your album!" says Bulbo. The Undertaker came and measured him for the handsomest coffin which money could buy—even this didn't console Bulbo. The Cook brought him dishes which he once used to like; but he wouldn't touch them: he sat down and began writing an adieu to Angelica, as the clock kept always ticking, and the hands drawing nearer to next morning. The Barber came in at night, and offered to shave him for the next day. Prince Bulbo kicked him away, and went on writing a few words to Princess Angelica, as the clock kept always ticking, and the hands hopping nearer and nearer to next morning.

He got up on the top of a hat-box, on the top of a chair, on the top of his bed, on the top of his table, and looked out to see whether he might escape, as the clock kept always ticking and the hands drawing nearer, and nearer, and nearer.

But looking out of the window was one thing, and jumping another: and the town clock struck seven. So he got into bed for a little sleep, but the gaoler came and woke him, and said, "Git up, your Royal Ighness, if you please, it's *ten minutes to eight!*"

So poor Bulbo got up: he had gone to bed in his clothes (the lazy boy), and he shook himself, and said he didn't mind about dressing, or having any breakfast, thank you; and he saw the soldiers who had come for him. "Lead on!" he said; and they led the way, deeply affected; and they came into the courtyard, and out into the square, and there was King Giglio come to take leave of him, and His Majesty most kindly shook hands with him, and the *gloomy procession* marched on—when hark!

Haw—wurraw—wurraw—aworr!

A roar of wild beasts was heard. And who should come riding into the town, frightening away the boys, and even the beadle and policeman, but Rosalba!

The fact is, that when Captain Hedzoff entered into the court of Snapdragon Castle, and was discoursing with King Padella, the lions made a dash at the open gate, gobbled up the six beef-eaters in a jiffy, and away they went with Rosalba on the back of one of them, and they carried her, turn and turn about, till they came to the city where Prince Giglio's army was encamped.

When the King heard of the Queen's arrival, you may think how he rushed out of his breakfast-room to hand Her Majesty off her lion! The lions were grown as fat as pigs now, having had Hogginarmo and all those beef-eaters, and were so tame anybody might pat them.

While Giglio knelt (most gracefully) and helped the Princess, Bulbo, for his part, rushed up and kissed the lion. He flung his arms round the forest monarch; he hugged him, and laughed and cried for joy. "Oh, you darling old beast, oh, how glad I am to see you, and the dear, dear Bets—that is, Rosalba."

"What, is it you? poor Bulbo!" said the Queen. "Oh, how glad I am to see you," and she gave him her hand to kiss. King Giglio slapped him most kindly on the back, and said, "Bulbo, my boy, I am delighted, for your sake, that Her Majesty has arrived."

"So am I," said Bulbo; "and *you know why*." Captain Hedzoff here came up. "Sire, it is half-past eight: shall we proceed with the execution?"

"Execution! what for?" asked Bulbo.

"An officer only knows his orders," replied Captain Hedzoff, showing his warrant, on which His Majesty King Giglio smilingly said, "Prince Bulbo was reprieved this time," and most graciously invited him to breakfast.

XVII

How a Tremendous Battle Took Place, and Who Won It

As soon as King Padella heard, what we know already, that his victim, the lovely Rosalba, had escaped him, His Majesty's fury knew no bounds, and he pitched the Lord Chancellor, Lord Chamberlain, and every officer of the Crown whom he could set eyes on, into the cauldron of boiling oil prepared for the Princess.

Then he ordered out his whole army, horse, foot, and artillery; and set forth at the head of an innumerable host, and I should think twenty thousand drummers, trumpeters, and fifers.

King Giglio's advanced guard, you may be sure, kept that monarch acquainted with the enemy's dealings, and he was in no wise disconcerted. He was much too polite to alarm the Princess, his lovely guest, with any unnecessary rumours of battles impending; on the contrary, he did everything to amuse and divert her; gave her a most elegant breakfast, dinner, lunch, and got up a ball for her that evening, when he danced with her every single dance.

Poor Bulbo was taken into favour again, and allowed to go quite free now. He had new clothes given him, was called "My good cousin" by His Majesty, and was treated with the greatest distinction by everybody. But it was easy to see he was very melancholy. The fact is, the sight of Betsinda, who looked perfectly lovely in an elegant new dress, set poor Bulbo frantic in love with her again. And he never thought about Angelica, now Princess Bulbo, whom he had left at home, and who, as we know, did not care much about him.

The King, dancing the twenty-fifth polka with Rosalba, remarked with wonder the ring she wore; and then Rosalba told him how she had got it from Gruffanuff, who no doubt had picked it up when Angelica flung it away.

"Yes," says the Fairy Blackstick, who had come to see the young people, and who had very likely certain plans regarding them. "That ring I gave the Queen, Giglio's mother, who was not, saving your presence, a very wise woman; it is enchanted, and whoever wears it looks beautiful in the eyes of the world. I made poor Prince Bulbo, when he was christened, the present of a rose which made him look handsome while he had it; but he gave it to Angelica, who instantly looked beautiful again, whilst Bulbo relapsed into his natural plainness."

"Rosalba needs no ring, I am sure," says Giglio, with a low bow. "She is beautiful enough, in my eyes, without any enchanted aid."

"Oh, sir!" said Rosalba.

"Take off the ring and try," said the King, and resolutely drew the ring off her finger. In *his* eyes she looked just as handsome as before!

The King was thinking of throwing the ring away, as it was so dangerous and made all the people so mad about Rosalba; but being a

Prince of great humour, and good humour too, he cast eyes upon a poor youth who happened to be looking on very disconsolately, and said—

"Bulbo, my poor lad! come and try on this ring. The Princess Rosalba makes it a present to you."

The magic properties of this ring were uncommonly strong, for no sooner had Bulbo put it on, but lo and behold, he appeared a personable, agreeable young Prince enough—with a fine complexion, fair hair, rather stout, and with bandy legs; but these were encased in such a beautiful pair of yellow morocco boots that nobody remarked them. And Bulbo's spirits rose up almost immediately after he had looked in the glass, and he talked to their Majesties in the most lively, agreeable manner, and danced opposite the Queen with one of the prettiest maids of honour, and after looking at Her Majesty, could not help saying—

"How very odd! she is very pretty, but not so *extraordinarily* handsome."

"Oh no, by no means!" says the Maid of Honor.

"But what care I, dear sir," says the Queen, who overheard them, "if *you* think I am good-looking enough?"

His Majesty's glance in reply to this affectionate speech was such that no painter could draw it. And the Fairy Blackstick said, "Bless you, my darling children! Now you are united and happy; and now you see what I said from the first, that a little misfortune has done you both good. *You*, Giglio, had you been bred in prosperity, would scarcely have learned to read or write—you would have been idle and extravagant, and could not have been a good King as now you will be. You, Rosalba, would have been so flattered, that your little head might have been turned like Angelica's, who thought herself too good for Giglio."

"As if anybody could be good enough for *him*," cried Rosalba.

"Oh, you, you darling!" says Giglio. And so she was! and he was just holding out his arms in order to give her a hug before the whole company, when a messenger came rushing in, and said, "My Lord, the enemy!"

"To arms!" cries Giglio.

"Oh, mercy!" says Rosalba, and fainted of course.

He snatched one kiss from her lips, and rushed *forth to the field* of battle!

The Fairy had provided King Giglio with a suit of armour, which was not only embroidered all over with jewels, and blinding to your eyes to look at, but was water-proof, gun-proof, and sword-proof; so that in the midst of the very hottest battles His Majesty rode about as calmly as if he had been a British Grenadier at Alma. Were I engaged in fighting for my country, *I* should like such a suit of armour as Prince Giglio wore; but, you know, he was a Prince of a fairy tale, and they always have these wonderful things.

Besides the fairy armour, the Prince had a fairy horse, which would gallop at any pace you please; and a fairy sword, which would lengthen and run through a whole regiment of enemies at once. With such a weapon at command, I wonder, for my part, he thought of ordering his army out; but forth they all came, in magnificent new uniforms, Hedzoff and the Prince's two college friends each commanding a division, and His Majesty prancing in person at the head of them all.

Ah! if I had the pen of a Sir Archibald Alison, my dear friends, would I not now entertain you with the account of a most tremendous shindy? Should not fine blows be struck? dreadful wounds be delivered? arrows darken the air? cannon balls crash through the battalions? cavalry charge infantry? infantry pitch into cavalry? bugles blow; drums beat; horses neigh; fifes sing; soldiers roar, swear, hurray; officers shout out "Forward, my men!" "This way, lads!" "Give it 'em, boys!" "Fight for King Giglio, and the cause of right!" "King Padella for ever!" Would I not describe all this, I say, and in the very finest language too? But this humble pen does not possess the skill necessary for the description of combats. In a word, the overthrow of King Padella's army was so complete, that if they had been Russians you could not have wished them to be more utterly smashed and confounded.

As for that usurping monarch, having performed acts of valour much more considerable than could be expected of a royal ruffian and usurper, who had such a bad cause, and who was so cruel to women—as for King Padella, I say, when his army ran away, the King ran away too, kicking his first general, Prince Punchikoff, from his saddle, and galloping away on the Prince's horse, having, indeed, had twenty-five or twenty-six of his own shot under him. Hedzoff coming up, and finding Punchikoff down, as you may imagine, very speedily disposed of *him*. Meanwhile King Padella was scampering off as hard as his horse could lay legs to ground. Fast as he scampered, I promise you somebody else galloped faster; and that individual, as no doubt you are aware, was the Royal Giglio, who kept bawling out, "Stay, traitor! Turn, miscreant, and defend thyself! Stand, tyrant, coward, ruffian, royal wretch, till I cut thy ugly head from thy usurping shoulders!" And, with his fairy sword, which elongated itself at will, His Majesty kept poking and prodding Padella in the back, until that wicked monarch roared with anguish.

When he was fairly brought to bay, Padella turned and dealt Prince Giglio a prodigious crack over the sconce with his battle-axe, a most enormous weapon, which had cut down I don't know how many regiments in the course of the afternoon. But, Law bless you! though the blow fell right down on His Majesty's helmet, it made no more impression than if Padella had struck him with a pat of butter: his battle-axe crumpled up in Padella's hand, and the Royal Giglio laughed for very scorn at the impotent efforts of that atrocious usurper.

At the ill success of his blow the Crim Tartar monarch was justly irritated. "If," says he to Giglio, "you ride a fairy horse, and wear fairy armour, what on earth is the use of my hitting you? I may as well give myself up a prisoner at once. Your Majesty won't, I suppose, be so mean as to strike a poor fellow who can't strike again?"

The justice of Padella's remark struck the magnanimous Giglio. "Do you yield yourself a prisoner, Padella?" says he.

"Of course I do," says Padella.

"Do you acknowledge Rosalba as your rightful Queen, and give up the crown and all your treasures to your rightful mistress?"

"If I must, I must," says Padella, who was naturally very sulky.

By this time King Giglio's aides-de-camp had come up, whom His Majesty ordered to bind the prisoner. And they tied his hands behind him, and bound his legs tight under his horse, having set him with his face to the tail; and in this fashion he was led back to King Giglio's quarters, and thrust into the very dungeon where young Bulbo had been confined.

Padella (who was a very different person in the depth of his distress to Padella the proud wearer of the Crim Tartary crown), now most affectionately and earnestly asked to see his son—his dear eldest boy—his darling Bulbo; and that good-natured young man never once reproached his haughty parent for his unkind conduct the day before, when he would have left Bulbo to be shot without any pity, but came to see his father, and spoke to him through the grating of the door, beyond which he was not allowed to go; and brought him some sandwiches from the grand supper which His Majesty was giving above stairs, in honour of the brilliant victory which had just been achieved.

"I cannot stay with you long, sir," says Bulbo, who was in his best ball dress, as he handled his father in the prog, "I am engaged to dance the next quadrille with Her Majesty Queen Rosalba, and I hear the fiddles playing at this very moment."

So Bulbo went back to the ball-room, and the wretched Padella ate his solitary supper in silence and tears.

All was now joy in King Giglio's circle. Dancing, feasting, fun, illuminations, and jollifications of all sorts ensued. The people through whose villages they passed were ordered to illuminate their cottages at night, and scatter flowers on the roads during the day. They were requested, and I promise you they did not like to refuse, to serve the troops liberally with eatables and wine; besides, the army was enriched by the immense quantity of plunder which was found in King Padella's camp, and taken from his soldiers; who (after they had given up everything) were allowed to fraternise with the conquerors; and the united forces marched back by easy stages towards King Giglio's capital, his royal banner and that of Queen Rosalba being carried in front of the troops. Hedzoff was made a Duke and a Field-Marshal. Smith and Jones were promoted to be Earls; the Crim Tartar Order of the Pumpkin and the Paflagonian decoration of the Cucumber were freely distributed by their Majesties to the army. Queen Rosalba wore the Paflagonian Ribbon of the Cucumber across her riding-habit, whilst King Giglio never appeared without the grand Cordon of the Pumpkin. How the people cheered them as they rode along side by side! They were pronounced to be the handsomest couple ever seen: that was a matter of course; but they really *were* very handsome, and, had they been otherwise, would have looked so, they were so happy! Their Majesties were never separated during the whole day, but breakfasted, dined and supped together always, and rode side by side, interchanging elegant compliments, and indulging in the most delightful conversation. At night, Her Majesty's ladies of honour (who had all rallied round her the day after King Padella's defeat) came and conducted her to the apartments prepared for her; whilst King Giglio, surrounded by his gentlemen, withdrew to his own royal quarters. It was agreed they should be married as soon as they reached the capital, and orders were despatched to the Archbishop of Blombodinga, to hold himself in readiness to perform the interesting ceremony. Duke Hedzoff carried the message, and gave instructions to have the Royal Castle splendidly refurnished and painted afresh. The Duke seized Glumboso, the

Ex-Prime Minister, and made him refund that considerable sum of money which the old scoundrel had secreted out of the late King's treasure. He also clapped Valoroso into prison (who, by the way, had been dethroned for some considerable period past), and when the Ex-Monarch weakly remonstrated, Hedzoff said, "A soldier, sir, knows but his duty; my orders are to lock you up along with the Ex-King Padella, whom I have brought hither a prisoner under guard." So these two Ex-Royal personages were sent for a year to the House of Correction, and thereafter were obliged to become monks of the severest Order of Flagellants, in which state, by fasting, by vigils, by flogging (which they administered to one another, humbly but resolutely), no doubt they exhibited a repentance for their past misdeeds, usurpations, and private and public crimes.

As for Glumboso, that rogue was sent to the galleys, and never had an opportunity to steal any more.

XVIII
How They All Journeyed Back to the Capital

The Fairy Blackstick, by whose means this young King and Queen had certainly won their respective crowns back, would come not unfrequently, to pay them a little visit—as they were riding in their triumphal progress towards Giglio's capital—change her wand into a pony, and travel by their Majesties' side, giving them the very best advice. I am not sure that King Giglio did not think the Fairy and her advice rather a bore, fancying it was his own valour and merits which had put him on his throne, and conquered Padella: and, in fine, I fear he rather gave himself airs towards his best friend and patroness. She exhorted him to deal justly by his subjects, to draw mildly on the taxes, never to break his promise when he had once given it—and in all respects to be a good King.

"A good King, my dear Fairy!" cries Rosalba. "Of course he will. Break his promise! can you fancy my Giglio would ever do anything so improper, so unlike him? No! never!" And she looked fondly towards Giglio, whom she thought a pattern of perfection.

"Why is Fairy Blackstick always advising me, and telling me how to manage my government, and warning me to keep my word? Does she suppose that I am not a man of sense, and a man of honour?" asks Giglio testily. "Methinks she rather presumes upon her position."

"Hush! dear Giglio," says Rosalba. "You know Blackstick has been very kind to us, and we must not offend her." But the Fairy was not listening to Giglio's testy observations, she had fallen back, and was trotting on her pony now, by Master Bulbo's side, who rode a donkey, and made himself generally beloved in the army by his cheerfulness, kindness, and good-humour to everybody. He was eager to see his darling Angelica. He thought there never was such a charming being. Blackstick did not tell him it was the possession of the magic rose that made Angelica so lovely in his eyes. She brought him the very best accounts of his little wife, whose misfortunes and humiliations had indeed very greatly improved her; and, you see, she could whisk off on her wand a hundred miles in a minute, and be back in no time, and so carry polite messages from Bulbo to Angelica, and from Angelica to Bulbo, and comfort that young man upon his journey.

When the Royal party arrived at the last stage before you reach Blombodinga, who should be in waiting, in her carriage there with her lady of honour by her side, but the Princess Angelica! She rushed into her husband's arms, scarcely stopping to make a passing curtsey to the King and Queen. She had no eyes but for Bulbo, who appeared perfectly lovely, to her on account of the fairy ring which he wore; whilst she herself, wearing the magic rose in her bonnet, seemed entirely beautiful to the enraptured Bulbo.

A splendid luncheon was served to the Royal party, of which the Archbishop, the Chancellor, Duke Hedzoff, Countess Gruffanuff, and all our friends partook, the Fairy Blackstick being seated on the left of King

Giglio, with Bulbo and Angelica beside her. You could hear the joy-bells ringing in the capital, and the guns which the citizens were firing off in honour of their Majesties.

"What can have induced that hideous old Gruffanuff to dress herself up in such an absurd way? Did you ask her to be your bridesmaid, my dear?" says Giglio to Rosalba. "What a figure of fun Gruffy is!"

Gruffy was seated opposite their Majesties, between the Archbishop and the Lord Chancellor, and a figure of fun she certainly was, for she was dressed in a low white silk dress, with lace over, a wreath of white roses on her wig, a splendid lace veil, and her yellow old neck was covered with diamonds. She ogled the King in such a manner that His Majesty burst out laughing.

"Eleven o'clock!" cries Giglio, as the great Cathedral bell of Blombodinga tolled that hour. "Gentlemen and ladies, we must be starting. Archbishop, you must be at church, I think, before twelve?"

"We must be at church before twelve," sighs out Gruffanuff in a languishing voice, hiding her old face behind her fan.

"And then I shall be the happiest man in my dominions," cries Giglio, with an elegant bow to the blushing Rosalba.

"Oh, my Giglio! Oh, my dear Majesty!" exclaims Gruffanuff; "and can it be that this happy moment at length has arrived—"

"Of course it has arrived," says the King.

"—And that I am about to become the enraptured bride of my adored Giglio!" continues Gruffanuff. "Lend me a smelling-bottle, somebody. I certainly shall faint with joy."

"*You* my bride?" roars out Giglio.

"*You* marry my Prince?" cried poor little Rosalba.

"Pooh! Nonsense! The woman's mad!" exclaims the King. And all the courtiers exhibited by their countenances and expressions, marks of surprise, or ridicule, or incredulity, or wonder.

"I should like to know who else is going to be married if I am not?" shrieks out Gruffanuff. "I should like to know if King Giglio is a gentleman, and if there is such a thing as justice in Paflagonia? Lord Chancellor! my Lord Archbishop! will your Lordships sit by and see a poor, fond, confiding, tender creature put upon? Has not Prince Giglio promised to marry his Barbara? Is not this Giglio's signature? Does not this paper declare that he is mine, and only mine?" And she handed to his Grace the Archbishop the document which the Prince signed that evening when she wore the magic ring, and Giglio drank so much champagne. And the old Archbishop, taking out his eyeglasses, read—"This is to give notice, that I, Giglio, only son of Savio, King of Paflagonia, hereby promise to marry the charming Barbara Griselda, Countess Gruffanuff, and widow of the late Jenkins Gruffanuff, Esq.'"

"H'm," says the Archbishop, "the document is certainly a—a document."

"Phoo!" says the Lord Chancellor, "the signature is not in His Majesty's handwriting." Indeed, since his studies at Bosforo, Giglio had made an immense improvement in caligraphy.

"Is it your handwriting, Giglio?" cries the Fairy Blackstick, with an awful severity of countenance.

"Y—y—y—es," poor Giglio gasps out, "I had quite forgotten the confounded paper: she can't mean to hold me by it. You old wretch, what will you take to let me off? Help the Queen, some one—Her Majesty has fainted."

"Chop her head off!"
"Smother the old witch!" } exclaim the impetuous Hedzoff, the ardent Smith, and the faithful Jones.
"Pitch her into the river!"

But Gruffanuff flung her arms round the Archbishop's neck, and bellowed out, "Justice, justice, my Lord Chancellor!" so loudly, that her piercing shrieks caused everybody to pause. As for Rosalba, she was borne away lifeless by her ladies; and you may imagine the look of agony which Giglio cast towards that lovely being, as his hope, his joy, his darling, his all in all, was thus removed, and in her place the horrid old Gruffanuff rushed up to his side, and once more shrieked out, "Justice, justice!"

"Won't you take that sum of money which Glumboso hid?" says Giglio; "two hundred and eighteen thousand millions, or thereabouts. It's a handsome sum."

"I will have that and you too!" says Gruffanuff.

"Let us throw the crown jewels into the bargain," gasps out Giglio.

"I will wear them by my Giglio's side!" says Gruffanuff.

"Will half, three-quarters, five-sixths, nineteen-twentieths, of my kingdom do, Countess?" asks the trembling monarch.

"What were all Europe to me without *you*, my Giglio?" cries Gruff, kissing his hand.

"I won't, I can't, I shan't—I'll resign the crown first," shouts Giglio, tearing away his hand; but Gruff clung to it.

"I have a competency, my love," she says, "and with thee and a cottage thy Barbara will be happy."

Giglio was half mad with rage by this time. "I will not marry her," says he. "Oh, Fairy, Fairy, give me counsel?" And as he spoke he looked wildly round at the severe face of the Fairy Blackstick.

"'Why is Fairy Blackstick always advising me, and warning me to keep my word? Does she suppose that I am not a man of honour?'" said the Fairy, quoting Giglio's own haughty words. He quailed under the brightness of her eyes; he felt that there was no escape for him from that awful inquisition.

"Well, Archbishop," said he in a dreadful voice, that made his Grace start, "since this Fairy has led me to the height of happiness but to dash me down into the depths of despair, since I am to lose Rosalba, let me at least keep my honour. Get up, Countess, and let us be married; I can keep my word, but I can die afterwards."

"Oh, dear Giglio," cries Gruffanuff, skipping up, "I knew, I knew I could trust thee—I knew that my Prince was the soul of honour. Jump into your carriages, ladies and gentlemen, and let us go to church at once; and as for dying, dear Giglio, no, no:—thou wilt forget that insignificant little chambermaid of a Queen—thou wilt live to be consoled by thy Barbara! She wishes to be a Queen, and not a Queen Dowager, my gracious Lord!" And hanging upon poor Giglio's arm, and leering and grinning in his face in the most disgusting manner, this old wretch tripped off in her white satin shoes, and jumped into the very carriage which had been got ready to convey Giglio and Rosalba to church.

The cannons roared again, the bells pealed triple-bobmajors, the people came out flinging flowers upon the path of the royal bride and bridegroom, and Gruff looked out of the gilt coach window and bowed and grinned to them. Phoo! the horrid old wretch!

XIX

And Now We Come to the Last Scene in the Pantomime

The many ups and downs of her life had given the Princess Rosalba prodigious strength of mind, and that highly principled young woman presently recovered from her fainting-fit, out of which Fairy Blackstick, by a precious essence which the Fairy always carried in her pocket, awakened her. Instead of tearing her hair, crying, and bemoaning herself, and fainting again, as many young women would have done, Rosalba remembered that she owed an example of firmness to her subjects; and though she loved Giglio more than her life, was determined, as she told the Fairy, not to interfere between him and justice, or to cause him to break his royal word.

"I cannot marry him, but I shall love him always," says she to Blackstick; "I will go and be present at his marriage with the Countess, and sign the book, and wish them happy with all my heart. I will see, when I get home, whether I cannot make the new Queen some handsome presents. The Crim Tartary crown diamonds are uncommonly fine, and I shall never have any use for them. I will live and die unmarried like Queen Elizabeth, and, of course, I shall leave my crown to Giglio when I quit this world. Let us go and see them married, my dear Fairy, let me say one last farewell to him; and then, if you please, I will return to my own dominions."

So the Fairy kissed Rosalba with peculiar tenderness, and at once changed her wand into a very comfortable coach-and-four, with a steady coachman, and two respectable footmen behind, and the Fairy and

Rosalba got into the coach, which Angelica and Bulbo entered after them. As for honest Bulbo, he was blubbering in the most pathetic manner, quite overcome by Rosalba's misfortune.

She was touched by the honest fellow's sympathy, promised to restore to him the confiscated estates of Duke Padella his father, and created him, as he sat there in the coach, Prince, Highness, and First Grandee of the Crim Tartar Empire. The coach moved on, and, being a fairy coach, soon came up with the bridal procession.

Before the ceremony at the church it was the custom in Paflagonia, as it is in other countries, for the bride and bridegroom to sign the Contract of Marriage, which was to be witnessed by the Chancellor, Minister, Lord Mayor, and principal officers of state. Now, as the royal palace was being painted and furnished anew, it was not ready for the reception of the King and his bride, who proposed at first to take up their residence at the Prince's palace, that one which Valoroso occupied when Angelica was born, and before he usurped the throne.

So the marriage party drove up to the palace: the dignitaries got out of their carriages and stood aside: poor Rosalba stepped out of her coach, supported by Bulbo, and stood almost fainting up against the railings so as to have a last look of her dear Giglio.

As for Blackstick, she, according to her custom, had flown out of the coach window in some inscrutable manner, and was now standing at the palace door.

Giglio came up the steps with his horrible bride on his arm, looking as pale as if he was going to execution. He only frowned at the Fairy Blackstick—he was angry with her, and thought she came to insult his misery.

"Get out of the way, pray," says Gruffanuff haughtily. "I wonder why you are always poking your nose into other people's affairs?"

"Are you determined to make this poor young man unhappy?" says Blackstick.

"To marry him, yes? What business is it of yours? Pray, madam, don't say 'you' to a Queen," cried Gruffanuff.

"You won't take the money he offered you?"

"No."

"You won't let him off his bargain, though you know you cheated him when you made him sign the paper?"

"Impudence! Policemen, remove this woman!" cries Gruffanuff. And the policemen were rushing forward, but with a wave of her wand the Fairy struck them all like so many statues in their places.

"You won't take anything in exchange for your bond, Mrs. Gruffanuff," cries the Fairy, with awful severity. "I speak for the last time."

"No!" shrieks Gruffanuff, stamping with her foot. "I'll have my husband, my husband, my husband!"

"You SHALL HAVE YOUR HUSBAND!" the Fairy Blackstick cried; and advancing a step, laid her hand upon the nose of the Knocker.

As she touched it, the brass nose seemed to elongate, the open mouth opened still wider, and uttered a roar which made everybody start. The eyes rolled wildly; the arms and legs uncurled themselves, writhed about, and seemed to lengthen with each twist; the Knocker expanded into a figure in yellow livery, six feet high; the screws by which it was fixed to the door unloosed themselves, and Jenkins Gruffanuff once more trod the threshold off which he had been lifted more than twenty years ago!

"Master's not at home," says Jenkins, just in his old voice; and Mrs. Jenkins, giving a dreadful *youp*, fell down in a fit, in which nobody minded her.

For everybody was shouting, "Huzzay! Huzzay!" "Hip, hip, hurray!" "Long live the King and Queen!"

"Were such things ever seen?" "No, never, never, never!" "The Fairy Blackstick for ever!"

The bells were ringing double peals, the guns roaring and banging most prodigiously. Bulbo was embracing everybody; the Lord Chancellor was flinging up his wig and shouting like a madman; Hedzoff had got the Archbishop round the waist, and they were dancing a jig for joy; and as for Giglio, I leave you to imagine what *he* was doing, and if he kissed Rosalba once, twice—twenty thousand times, I'm sure I don't think he was wrong.

So Gruffanuff opened the hall door with a low bow, just as he had been accustomed to do, and they all went in and signed the book, and then they went to church and were married, and the Fairy Blackstick sailed away on her cane, and was never more heard of in Paflagonia.

AND HERE ENDS THE FIRESIDE PANTOMIME.

Reading Guide

The stories in this volume are better suited to more mature readers who prefer their fiction to have depth of meaning. Themes of human emotion and endeavour help the reader find affinity with the characters within. They are wholesome tales, a far cry from the simple fairy stories we saw in Volume One and a step above those in Volume Six, bringing the narrative style closer to the fictions preferred by adults.

Thackeray's play, *The Rose and the Ring*, which forms the second part of this volume, may appear at first glance to be a type of fairy tale, yet upon deeper reading we reveal the reason it was included in this volume. The story, written as a gift to Thackeray's own children, is a satire which revolves around the lives and fortunes of four young cousins. It challenges the ideals of beauty and marriage, and to an extent, the attitudes of the monarchy. Today's readers may consider these timeless themes to be perpetually relevant while reflecting on the perspectives of our modern culture.

- A. Kennedy, curator of *The Harvard Classics Project*

The first part of this volume consists of stories by modern writers dealing mainly with life in our own day. They are, of course, meant for the older children, and both the style and the situations call for more maturity on the part of the reader. The lure of the extraordinary is now dispensed with, and instead these tales supply the interest that comes from recognizable truth to experience.

When a boy reaches a certain stage in his development he is apt. to become impatient of the fantastic and impossible in fiction. The sense of fact which his everyday life and most of his study in school have been cultivating finally becomes the dominant element, and it tends to reject summarily all that offends it. For some years now the physical is in the ascendant, and the child is passing through the most precarious period of his life. The imaginative and ideal elements were never more important than at this time, and yet these are precisely what he is most likely to reject in his reading. The lavish use of such qualities in the books of his earlier years is now merely irritating to him, and a substitute is urgently needed.

It is at this point that wholesome modern fiction of a more realistic type can serve a lofty educational purpose. The care of the best modern writers of fiction for accuracy of detail, for faithfulness to local colour, for technical exactness in the description of both internal and external matters, appeals to a youth just beginning to pride himself on his grasp of reality, and lays him open to whatever else the writer may have to offer. What these stories have to give is a number of pictures of life, presented vividly and convincingly, and in proportion to their truth and vigour serving as a kind of vicarious experience. The reading of such fiction, with a lively realisation of the scenes and characters, is not only an exercise of the imagination abundantly rewarded by the pleasure obtained, but is also a moral gymnastic, through its stretching and supplying of the capacity for sympathy with one's fellows.

The list of fiction contained in these volumes, representing the imaginative product of almost all races and times, is fitly closed by the gift made to the children of England of a story for themselves by the master of English novelists, William Makepeace Thackeray.

- William Allan Neilson

Suggested Books

The following is a list of original stories for the more mature reader. All of these titles have now entered the public domain, and should be easy to find on websites such as Project Gutenberg, The Internet Archive and HathiTrust, if not in your local library.

- *The Madness of Philip, and Other Tales of Childhood* by Josephine Daskam Bacon
- *The Lonesomest Doll* by Abbie Farwell Brown
- *Richard Carvel* by Winston Churchill[1]
- *The Moonstone* by Wilkie Collins
- *John Halifax, Gentleman* by Dinah Maria Mulock Craik
- *The Adventures of Sherlock Holmes* by Arthur Conan Doyle
- *An Egyptian Princess* by Georg Ebers
- *The Captain of the Gray-Horse Troop* by Hamlin Garland
- *King Solomon's Mines* by H. Rider Haggard
- *L'Abbe Constantin* by Ludovic Halévy
- *The Prisoner of Zenda* by Anthony Hope
- *Rupert of Hentzau* by Anthony Hope
- *Deephaven* by Sarah Orne Jewett
- *Stover at Yale* by Owen Johnson
- *The Varmint* by Owen Johnson
- *Cadet Days: A Story of West Point* by Charles King
- *Kim* by Rudyard Kipling
- *Bob, Son of Battle* by Alfred Ollivant
- *A Captured Santa Claus* by Thomas Nelson Page
- *The Seats of the Mighty* by Gilbert Parker
- *The Jester of St. Timothy's* by Arthur Stanwood Pier
- *Mrs. Wiggs of the Cabbage Patch* by Alice Hegan Rice
- *The Wreck of the Grosvenor* by William Clark Russell

---

[1] This Winston Churchill was a celebrated American novelist, and should not be confused with the infamous Prime Minister of Great Britain.

- *The Biography of a Grizzly* by Ernest Thompson Seton
- *Kidnapped* by Robert Louis Stevenson
- *Monsieur Beaucaire* by Booth Tarkington
- *When Patty Went to College* by Jean Webster
- *Rebecca of Sunnybrook Farm* by Kate Douglas Wiggin

About this Book

This is a new edition of *Stories of To-Day: Volume 9 of The Junior Classics*, originally published by P. F. Collier and Son in 1918. All volumes of *The Junior Classics* are now available in the public domain. This edition has been enhanced and expanded by The Harvard Classics Project for a new generation of readers, featuring a reading guide, list of suggested books for further exploration, and additional illustrations.

In particular, this volume has been edited and reformatted for an improved reading experience both digitally and in print. The main content of the text remains largely unchanged, save for a few minor errors and spellings. However, if you compare the visual layout to that of the original published volume, you will notice several changes, including chapter divisions, drop caps, formatting, and illustrations. I trust that these changes will improve the experience of reading this volume, while ensuring the content is easily accessible, whether you read for pleasure, to supplement homeschooling or provide some foundation for a *liberal education*.

Digital readers will find that the several of the original illustrations contained in this edition are in full colour. Unfortunately, the additional cost for colour in the print editions outweighs the benefits of value and distribution, so at this time I'm afraid you are only able to view these in black and white on the paper page.

Additional images, including those used in chapter divisions and to decorate chapter endings are sourced from the public domain and FreePik.com.

Should you discover any errors or mistakes, I would be very grateful if you could forward these to hello@amandakennedy.co.uk to be corrected.

Titles in *The Junior Classics Series* of Books

The original *Junior Classics* series, published in 1918, comprised of 10 volumes as follows:

- Volume 1: *Fairy and Wonder Tales*
- Volume 2: *Folk Tales and Myths*
- Volume 3: *Tales From Greece and Rome*
- Volume 4: *Heroes and Heroines of Chivalry*
- Volume 5: *Stories That Never Grow Old*
- Volume 6: *Old-Fashioned Tales*
- Volume 7: *Stories of Courage and Heroism*
- Volume 8: *Animal and Nature Stories*
- Volume 9: *Stories of To-Day*
- Volume 10: *Poems Old and New*

The Harvard Classics Project hopes that all titles in this series will be available for purchase in their updated paperback format from Amazon.

www.harvardclassics365.com

Printed in Great Britain
by Amazon